SOFIA NOVA

MARADONIA AND THE GUARDIANS OF THE PORTAL

ILLUSTRATIONS BY
MARINA TERKULOVA TESCH

MASCOT BOOKS
an imprint of Amplify Publishing Group

MASCOT® BOOKS
an imprint of Amplify Publishing Group

www.mascotbooks.com

MARADONIA AND THE GUARDIANS OF THE PORTAL

For more information, please contact:
Mascot Books, an imprint of Amplify Publishing Group
620 Herndon Parkway, Suite 220
Herndon, VA 20170
info@mascotbooks.com

Library of Congress Control Number: 2023921114
CPSIA Code: PRV0424A
ISBN-13: 978-1-63755-761-7

Printed in the United States

To my husband and my family for always believing in me, but especially for my father, who encouraged me to pursue my dreams as a writer.

CONTENTS

PROLOGUE

The moon's aura glowed brightly, forming a wide, eerie circle of light that illuminated everything below it. Captured by the moonlight, a silhouette of a woman took shape, sitting on a rock by the water's edge. The mysterious woman had alabaster skin, the identical color of the moon. Her wet hair sparkled with moisture, and her turquoise eyes glinted with energy as she watched the ocean. Waves crashed against the jagged rocks, throwing cascades of seawater high into the air around her.

She took a deep breath of the crisp air before speaking into the wind, "The world is changing. There are forces that lust for more power."

The wind howled. Somewhere in the depths of the forest behind her, drums began to beat.

"Much has been given to the world," the woman continued, "yet it wants much more. Nations against nations. Soon, unseen kingdoms will be pulled into the final conflict."

The woman lifted her arms heavenward. On the horizon, dark clouds began to form, staining the immaculate sky. Lightning flashed, followed by the rumble of thunder. The sounds of nature all joined the bellowing of tribal drums, building to a crescendo.

She threw back her head and cried, "The prophecy has yet to be fulfilled!"

A whiteness grew across her eyes, consuming the turquoise. Her voice rose in power, matching the intensity of the storm building all around her.

"It has been foretold. In our greatest time of need, two will come. To unite. To redeem. To encourage! They will face seven challenges and, if they survive, will prove themselves worthy!"

As soon as these words were spoken, the drums stopped. The woman dove off the rocks and into the icy waters of the sea. Far out to sea, too far for human legs to have propelled her so swiftly, the woman reemerged; her glistening head lifted above the roaring waves.

"And now," she cried into the storm, "the real battle begins."

As heavy rain began to fall, the woman's head sank beneath the churning waters. A huge splash erupted as her fishtail slapped against the water.

CHAPTER ONE

THE PERFECT STORM

NOT FAR AWAY, a midsize cargo vessel rocked helplessly as storm waves surged onto its decks. Written on the prow was *Unstoppable Barracuda*. Lightning flashed through the sky, and the GPS navigation system monitor went completely blank.

On the bridge, Captain Hazelton leaned into the wind and rain that howled through the broken window in front of him, struggling to control the wheel and keep the ship on course. He repeatedly rubbed his foggy glasses with his fingers, but rain and seawater blurred his vision once again.

"This damn wind is pushing us too far off course!" Captain Hazelton shouted to Clayton, his young and skinny first mate.

"Our cargo is shifting, Captain!" Clayton yelled back over the howl of the wind, barely staying upright by clinging onto the handrail.

"I haven't seen a storm this bad for decades," the captain grunted, exhausted from his unsuccessful attempts to steer the ship. Hazelton's lined, leathery face peered into the inky darkness above the raging waves. From cloud to cloud, he watched lightning flash, not white but blue and green. Hazelton blinked at it incredulously. He thought he had seen it all.

"It's . . . it's unnatural," he whispered, fear in his voice.

"Insane!" Clayton shouted, gawking at the otherworldly flashes of blue and green.

Another wave crashed over the bow. Water surged through the broken window. Hazelton gritted his teeth, holding on to the steering wheel for support. The rain beat even harder, hammering down like hail.

"Captain! Too much water is entering the vessel. Do we abandon ship?"

Captain responded, "My ship never fails! It's *unstoppable*."

Clayton lost his grip and went sliding across the floor of the bridge.

One deck below the bridge, through their room's window, Maya and Joey Swanson watched another massive wave crash against the ship, engulfing the deck. Fifteen-year-old Joey stayed at the window, holding fast to the sill, knees bent, swaying with the ship. Maya, one year older than Joey, was sitting on the bed, shouting into her phone, hoping their parents could hear. The siblings were two of only eight passengers aboard the cargo ship. They were heading back from a trip abroad to see faraway family and, since their father was good friends with Captain Hazelton, they had the opportunity to experience life on the ocean waves on their return.

"It's just a little rainstorm, honey," their mother reassured them over speakerphone. "Just a few more days and you'll be back home."

"I know," Maya said, her throat tight with nervousness.

"Captain Hazelton has a great vessel. He will get you to the port safely," their father said. He sounded distant in the background.

"I know," Maya croaked again.

Joey shouted, "I've got everything we need. Flashlights, knives, grandpa's compass, you name it! Don't worry about us!"

"Why did you take all those things?" his dad asked.

"Uncle John said he would take us camping on his land, so I thought I . . ."

"Sorry, son. What did you say? You're breaking up," his dad said. A moment later the call was lost.

Suddenly, the vessel jolted. Joey stared out the window, perplexed and excited. "Did we just hit a reef?"

"There aren't supposed to be any of those all the way out here," Maya replied, her voice croaking from shouting.

"I know!" Joey yelled. "We must be way off course!"

Maya felt her stomach lurch as the entire vessel listed. "Do you think we're going to sink? I don't want to die!"

Joey grabbed her shoulders and looked her in the eyes. "I'll get us out of here. We're not going to die. Just do as I say, and we'll be fine."

"Let's find Captain Hazelton," Maya pleaded. She appreciated Joey's self-confidence, but a few days camping on Uncle John's land was hardly a test of his leadership ability.

On the open deck, Maya was hit with the raging wind and rain. She clamped her hands around the railing and inched herself toward the only other passenger room. The room was just a few doors down from her own, but it felt like miles away.

"Look out!" someone screamed.

Maya looked up to see a flash of green lightning and then a heavy wooden barrel falling toward her.

At the last moment, Maya was pulled back and thrown onto the deck, barely escaping being crushed. Clayton, her rescuer, was not so lucky. The loose barrel bounced off the deck at an awkward angle and hit Clayton full force, knocking him overboard. Maya screamed his name as she looked for him in the water. Another bolt of lightning tore through the sky, accompanied by the bellow of thunder. She turned to look for a floatation device. Maya exhaled with relief when she found a life ring attached to the railing. She fumbled to remove it, finally releasing it and throwing it into the direction of Clayton's fall. However, Clayton was nowhere to be seen.

"Somebody, help!" Maya shouted, blinking through tears and rain.

"I'll tell the captain!" another crew member shouted.

Then the boat suddenly jolted. Afraid of joining Clayton in the churning sea, she lunged for the nearby door, opened it, and fell inside. The wind slammed the door shut behind her.

Gordon Huang was, as always, sitting at his desk with headphones on, tending to his stacks of computer drives and scientific equipment. Gordon had been secretive about his high-tech gear for the whole one-week trip, and Maya and Joey had given up asking him questions about it. All Gordon would say was that he was involved with some kind of scientific-transportation program.

Although only twenty-eight years old, Gordon had recently completed his PhD in electrical engineering. That accomplishment, unlike his current work, was something Gordon had been happy to talk about at dinner. Whenever Joey had spoken to Gordon, they talked about how expensive all that equipment must be, which made Maya roll her eyes each time.

Gordon was swaying back and forth more than usual and tilted at a more acute angle than normal, but otherwise it was just another day at sea with his equipment.

Staring up at Gordon from the floor, Maya couldn't believe he was just sitting there like nothing was happening. Maya hated to admit that even in the midst of a life-threatening storm, she was mesmerized by Gordon's wavy black hair, high cheekbones, and small, pointed nose. He was brilliant and handsome, and Maya had a crush on him the very first moment they met. As something ice cold covered her feet, she stopped gazing at Gordon. Seawater was rising inside the cabin.

"The ship is sinking!" Maya screamed.

Gordon, completely engrossed by whatever he was working on, leaned forward to stare more closely at his massive flat-screen computer monitor. He clamped the headphones down onto his ears, tighter, and started shaking his head.

"I can't believe it," Gordon said. "It's here. We are so close!"

Then, the giant monitor finally obeyed the motion of the tilting ship and fell to the floor, shattering. Gordon leapt up and shouted in distress, whipping off his headphones.

Finally noticing Maya, he shouted, "You can't be in here."

Joey burst into the room. "We need to get to the lifeboat! The ship is coming apart!"

"What are you talking about?" Gordon yelled.

"I came to tell you that," Maya said to Gordon as Joey pulled her up from the floor. "Come on! We gotta go."

"But my work," Gordon said. "We're so close! We're here! I've finally found what we've been searching for!"

"We must go—*now*!" Joey repeated. "The lifeboat is waiting!"

Joey raced to Gordon and started pulling him toward the door just as the ship tilted even deeper. Seawater poured through the open door, now up to their knees. Gordon frantically unplugged a hard drive and stuffed it into an orange survival bag. Joey pulled on Gordon's arm.

"*Come on!* No more waiting," Joey said frustrated. Then he grabbed Maya by the arm too and dragged her to the door, sloshing through the high water. The trio finally emerged onto the open deck to see crew members jumping into the last lifeboat on the water. Huge containers of cargo had been tossed overboard and were bobbing up and down in the ocean. Floating near Maya was a single life jacket. She grabbed it.

"We need our backpacks!" Maya shouted to Joey. He pointed to his back, where both bags were hanging.

"I've got them! Please, we have to jump now!"

Suddenly, an enormous bolt of blue lighting struck the bridge of the ship. A tremendous CLANG shook the entire vessel so hard that the siblings barely kept their balance. Gordon was staring, pale-faced, into the raging waves. Terror was in his eyes. "I can't do it. I'll wait for the lifeboat to come back. Maybe we won't sink."

"Gordon," Maya said, "you have to! It *is* sinking."

"I can't do it!" he repeated.

Without any thought, Joey pushed Gordon overboard. Maya saw Gordon's surprised face as he fell, hugging his orange survival bag to his chest.

"Hold on to me and don't let go," Joey shouted to his sister. Joey handed Maya her backpack, then they climbed over the deck railing together. Now that she was faced with it, Maya was just as scared of jumping as Gordon had been.

Joey counted. "One, two . . ."

"No!" Maya objected.

"Three!" Joey jumped, pulling Maya with him.

The siblings splashed into the ocean and fought their way to the surface, still holding hands.

"Don't let go!" Joey repeated. Maya gulped breaths of air as waves tumbled over them.

"Look!" she heard Joey say. She turned to see Gordon being pulled into a nearby lifeboat.

"Swim to the boat!"

Maya felt an adrenaline rush. She started kicking her legs and using her free hand to swim as she clung onto Joey's arm with the other.

"Almost there," Joey said, panting.

A huge wave crashed down, pushing the siblings underwater. Maya lost her grip on her brother's arm. Fighting to the surface, Maya saw Joey drifting further from her. He tossed the life jacket straight into her outstretched hand. She clung to it. Then Joey disappeared under the water. Another wave rolled over, sending Maya down into the depths.

Clutching the life jacket, Maya popped back up like a buoy, coughing out water. Joey was nowhere in sight.

Hearing yells behind her, Maya turned and caught a glimpse of Gordon's lifeboat moving away from her in the tall waves. She kicked her legs with all her might. When the next huge wave passed, though, Maya lost sight of the lifeboat and everything else. It was just her and the dark waters of the ocean.

"Joey! Gordon! Captain Hazelton!" Maya screamed, receiving no response. To her left, she saw Clayton pop up with some blood dripping down his forehead.

"Help me!" Clayton waved to her.

Maya started swimming toward him. But suddenly, Clayton let out a yelp and was pulled under the choppy water. Maya's breathing raced even faster. The only thing she could think was, *sharks*.

Her heart beating hard, she scanned the surface for anything to climb onto. She saw some wooden panels and began swimming with every ounce of strength she had left.

During what felt like a lifetime of waiting to be pulled under by a shark, Maya finally reached a large panel and scrambled on top of it. She coughed, spitting out seawater, and then drifted helplessly.

A flash of bright green and blue light caught her eye. Oddly, it didn't come from the sky; it came from under the water. Maya was shocked to see a glowing fish-like fin. But then, Maya's blood froze as she saw triangular fins circling her. The sharks! She pulled her legs and arms up and hugged herself, struggling to stay aboard her panel. She couldn't see the lifeboats, crew members, or Joey.

Maya tried to concentrate. She breathed in and out, but it was as if there was not enough oxygen in the air. She closed her eyes and finally surrendered to the storm in exhaustion. Feeling hopeless, tired, and alone, she began to fade into a dreamlike state. However, from a distance, she heard voices. Beautiful voices, like a glorious choir singing a troubled melody to her.

"Maya, Maya. Come and help us," they sang. The enchanting melody echoed through her mind.

"What?" Maya murmured, her eyelids getting heavy.

"Maya, come and help us."

CHAPTER TWO

THE MISSION

THE EARLY HOURS OF DAWN BROKE through the clouds over the Pentagon outside Washington, DC. Deep underneath it, military personnel and staff were rushing in to sit at a long table. Under Secretary of Defense Joanna Johnson strode into the conference room. Everyone in the room rose to their feet.

Joanna's curly hair was tied in a bun, and she dressed professionally with long pants and her shirt, buttoned all the way to the top, with a collared jacket over the top. There was no doubt she meant business. Indeed, she was considered one of the top African American women in a position of real power in the US President's cabinet. Joanna straightened herself and motioned to the attendees of the meeting to sit.

At that moment, elderly Doctor Huang shuffled to Joanna and placed a coffee cup down in front of her with a trembling hand. Coffee accidentally sloshed onto the table. Huang looked at the Under Secretary with wet, red eyes.

"Oh! I'm terribly sorry, Ms. Johnson," Doctor Huang said, his voice wavering. "Please, allow me to bring you a napkin."

Joanna placed her hand on Huang's shoulder. "Don't give up hope, doctor. There is always hope. And I appreciate the coffee, but we have assistants for that. Please, sit down."

Huang nodded almost imperceptibly.

"Chop, chop," General Stanton said quickly, still standing. "What is the reason for this urgent meeting? I'm due back in Congress to make sure the new budget passes." General Stanton sniffed, making it obvious what he thought of politicians who didn't put the defense of the country above all other things.

"Neither of us really has time," Admiral Wells began, "to listen to more of Doctor Huang's 'special projects' right now. What is it now? Unicorns from Mars?"

"Time traveling fairies?" General Stanton added, chuckling.

"Sit down," Joanna said sharply. "Both of you. And listen."

Both military men glared at her but took their seats. Doctor Huang sank into his chair, looking lost and forlorn. Everyone grew quiet. The general exchanged looks with the admiral. Something about this meeting was, indeed, very serious.

Joanna took a sip of coffee to gather her thoughts. Her faith in Doctor Huang's unusual theories and proposals had put her in uncomfortable situations in the past. This time, though, it seemed to be different.

"Before we begin," Joanna said evenly, "let me say that this is confidential information, and the Department of Defense will not tolerate any leaks." She looked straight at Admiral Wells. "Especially to the press."

Admiral Wells cleared his throat and repositioned himself in his chair.

"Everything I do," Wells said, "is in the best interests of protecting this great country."

"As you know," Joanna continued, "Doctor Huang, from the University of Iowa, is one of our leading quantum physicists."

General Stanton leaned over to whisper to Admiral Wells just loud enough for all to hear, "One of our top loony birds, she means."

Wells cracked a smile. Joanna slammed her hand down on the table so hard that more coffee sloshed onto the table.

"Enough! Have some respect. Our government sponsors Doctor Huang."

The older men blinked at her, shocked and embarrassed, like class clowns disciplined by the teacher. Joanna took a deep breath and continued, "We have received news that the Chinese have already launched their 'Micius Project.' Therefore, this upcoming mission must be absolutely top secret."

"The Chinese?" General Stanton said, rubbing his chin.

"Which mission?" Admiral Wells asked.

"Doctor Huang has proposed an expedition to our board after developing a computer program that identifies magnetic portals. His research suggests that there are several of these portals spread out across the planet."

"Portals?" General Stanton demanded. "Portals to where?"

"We don't know yet," Joanna said, rubbing her eyes. "All we know so far is that they exist, thanks to the confirmation of Doctor Huang's work."

"Actually," Doctor Huang sighed, "thanks mostly to my son's work . . . Gordon's work. He's the one who combined my hypothesis with actual science. He should be here, not me."

"Then where is he?" Admiral Wells huffed.

Doctor Huang blinked at the ground. "He . . . he's dead."

"Missing," Joanna corrected. "He was conducting field tests with the new locating apparatus when his ship went down last night."

A tear leaked from Huang's eye and crept down his face.

"We're sorry for your loss, doctor," Wells said, finally with some sympathy in his voice. "We're listening. Perhaps you can tell us more about these portals."

Huang took a deep breath. "Gordon's work proves beyond a doubt that portals exist. What we don't know is where they lead. And we've never known the possible location of any. Until last night."

"Before we lost contact with Gordon's ship," Joanna said softly, "he sent a radio message. Apparently, he has strong evidence that he located a portal, or at least the general location of one."

General Stanton leaned forward. "So, this portal can transport you from one place to another."

Doctor Huang nodded. "Yes. All our research points to the fact that you can enter a portal from one part of earth and emerge through another, somewhere else."

Admiral Wells's eyes lit up. "You mean . . ."

Joanna nodded. "Teleportation."

Stanton jumped to his feet. "Do you understand the military implications? If we could transport soldiers from one place to another immediately, it would give us an advantage that no power on earth could match."

"We'd be invincible!" Wells added. "We could attack with no warning, giving the enemy no chance whatsoever."

"Or," Joanna added, glaring at them, "we could transport resources, food to the starving, medicine to the sick. The humanitarian applications are endless."

General Stanton sat down, frowning. "Of course," he said, "but we should look at this as a defensive opportunity as well."

"In any case," Wells said, "if this is true, we cannot take any chances of these portals falling into the hands of another nation. The United States must be first to find them and secure them."

Joanna sighed. "Yes, that we agree upon. Which brings us to the 'Flying Bird Expedition.' Admiral, you will prepare a Navy vessel and crew to accompany Doctor Huang and his team. Together you will sail to the spot where Gordon's ship was last located and begin the search for the portal. We don't know what or who you'll encounter, so I need your best security team aboard."

"I know just the young lady for the job," Wells said, grinning.

Joanna passed out a report for all to read.

"This is what we know. Now, I want to be clear that under no circumstances are you to—" Joanna paused as her assistant rushed into the room to hand her a message. Joanna's eyes went wide, and she looked at her assistant. "You're positive?" she asked.

Her assistant nodded, enthusiastically. A smile spread across Joanna's face.

"Doctor," she said. "We have located Gordon."

Huang's head shot up. "What? Really?"

"His lifeboat was picked up by a fishing vessel. It seems he and two others are the only survivors. Gordon is on a military transport heading to San Diego right now."

"Which is exactly where we should depart from, given the coordinates of where his ship went down," Wells said, studying the report.

"He's alive," Huang said softly. "My son's alive!" Then he jumped up and hugged Joanna.

"Yes, I'm happy for you," she said, patting his back.

General Stanton leaned over to whisper to Admiral Wells, "Imagine the possibilities. Finally, something useful from Huang."

The smile of Admiral Wells turned into a large smirk. "I love it when we win."

CHAPTER THREE

STRANDED

Maya's eyes were crusted with sand and salt. As they slowly opened, she saw a flock of pelicans flying overhead. Seagulls shrieked nearby. A churning in her stomach made her roll over onto her front, and she coughed up seawater.

After a few minutes, Maya stood up on shaky legs and looked around. Before her was the open sea. Turning on the sand, she saw a tropical rainforest behind the thin stretch of beach. A tall mountain rose behind the trees. *Where am I?* she thought.

Debris from the *Unstoppable Barracuda* was strewn across the beach. Maya called out as loud as she could. "Joey, where are you?"

With her legs trembling, Maya walked to the edge of the shore, inspecting what was left of the ship. Something long and thin caught her eye in the gentle waves lapping at the shore. Maya approached the figure, afraid, and then stepped back suddenly. The brown hair, thin limbs . . . was it?

"Joey?" she croaked, terrified.

Maya waded into the calm shallows and around the body to see the face, needing to find out the identity of the corpse but also not wanting to. As she looked down, Maya's hand shot to her mouth. Then, raising her eyes, she exhaled loudly and then sobbed. It was Clayton. Lifeless, mauled, and drifting back and forth in the surf. *Poor man*, she thought.

Just then, a voice shouted in the distance. She spun around to see her brother running toward her, a tree branch in one hand, sharpened into a spear. Maya ran to her brother and hugged him.

For a long moment, the siblings embraced one another.

"Are you okay?" Joey asked.

"I think so . . . at least better than poor Clayton," Maya choked, overwhelmed with sadness.

"He was better than all of them, I think," Joey said softly. "There's another body down that way," he said, pointing behind him.

"How awful," Maya said, her heart breaking.

"It is, but we are alive and must make it through," Joey said, hugging her again.

Maya pulled away and asked, nodding to the spear, "What's that for?"

"As I searched for you, I figured I might as well prepare a weapon."

"Smart," Maya said, marveling at her brother's clear-headedness. "For once," she added.

"I'm starving! Maybe we can use it to catch fish," Joey said. "Man, what I wouldn't give for a five-course meal right now."

Maya pointed to the tree line. "There are banana trees just behind those rocks. Easier than spearfishing!"

At that moment, an eerie, high-pitched sound emerged from the jungle. Maya stepped closer to Joey. "What was that?" she said.

"I don't know," Joey raised his spear and peered into the thick trees. "It almost sounds human."

"Almost," Maya whispered.

Joey stepped toward the jungle.

"What are you doing?" Maya exclaimed.

Joey looked deep into her eyes. "No one's going to help us right now. We have to fend for ourselves. If there's something in there, we need to know what it is. Maybe there is someone who could help us figure out where we are."

Maya shook her head. "Maybe it could eat us."

"Well, we can't be helpless. We need food. We need water. We need to move." Joey took his sister's hand and started leading her toward the trees. Maya immediately let go.

"Come on, Maya! Why do you always have to be such a wuss? I've got this situation under control. Trust me. I know what I'm doing," Joey said with extreme confidence.

"Wait . . . let's not rush in there yet. We can grab those bananas. You can catch some fish."

He looked down at her disapprovingly.

"Look, I . . ." Maya's voice began to shake. "I'm not like you. You're a go-getter. You're always so confident, so sure of everything, but for once, can't you just listen to me? Let's just wait here, where it's safe. Please."

Joey took a deep breath, feeling defeat. He noticed that Maya's eyes were watery and full of fear.

It was in this moment that a thought struck him: *Sometimes a leader needs to understand the needs of his followers and do what's right for them, not just for himself. Maybe with some food, Maya would feel better*. Joey agreed with himself, finally appreciating his elective course in leadership skills.

"Okay. Just tell me one thing."

"What?" Maya's eyes betrayed the fear she still felt.

Joey lifted up his spear and started hopping from one foot to the other, imitating a caveman. "Which do you like better? Sushi or grilled fish?"

It worked. Maya smiled.

An hour later, Maya and Joey were sitting around the fire they'd built. Banana peels and opened coconuts surrounded them. Maya took off her

sneakers and put them next to the heat to dry off any remaining moisture. They also cleaned their backpacks and dried them out.

Joey was finishing up cooking fish over the fire on his spear. He had used a pocketknife from his backpack to gut and debone the fish, earning him an approving look from Maya.

"Thanks to my survival guide, I pretty much packed everything we need," Joey said.

Joey placed the fish on a palm leaf and cut it in two, giving one half to his sister on another leaf.

"It isn't filet mignon and lobster tail," he said, "but it'll do."

The food had helped give Maya energy, Joey knew, and she was feeling a little better. Still, though, it was obvious Maya was stressed.

"Ugh. I tried drying out our phones and my laptop, but they're dead! Basically, everything in my bag is trashed, except the flashlights," Maya blurted. "We're hopelessly stranded."

"Well," Joey said, trying to keep his voice light, "no help has come yet, that's true. But give it time. We've only been on this island since last night. I still think help will come."

It almost seemed like he enjoyed being lost in the jungle and stranded on an island. He felt like a hunter in the game of life. A drop of water plopped onto Maya's fish. She looked up to see rain clouds rolling in.

"Well, hopefully it will come soon," Maya said.

Joey didn't like the look of the storm clouds at all.

"Come on, let's eat as we walk," he said, rising to his feet. "And look for more fruit trees. I'm still hungry."

"You're always hungry," she remarked.

The siblings made their way to the edge of the jungle and turned, walking on the sand along the line of trees.

"Man, what I wouldn't give for a Land Rover right now." Joey laughed. "Or one of those new ATVs with fat tires and the sports package."

Maya rolled her eyes. "You and your luxurious tastes."

"Hey, what's wrong with wanting the best?"

"You mean the most expensive."

"That, too!" Joey grinned.

"I'd be happy with *anything* that didn't involve walking right now," Maya said.

After a few minutes of walking, Maya pointed. "Look. The mountain comes all the way to the beach over there."

The siblings headed in that direction. When they got closer, Joey saw a gap in the trees. "I see something over here."

Maya studied the opening in the foliage. "You're right. It looks like a cave."

Just then, rain started falling steadily in large drops.

"Come on. Maybe we can find shelter inside," he said. They arrived and pushed through a few low bushes to reach the cave's entrance.

Maya hesitated. "Wait, let's find out if there's anything dangerous inside."

But Joey had already entered the cave. Heavy rain started pelting Maya's head, so she had no choice but to follow. The cave's opening was wide, but its ceiling was a few feet taller than Maya. Her brother was waiting for her just inside. He put his hand up for her to stop.

Maya strained her ears and then heard it. The eerie, high-pitched sound; the same strange sound they heard on the beach.

"It's coming from deep in the cave," Joey suggested.

"No, it's something else," Maya said, listening closer. "Now all I hear is the sound of a waterfall. Strange."

Joey nodded. "You're right. A waterfall means freshwater. A river. Maybe we can drink from it."

Maya pulled a flashlight from her backpack. Luckily, it worked. She ran its beam over the cave walls and the pointed, wet rock formations above their heads.

"Whoa," Joey said. "Look at all those, uh, stalagmites."

"Stalactites," Maya corrected. "Stalagmites grow upward."

Maya trained her flashlight beam on one of the stalactites and followed the formation. But this revealed hundreds of bats hanging down with their wings draped around them.

Quickly, Joey clamped his hand over Maya's mouth. He raised his finger to his lips in a silent "Ssshhh."

Joey took her hand and started walking deeper into the cave. Maya pulled back, but Joey nodded forward and mouthed the words, "Come on!"

Maya stood still for a moment, scared. *If only I was as brave as my brother*, she thought, but despite feeling vulnerable, she quietly followed.

CHAPTER FOUR

TUNNEL OF MYSTERY

THE WALLS OF THE CAVE were made up of thin layers of rock, each a slightly different color. Tiny crystals glistened whenever the flashlight's beam shone over the rock formations. The sound of droplets echoed throughout the cavern as water fell from the ceiling and walls of the cave. The air smelled dank.

Maya followed Joey with trepidation as they continued to venture deeper into the cave. As they walked deeper and deeper, she noticed layers of yellow, red, and purple rock. If she hadn't been so frightened, she'd have thought the cave was very beautiful.

After a while, Joey turned around and started walking backward.

"No more bats," he chuckled, looking up.

"You should probably look where you're going," Maya said with a hint of annoyance.

"Maya, I know what I'm doing," he replied.

"Don't be stupid. You're going to—"

Of course, at that moment, Joey fell backward and disappeared from view. Maya gasped. She heard him tumbling and rolling. Immediately, she rushed to the spot where he had fallen. There was a long, steep slope, and she could see Joey's flashlight bouncing away from her until it came to a stop far below.

"Joey! Are you okay?" Maya called as loud as she dared, still imagining bats all around her.

A cloud of dust rose from Joey's landing spot. Coughing, Joey got to his feet and patted off some of the dust from his pants. "Well, that was intense. I'm all right, though," he said, analyzing his body. Then, looking up at Maya, said, "Here, follow my light."

Maya carefully picked her way down the gravel slope, guided by Joey's flashlight. At the bottom, Maya raised her eyes and noticed the vaulted hall of rock they were standing in. There were three tunnel openings: to their left, right, and straight ahead.

"Which way do we go?" Maya said.

"I've always thought that the best way forward is always straight ahead," Joey said.

Maya couldn't think of a better choice, so she nodded.

After what felt like hours of walking, Maya started to wonder if they should turn back. Although he wouldn't admit it to his sister, Joey did too.

Suddenly, Maya gripped Joey's arm. "Turn off your flashlight," she said with urgency.

Joey cocked his head in confusion but obeyed. Once both beams were out, the siblings noticed a light coming from around the upcoming bend in the tunnel. As they turned the corner, cautiously, Maya and Joey both shielded their eyes from the brightness that they were not accustomed to.

Maya peeked through her fingers, squinting. A perfect shaft of pure white light was beaming down from a crack in the ceiling. The beam struck a blue, glassy stalagmite growing from the rocky ground, refracting an array of brilliant colors across the tunnel. Spots of blue, green, and purple light glistened all over the walls of the tunnel. Looking at the stalagmite made their eyes hurt. Maya closed her eyes again. When she opened them, she saw Joey kneeling at a hand-carved figure of a woman with a fish tail. The figure was no bigger than a meter.

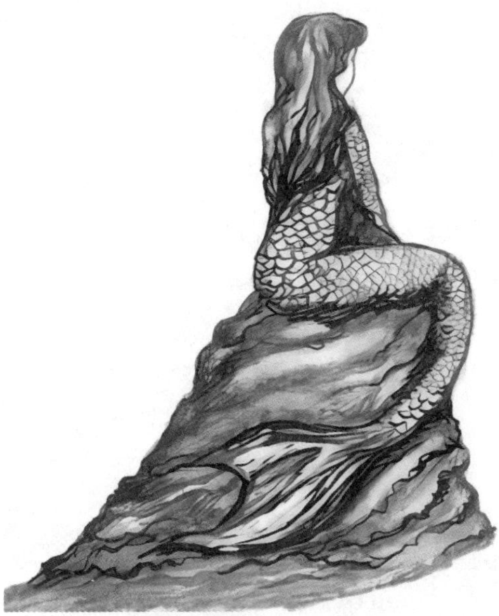

Who made this? And why is it inside this cave? Maya thought.

"It has jewels attached to it!" Joey gasped. Joey circled the statue and then began pushing and pulling it.

"Joey!" Maya protested. "That's not right! It's not ours."

"We can't leave all this treasure here," Joey said, still grappling with the mermaid.

Just as Maya was about to intervene, they heard a loud crack. The figure broke free of its base and was now in Joey's hands. Its glow seemed to dull right away.

"I've got it!" he said, victorious. Maya gasped and held her breath.

There was an eerie moment of silence between the siblings as a strange presence entered the cave like a mist. Maya's stomach churned, and chills ran down her spine, causing goosebumps to form all over her arms and legs. She could feel her heart pounding within her chest. A faint sound of falling pebbles could be heard.

"Joey? I have a strange feeling that you should probably put the statue back and not touch it anymore," she said.

"What do you mean? C'mon. Just look at it," Joey said as he gazed into the glowing statue. "This thing belongs in a museum!"

Now larger pebbles rolled down the slope, kicking up dust into the air. Maya sneezed. Then they felt a vibration as the walls of the tunnel began to tremble. Larger chunks of rock began to fall from the ceiling. The siblings heard another rumbling, this time far behind them. The sound grew louder, turning into a deafening roar.

"Put it back!" Maya called.

"No way!" Joey snapped, clutching the statue closer to his chest. The ground continued to shake, now violently, like an earthquake. Maya's flashlight fell to the ground. With the floor trembling, she tried to remain upright. She screamed, "Put it back right now before the walls come down and bury us alive!"

A chunk of rock, the size of a basketball, narrowly missed Maya's head, and she persisted, "Just listen to me for once or we'll be dead!"

Finally realizing the seriousness of the scenario, Joey set the statue back onto its foundation. Immediately, everything stopped shaking, and the statue glowed brighter than before. Maya shielded her face, as her eyes adjusted to the bright, glowing beams. When she finally reopened her eyes, she saw many of the colorful stalagmites and stalactites on the ground, broken all around them. Dust descended through the air, twinkling as it passed through the light beams.

A small crack at the top of the cave let in just enough light for Joey to notice an opening. He climbed over a few of the fallen rocks and peered into it. It seemed to be just wide enough for the siblings to crawl through. Joey pointed his flashlight into the tunnel to get a better look at where the opening led to, but its beam didn't reach far.

Maya picked up her flashlight, then heard a sound. "Listen, Joey," she whispered.

Joey strained to listen. It sounded like the howling of a mighty windstorm, approaching quickly. His face went white.

"Go!" he yelled.

Maya started scrambling through the tight tunnel on all fours. It wasn't easy with her backpack on. The beam of her flashlight bounced wildly across the rocky walls as she rushed along the jagged ground, hurting her palms and knees. She could hear Joey behind her, crawling desperately.

Then, screeching and flapping filled the space around them. Bats poured through the narrow tunnel, and the siblings pushed themselves to crawl faster. Maya wanted to cover her ears, but she had to make it out of the tunnel as fast as she could.

"Go faster, you slow poke!" Joey yelled.

Bats were slamming against Joey's legs. Maya felt one of the bats land on the strap of her back pack and then start nibbling her shoulder. Another got caught in her hair and flapped its frantic wings in her face, beating against her cheeks. Inches away, she could see the creature's bulging, glowing eyes and its fangs gleaming. Maya screamed and slapped it away, but hundreds more surrounded her, flapping and screeching.

"Go, go, go!" Joey insisted.

Through the flurry of wings, Maya saw light in front of her. She raced on her hands and knees as fast as she could and suddenly found herself falling. Joey tumbled out behind her.

Both slid down a gentle hill and came to a stop at the bottom, curled up in the fetal position. Hundreds of bats poured out of the tunnel's mouth behind them.

Finally, the screeching faded. Maya was panting hard, eyes still shut. Under her hands, she felt soft grass. Her fingers bunched up, gripping blades of grass like it was a miracle. Breathing heavily, she slowly opened her eyes. "I think they're gone," she said.

At that moment, there was a rumbling.

"Look out!" Joey screamed as he grabbed Maya by her backpack. Behind them, a rockslide blocked the opening of the cave, and more rocks bounced toward the siblings. The two rushed away as fast as they could, running until they no longer heard the crashing rocks.

They stopped, and Joey took a deep breath of moist air. Looking at their surroundings, he cocked his head. "Why does everything look different?"

Maya was wondering the same thing.

In front of them was a jungle, taller and thicker than anything they'd ever seen.

"Everything is oversized," Joey said. "The bushes, the leaves, those trees are crazy tall! And look at that fog over there on that hill. It's nearly black."

Maya looked up. The sky was strange too. Tones of pink and dark purple streaked through the blue. Sitting silently, wondering, the siblings began to hear the croaking of frogs and buzzing of insects.

"I see the moon, but it feels like early morning," Joey noticed. "When we entered the cave from the beach, I could've sworn it was almost dark."

Leaves rustled behind them.

In one fluid motion, Joey grabbed the knife from his backpack and jumped up, turning to face the sound. At that moment a sloppy piece of mango hit him in the face. "What the?" he said, wiping his cheek.

A moment later, a small monkey emerged from the bushes. Mostly golden brown, the monkey had darker spots on its fur, like a cheetah. It grinned at Joey and started snickering.

Maya giggled. "It's laughing at you."

The monkey picked up another piece of mango and, again, hit Joey's face with it. Joey turned away, sticky chunks of fruit glued to his cheek. Maya laughed even harder as he wiped the mess off his face again. Joey grunted, rubbing his hand on the grass while giving Maya a look. "You're laughing at me too?"

"Sorry!" Maya said, giggling. "I can't help it!"

As Joey lifted his backpack to his shoulders, the monkey hopped over, jumped up on Joey's leg, and zoomed up to his shoulder.

"Look," Maya said, "he likes you."

Joey held back a smile. "Yeah, well the feeling isn't mutual."

The monkey unzipped Joey's backpack and pulled out a banana.

"He's just hungry," Maya added.

"He's got a heck of an arm," Joey said, finally grinning.

"And perfect aim," Maya laughed.

Then the monkey jumped to the ground, holding something in each hand. "Oh no you don't!" he called, chasing the monkey.

"What is it?" Maya asked.

"He's got Grandpa's compass!"

Joey dove for the monkey, but the little creature was too fast, and Joey landed face first in the grass. The monkey pranced around him, chittering, holding up his treasure. Without thought, Joey began chasing the monkey through the trees. Maya gathered up her backpack and ran after them. The pair followed the monkey a short way into the jungle but were no match for his speed and dexterity.

"Wait," Maya said. "Should we really be going deeper into this jungle?"

Joey stopped, catching his breath.

"Sit for a minute," Maya said.

They sat, and Maya started wiping Joey's face. He tried to brush her off, eyes darting, trying to locate the compass thief.

"Be still," Maya scolded. "You've got blood on your face from the bats." She pulled her first-aid kit from her backpack and put some antibacterial salve on his wounds.

"I guess my one survival item came in handy. Now fix me," she said, turning around and pointing at the cuts on her shoulder. Eyes still searching for the monkey, Joey applied the ointment.

Back on their feet, they soon found the monkey sitting in a high branch of a nearby tree, peeling a banana. The monkey gulped down the fruit and smiled at the siblings as if he didn't have a care in the world.

"That little creep is mocking me," Joey said. "We need to catch him."

"Are you serious?" Maya said. "Look at you. We need to get back to the beach and make shelter in case someone comes searching for us."

"No, no, no. That compass was Grandpa's! He led his platoon out of the jungle in Vietnam with it, and now it's my duty to look after it," Joey said, striding toward the monkey's tree. The monkey grinned down and leapt to the branch of another tree. He looked back to be sure Joey was behind him, then continued jumping from tree to tree. Joey followed.

"Forget it!" Maya called. "Just be happy we're still alive!"

"I'll be happy when I get that compass back," Joey said, not turning around. Nothing else mattered. He marched ahead, pushing the branches aside as he headed deeper into the jungle.

Maya groaned and started jogging after her brother. "Every time it's the same. Always me following you. One day, you're going to do the smart thing and follow me!"

CHAPTER FIVE

TWILIGHT

AFTER THE SUN KISSED THE HORIZON GOODNIGHT, the moon revealed itself in all its glory and an ambient twilight bathed the land in vibrant hues of purple and pink.

High on a nearby hill, a mysterious black fog billowed and swirled. Hundreds of tiny leaves blew away in the gust of wind, and when the trees on the hill became bare, with not a single leaf in sight, three figures materialized in the fog. The figures took shape, and after a moment, three tall women stood in silence as they gazed down upon the land. From the edge of the hilltop, they surveyed the horizon, watching every movement. Behind them, their ancient violet cloaks undulated in the wind.

In the center stood Andromeda, the oldest and most powerful among the fairy witches. On her left stood her sister Lilith, and to her right the youngest of the three, Mui. Their eyes were piercing and darkly mesmerizing, and they had hair so long that it stretched all the way to the floor. Their skin, though pale in shadow, took on a sparkling tone when caressed by the dim moonlight.

High above, five ravens broke the silence as they cried out and circled the three women. Andromeda looked up and waved her hand toward the sky. She was tall and regal, her face that of a stern middle-aged woman.

"Yes, my little ones. Tell me what you have seen," she asked the birds. The largest raven swooped down to perch on Andromeda's outstretched forearm and bowed its head.

"Mistresses," the raven croaked, "we have seen two children on the shore."

"Yes, we can see!" Lilith hissed. "We noticed some movement, as well. What good are you as scouts if you only tell us what we already know?"

Mui added in her delicate, childlike pitch, "We also saw that the seer's pet, that ridiculous monkey, seemed to be frolicking close by." Mui appeared to be not yet a teenager, young and innocent on the outside. On the inside, though, like her sisters, there brewed a terrible, dark power and an ill temper.

"What kind of children are they?" Andromeda asked. "I couldn't tell from the distance. Elfin children?"

"No, mistress," the raven said. "They are something unusual. It is troubling us."

Andromeda's eyes narrowed. "What do you mean?"

The raven nodded. "Human."

"Human?" Lilith repeated icily.

Mui gasped in her dainty way, but a hint of fear crossed her young face.

"Oh, very interesting," Andromeda said, not showing any sign of emotion. "Have you told anyone?"

"No, mistress. Only you. Of course, only you."

Andromeda ran her long fingers down the back of the raven. Rather than comfort the bird, her touch made the bird squint and cringe. Lilith snickered at her sister's pet.

"Good. Do not speak to anyone else about what you have seen," Andromeda instructed. "Return to these children and keep watch. Then come back and tell us more."

"Yes, my lady!"

The raven bowed and took off into the air to join his brothers above. The five ravens flew away with great speed.

For a long moment, the three sisters watched as the ravens glided through the fog and into the jungle.

"Human children? How could that be?" Lilith whispered just loud enough for her sisters to hear.

"The prophecy," Mui breathed.

Andromeda raised her hand. "Indeed, this does sound like that which has been foretold. How was this unforeseen on our part when we have the ability to see everything? Perhaps, these children may not be who we think they are. However, we must not take this event lightly. We must learn more."

A tiny butterfly nearby was caught in the light breeze. When Andromeda saw it, she effortlessly captured it in her bony fingers, trapping it in her palm and bringing it close to her face. While the helpless butterfly fluttered, Andromeda analyzed the insect before she spoke again.

"*Even if* they are the fulfillment of the prophecy, they have many challenges to face. Remember, they are mere human, mortal children. Incredibly vulnerable."

Mui turned to her older sister. "But if they are the ones of which the prophecy speaks, we cannot allow them to fulfil their destiny."

"This is the wrong time for humans to mingle with our plans. King Palazar is already preparing to go to war with the guardians of the portal. We must tell him of these children before they can interfere in any way," Lilith said.

"You are right, dear sister," Andromeda said in her low, even tone. "We cannot underestimate these intruders; however, there is no doubt that our king will surely win the battle."

"Do you see what I see?" Lilith hissed as her body moved in a subtle slither. Her skin glistened in the moonlight.

"The Seven Kingdoms shall fall into our hands," Mui responded in her childish pitch.

"Let's wait and see who these children really are." The slightest smile crossed Andromeda's face as she closed her palm. The tiny butterfly she had held crumbled to the ground.

At that same moment, a deep rumbling was heard far out on the edge of the jungle. The three fairies watched as a massive landslide began to fall where the entrance to the cave was located. Dust lifted high into the atmosphere, reaching for the moon as it rose in the sky.

CHAPTER SIX

THE PROPHECY

"YUCK," JOEY SAID, glaring down in surprise at the black mud he had just stepped in.

An oversized toad hopped through the mud until it found a flat rock. The bumpy toad with strange blue markings turned and stared at the siblings, as if it hadn't seen a person before. Then it began croaking loudly, joining in with the chirping crickets. Joey stared at the toad for a moment, before reaching for a large branch above him to pull himself to higher ground. Neon purple birds fluttered out of the trees when he snapped the branch.

"Ow," Maya said, slapping her neck. "First a jungle, now a swamp filled with the biggest mosquitoes I've ever seen." Maya pouted in disgust. "Nice job, Joey. Let's just follow a monkey into the jungle."

The lush jungle trees were densely entwined with green vines that stretched between them, connecting them to one another. Since they'd entered the jungle, the colorful twilight began to darken by the minute. Suddenly, a slight snicker drew their eyes up into the branches.

"There he is!" Joey shouted.

The monkey smiled down, then started taunting them by slapping his neck, pointing to his feet, and snickering even louder until he fell over on his branch, rolling with amusement.

Joey fumed. "I'd say monkey stew sounds pretty tasty right about now." The monkey stopped frolicking and stared at him in disbelief.

"Oh, I assure you," said a distant voice, "that monkey is all skin and bone. He'd be tough chewing for sure."

A frail man emerged from the trees in front of them, chuckling to himself. Maya and Joey stared at the man's long, beaded dreadlocks, brown robe, and seashell necklace.

"It's okay, Bubah," he said to the monkey. "Maya and Joey are our friends."

The siblings turned to each other with the same questioning look. The monkey nodded in agreement, grinned, and hopped down onto the mysterious man's shoulder. The man spread out his hands, palms up.

"We welcome you to our land. My name is Oraculus. You've already met Bubah."

The monkey proudly puffed out his chest.

"He gets excited when we have visitors, and you are very special visitors indeed." Oraculus took the compass from Bubah's furry hand and held it out. "I believe this is yours."

"Thanks," Joey said as he accepted the compass.

He looked down at his muddy feet, hesitating.

Oraculus smiled. "All is not always as it seems. The swamp you speak of is no more than a muddy stream. You may jump right over it."

Without question, the siblings hopped over the muddy water.

"First of all, how do you know our names?" Maya asked suspiciously.

"The jungle whispers. You only need listen."

The look on Maya and Joey's faces made Oraculus chuckle once more. His face had a slight glow.

"Well, truth be told," Oraculus confided, "he told me." Oraculus nodded to the monkey on his shoulder.

"What do you mean? He can talk?" Joey said.

"In his own way," Oraculus said, petting Bubah on the head. Turning back to the siblings, Oraculus grew serious. "I have been waiting for you both for a very long time."

"How?" Maya asked. "We've only been stranded here since last night."

Oraculus interrupted her in a strong, clear voice. "Long ago, a prophecy was foretold that, in our time of greatest need, two children shall come from a foreign land and overcome the principalities of evil by uniting the people. They shall be called the Encouragers. And that time is now."

Joey and Maya looked at each other, confused.

Joey scrunched his face, "Yeah. Okay. That sounds great, but I don't think we're interested, buddy. We actually just need to find a way to get back home. Or even send a message out, so someone can find us. Do you have a phone we can use?"

Oraculus was nodding and said with a singing voice, "Unfortunately, there is only one way for you to return home. You must fulfill your destiny. Thus, it has been foretold by—"

"The prophecy," Maya said, finishing for him. "Riiiight."

Maya turned her back on Oraculus and rolled her eyes at Joey. He nodded, getting the message: this guy was nuts!

Joey sighed. “Okay, I get it. But what kingdoms are you talking about? It’s all jungle and mosquitoes and toads around here. Are there other people on this island?”

“Others, yes. People, no.” Oraculus stated, “This is the Land of Maradonia.” He bowed his head briefly, in respect.

“The land of what?”

“In your world, they call this island Husario. But we know this place as the Land of Maradonia.” Oraculus closed his eyes. “Don’t you feel a different energy on this island? Surely you feel it.”

“I don’t feel anything except really sweaty,” Joey said. “And the worst part is that my brand-new kicks are filthy!” He looked at his feet mournfully.

“Extend your mind,” Oraculus said, rocking back and forth. “Feel the vibration of the entire universe beneath your feet. Feel the breath of the world on your face. Feel—”

Maya interrupted, “The swelling of my feet and bites on my back?”

“No!” Oraculus raised his voice.

Maya and Joey went silent.

Oraculus continued, "These are the foolish thoughts that consume the weak-minded."

A light breeze swept through the trees. Crickets began chirping louder and then the frogs chimed in, as well.

Maya sighed and closed her eyes. She took a deep breath as a cool breeze swept through her hair. Her mind quieted.

"*Maya.*"

She heard it. "*Maya*," they sang, "*come and help us.*"

"Wait," Maya gasped. "I heard it. I heard them!"

Oraculus smiled. "Have you heard these voices before?"

"Yes," Maya whispered. "How did you know that?"

Oraculus laughed with only his eyes, as he put his hands in the pockets of his coat. The little monkey straightened itself up onto the old man's shoulder and chattered.

"Sir," Joey said, shaking his head, "there must be another way. We didn't come here to encourage anyone. We're stranded and probably need some encouraging ourselves. Our ship hit a reef, and we are the only survivors."

"And yet you two were the reason the ship sank," Oraculus said.

"Whoa! That's not true!" Maya exclaimed, putting her hands on her hips.

"Yeah," Joey said, growing angry, "how can you say my sister and I are responsible for the ship sinking and our friends dying?"

"I did not say you were responsible. But I can tell you that it was no ordinary storm. It was created by the rulers of the ocean who pushed your ship into the dangerous reefs off the coast of Maradonia." He turned to Maya. She could only stare at Oraculus in disbelief.

"And," Oraculus continued, "you were not the only survivors."

"What?" Joey gasped. "Wait, who else made it? Is the captain all right? What about—"

"Gordon!" Maya blurted. "Is Gordon alive?"

"Indeed," Oraculus said, taking a deep breath. "He too will have his part to play in this before it is over."

“But how will we get home?” Joey said.

“Let me show you something.” Oraculus turned to leave.

Maya was trembling at what she had already heard. “Honestly, I think I’ve seen enough. Can’t you just answer our question?”

“Tough times never last. Only tough people last.” Oraculus turned to face them. His eyes looked wet. Then, in a voice that reverberated around the jungle like thunder, he declared, “Your journey through Maradonia has just begun. I can tell you right now that you have much more to see and accomplish . . . perhaps more than I would wish upon anyone. But that is not my choice.”

Oraculus continued to walk away from them, entering deeper into the jungle. On his shoulder, Bubah turned to the siblings and beckoned them. Maya and Joey looked at each other. Without a word, they followed.

The crickets and frogs resumed their music even louder, but now in sync. As the moon rose through the sky, an eerie, dark fog slowly consumed the jungle.

CHAPTER SEVEN

SERGEANT ILONA

Doctor Huang was bouncing as he walked out of the hanger of the military airfield in the forests of eastern Virginia. Admiral Wells struggled to keep up.

"Slow down!" Wells puffed. "Our plane isn't even ready yet."

"Sorry, Admiral," Huang said as his smile widened, "I just can't wait to see my son!"

"Yes, yes," Admiral Wells said, waving his arm, "we're all very happy for you that he's alive. Just remember, Doctor, the Flying Bird Project isn't your little science experiment anymore. It is of the utmost importance and urgency where our country's defense is concerned."

Huang stopped. "Believe me, I know what side my bread is buttered!"

Admiral Wells squinted his eyes and grimaced. It was clear that he was not amused. Huang laughed, patting Wells on the shoulder. "But really, Admiral, when you think about what we're about to discover, the implications are astounding! Not only for practical purposes, as you say, but for the entire history of scientific advancement and universal exploration! We're about to revolutionize the theories of Einstein and Newton!"

Wells placed his large hand on the scientist's shoulder and pressed down. "I think you need to understand how dead serious I am. If another one of your fantasy projects fails, that means that our entire funding will be cut in half. That means my head is on the line." Wells clenched his teeth, adding, "Do you understand?"

Doctor Huang stared into the admiral's unflinching eyes, although the pain in his shoulder was making him wince. "Yes, sir," he said through the pain. "Of course. None of this would be possible without government funding. I understand."

Wells didn't let up on the pressure. "If anything goes wrong, you report *directly to me*. Not the Under Secretary of Defense, the do-gooder. You report to me and only me."

"B-b-but," Huang stuttered, "the chain of command dictates—"

"I am the only chain of command you need to acknowledge," Wells bellowed. "Is that understood?"

Huang was leaning under the weight of Wells's hand, feeling like his shoulder was on fire. "Yes, sir!"

Wells removed his hand. "Now, moving forward, I arranged an excellent team to protect you and your scientists." Then something on the far-left side of the hanger caught his attention. "Ah, there she is."

Huang turned to follow the Admiral's gaze. Out on the tarmac, next to their transport plane, a young woman in a tight-fitting black tactical suit was being attacked by three men in camouflage combat uniforms.

Huang gaped in astonishment. "What's going on? We have to help her!"

Wells grinned. "No, we don't."

The young woman moved swiftly as she jumped over the leg of the man in front of her. Another man charged at her with a knife. She completed a leg swing, launched her body into the air, and completed a full spin, connecting her booted foot with the second man's jaw. He tumbled to the floor.

The young woman smirked, then a third man seized his chance and grabbed her blonde ponytail from behind. He yanked her head down, bringing his knee up. The back of her head slammed down and up, brutally.

"Hey!" Huang called out, moving forward. "Admiral?"

"Wait," Wells commanded as he held back Huang with an arm across his chest.

The woman shook off the blow and chuckled. Her attacker stepped back, surprised at her resilience and ability to take pain. The young woman circled him with a playful smile and said, "Didn't your mother ever tell you not to pull a girl's hair?"

In a flash, she dove forward, turned a somersault, and kicked the man straight in the face with the back of her boot. He wobbled for a moment, closed his eyes, and fell. Then the young woman caught sight of Admiral Wells and Doctor Huang.

"Ilona," Wells called. "Still keeping up the practice in the most unlikely of settings, I see." Wells chuckled and walked toward her. Confused, Huang followed.

"Oh," she said, taking a deep breath. "Hi, Dad. Was just doing a little warmup exercise with the boys. Lack of readiness is a lack of strength, sir."

"This is your daughter?" Huang said. "And you let her face these dangers? What is she, eighteen years old? Twenty?"

Wells snorted. "Twenty-five. She's already faced more dangers than you'll ever know. So rest assured."

Her first attacker rolled over and attempted to get up. With her boot on his back, she flattened him back to the ground. She told him, "That's what you get for lying to me about your girlfriend. Cheater."

Wells smirked.

Ilona stood to attention. "Just putting these boys in their place, sir. Victory never blesses the weak, nor those who take you out on a date and lie about not having a girlfriend."

"At ease," Wells said.

Ilona relaxed and began fixing her ponytail.

"Ilona, I'd like to introduce you to Doctor Huang. One of the important civilians under your protection for this mission."

Huang blinked at her.

"You are in good hands, Doctor Huang," Ilona confidently said, giving him a wink.

Then another voice from behind interrupted them, "Huang, you old computer jockey, how are you?"

Professor Mundi walked from the hanger as briskly as his three hundred pounds would allow.

"Professor!" Huang replied. "So good to see you after so many years, my good friend."

The two men greeted each other with a friendly hug, then Mundi turned to Wells and Ilona.

"At your service, good people. I am Octavius Mundi of Oxford, England," he said, removing his tweed cap and bowing dramatically.

Ilona looked disapprovingly at Mundi's round stomach and ruddy cheeks. "And you are professor of what, exactly?" she said, raising an eyebrow.

Admiral Wells gave his daughter a look. "Have some respect."

"My apologies, Professor," Ilona quickly added, looking at the floor. Her face flushed red. "I was just curious."

"I chair both the departments of Paranormal Sciences and Fantasy Literature," Mundi said. He pulled out a handkerchief from his pocket and wiped the sweat off his forehead.

"Don't be too impressed," Doctor Huang joked. "He's also the only staff member in each department."

"Huang, you old test-tube chugger, let's catch up. Come, our chariot awaits!"

Mundi chuckled as he pushed Huang toward the private transport plane.

"Paranormal?" Ilona said incredulously, watching them walk off. "Fantasy?"

"Strange as it may seem," Wells said to his daughter in all seriousness, "his expertise might be just what's needed on this mission. You've been briefed, have you not?"

"I have, sir."

"Good. Your future depends on it." Her father took a step closer. "I had to pull a couple of strings with Lieutenant Kreeger to get you on this mission. This is your chance, Ilona, to prove to the rest of them who you are meant to be. You will do whatever it takes to make this mission a success. Is that clear?"

Ilona grinned like a cat finding her mouse. "Crystal clear, sir!"

After Ilona gave her father a hug, she saluted him and marched toward the plane full of fresh energy.

CHAPTER EIGHT

THE DECISION

THE FOG CREATED A DENSE MIDST as it crept through the overgrown leaves of the jungle.

Maya shivered and rubbed her arms. “It’s a little chilly.”

Colorful lanterns festooned Oraculus’s island home. Maya and Joey sat cross-legged on the floor. In between them, a fire crackled in the pit and

danced in the moonlight. The little monkey relaxed in his tiny hammock, showing its teeth in between messy bites of a strange, purple fruit. Joey's stomach rumbled.

"Smells good," he said, nodding to the pot brewing on the firepit. "What is it?"

"Rat stew," Oraculus replied, sprinkling a pinch of fresh herbs into the bubbling broth.

"Ew!" Maya began to gag.

"Just kidding!" Oraculus chuckled. "It's an eastern Maradonian dish made with fresh fish."

Oraculus spooned generous portions of the stew into banana leaf bowls and handed them to Maya and Joey.

"Whatever this is," Joey said through a huge mouthful of stew, "it's amazing."

The monkey scampered down a pole and placed a large, yellow flower in Maya's hair.

"Aw, thank you," Maya smiled. The monkey bowed deeply.

"You've come to no ordinary world," Oraculus said as he poked at the stew before placing a portion into another bowl for himself. "We are not like your human world. This is a world between the worlds." Oraculus took a deep breath as he turned his eyes to the floor, "Unfortunately, for many generations, the people here have suffered under the many attacks of the evil King Palazar."

"But there will always be wars," Maya replied as she inched closer to the firepit in the middle of the hut.

"This coming war is no ordinary war," Oraculus looked up solemnly. "It is a battle for ultimate power. And if King Palazar is victorious over the Seven Kingdoms here, he will then set his eyes on your human world, too."

"But what do you mean by 'a world between the worlds'?" Joey asked after he'd gratefully swallowed a spoonful of fish stew.

The light of the moon was a beacon between the trees casting both shadow and light over the jungle floor. Maya inched even closer to the firepit as it crackled close to her feet. The warmth comforted her entire body.

"The Land of Maradonia is a bridge to the unknown. That is why I mention that the war we are about to see is about control and power," Oraculus said. "You must understand, Maradonia is the key to the main portal, which is the entrance to the rest of the universe."

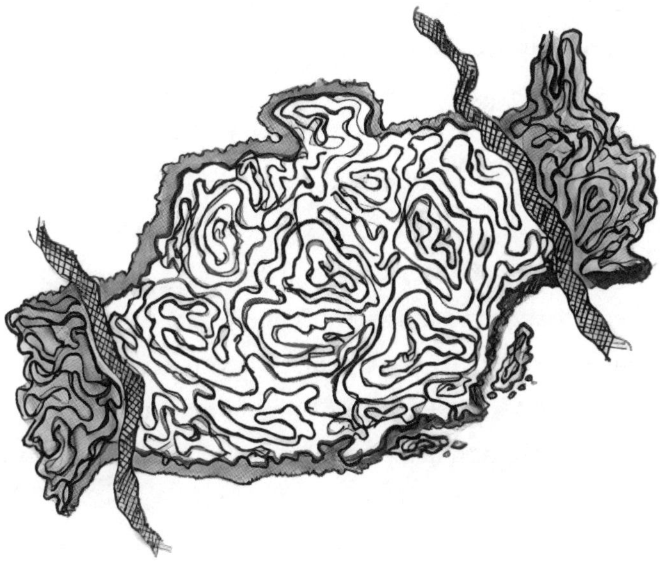

"Like a traveling portal?" Joey eyes betrayed doubt, but he asked, "Maybe it can take us home?"

Just then, an eerie screech rose from the depths of the jungle. Maya looked out of the hut's door in time to see several ravens rise over the trees and fly off.

Oraculus furrowed his eyebrows.

"I suspect those may be spies of King Palazar." He leaned in closer to the siblings, whispering, "I can feel that the air has changed. I foresee that King Palazar will soon declare war over the land of Maradonia because the portal's guardians, the mermaids, have grown weaker."

With this, Joey burst out laughing. "Mermaids? Come on, man. Seriously? This is fantasy." He waved his wooden spoon and added, "I'm sorry, but I think you've been stranded on this island a little too long!"

Oraculus stiffened his back. "Don't be ignorant. It has to do with faith, my boy! All great leaders have one common gift. Faith! Faith is like a magnet in your heart and a compass in your head. Never forget. When you handle yourself, always use your head, and when you handle others, always use your heart."

Maya nodded. It was good advice. As crazy as it seemed, she couldn't help but trust his words.

Joey, on the other hand, sighed, fearing Oraculus's talks were just a dead end of nonsense.

"You didn't come here by accident," Oraculus continued, his mood lightening. "*You must fulfill your destiny.* It is the only way you can return safely to your old world. Help the mermaids and defend the portal. In return they will help you get back to your own world."

Maya couldn't explain it, but Oraculus's words rang true in her heart. She didn't know why she believed him—she simply did.

"Well," Maya finally admitted. "I also have mixed feelings about all this." For a moment, she felt dizzy. "This just all feels . . . unreal."

"It does, doesn't it?" Oraculus said, peering into her eyes. "The most powerful truths sometimes knock us off balance when they are new to us. This is your mind seeking equilibrium in the storm of knowledge."

"So, that's it?" Joey asked in disbelief. "We're stuck in a different world and our only way home is to help these mermaids?"

Oraculus slowly got up and brushed the sand from his robe. "I will leave you to discuss your choice. The decision must be yours and yours alone. I am merely the messenger." Oraculus looked down at the siblings, then strode toward the bamboo door, where he stopped.

"But be warned," he said. "King Palazar's spies are everywhere. They may already know you are here. Once the Forces of Darkness know you have entered the land, they will do everything they can to find you and kill you. If you take the responsibility of fulfilling your destiny, you become an enormous threat to all of them.

"It comes down to this: every living thing in this world serves one of two forces. The Forces of Light, or the Forces of Darkness. Here, the Forces of Darkness are ruled by Palazar. He presents illusions of power, greed, and self-glory. Anyone who follows these illusions will be lured into his kingdom. But the Forces of Light are illuminated forever by peace, love, and wisdom."

With that, Oraculus left the hut. The monkey stared at the floor, silently, understanding the risks to his new friends.

"I think he left out *unicorns and ogres*," Joey scoffed.

"Joey—" Maya began.

Joey exhaled loudly. "Come on, sis! Don't be stupid. Do you really believe this guy? It's nice that he sheltered us and fed us, but Forces of Darkness? Portals? Mermaids? It's nuts! It's like something from a fairy tale."

"Fairy tales and myths come from somewhere you know," Maya said, more to herself. "Many of them are based on ancient, somewhat true, stories."

Another eerie howl escaped from the depths of the jungle, this time further away. The siblings looked through the bamboo curtain to see the lingering fog start to roll in with unnatural speed. Then a strange silence hung over the whole jungle, as if everything around them was waiting for something to happen. Maya felt goosebumps rise on her arms and legs.

"You believe him?" Joey asked in a much quieter voice.

His sister took a deep breath. "When I was in the ocean, I heard voices that came out of nowhere. I believe opportunities come only once in a lifetime. I believe that we're stranded on a really strange island, and that there's a monkey that's smarter than he should be!"

Bubah chirped, nodded, and showed his teeth with pride.

"So, you want to go on this quest to help some *mermaids*?" Joey mocked. Then he added, "Man, I can't believe I just said that."

"Do you have a better idea? How else are we getting home?"

Joey grumbled into his empty bowl. "Honestly, I'm not sure. I mean we could wait on the beach and continue being stranded until help comes. But what if nobody comes to our rescue? How long can we survive on this island?" Joey continued to stare into the fire, unsure of his own thoughts.

Maya lifted her head. "I don't know how to describe it. Somehow, in my heart, I believe Oraculus. Let's take a chance."

Joey looked intently into his sister's eyes. He placed his hand on her shoulder. "Maya, you know, if that's what you believe, that's good enough for me."

At that moment, the monkey chittered, happily hopping on his hammock from foot to foot.

"Sounds like our guests are listening to their hearts, Bubah," Oraculus said from the doorway. "The best advisor any leader could have is their own heart."

The monkey jumped on Joey's shoulder.

Joey chuckled. "Looks like we're friends now, huh?"

"It is time, then," Oraculus continued, "for you to journey to the lagoon."

He grasped both of Maya's shoulders. Maya was surprised to see in Oraculus' eyes what looked like two miniature storms. Dark clouds drifted through them. In each eye, she saw tiny bolts of lightning.

"This is your first leap of faith," Oraculus said. "But it won't be your last. Remember, both of you have been given a spiritual gift. You must discover what that is. Each gift is given individually, and each is special in its own way."

CHAPTER NINE

STRENGTH

After they had rested in the hammocks set up by Oraculus, they felt better. As crazy as it seemed, they were ready to take on this adventure.

The compass needle rocked back and forth until Joey determined the right direction.

"Still working," he confirmed. "All we need to do to find the lagoon is to follow the river due north, just like Oraculus said."

That was the only instruction the old man had given them, no other hints or suggestions. *If we are going to get through this,* Joey thought, *we are going to have to do it with our own wits.*

It was a luminous morning. Sun beams broke through the forest as glowing bugs, butterflies, and bees flew through the air with golden sparkles floating behind them. As the siblings passed through the sea of trees, strange birds flew off into the sky like tiny rockets, singing sweet songs. Maya's heart was filled with enchantment as she gazed at the forest and the trees surrounded by glistening smoke. It seemed that the deeper they ventured into the forest, the more vibrant the colors became. She took a deep breath and filled her lungs with oxygen.

After walking for over an hour, Maya's feet ached from scrambling over the loose rocks and pebbles that lined the river's edge.

"Wait," she heard Joey say.

Maya followed Joey's pointing finger. So far, the forest had led them to a rocky stretch of riverbank to walk along. But now the forest was closing in. In front of them, the trees and overgrown bushes were blocking the way, growing right up to the water's edge as far as they could see.

"What do we do now?" Maya asked, sitting down to rest on a boulder. She wiped the sweat off her forehead with the sleeve of her shirt.

Joey smirked. "I've got something in my backpack you don't know about," he said.

"And what would that be?" she asked, slightly irritated.

Joey dropped his backpack and pulled out a long knife.

"Dad's machete!" Maya said.

"The best thing I packed!" he said, taking a practice swing. "Failing to prepare is preparing to fail," Joey added, proudly. "And I don't plan on failing."

Joey hacked at several hanging plants that were blocking their way. The sharp blade sliced right through them. Within minutes, large drops of sweat poured down Joey's face.

They stuck close to the riverbank and continued working their way through the bushes, gigantic jungle plants, and woody vines. Suddenly, Joey stopped.

"Don't take another step," he whispered.

Following his gaze, Maya turned to look at the river. Hungry eyes were looking back at them from the water's surface. A creature that resembled a crocodile was eyeing them from a short distance. Three times the size of a regular crocodile, it looked prehistoric. Its bumpy scales vibrated, rippling the black water. Then, the siblings realized there were more than one.

"Let's go!" Joey shouted, bolting into the jungle.

The hungry crocs moved with speed, lumbering up the muddy bank, piling over one another, their jaws chomping, trying to grab the siblings. But they couldn't reach them and seemed to be reluctant to venture too far from the water. Maya looked back and was relieved they were holding back.

Maya followed Joey back into the dense jungle. Leaves and vines struck her hard as she rushed through the overgrown vegetation.

Joey stopped so quickly that Maya ran right into his backpack.

"Are they gone?" Joey asked, breathless.

Maya nodded, unable to speak.

They were standing under a huge banana tree that was entangled with an exotic air plant with hundreds of roots hanging down from it. Joey lifted up his machete.

"What is it now?" Maya exclaimed, hands on her hips. It took her a long moment to examine the roots, until she saw it herself. Then she froze. Joey seemed terrified, too.

In front of them, wrapped around a fallen tree, was a gigantic snake. Its eyes shone bright red, its tongue flicking in and out. Its thick body sparkled with what appeared to be gemstones.

"Ssssooo," the snake hissed, "you think you can tresssspasss in my territory?"

"We didn't know we were trespassing," Joey said with nervousness in his voice. "We are just passing through."

Maya was amazed at how quickly Joey shook off the fact that this snake was *talking*! The tiny jewels on the snake's skin glistened and danced. The beams of sunlight that poured through the trees sparkled in a mesmerizing way.

"You're . . . you're very beautiful," Maya commented.

The snake turned her head and began slithering closer to the siblings.

"Yessss," the snake hissed, "yesss, I am. They call me Munasa." The snake beckoned with her ruby-colored eyes. Maya tensed, as if she were paralyzed. Her heart began to pound through her chest, while her hands began

to sweat. She rubbed them on her pants. Maya took a moment to compose herself to hide any sense of fear. Her brother, on the other hand, confidently inched forward, saying, "Please let us pass; we won't bother you."

"I understand. But you may *not* passsss through my territory."

"But we have to," Joey said, standing up straight. "There's no other way we can go."

Maya shivered. She turned her eyes from Munasa's jewels to stare at her brother. Joey had more inner strength and bravery than she had given him credit for.

"Isss that ssssso?" Munasa said revealing large venomous fangs. She slithered closer, her body moving side to side.

Suddenly, a disturbance in the air made the snake look up. Maya looked up to see seven white doves cooing in the tree overhead. Munasa hissed in disgust.

"You!" Munasa spat. Her fangs dripping with venom.

To Maya's surprise, the largest of the doves flew down from the tree to land on her shoulder. Before Maya could react, the dove spoke, "You must follow me!"

Munasa gazed deeply into Maya's eyes.

"And jussst who are you then, that the wretched dovessss come to your aid?"

"Don't answer," the dove said in her airy voice. "Munasa is a spy to the dark realm, possessed by King Palazar."

Munasa slithered a few feet closer to Maya and Joey.

"Stay where you are," Joey warned, taking a step back and raising the machete.

"If these foul birdssss appear, sssomething unusual is going on. Sssomething important." The large snake rose higher and higher, stretching her bejeweled body twice the height of Maya and Joey.

The delicate white dove whispered into Maya's ear again. "My sisters and I have been ordered to follow you. I am Libertine, and I must guide you when you are in need." The dove spoke louder, so Joey could hear, "Munasa will deceive you. She will kill you. Defend yourselves!"

"B-but," Maya stammered, "I-I don't want to fight. I don't want to—"

Suddenly, Munasa gave a mighty hiss and lunged at the siblings. Her mouth spat venom at Joey, who was quick enough to leap out of the way.

The venom landed on the hanging roots of an air plant and quickly burned straight through them, like acid.

Without a second thought, Joey swung the machete and connected with Munasa's neck. Maya gasped in horror. The snake's head had come right off!

Munasa screeched as her long body lashed around on the ground and then, finally, curled in on itself. Her eyes now burned a vivid red. They pulsed a final burst of color, and then grew dark.

A strange silence surrounded the siblings. Maya held her breath in awe, her gaze fixed on the massive, headless snake on the grass.

"Joey," she finally squeaked. "That was just . . ."

"Unbelievably heroic? Awesome?" Joey grinned, adrenaline rushing through his whole body. He triumphantly held the machete aloft with one hand and, with the other, pounded on his chest like a gorilla.

But as relieved as Maya was, she also felt sorry for the snake. "That poor creature. I mean, I don't think I could have done that," Maya whispered.

"Well," Joey said, gathering up an oversized banana leaf, "it was either us or the snake. Look at it from that perspective."

"He's right, Maya," the dove said and took off into the sky to join the other doves.

Joey watched them fly away, then turned to his sister. "A worried person sees a problem," he said. "A concerned person solves the problem." Joey wrapped the snake head in the banana leaf and pushed it into his backpack. "Leaders must keep their cool," he added with a new confidence, "when those around them are lost to despair. A quote by my teacher."

"Wait," Maya said in shock. "You're keeping *that*?"

Joey shrugged. "It's covered in jewels. It's gotta be worth a fortune!"

After a moment's shock, Maya laughed hard, and kept laughing hysterically. Not because she thought the whole situation was funny, but because she was overwhelmed with the strangeness of it all. Her hysterical laugh turned into a torrent of tears. She sat down on the ground and curled up, her face in between her knees. Joey gave her a moment to gather herself before he said anything.

"Are you okay?"

"Did that really happen?" she mumbled, trying to control her thoughts. Her anxiety kicked in. "I mean, I can't believe it."

"What do you mean?" Joey asked.

"Think about it. We're shipwrecked. We meet some island man, a bunch of killer crocodiles, a talking snake, talking doves, and now we're looking for mermaids? What is going on?"

"I don't know, but we're here, and this is real. We've got to keep moving and find those mermaids if we're ever going to see Mom and Dad again," Joey said, resting a hand on his sister's shoulder.

Maya nodded but didn't move.

"Come on," Joey said, pulling his sister back up. "We'll pass through easily now that we don't have to worry about *tresspassssing*," he drawled, mocking Munasa.

Maya rolled her eyes but smiled. She took a deep breath and ran her fingers through her hair. Having Joey by her side was filling her with strength. He seemed to be able to tackle anything. It was a side of him that she had never noticed before.

"Okay, I'm ready," she said, wiping the tears away.

"Then it's onward we go," Joey announced. He turned to the overgrown jungle plants and started swinging the machete at them with a new vigor.

CHAPTER TEN

KING PALAZAR

Mount Hailstone rose like a jumble of dirty, icy daggers above the soft, snowy peaks of the neighboring mountains. On the far side of the mountain was the frigid sea. Roaring waves crashed over the jagged rocks and howling winds battered the base of the mountain like a giant fist.

Mount Hailstone had been home to the deities of the dark realm for a thousand years. In V-formation, a murder of crows constantly circled its blue-gray summit. Ramparts and battle camps had been carved into the side of the frozen mountain, and a deep chasm separated the stronghold from the adjacent mountains on one side. A thin rock bridge spanned the glowing blue abyss and disappeared into Mount Hailstone's foreboding entrance, carved into the image of a skull with sharp fangs, as tall as twenty men.

Deep inside Mount Hailstone, among the roots of the mountain, was the Chamber of the General Council. Ancient columns rose from the chamber's floor to support the rocky ceiling. Ominous red stains blotched the stone floor. In the center of the cavernous room was an oval table, hewn from the icy rocks jutting up from the floor.

A congregation of twelve rulers now sat at the table, whispering to each other. These rulers represented all the underworld creatures who had, for eons, sworn allegiance to King Palazar and his reign. Countless generations of evildoing had corrupted the creatures, and they moved in the shadows of the Council Chamber like something from a nightmare. Gnomes, goblins, ogres, dwarves, trolls, titans—all were accounted for, along with several unclassified creatures.

A platoon of hooded dwarves, the royal guards, marched from their places among the columns and opened the tall doors at one side of the room. Everyone arose from their seat as King Palazar entered. No one knew how old Palazar was. It was clear, though, that after hundreds of years, the evil and hatred he stoked in his heart had spread throughout his body, corrupting it.

Palazar's bulky frame stood a full ten feet tall. But his once-white skin was now burnt and splotched. His once-piercing amber eyes now burned a sickly green. His battle uniform and flowing cloak were made of bumpy, black leathery skin.

He walked with a confidence and purpose that demanded absolute respect—and fear. Palazar strode to his seat at the oval table and stared down at those under his command. All eyes lowered. Palazar waved his hand for them to be seated.

When he spoke, his dark, icy voice boomed in echoes bouncing all around the cavern walls: "I declare the General Council to be inaugurated." He sat upon his throne with great satisfaction, his stare sweeping across those seated before him. However, the three chairs next to his own were empty. His fairy witches were late. Their insolence burned like a red-hot coal in Palazar's stomach. "Everyone at this table may speak freely and openly. All new ideas are welcome here," he announced.

The titan Orphilios, flanked by his two brothers, was first to speak. "My brothers and I have several items to discuss."

Palazar nodded to a servant dwarf to fill his wine goblet, then spoke. "Let's hear them. But let me remind you, there is only one task before us. The Kingdom of Mermaids must be destroyed so we may capture the eternal portal inside their Crystal Cathedral."

Orphilios's brother, Marcarios, spoke up. "Yes, sire. But first we must discuss the matter of who will have access to the portal once we control it. Will we, the titans, have full access to the site, or is it to be reserved for the king and his son?"

A distasteful sneer crossed his face. "It has been one year," Palazar said, "since my son, Plouton, failed our kingdom—and failed me—by suffering defeat at the hands of the mermaids and their queen, Aquamarisha. It was an experience we will not soon forget."

Many around the table swallowed hard at the memory of Palazar's rage the day he had killed his own son.

"We have every confidence that my only remaining son, Abbadon, fully understands the repercussions of defeat," Palazar continued. "Since his brother's failure, Abbadon has been preparing to avenge us. And to destroy the mermaids once and for all."

Palazar nodded to the hooded dwarf to open the doors again. Prince Abbadon walked in, wearing full battle armor. His heavy footsteps caused the wine goblets on the table to tremble. Abbadon's height, bulk, ravaged skin, and sneer made it obvious who his father was. Though young, Abbadon's appearance still struck fear into many seated around the table.

The third titan brother, Remmilos, slammed his armored fist onto the icy table. "And we are to put our faith in one more of your sons? And those fairy witches who failed us last year and don't even have the respect to attend our meeting?"

Raven after raven suddenly flew into the room, circling the table and squawking terribly. The titans lowered their heads and swatted at the birds, which flew up to perch on the high chandeliers and, after one final clamor of piercing calls, fell silent.

Just then, the three fairies entered the room through the open doors, led by Andromeda. On her left, Lilith slithered, and young Mui stepped lightly on Andromeda's right. All three folded their pointed wings under their cloaks.

Andromeda bowed deeply. "King Palazar, Rightful Lord of the Underworld, Ruler of Darkness, and soon to be Emperor of the Seven Kingdoms, we fairies beg your forgiveness for our lateness. We mean no disrespect. Our delay is due to the disturbing discoveries we have made on your behalf, and the troubling news we carry."

Whispers again circled the table as the rulers wondered what the fairies meant.

"My king, we request an immediate, private conference to share what we have seen," Andromeda said as she laid a palm upon the icy table. The motion sent tiny snow particles up into the light.

Palazar looked around the room at the troubled faces. His electric green eyes came to rest on the titan brothers. Remmilos held Palazar's gaze, his face full of anger and rebellion.

"You will tell us now, sisters," Palazar said. He opened his arms wide and grinned. "We have no secrets here."

"But my lord, what we have to say—" Mui began in her airy voice.

"I demand you to speak!" Palazar shouted.

Andromeda stepped protectively in front of Mui. "As you insist," Andromeda said giving her sister a look. "Our news is most disturbing. We have seen two children."

"Children?" Palazar scorned.

"Humans, sire," Lilith confirmed. "Here in the land. A brother and sister."

Several anxious voices around the table repeated the words in dismay.

"Silence!" Palazar shouted. All went quiet. "For one full year," the king continued, bottling his rage, "we have prepared the greatest armada Maradonia has ever seen. We have built weapons never before imagined; weapons created specifically to destroy the mermaids where we've never been able to attack them before—in their very own waters. My son is ready. Our forces are ready, and you are worried about children?"

"But, sire," one of the dwarves' delegation said fearfully, "the prophecy."

Palazar jumped to his feet. "Silence. I have heard enough! Superstition, folklore, bedtime stories. Are we infants to tremble at the words some mermaid-witch uttered three hundred years ago as she lay dying under my sword?"

The room fell silent.

Palazar crossed the room to face his son. He placed his hands on

Abbadon's shoulders. "I place my trust in iron, in our power and strength, in vengeance, and in our numbers!" Fuming, Palazar turned to the rulers sitting at the table. "I now invoke the ancient pledges. It is time to fulfill your promises and prove your loyalties. Each of you shall provide me with one thousand warriors to man our ships. They will obey my son and watch the mermaid queen perish under his blade!"

"One thousand warriors?" Orphilios shouted. "That means we will leave our own lands defenseless!"

"That means victory!" Palazar shouted even louder.

"My *king*," Remmilos said, sneering the word. "You have not answered our question. Will we titans have access to the portal once we control it?"

Palazar walked slowly back to his chair and sat. For a long moment, there was silence in the hall until Prince Abbadon, gesturing toward his father, said, "There is only one king here. You would do well to remember that."

King Palazar nodded approvingly.

That was the moment when the titan, Remmilos, stood up from his seat. In all his armor, he stood tall and barbaric. His eyes screamed for war as he declared, "If you cannot respect our people, then I say we need a change of leadership."

An icy howl of wind blew through the palace, leaving a trace of snowflakes across the floor. An eerie silence fell upon the room. Remmilos looked around nervously. "Why has everyone become silent? Now is the time to speak."

King Palazar closed his eyes and slowly lowered his hands to the icy table, anger rising from the depths of his soul. It circulated through his chest and into his head. When he opened his eyes again, he turned his hands over and two glowing fireballs were hovering over his palms. The fear of death fell over the hall like a fog. A raven croaked, breaking the silence.

Andromeda stepped forward to face the titan. "You have no right to criticize our anointed king!"

Remmilos stared uncertainly at the fireballs in Palazar's hands yet continued, "But King Palazar told us all to speak freely and openly."

Andromeda stepped back quickly when she saw the king rise from his seat. Palazar stared pitilessly at Remmilos. The fireballs in the air glided forward and merged into one, floating over the table. Lowering his head at Remmilos, Palazar slapped his hands together and made a swift pushing motion.

The large fireball raced across the table and struck Remmilos through his armor. He screamed in agony as the fire consumed him from the inside out. After several terrible seconds, the fire finally dissolved the titan. All that was left was a wisp of smoke.

The remaining titan brothers, Orphilios and Marcarios, kept looking at the seat where their brother had sat a moment earlier. As brutal thoughts rushed through their minds, the two remaining titans became consumed with raging hatred against Palazar but remained silent.

Everyone else traded horrified looks and held their breath. Palazar shrugged and sat back down as if nothing had happened. He gulped down his glass of wine, then said, "A change of kingship is unconceivable. Any other questions?"

No one dared speak.

"Sire?" the dwarf ruler said quietly. "How do we know the mermaids won't use the portal to call for aid, as in times past?"

"Help? From whom?" Palazar laughed. "The Seven Kingdoms are fractured. There is mistrust. It has been centuries since one kingdom came to the aid of another. The mermaids are alone; they have no one."

The rulers nodded their heads, knowing the truth of it.

"Now is the time," Palazar continued. "When the kingdoms are divided, one by one they shall each fall, and we conquer the greatest prize of all."

"Yes, yes!" the rulers responded, gaining courage.

"After all these centuries, the whole universe is within our grasp," Palazar said, raising his voice. "The time has come. The war has begun. Summon your warriors immediately!"

Many began to rise, eager to do the king's bidding, but Andromeda's voice kept them in place.

"My lord," Andromeda said. She moved forward, her wings glistening. "I desire to find out more information about the human siblings. Prophecy or no, it is alarming. Allow my sisters and I to investigate."

"Again with these children?" he scoffed. The undisputed king threw back his head and laughed. "What can two mere children possibly do to us?" A terrible grin crossed Palazar's burnt face. "Go and play with them. I have seven kingdoms to conquer."

CHAPTER ELEVEN

SUNFLOWERS

MAYA AND JOEY LOOKED DOWN from their tall hill over what looked like an ocean of endless yellow flowers. The river curved off to their right. Joey nodded to his compass, then pointed over the flower field.

"Due north is that way," he said.

"Is this beautiful or what?" Maya gasped. "I can't even see where it ends."

The sunflowers were four or five times the size of the ones that grew in their mom's flower garden. That made them more than twenty feet tall. Joey agreed that the flowers in front of him were stunning, but he couldn't share Maya's enthusiasm.

"Who cares?" Joey muttered. "The fact is, it's not going to be easy to cross."

Beyond the mile-wide field of gigantic flowers was higher ground, hills that rose to the horizon.

He sighed. "I don't see another way."

Maya grinned. "At least we get to walk through a field of something beautiful!"

Maya jumped up and down, clapping her hands. As she did so, hundreds of orange birds flew from the sunflower field. Maya laughed. "Don't let me scare you, little friends," she called out to the birds, but they were already disappearing.

Joey scowled at Maya but didn't say anything. Her positivity had begun to annoy him. He swatted a large leaf with his machete.

Maya ran into the forest of sunflowers. Joey took one last look around for danger then followed her. He found his sister spinning among the sunflowers, from one tall stem to the next.

"Look at the size of this," she said, hiding playfully behind one of the sunflower leaves.

Huge butterflies fluttered around the flower petals. With every beat of their wings, a tiny ding was heard. It sounded like wind chimes.

Joey pushed at a sunflower stalk. It was wider than his head and didn't budge an inch. "These stalks are like trees," he said.

"And the flowers smell delightful," Maya said, inhaling deeply.

Joey didn't like the idea of making their way through the thick, unnatural flowers, but Maya's good humor was infectious.

"I guess you're right. They are pretty, aren't they?" he admitted, catching Maya's arm as she swung around a particularly broad stalk.

"But we need to keep the river to our right," he reminded her. "We want to keep going dead straight. Stay near me."

"I can still see the river," Maya replied cheerfully.

"Follow me," Joey said. "I've got the compass, and I will make sure we keep heading north."

"Yes, sir," Maya said, saluting. Joey smiled. As annoying as it could be, Maya's playfulness was good to see after all that they had been through.

After only a few minutes of walking through the maze of thick stalks, Joey realized the space between the sunflowers was becoming tighter and everything around him was growing darker. He looked up. Enormous petals like umbrellas covered his view. He plodded forward, Maya a few steps behind. Joey had to squeeze himself through openings in the stalks. They were so dense and strong that pushing on them did little good.

"Wow, they're even bigger here," Maya said from behind him. Their path was so narrow, she couldn't stand next to him.

Joey turned to look at his sister. "I can't see or hear the river anymore, can you?"

Maya shook her head. "Good thing we have the compass."

Joey nodded. "Yeah, follow me."

He got down on all fours and started crawling forward. Since the stalks leaned into each other as they grew, this felt like the best plan. There was more space for them to pass down low.

It was hard going forward, but Joey found his way through the maze of stalks. Looking up, he could only see flower after gigantic flower, all merging together to form a solid canopy, blocking out the sun and sky. They had to use their flashlights.

Maya kept her eyes on Joey's sneakers. But when her backpack snagged on a stalk, she had to twist sideways to release herself and get through. Maya popped through the tangle of stalks, breathing heavily.

Maya sat with her back against a stalk and calmed her breathing. "Okay. I'm good. Are we still going in the right direction?"

There was no reply, and Maya didn't hear any sign of her brother.

"Joey?" she called out loud. No answer. She yelled again. "Where are you? I can't hear you."

Fear gripped her heart. Was she lost?

She started crawling forward quickly, thrusting herself between the narrow gaps in the stalks, pushing through with all her strength, before suddenly popping out onto open ground. Before her was the higher ground and hills.

"Where are you?" she called out. "I'm through."

She closed her eyes to focus on listening. No response. It became eerily silent. Maya spun around to peer into the sunflower field, but she couldn't see further than a few feet inside of it. The sunflower stalks creaked back and forth in the soft wind. The river was far off now.

She thought, *Joey must have gotten through first and scouted the higher ground up ahead.* She stood up, brushed off her knees, and walked toward the hills.

Meanwhile, in the middle of the sunflower field, Joey was slashing at a stalk with his machete. He was able to get off his hands and knees and walk, but there still wasn't enough room for him to take a good swing. After four or five little hacks, the machete didn't bite into the stalk at all.

"Maya!" Joey yelled again. He had been calling for his sister over and over with no response. Suddenly, the sunflower stalks gave way to a bamboo forest. The tall, green bamboo shoots were so thick that they were like a curtain. Joey felt dread gripping his heart. He opened his compass again. He knew he had drifted west because the river was nowhere in sight.

"Oh man, this must be the wrong way. What should I do?" he asked out loud. "Should I crawl back into the sunflower field and try to reach the hillside again? So far, I've had very little luck in there. Or should I make my way through this bamboo and find the river?"

Joey stood still, uncertain. The feeling that he had lost his sister in a foreign land crept into his mind. He closed his eyes and focused.

"Okay," he said. "I'm positive that no good comes from concentrating on the negative." A small smile pulled at his lips. That quote always made Joey feel better.

"So," he continued. "I won't stand still. And I won't go backward. Maybe Maya made it to the river. If I was unable to make it through the sunflowers, chances are she didn't make it either."

Joey realized going back to the river made the most sense. He pulled his machete back and hacked into a bamboo shoot. The blade sliced through it, but the surrounding bamboo leaned over to fill the space. The solid curtain looked no less impenetrable. Joey sighed, taking a deep breath. This was going to take some time.

"Leadership is a privilege," he huffed. "With privilege comes responsibility. I am responsible for my sister, and I won't fail."

He drew back and sliced even harder. Two more bamboo shoots fell. Joey nodded with satisfaction and kept swinging his machete.

CHAPTER TWELVE

ENTANGLEMENT

THWACK.

The blade struck deep into the wooden post wrapped in mooring lines. Ilona walked to the post and retrieved her throwing knife. She walked back twenty paces this time and threw the blade again. Again, it struck the post dead center. Three inches in either direction, the blade would have flown into the bay.

Behind Ilona, docked at the military wharf in San Diego, California, floated the *Explorer 2*. This was the vessel that would carry the science team to the island of Husario. Around her, US Navy personnel rushed around the wharf with forklifts and dollies, loading the ship with large wooden boxes marked in red labels that read "FLYING BIRD."

"Careful, careful!" Doctor Huang called out to a beefy lieutenant, who was instructing a driver on the forklift. "That equipment is one of a kind. Irreplaceable and expensive!"

Lieutenant Kreeger had been watching but turned his attention to the ship. The vessel itself was an unusual sight. It was chunky, boxy, and almost sinister looking. The Navy's most advanced craft, *Explorer 2,* was covered in black metal shielding. The high-tech metal plates were made of an experimental cloaking alloy that absorbed sunlight and were angled to deflect radar and other tracking technologies. As promised by the intelligence team, *Explorer 2* was harder to locate than any other vessel in the world.

THWACK.

Doctor Huang turned to see Ilona walking toward her blade again. As she removed her knife, he saw what he had been looking for. Behind Ilona, on the wharf, his son was walking toward the ship.

"Gordon!" Huang called. He ran to his son and embraced him. Gordon hugged his father in return. Huang pulled back and held his son's shoulders. Gazing into his face he said, "You'll never understand how happy I am to see you and hold you in my arms again," Huang said. "Unless you ever become a father yourself one day."

Gordon nodded. A good-humored smile showed itself on his handsome face.

THWACK.

Gordon turned to see Ilona stride to her blade.

Huang shook his head. "Our security officer is very . . . impressive."

"Very," Gordon said, unable to take his eyes off Ilona.

"Gordie!"

Gordon suddenly found himself in the suffocating embrace of Professor Mundi. "My boy, you are a sight for sore eyes!"

"Thank you, Professor," Gordon chuckled, pulling himself free of the large man's grip.

"Anything new?" Gordon asked his father.

Huang knew what his son was referring to and dove right in. "It seems our Chinese friends are close to a breakthrough," he said, growing serious. "Our contacts in Beijing report that they've made progress with their photon entanglement. Yesterday, they successfully interacted with their satellite in high earth orbit."

"You mean data transfer?" Gordon's eyes lit up.

"Yes," his father said. "They have successfully teleported information on a photon."

Gordon pulled his father to a quieter area behind crates full of fruit where no one could overhear. Mundi followed, swiping at a moth flitting around his head.

Gordon lowered his voice. "They're moving quicker than we thought then."

"Photon entanglement?" Mundi asked. He finally swatted the moth in the other direction.

Gordon nodded. "Einstein called it 'spooky action.' Even he couldn't explain it. In certain situations, particles can somehow remain connected to each other—and actually act on each other—even when they are physically very far apart."

"As far away as earth to the satellite in this case," Huang interjected.

"For instance," Huang explained, "push on one and it pushes on the other."

"Or," Gordon said, "imprint one with data, and it transfers that data to the other."

Mundi's eyes widened. "Unbelievable. It sounds like science fiction. My favorite." He chuckled and grabbed an orange from the nearby crate and started peeling it. He offered a piece to Gordon and his father. Gordon grabbed a slice.

"You're right, Professor Mundi. Much of modern science sounds like fiction these days. I realized when I was out on the water," Gordon said as he looked into the horizon, "that we were close to the energy source, and then that storm came out of nowhere. I'll have to reevaluate the data before making any statements, but this is an exciting development."

"This is one of the reasons you are here, professor," Huang said, turning to his old friend. "We might need your imagination and knowledge of folklore. As scientists, we are entering unknown realms. You could say that our work is where science meets magic."

Gordon snorted. "I would say our work is where science meets more science—just previously unknown science."

Mundi lowered his head dramatically and bowed. "I'm happy to be of service any way I can."

"Glad to have you aboard," Gordon said. Then his thoughts took him back to the seriousness of the project. He furrowed his eyebrows. "Our competitors might be on the edge of discovering the full teleportation of organic material."

Mundi blinked. "You mean people? Teleporting people?"

"Professor," Huang said, "this portal we are searching for on Husario is rumored to do exactly that. Technically, we are on a mission based merely on theory."

"However, since the Chinese are getting closer to their own findings, our mission just became even more crucial." Gordon said, waving the moth from his face again.

"And time sensitive," his father added.

SWISH—THWACK.

Ilona's throwing dagger whizzed between Gordon and Huang's faces, missing each by mere inches. It stuck into the fruit crate right behind them. All three turned.

Ilona strode forward, her face hard as stone.

"Are you mad?" Mundi exclaimed. "Throwing a knife right between us? What if you'd missed?"

Ilona stepped between them. She grabbed the hilt of her knife and pulled it out. Pierced on the tip of it was the moth. She wiped the dead insect on her leg and looked into Mundi's eyes.

"I never miss," she said, and strode off.

"Now she," Gordon said, "is quite a woman."

"A very reckless woman, I must say," Mundi huffed, and walked toward the ship. He threw the rest of the orange peel off the dock and into the ocean.

Gordon felt his father push something hard and cold into his hand. He looked down. It was a small, black pistol. At first, Gordon gave his father a questioning look, then tucked the handgun into the back of his jeans, under his shirt.

Huang looked deep into his son's eyes.

"Keep it in case something goes wrong," Huang said. "I know I can trust you. And Mundi. But I can't say the same about anyone else on this mission."

Gordon followed his father's eyes to Ilona. She was staring at them, tossing the knife up and down in her hand.

CHAPTER THIRTEEN

THE POOL OF BACCHUS

Overlooking the field, high on the hill, Maya couldn't see any movement among the sunflowers. There was no sign of her brother.

"Joey!" she called. It was part yell, part sob. As anxiety overwhelmed her, hundreds of thoughts raced through her mind all at once. *How could I fall behind? I've always hated being alone. Now I'm all by myself in such a strange land.*

"I wish the doves were here," she said. "Honestly, I wish anyone were here."

Hopelessness crept into her heart. Maya sat down on a rock and began to cry. *If Joey was here all alone, what would he do?* Maya sniffled and wiped her eyes. *He wouldn't be sitting around, crying. No, Joey wouldn't be sad and motionless, like me. He's out there right now trying to find me. Of course he is.*

Maya hopped to her feet. "This is my challenge, isn't it?" she said. "My own personal challenge is to have faith and believe in myself, so that's exactly what I'm going to do!"

She looked down at her dirty shoes. It only took one step to start any journey. She inhaled a deep breath and took that first step, and with every step after that, her spirits rose. She took a moment to appreciate her own strength. She wasn't waiting, or crying, or too scared to do anything—she was moving forward. She was grateful for it. And it gave her courage.

Maya turned from the sunflowers to look over the opposite side of the hill she was standing on. There were other hills in that direction, higher than the one she was on. However, at the bottom of her own hill was what looked like a valley.

Scanning the area, she saw something sparkle. She squinted. It was—water. It was then she realized she was thirsty. She headed right for it and soon reached the edge of the pool, but up close, she saw this was not water at all. The liquid looked thicker than water. Its surface was murky and oily. She couldn't see the bottom of the pool. She bent down to get a better look and slowly inserted a finger into the liquid. It was sticky. Maya's finger started feeling warm and numb. Then the sludgy liquid became heavy, as if something were pulling her finger deeper into the substance.

Surprised, Maya jerked her hand back. When she did this, she lost her balance and fell into the thick liquid. As she sank, her heart raced. She tried spinning her body around, looking frantically for anything to grab hold of, but her body sank deeper into the swampy pool. Her body began to tingle and feel strangely numb.

The dove with a golden tail feather landed in front of her, on the bank.

"Libertine!" Maya gasped. "Oh, thank God."

The dove replied cautiously, "Be still, young one. The more you struggle, the deeper you will sink. You must keep your head above the water."

Maya closed her eyes and forced her body to relax, chanting in her mind, *I can do this, I can do this*, as tears streamed down her cheeks.

Libertine cooed, "We will find your brother. Three of my sisters will stay here with you. The other three will come with me."

Maya willed herself to keep still. "Please hurry!"

Libertine shot into the sky, followed by three of her sisters. The doves quickly spread out over the sunflower field. It didn't take long for Libertine to spot the fallen bamboo. She flew down into the area, and her sisters followed. Just as Joey broke through the last of the bamboo and stood, panting, near the bank of the river, the four circled his head.

"Hurry and follow us as fast as you can," Libertine commanded. "Maya has fallen into the Pool of Bacchus!"

"The pool of what?" Joey asked.

"No time to explain, but know she is in grave danger. Come!" Libertine said.

The four doves started flying upriver, but Joey was standing still. Libertine circled back.

"What are you waiting for?" the dove asked.

Joey's eyebrows formed a V on his forehead. "I'm not so sure," he said.

"What? Why?" Libertine landed on a rock nearby.

"Because you're a talking bird for one," Joey said incredulously. "That takes a little getting used to, you know? Plus, I did pretty well by myself just now, getting out of that maze. I'm not sure I want to just go and follow you now."

"It is true you do not know us well," Libertine admitted. "But back with Munasa—didn't we give you good advice? Didn't we warn you of her attack?"

Joey thought about it. "Yes, you did. But I don't know if I want to trust my life—and Maya's—to someone else. I don't want to follow you blindly when I have faith in myself, too."

Libertine was nodding. "You have done very well so far. Admirably well. But a leader doesn't always lead. Sometimes you must know when to lead, and when to follow."

Joey heard the truth in the bird's words. As odd as it seemed, he did trust Libertine. And he realized that, in this moment, it would indeed be smarter to follow rather than lead.

"Okay," he said. "That makes sense. This is your land. You lead, I'll follow."

"Good," the dove said in her gentle voice. "But hurry! If we don't reach her quickly, she will die!" Libertine lifted into the air and beat her wings, hard, leading him upriver. Joey took off after her, running.

"Hey!" he called out. "Why aren't we sticking to the river if Maya is over that way?"

Just then, Joey saw that Libertine had led him to a grassy lane that cut directly from the riverbank to the bottom of the nearby hill that marked the end of the sunflower field.

Joey, sprinting down the pathway, thought, *I never would have found this on my own.*

"Hurry, young one," Libertine called back to him. "The pool is toxic. She doesn't have much time!"

Joey ran even faster.

At the pool, Maya had tilted her head back. The noxious liquid was now up to her ears. Libertine's sisters were hopping up and down on rocks, speaking words of encouragement to her.

One of them bobbed her head and said, "Hold on. I hear them coming!"

"Hurry!" Maya called with every last breath she had. Her entire body was numb and her chest heavy with unimaginable pressure.

"I'm here!" Joey yelled, coming into view and seeing the pool. He ran to the edge of the water, huffing.

"Don't touch it!" the doves warned.

Maya gasped with tiny, short breaths. "I feel terrible," she said in between breaths. "Something is happening to me in here! Don't let it get you."

Joey frantically surveyed his surroundings, then rushed into the bushes. After three quick machete cuts, Joey was back in front of his sister, kneeling on the same rock she had slipped from. Joey held a long branch. He grabbed the rock with one hand and used the other to extend the branch to Maya. It touched the pool just inches from Maya's head.

"Grab it," Joey called. "Lift your arm out and grab it!"

Maya struggled to lift her arm through the muck. "It's . . . it's too hard!"

"C'mon!" Joey yelled. "On the count of three, give it everything you've got. Ready?"

Maya summoned every ounce of strength to her arm, but a heavy weight was pulling her back down into the pool. Maya fought and fought, urging her arm upward until, finally, her hand popped out of the black muck and grabbed hold of the branch. Joey took the branch in both hands, leaned back, and pulled.

"Pull, Joey, pull!" the doves cheered.

Slowly, Maya inched closer to shore. Joey pulled even harder, trembling and grunting with the effort. Finally Maya made it to the base of the rock. He reached down into the pool, took hold of Maya's arm and pulled. Then he leapt back from the rock to the shore, and with one final pull, Maya popped free of the pond. Overcome with the effort, Joey fell to his stomach. The siblings lay side by side on the rocky shore of the pool, panting.

"We did it," Joey gasped.

Joey lifted his hand to wipe mud from Maya's face, only to realize his arm was becoming stiff. It began to feel like it weighed a hundred pounds. Joey felt little pinpricks from his shoulder to his fingers. Investigating his arm, Joey saw that it was encased in the same black mud that covered most of Maya. The mud was half liquid, half solid—and getting stiffer as it dried.

"What's going on?" he asked, swinging his arm around like it wasn't part of his body anymore.

"Maya?" Joey looked in horror to see that Maya's eyes were closed and her breathing was shallow.

"Wake up! Please," Joey tugged at Maya's muddy arms. The skin on her face started to turn blue.

Libertine flapped her wings up and down as she chirped, "We must get her to the river! The toxic Pool of Bacchus carries a liquid that dries in the air and builds a cover like stone. You must wash it off as soon as possible. Otherwise, Maya will die of the liquid stone's intoxication."

Joey closed his eyes, concentrating. "How do we get there?" he asked, his trust in Libertine now complete.

"Follow us."

Joey pushed himself onto his feet. His arm felt so heavy that he was tilting to one side. He felt dizzy and grabbed onto a rock for support.

"You are already feeling the toxic influence of the pool," Libertine said as she flew into the air, joining her sisters circling overhead.

Joey took a deep breath and squatted in front of his sister. He turned, facing away from her. With his good arm, he reached back and lifted Maya's arms onto his shoulders. With all his strength, Joey slowly stood up. His legs trembled, but he got Maya up onto his back and started staggering forward.

"Follow us!" Libertine chirped. The doves started flying along the crest of the hill, toward the river.

Joey's encrusted arm felt like hot lead, and Maya was growing stiffer and heavier. After just a few minutes, the load was nearly too much for Joey to bear. The doves took turns flying down to Joey, saying, "You can do it. Halfway there. We're getting close."

Meanwhile, Maya was in a dream state of mind. She saw herself and her brother walking through an icy forest. She felt her body temperature drop, and her breath fogged when she exhaled. Snow started building up on the ground with every step she took. Then she felt a sense of urgency as they started running through the frozen forest . . .

"Just a little bit farther," she heard her brother say.

Then, somehow, they reached a palace that was engraved into the mountain. Ocean waves battered the sides, crashing back and forth. It became harder for her to breathe, and her mind raced in confusion. *Where were they?*

Joey was in a blur of pain and fatigue. He was staring at his sneakers, willing each step to happen, and then staring at his feet in surprise when it did.

"All right, this will have to do," he heard Libertine call out. That was all Joey needed to hear. He squatted down, allowed Maya to slip off his back, and then fell over into soft, wet grass. He felt a flurry of wings and knew Libertine had landed nearby. A prolonged crashing sound was coming from the area just to his right. Joey opened his eyes and saw that he was at the riverbank.

"Okay," he panted, "now what?"

Libertine replied, "You must deliver Maya to the heart and source of the river's energy."

Joey followed the bird's eyes. Near to where he was lying, rapids frothed among rocks. But then the river disappeared. Joey blinked at the sight.

"Wait, isn't that a—"

Libertine nodded. "A waterfall."

Maya groaned, muttering words that made no sense.

"The toxins," Libertine said. "She's almost out of time. Soon the madness of Bacchus will overtake her completely. If you don't move now, she will be lost inside her own mind."

Without a second thought, Joey staggered to his feet. He lifted Maya up in a hug and dragged her to the water's edge. Joey was scared to see no recognition, no intelligence in Maya's half-open eyes. It looked like her eyes were foggy. Joey shivered with fear.

With a deep breath, he launched them both into the icy river. The current took hold of them immediately. Unable to guide them, Joey did everything he could to keep Maya's head above water as the river swept them over the rapids and straight over the edge of the tall waterfall, when Joey lost hold of Maya. He felt his body fly through the mist; then he felt the impact as he landed in the plunge pool. He sank down deep into the crystal-clear pool. Kicking hard, Joey broke the surface and immediately looked for his sister.

Still in her dream state of mind, Maya saw the ocean waves beating against the mountain palace. She watched in fear as the waves grew bigger and bigger forming into a terrifying tsunami. When Maya tried to run, it was in slow-motion. She saw her brother as he ran away faster and disappeared. She tried to follow, until she was totally consumed by the tsunami. The massive wave overpowered her and swallowed her into the depths of the ocean. She tried reaching the surface of the water, but the water blurred her vision, and she didn't know which way was up. Maya kicked with all her strength but couldn't reach the surface. She was sinking deeper and deeper into the depths.

"Maya," the voices sang, "come and help us!"

Her lungs felt like they would burst. She couldn't reach the surface of the water.

"Maya, help us!" The voices were pleading with her.

Her arms felt like they were made of stone. It was hopeless. She'd never reach the surface. She would drown. And she would not be able to help the mermaids. Maya opened her mouth to scream under the water. Unable to move her body, the waves crushed her and pushed her deeper and deeper until she felt every molecule of oxygen leave her lungs.

"She's here!" Libertine called out to Joey.

Joey spun around, searching. "I don't see her!"

"Through the waterfall!" came Libertine's reply. "Follow my voice! This way!"

Joey kicked his feet and paddled with his one good arm, his other regaining its strength slowly. He made it back to the waterfall and swam through the torrential downpour. Wiping his eyes, Joey saw all the doves surrounding Maya. She was half in, half out of the water, resting upon a narrow shelf of stone. Joey pulled himself up, next to his sister.

"Rub off the mud!" Libertine said. "Quickly!"

Joey started pulling the remaining mud off Maya's face in gobs. Once her face was clear, he set to work on her arms, legs, and upper body, saying, "Come back to me, Maya! Please come back!"

Maya heard his voice as if it came from the end of a tunnel. Panting, she gulped huge mouthfuls of crisp air, sensing her consciousness struggling to wake up. Finally, she awoke. Gazing up at a strange boy with white doves flying above, she whispered, "Who are you?"

"No, stop that!" Joey shouted. "Fight it!"

Painfully, Maya moved her head and looked around. Everything was vivid. She took another deep breath.

Joey was looking down at her with fear and concern.

Maya massaged her forehead, mumbling. It was as if someone hit her on the head with a bag of bricks. "I have the worst headache," she croaked.

Maya thought about what she had just experienced. *What was that all about? A vivid dream?* The confusion stuck with her for a long moment. After inhaling a deep breath of fresh air, she shook off the feeling of uncertainty and exhaled. Her mind was coming back to her, and she looked again at her brother, smiling. *Joey.*

"You really saved me," Maya whispered.

"I had help," Joey admitted, nodding to the cooing doves.

"Promise me one thing," Maya said, still regaining her strength.

"Sure, okay, what?" Joey said, ready to promise anything, joyful that his sister had been brought back from the edge of madness.

"When we're back in our world when this is over," she said.

"Yes?"

"Don't ever let me take one of those fancy mud baths that people say are *so* good for you."

Joey's face went blank, but then he exhaled loudly and laughed.

CHAPTER FOURTEEN

DISCOVERY

In the choppy seas, Doctor Huang gripped the railing in a corridor of *Explorer 2*. Outside on deck was worse, but Huang felt constantly queasy wherever he went.

At least I'm not vomiting anymore, the scientist thought to himself, grimly.

Gordon hadn't shown up for breakfast again. And he still wasn't answering the phone in his cabin. Huang rounded a corner in the hallway to find Ilona leaning against a bulkhead, staring at him, expressionlessly. The woman always seemed to appear out of nowhere. She also seemed to know everything that happened aboard *Explorer 2*.

"Ah, good morning, young lady," Huang said, trying to suppress the churning of his stomach.

"This is a military operation, Doctor," Ilona said, standing up straight. "I believe it is more appropriate for you to address me as Sergeant Wells."

"Ah yes, you're right," Huang said, wiping the sweat from his forehead. "Good morning, Sergeant. Do you happen to know where my son is?"

"He's in his mancave. Where else would he be?"

The ship tilted to one side. Huang gripped the railing, hard. He felt his stomach churn again and closed his eyes as he took several deep breaths. Ilona stared at his shaking hand, making it perfectly clear what she thought of the man's weakness, then walked straight down the hallway, as steady as if the ship were in dry dock.

Huang shook his head. He'd have to keep his eye on Ilona for sure. He labored onward until he finally reached his son's door and knocked. There was no reply.

"Gordon?" he called to the door.

Huang tried the doorknob. It was unlocked.

He opened the door and looked into the large room that served as Gordon's laboratory. An eerie glow emanated from several large, flat-screen monitors at the back of the room. Otherwise, the room was dark. Huang could just make out a mess of sheets on the couch against one wall. He shook his head. Evidently, Gordon had been sleeping in his lab as well. Huang felt around on the wall for a switch and flicked on the overhead lights.

"Turn them off!" Gordon shouted.

Huang saw his son kneeling at a tall bank of computer hard drives, his hand covering his eyes.

"Gordon," Huang said, "you're turning into a vampire."

Gordon scrambled to the wall and flicked off the lights.

"Some of us call it working," he said to his father with a hint of bitterness.

"Some of us call it obsessing. I haven't seen you in two days," Huang said. "Have you slept at all?"

Gordon sat at his desk and waved his hand dismissively. "Here and there."

Huang crossed the room to stare at the computer monitors. "Anything new?"

"I'd have told you if there were," Gordon said, typing furiously on his keyboard.

"Have you tried triangulating the infrared—"

"Of course I have," Gordon interrupted. "I think it's safe to say I've tried everything you might think of, and then about half a million other things."

Huang sighed. He had to admit—his son was brilliant. A pain in the neck sometimes, but brilliant.

With just a few glances at the data streaming across the side monitor, Huang knew his son was right. Gordon was certainly more adept at this type of fieldwork than he was.

"But I'm also glad you're here," Gordon said.

"Oh? Is that so?" his father replied.

Gordon spun in his chair to face his father and said, "Dad, have you given any recent thought to the commercial applications of the portal?"

"I'm more concerned at the moment with actually finding it," Huang said, sitting down on the couch. "We have the general location you identified, and we have the name of the island. Husario. Funny thing is, no one seems to know exactly where it is. The last time it showed up on a chart was nearly a hundred years ago. And now it doesn't seem to be where it's supposed to be."

Gordon sighed and stared up to the ceiling.

"But what I'm saying is," Gordon said, leaning to turn up the booster on one of the satellite relays, "someone's going to make billions off the portal. And they never would have found it without our work."

Huang nodded. "Yes, of course you're right. But we are scientists and—"

"'And we pursue science and discovery for their own sake,' right," Gordon said in a mocking tone.

"Gordon. We've been through this all before. We're being paid very well for our work."

"Pennies, next to what it's worth," Gordon scoffed. "Without our years of work, they'd never even know about the portal."

Huang sighed. "This is a military operation. Without their funding, we wouldn't be here or have made any discoveries in the first place."

"But—"

"You have a point, son. Scientists have a long history of being denied their just rewards by industry and government. But this is different. Think of what the world could accomplish with teleportation. The beneficial possibilities are endless. We are doing this for the greater good of the world."

"Come on, Dad! Don't be ignorant." Gordon's tone surprised his father. "Aren't you concerned those generals and admirals are going to use it for their own benefit and keep the entire world under their control?"

"I doubt they'd take it that far."

A heavy silence fell between father and son.

"I don't," Gordon said. He lowered his head and ran his fingers through his hair in frustration. "Dad, listen. The ones who should profit from this discovery are us. You and me. Period."

Behind Gordon, on the navigational display, a red light began blinking on and off.

Huang nodded to the red light. "What is that?"

"What is what?" Gordon said, irritated.

The speakers on Gordon's desk started beeping. Gordon's eyes went wide, and he spun around in his chair to face his screens.

"Is that—?" Huang began.

"Hold on!" his son barked. "Let me check the redundant systems." Gordon's fingers flew over the keyboard. He reached over and tapped digital buttons on a touchscreen off to one side. Then he leaned back in his chair.

"Gordon, bring up the infrared signature."

"It's there," he said, annoyed, waving at another, smaller screen. Huang turned to see a pinprick of orange light on an otherwise black screen divided with trajectory lines.

Gordon scribbled on a piece of paper. "Three hundred and twenty-four nautical miles, on a course of seventy-six-point-four degrees." Gordon slammed his hand down on the desk. "We've found it! We've found Husario!"

The look on his father's face was one of stunned delight. A moment later, both men jumped to their feet and embraced.

On the back wall, behind a small mirror, a video camera lens whirled softly, zooming in. Two decks beneath them, in her private security cabin, Ilona stared at the image of father and son on one of her many security screens. She picked up her satellite phone, hit speed dial and smiled. Her father picked up the call on the first ring.

"Admiral," she said proudly into the phone, her smile widening across her face. "We've found it."

CHAPTER FIFTEEN

LAGOON OF THE MERMAIDS

"THIS FEELS WONDERFUL," Maya murmured. She took a deep breath as the aura of nature filled her lungs. The sound of the waterfall soothed the siblings as they lay on sweet smelling grass. Now the warm sunlight had dried them off completely. After all they had been through, the past hour of rest had done wonders for their bodies and souls.

"Here is the second one!" Libertine chirped. Maya opened one eye to see all seven doves flying toward her. They were carrying her backpack through the air and gently dropped it into the tall grass next to Joey's.

"Libertine, you and your sisters are amazing," Maya said, patting the dove on her head. Libertine cooed appreciatively and bowed.

"You have done well by trusting your inner faith," Libertine said. "Every time someone makes a leap of faith, he or she reaches a higher level of knowledge. And vision." She fluttered her glowing white feathers. "You are on your way to becoming mighty leaders. If you can give hope and encouragement to those who need it most, you will be true leaders."

The wind picked up in the distance. In response, many of the tall trees swayed back and forth, colorful particles glistening on the bark. Tiny leaves floated across the sky. The wind seemed to echo with the sound of chimes.

"But we must hurry," the white dove added, sniffing the air. "I fear we don't have much time."

Libertine and her sisters took flight. Maya watched them until they disappeared over the hills to the north.

The siblings began to follow the pathway Libertine had pointed out. All around them were fields of blue-green grass. On the path, the grass had been trodden down to the soft, brown dirt. Evidently creatures used the path regularly.

They entered an area where tall palm trees grew in clusters, and soon they came upon a group of rocks on the side of the path, shaded by the massive palm leaves. Joey pulled a water bottle from his backpack and shared a drink with his sister. A light breeze rustled the trees around them as they sat to rest.

"There has to be some kind of explanation for this place," Joey chuckled.

"I can't explain it either, but it is what it is." Maya took a sip of water. "I wish I could tell Mom and Dad that we're alive and well. They must be so worried. If this is how we can get back home and get back to normal again, I'm all for it."

Maya and Joey sighed at the same time. It was as if they could read each other's mind. They both knew that, in this strange place together, their only hope was to believe what an odd man told them. There was a short moment of silence between the two.

Maya perked up. "Honestly, what I'm looking forward to the most is seeing real mermaids. Do you think that's really going to happen?"

Joey snickered. "That's where I draw the line. I know for a *fact* they don't exist."

"I guess we'll see." Maya shrugged and sat up from the rock. Another cold breeze swept through the air.

"Whoa," Maya said, looking around. "Do you hear something?"

"I hear the wind," Joey muttered, putting the water bottle in his backpack.

"No," she responded, quietly. "There's something else, underneath."

"It's not bats, I hope!" he said and chuckled.

The siblings focused on the sound. Suddenly, an enormous black cloud appeared in the sky out of nowhere, moving closer with high speed.

Joey stared down the path. "Whatever it is, it's getting louder."

The siblings shielded their eyes from the sun to catch a closer look at the fast-moving cloud. That's when they realized that what they were looking at was not a cloud at all. Hundreds of ravens were soaring through the air above them, screeching loudly. The huge, black birds circled them a few times, and their shrieking grew louder and more chaotic.

"Ugh! It sounds like nails on a chalkboard," Joey said, wincing and covering his ears.

Just then, the ravens stopped circling, formed a single line, and began to fly back the way they had come.

"It sounded like some sort of alarm," Maya furrowed her eyebrows. "I don't like it. Come on, let's walk faster."

They walked on for several minutes until they turned a corner on the path. Through a line of palms, an incredible sight came into view: a beautiful beach. The sand was so pure white, it hurt their eyes. Not far ahead, lapping at the sand, was a massive lagoon. The mountains on the far side seemed very distant. To their right, through the thick palm trees, they saw glimpses of a rocky shore that ended in cliffs dropping into the open ocean. To their left were more mountains, forming a circle that protected the lagoon.

It seemed that their path was the only way to the lagoon. Apart from a narrow channel that connected the lagoon to the ocean on the far side, the mountains blocked all other access.

Without a word, the siblings walked over the soft sand. Large, flat rocks dotted the area where sand met water. When they reached the edge of the shore, Maya gasped. The siblings stood in awe as they pondered the unique lagoon.

Brightly colored fish of all sizes darted and frolicked in the crystal-clear water. Joey pointed to rings of yellow, orange, and red coral, stretching out into the water until the lagoon floor seemed to fall off and disappear into the depths. Remarkable and unique coral of all sorts grew along the shoreline too.

The longer Maya stared into the water, the more she believed she could hear the whispering voices again, the same ones she heard in the ocean after the shipwreck. She looked closer and thought she saw dark shadows move below. Her heart skipped a beat.

Suddenly, sounds of small splashes came from the water off to their right. Maya and Joey turned to look. All they saw were small ripples on the surface, spreading out in circles. Then, splashes came from their left. They spun to their left, but again only saw circular waves.

"What's that?" Maya thrust out her finger, pointing to something that was approaching the shore, something big enough to create a wake behind it.

"It's moving fast," Joey said, taking a step onto the large, flat rock in front of him to get a better look.

Suddenly, a figure leapt out of the water and slid to a stop on Joey's rock. Maya's hand flew to her mouth as she took in the sight. Joey blinked at the creature before him, his mouth dropping open.

The mermaid's scales were blue and green and shimmered like sequins. Her tail flashed and glimmered in the sunlight as she slapped it down on the rock, hard.

"I don't believe it," Joey whispered.

"She's gorgeous," Maya breathed.

The mermaid's soft, violet hair fell all the way down her back. Her face was diamond-shaped, with high cheek bones. She wore a top woven of sea grass and covered with shells. Her tail began just below her belly button—and she was carrying a strange glowing spear. Its sharp point glinted. The mermaid cocked her head, seeming to be just as curious of Maya and Joey's appearance as they were of hers.

"Who are you?" the mermaid said. She lowered the spearhead toward them. Her loud, clear voice was as sharp as her spear.

"She's exactly like I imagined," Maya said, still in awe.

"Why are you here?" the mermaid demanded, even louder. She had an interesting accent. Her voice sounded like bubbles rising from the ocean.

"I gotta be dreaming," Joey mumbled.

The spear glowed brighter, as if it were charged with electricity. The mermaid's eyes began to sparkle in a shade of dark purple. "Leave this place at once or you will drown in the bottom of our lagoon."

Maya opened her arms, palms up, in a sign of peace. "We are here because your queen has sent for us," she said.

"Lies! We accept no visitors," the mermaid declared. "Our queen would never send for—whatever you are. You were warned!"

At that moment, two more mermaids jumped onto the rock and immediately grabbed Joey by his ankles.

"Joey!" Maya yelled, running toward him.

She reached for Joey's hand, but it was too late. The mermaids pulled him straight into the water. Within a moment, he was gone, under the surface, leaving Maya alone on the sand bank.

"No!" Maya called. "Stop! You have to believe me!"

Cruel laughter echoed all around the lagoon. "Oh, no," the mermaids mocked, "Joey, Joey! No!"

Then the laughing mermaids disappeared under the water. All that was left were the ripples in the water and a light mist that swirled on the surface of the lagoon. Maya was left in silence. *This can't be happening! What do I do?* she thought.

"Please!" Maya screamed even louder, collapsing to her hands and knees. "I'm Maya, and your queen has sent for us!"

At that moment, another mermaid leapt onto the rock. She appeared taller than the rest and wore a necklace of green, sparkling gems.

"Maya?" the new mermaid said, staring at her. "Did you say that is your name?"

"Yes!" she said, on the verge of tears. "Please! Help my brother! We can't breathe underwater!"

The dark-haired mermaid sank into the water, without a splash. Moments later, Joey was thrown high into the air, and he landed on the sand bank with a thud. Maya ran to him and started slapping his back as he coughed up water and gasped for air.

Meanwhile, the dark-haired mermaid slipped up onto the rock again and snapped at the mermaid with the spear, "How dare you treat our guests like this!"

The first mermaid spoke with edge and authority. Her hair shimmered in vibrant tones of purple. "This is our territory. My patrol and I are obligated to protect this shore."

The dark-haired mermaid's eyes flashed. "Have you not listened to Queen Aquamarisha? She is expecting these humans."

"Humans?" the first mermaid repeated. "They look like hairless dwarves. Or ugly elves." Sneering at Maya, the mermaid jumped back into the lagoon. Maya saw the water rippling in many places. Maya was indignant. *Ugly elves?*

Then, a dozen mermaid heads emerged, all of them staring curiously at the siblings.

Joey sputtered, "I just saw my life flash before my eyes."

"And I got called a hairless dwarf!" Maya said.

"My apologies, humans. Mermaids are not unfriendly folk until we feel threatened. I am Crystalline," the dark-haired mermaid said. "We are the warrior mermaids of Awanata. We are the most feared warriors in all of Maradonia."

"We believe it," Maya said.

"You can say that again," Joey said, wobbling on his feet. He was soaked to the skin.

A silver-haired mermaid, much older than the rest, glided onto the rock.

"I am Persolia," she said, holding her head high. Fearlessness sparkled in her lavender eyes. "Forgive our young warriors. They have never met a human before, nor do they have the wisdom that comes from age and experience."

Maya saw the other mermaids staring at her. Some seemed happy, others were frowning. Several of them, including the first mermaid with the spear, were angrily whispering.

Persolia held up her hand and the mermaids grew quiet.

Maya bowed to Persolia. "We are ready to meet your queen. We were guided your way by a wise man. He mentioned a prophecy and that you are fighting an evil king."

Persolia nodded. "The wise man spoke the truth. Indeed, we have been expecting you. We are the guardians of the portal, the Crystal Cathedral. The crystals that adorn our holy site are not glowing as brightly as they have in generations past. Yes, we are strong, but we are losing power every day."

Even the aggressive mermaids lowered their eyes.

Confused, Maya said, "I don't know what to say, but we will help however we can."

Persolia nodded and her eyes turned vibrant. "Then you shall meet our queen, and she shall explain further." Persolia turned to face the other mermaids. On her silent command, with the flick of their tail fins, several warrior mermaids disappeared back under the water. The siblings saw them through the crystal-clear water of the lagoon begin plucking fish from the reefs. In a brief moment of time, the mermaids had deposited the wriggling, fresh fish on the flat rock.

"Eat these fish and you will regain your strength," Persolia said, cutting the tiny fish with a strangely shaped knife. "And enjoy the lagoon fruits," she said, motioning to strange fruit trees on the shore. "But wait here for our return. There are many who are very excited to see you."

Crystalline and Persolia slipped back into the water. The other mermaid heads sank below the surface. Maya was surprised to see that there wasn't a single ripple on the surface of the lagoon.

Joey sat down on the sand.

Maya's legs felt weak. She sank down to sit near Joey. "Believe in mermaids now?" she asked, punching her brother in the arm.

Joey onto his back in the sand and whistled up into the sky. He felt the sun beginning to dry his hair and clothes.

"If there's something on this island tougher than them," Joey said, "I sure don't want to meet it!"

"I'm hungry. Light a fire to cook the fish, and I'll go pick some fruit," Maya said.

CHAPTER SIXTEEN

PALAZAR'S ARMADA

THE WIND WHIPPED at King Palazar's cloak. Behind him rose the north face of Mount Hailstone. In front of him, the frigid tide rose over the rocky beach, almost touching his black leather boots. Palazar looked out over the bleak, rolling waves and smiled.

One hundred warships covered the horizon. The mighty vessels radiated a dark aura, even the sails. They sat low and heavy in the water, each carrying one hundred and twenty warriors.

The twelve rulers of darkness had responded to Palazar's command with one thousand warriors. All twelve thousand soldiers—dwarves, titans, trolls, goblins, and the rest—wore spiked armor made of black metal and held their own traditional weapons, including axes, swords, and crossbows.

Vultures landed at the edge of the rocks and watched carefully as the armada set off into the horizon. The scavengers knew that whenever these ships sailed, there would be meat.

Palazar turned to watch his servants on the docks finish loading the last of the wooden barrels. He placed his hand on Abbadon's shoulder. "My son," Palazar said. "We have done well. Many moons have passed, but in this time of planning, we have built a deadlier fighting force than Maradonia has ever seen. Our soldiers will outnumber the mermaids five to one."

In his black battle armor, Prince Abbadon bowed deeply. "Father, I assure you. Victory is ours."

Palazar stepped forward to the huge, ancient horn that had been hauled down to the shore for his parting address to the warriors. The horn looked like it had been sliced off a prehistoric creature. As their king approached it, all twelve thousand soldiers stopped their work to stand at attention, listening for their orders.

An eerie silence covered the bay. On the horizon, dark clouds began to form in the previously blue sky. Another strong gust of wind rushed through the air.

"Forces of Darkness!" Palazar shouted through the horn. His voice boomed over land and sea, amplified even further by the mountain behind him. The volume of his voice surprised even Palazar. *It is truly the voice of a god*, he thought to himself with pride.

"For centuries we have been disrespected," Palazar declared. "We have not taken our true place atop the Seven Kingdoms. Those times are past.

Today, we take the first step in the total conquest over all of Maradonia—and beyond."

A thunderous cheer erupted from twelve thousand voices. Together they sounded like the rumbling of a storm. War drums began to beat in sync. The soldiers' war cries joined the bellowing of deep drums, building to a crescendo. Palazar pulled out his sword from its scabbard. He held it up. The blade was razor sharp and had vanquished hundreds of foes.

Palazar beckoned Abbadon. His son stepped to his side and removed his battle helmet. Palazar raised the blade to Abbadon's face and, with one quick slice, opened a deep cut on his son's cheek. Abbadon did not flinch as blood trickled down his face. Palazar placed his palm against his son's cheek and then held up his bloody hand.

"This," he boomed into the horn, "is the first blood of the day. It will not be the last!" Palazar's cold eyes scanned the ships as if looking into the heart of each warrior under his command. "Do you pledge allegiance to Prince Abbadon, your commander?" he shouted.

"We pledge!" the warriors said, their voices echoing off the frozen cliffs of Mount Hailstone.

Palazar bellowed even louder. "Do you wish to sacrifice yourself to the Kingdom of Darkness?"

"We do," came the deafening reply.

"No mercy!" Palazar cried.

Thousands of throats screamed as one, "No mercy!"

The war drums beat louder, as the warriors chanted over and over again, "Death to Maradonia."

Two dwarf royal guards dragged a captured mermaid to the ancient horn and dropped her onto the sand at Palazar's feet. She was wrapped in a fishing net. Her body was thin, her tail dull and crusted with scabs. Her face, however, was held in perfect tranquility. Whatever she had endured in Palazar's dungeons had tortured her body but not damaged her spirit.

Palazar looked down at her in disgust. "Enemy scout, the only meaning of your life was to satisfy my warriors' bloodlust. It is more than you deserve."

The mermaid stared out to sea, unflinching. When Palazar lifted his hands into the air, the mermaid's body rose with them. War cries were heard coming from the ships; they sounded like raging animals. Higher and higher the mermaid floated, until she was lifted high in the air. Then the king's forces grew deathly quiet in awe and anticipation. A moment later she was gone and only her sparkling scales were left, floating on the water.

"Today the mermaids," Palazar bellowed. "Tomorrow the world!"

A terrible clanging erupted among the trolls, ogres, imps, and other creatures of darkness as they started beating their weapons against their shields and chest plates. The vibrating sound shook the pebbles and sand under the feet of the king and his entourage. The king's warriors started chanting his name.

"Pal-a-zar! Pal-a-zar!"

Vibrating with wrath, King Palazar turned to Prince Abbadon. "Return victorious, my son."

Abbadon bowed. "Yes, my king."

Palazar's eyes burned into his son's as he added, "Or don't return at all."

CHAPTER SEVENTEEN

THE CITY OF AWANATA

Dozens of mermaids began surfacing in the lagoon. The tips of their glowing spears were poking out of the water.

Persolia lifted her head and proclaimed, "Her Royal Highness, Queen Aquamarisha."

Maya and Joey scrambled to their feet. A jeweled crown rose from the water, followed by the most stunning face they had ever seen. Beauty and strength glowed from within.

Queen Aquamarisha's shiny hair seemed to alternate in color from blue to green to purple as sunlight glinted off it. Her body kept rising, levitating out of the water, until only the tail fluke remained underwater. Her purple robes flowed out around her, adorned with blue and gold gemstones. With one hand she grasped the large emerald on her golden necklace. It shimmered a deep green and seemed to be creating the soft glow that enveloped her.

All the mermaids bowed their heads simultaneously. Joey dropped to one knee and pulled Maya down beside him, whispering, "I've never met a queen before, but this is probably the proper thing to do, right?"

Maya nodded. She didn't know whether to look into Queen Aquamarisha's sparkling eyes or turn them to the ground in respect.

A smile played across the queen's face. "Maya and Joey," she said in a voice that reminded them of both fire and ice at the same time. "It was I who called you, with my mermaids, when you were adrift in the deadly ocean. I am pleased to see that you have answered my call."

"We have come to help," Joey said.

"If we can," Maya added.

Queen Aquamarisha nodded, and a young mermaid leapt from the water. Her body arced gracefully through the air, and she landed softly on the sand next to Joey. The landing of the mermaid was a surprise, but her exquisite beauty left him speechless.

"I am Princess Morgana," the black-haired mermaid announced to him. Morgana's alluring purple eyes reflected light like two flawless mirrors. Morgana seemed to be the same age as Joey, who could only mumble, "I . . . I'm . . . uh . . ."

Morgana giggled. "You're Joey. I know. I've heard a lot about you," she added.

Joey could only nod. Morgana beamed a smile that made him blush and sent a thrill of electricity through his body. His eyes instinctively met her eyes, and he smiled in response. Maya cleared her throat loudly to break the enchantment. Again, Morgana giggled as she handed two shells to the siblings as large and round as grapefruits.

"These are gifts from our queen," Morgana said. "They are from very rare water snails."

"Thank you," Maya said. "They're beautiful."

"Yeah, wow," Joey whispered, still staring at Morgana. "Beautiful."

Morgana tucked herself into a ball and sprang into the air. Turning a somersault, she entered the lagoon in a perfect, splashless dive.

"Now it is time to take you to our city," Queen Aquamarisha declared.

"But your majesty," Maya said, "we humans cannot breathe under water."

The queen laughed. "I know enough about your kind, my girl. The snail shells will enable you to breathe in the water. I have summoned two helpers to escort you."

"But—" objected Maya, who had not previously enjoyed swallowing seawater in the ocean. However, Aquamarisha tightened her fist on her emerald and slowly sank into the lagoon. The other mermaids disappeared underwater. Just then, two gray heads popped up through the surface of the lagoon.

"Look!" Maya gushed. "They look like dolphins!"

The two dolphins started clicking and whistling.

"Oh! They are dolphins!" she said, laughing.

They had strange metallic markings on their bodies.

"Perhaps they are our helpers," Maya said.

Maya and Joey began to make their way into the cool water. They quickly reached the edge of the shallow shore, where it dropped off into the deep. Maya stared into the depths of the lagoon. Her stomach sank. She did not want to be taken below the surface. For a long moment, she thought about all the crew members who died in the ocean, and Gordon.

One of the dolphins swam up to Maya and nuzzled her with its nose, seeming to understand her fear. When she rubbed its head, she suddenly felt calm. She trusted this animal and saw intelligence in its eyes.

She slowly lowered herself halfway into the water. Then, as if redirecting her thoughts, the dolphin swam around her and came up under one of her arms. The dolphin started chattering again.

"What is it?" Maya asked. "You're trying to tell me something, aren't you?"

Morgana's head appeared above water. "Koyo is reminding you to use your snail shell. Put it up to your mouth. Through it, you'll be able to breathe and even speak underwater."

Koyo bobbed his head up and down, playfully agreeing. Maya held on the dolphin and they disappeared underwater.

Joey looked at the second dolphin, then to Morgana, who had reappeared beside him. The mermaid smiled at him and held out her hand. "May I escort you myself, Joey?" she asked.

"Yeah, definitely!" he shouted, then caught himself and cleared his throat. "I mean, yes, please. That would be amazing."

The second dolphin clicked and whistled before disappearing underwater. Without hesitation, Joey walked out into the lagoon, took Morgana's hand, put the shell to his mouth, and let her pull him underwater.

Joey wasn't ready for the speed he was about to experience. With one swish of her tail, Morgana sent the two of them zooming above the coral reef. Joey felt a strong jerk in his shoulder as the mermaid swam even faster. In surprise, Joey gasped, and all the air left his lungs emerged in hundreds of tiny glowing bubbles. Joey instinctively let go of Morgana's hand. His heart hammered as he panicked and swam toward the surface. They were already so deep that the surface of the lagoon felt like miles above.

Morgana grabbed Joey before he could swim anywhere. With one swift motion, she reached for the snail shell in his hand and brought it up to his mouth. She nodded to him, encouragingly. Even underwater, the mermaid glowed with elegance. Unsure, Joey pressed his mouth against the shell's opening and breathed in fresh air.

"Whoa!" he exclaimed. "You were right. I can breathe. And talk!" His voice was amplified by the many chambers of the magical shell. Morgana laughed. It sounded to Joey like the delicate tinkling of fine crystal.

"Sorry for pulling you so hard," Morgana said with a slight pout. "Here," she said, "I think this will be better."

Morgana took Joey's arm and wrapped it around her waist. Then she wrapped her own arm around Joey's lower back, pulling him close.

"This will give you a better grip. Right?" she said, looking into his eyes. Feeling the touch of Morgana's skin sent shivers down Joey's spine.

"Yeah," he said through the shell in his mouth. "Much better!"

Morgana grinned. "Hold on to me," she said, and kicked her tail. They took off like a bullet. Bright fish darted out of their way. Morgana made quick turns, navigating the taller, waving coral formations that grew up from the bottom of the lagoon.

To Joey, the incredible speed and sharp turns were almost as invigorating as the feeling of being so close to the beautiful mermaid. Morgana nodded to him as they arrived at a cliff. This was where the bottom of the shallow lagoon dropped sharply into the depths. As the lagoon floor fell away, Joey felt like he had just jumped off a mountain ledge.

Flying through the water with such speed was an exhilarating feeling. Up ahead in the vast, clear waters, Joey saw Maya and the mermaids waiting for them to arrive. Morgana swished her tail, and they caught up to the group in seconds.

The warrior mermaids arranged themselves around Queen Aquamarisha, the siblings, and their escorts, forming a tight sphere. Joey saw the broad smile on Maya's face and knew she was enjoying the amazing experience as much as he was . . . *Well, maybe not quite as much,* he thought with a glance at Princess Morgana's stunning face.

The group moved downward. Dozens of species of creatures passed them by. Morgana tightened her arm around Joey with reassurance as they raised the speed. Joey looked up to notice that, although sunlight penetrated the clear water perfectly, they were traveling very far from the surface. Looking down again, he was amazed to see a stone gate appear. It seemed to be floating in the middle of the lagoon. The gate looked magical. They glowed in bioluminescent green and blue colors. As they approached, Queen Aquamarisha waved her hand and the ancient stone gates slowly swung open.

As Joey and Morgana passed between them, everything changed.

"Welcome to Awanata," Princess Morgana said.

From the outside, it appeared that there was nothing but water beyond the gates. Now that they were through them, the siblings saw they were entering a vast, hidden underwater city!

Joey stared in awe as the group swam over a busy city. Coral towers rose high from the bottom of the depths like living skyscrapers. Long, waving strands of kelp grew up around the buildings, intertwining with them. Around the towers were shorter structures, made of glowing rocks. These were homes. Joey watched mermaids and their children swim in and out of them. Many turned to stare at Joey and Maya. Maya waved to them. Some waved back, others just stared in bewilderment.

In between the fluorescent towers and homes were twisting crevices that led down to the unseen floor of the lagoon. Joey could not tell how deep the chasms were, but all the light seemed to be swallowed up by them. Some homes were built into the upper sides of the crevices, like caves carved into the rock.

Joey looked over to see Maya chatting with Queen Aquamarisha as they swam. They swam over a marketplace where mermen guarded food and goods.

"And over there," the queen was saying, "are the fruit gardens."

Beyond the market, Maya saw what looked like orchards. Strange, colorful fruits she didn't recognize were growing on tall plants that looked very much like trees. Maya's eyes widened with astonishment. After the fruit gardens, they saw huge rock formations and mountains with cave openings. Mermen were sitting at many cave entrances, alone, looking up quizzically at the royal procession.

Just as Maya was going to ask about the mermen caves, something came into view that made her shudder. Beyond the caves, Maya saw the mast of a ship reaching up from the lagoon floor. Then another. Some looked thousands of years old. Then she noticed modern ships and sailboats among the tall ships that must have been destroyed recently. The sheer number of sunken vessels was overwhelming. The ship graveyard made Maya feel very uneasy. Endless questions filled her mind. She thought about all the people who must have been on board and wondered how they had ended up there . . . and why there were so many of them.

Then she saw something that made it feel like her heart was climbing into her throat. One ship in particular reminded her very much of the *Unstoppable Barracuda*.

In her mind, she saw a flash of blue-green lightning. She felt the rolling of waves and the tilting of the *Barracuda* when it struck the hidden coral reef. She saw Clayton falling over the side of the boat.

The flashback struck her with a physical blow. Her muscles tensed. It felt as if her heart stopped beating for a moment. The snail shell fell from her mouth, and Maya gulped in a mouthful of water. Her body started convulsing. She was choking. Drowning.

She closed her eyes, kicked her legs, and flailed her arms, fighting to reach the surface she knew she could never reach. Suddenly, a strong hand grabbed her shoulder. The fingers felt like an iron vice. The snail shell was forced back into her mouth, and it sucked out the salt water from her throat.

"Breathe, Maya! Breathe!"

Maya opened her eyes. Aquamarisha was staring at her sternly. The greenish glow was surrounding the queen's body again. Maya was taken aback for a moment: The best word Maya could find for the queen's appearance at that moment was "deadly."

Maya took a deep breath. Air filled her lungs.

"Come," the queen commanded. "We will get you inside."

The ship graveyard was behind them now and they were swimming above a training ground. Mermaid soldiers were sparring with each other in forceful combat. Their powerful tails were strong enough to send a foe reeling head over tail for many yards. Other mermaid warriors were practicing their deadly skills with glowing swords and electric spears, sending waves of energy back and forth.

"And there," Maya overheard Morgana tell Joey, "is our destination. The Palace of Awanata."

Maya looked up from the military grounds to see a huge castle carved from a mountain of dark stone. Turquoise flags waved with the currents, but this was no fairy-tale castle. With its ramparts, guard houses, and armed guards, it looked more like a headquarters for war.

CHAPTER EIGHTEEN

NAVY CAMP

ILONA'S BOOTS WERE THE FIRST to jump off the landing craft onto the shore of Husario. Lieutenant Kreeger was next, followed by the handful of Navy crew aboard the inflatable craft. Behind, three more high-tech rubber rafts touched sand, and the rest of the advance team jumped out to form a perimeter.

Aboard a larger landing craft, Gordon, Huang, Mundi, and the boxes of Gordon's gear waited offshore for the all-clear. With hand signals, Kreeger dispatched three two-man teams, including Ilona, to scout the beach and tree line. After a few moments of surveilling the area, they saw no threats. Everything was calm and quiet. Ilona motioned for the scientists' raft to come ashore.

As soon as his raft touched sand, Gordon jumped out, lightly, while his father helped Professor Mundi ungracefully flop over the side of the boat and onto the shore. Gordon made his way to Ilona's side just as Kreeger and his partner returned.

"Lieutenant," one of the Navy men croaked in a gruff baritone. "We found the remains of a fire and some palm leaves that were used as plates. There are two sets of footprints." He nodded behind him at a group of rocks bordering the edge of the thick jungle of palm trees and bushes.

Lieutenant Kreeger squinted in concentration. "Barefoot? Or combat boots?"

"Neither, sir. They appear to be sneaker prints. Like athletic shoes."

Gordon's eyes widened. "Maya and Joey?"

"Who?" Ilona demanded, turning to Gordon.

Doctor Huang and Professor Mundi caught up to the group.

"The kids on the *Barracuda* with us," he explained. "It has to be them. I believe everyone else was accounted for. They are still missing."

Mundi huffed, out of breath, "What a blessing if those two youngsters survived."

Another Navy scout duo ran up. "Sergeant," the female soldier reported, "we found evidence that someone hacked their way through some foliage with a machete. Recently, too."

"Where?" Ilona asked.

The Navy woman pointed to an area down the beach.

Lieutenant Kreeger turned to the scientists. "Set up your instruments in the most defendable position, and we don't want any delay. We need to know in which direction to look for the portal."

"Right away," Huang replied. He and Mundi turned and walked back toward their boat.

Ilona noticed Gordon standing still, staring at her.

Kreeger noticed as well. "Geez, someone push this dude's eyes back into his head," the burly lieutenant joked.

Ilona sighed. "You, too, Gordon. Get to work."

Gordon grinned. "Yes, ma'am." He followed his father back toward his boat.

Ilona spoke into her radio. "We're making camp. Prep the bird."

"Prep the bird, copy," came the reply.

Onboard the *Explorer 2,* Navy workers grabbed hold of a large tarp on the highest deck and pulled. The camouflage covering came off, revealing a small, futuristic looking aircraft with its rotors folded back. It looked like a smaller version of a Blackhawk combat helicopter, but with space only for a pilot and copilot.

The latest in military technology, the aircraft had a sleek, black, angular hull that made it look like a lethal insect poised to strike. The Navy workers began unfolding its rotors and making preflight preparations.

"Alpha Team with me," Ilona said, jogging toward the tree line where the Navy woman had reported signs of activity. Kreeger and four Navy SEALs followed. They reached the area quickly and stopped. Ilona raised her automatic rifle, and the SEALs did the same, spreading out. Ilona stepped silently into the bushes. Even Kreeger paused for a moment to admire her catlike movements, perfectly graceful—and lethal. In just a few more steps they saw it—the cave.

"Clear," came the word from behind her. Ilona returned to her troops.

"They went through here," Ilona said, brushing off a strand of hair that blew over her face. "There's a small cave that we will want to—"

"Sergeant," another Navy man hissed. "Look."

He nodded to the side. Ilona raised her rifle and turned to see something she couldn't at first understand. She narrowed her eyebrows. Four large horns were poking through the thick foliage. Each was six feet long. They swayed forward, revealing a head the size of a refrigerator. The head had the thick skin and height of an elephant's but the rectangular shape of a rhino's. And it was deep blue.

"What in the—?" the Navy man whispered.

"Shh!" Ilona chastised, but too late.

The rhino-elephant creature swung its massive head toward the group. A soft stomping sound followed and, through the bushes, stepped the creature's baby. The baby was the size of a horse but moved awkwardly, as if very young.

Although the animal resembled a rhino, it was certainly something never before seen by human eyes. The mother creature glared at the Navy team and bellowed loudly in an abnormal beastly call. Ilona had to stop herself from covering her ears in pain.

Kreeger took aim at the mother creature's head and whispered, "Prepare to attack."

"Hold!" Ilona hissed.

With the prehistoric-looking beast's thick hide and incredible size, she wasn't sure bullets would have any effect other than infuriating it.

"Don't fire," she commanded. "Be still."

Frightened by the newcomers, the baby let out a small squeal and toddled back the way it came, crashing through the bushes. The mother stomped the ground so hard that Ilona's legs shook. Then it turned and followed its child.

The Navy team exhaled as one.

"You two," Kreeger motioned. "Follow them. Do not engage. Let's see if they can lead us to some kind of trail."

The two SEALs nodded and quietly followed the lumbering creatures, using the pathway the huge animals created in their wake.

Lieutenant Kreeger chuckled. "Well, we aren't in Kansas anymore." The Navy team laughed.

Ilona and the remaining soldiers walked back toward base camp. She was impressed to see that the team had already dug several concealed combat bunkers. The science tent structure was also set up. Ilona smiled to herself. This team worked fast.

The mobile lab tent was made of a solid frame covered in beach camouflage fabric. Through the open door, Ilona saw that Gordon and his father were already operating their locating equipment. As she approached, she heard the two men arguing.

"I don't want to talk about it anymore, Gordon," Huang was saying, exasperated. "I understand your point, but we made an agreement. You need to put all thoughts of personal gain out of your mind and focus on the job at hand."

"Dad," Gordon said in a harsh whisper, "did you see those animals out there with Ilona? Those creatures alone are worth millions of dollars to the right buyer, never mind the portal."

"Enough!" Huang shouted. "If nothing else, respect the fact that I am your father! Please, I'm telling you to be quiet!"

Ilona registered the disagreement but decided to hold off on asking any questions—until she could find a way to use their conflict to her advantage.

"How is it looking?" she asked innocently, stepping into the tent.

Both men turned to her. Huang looked sheepish, like he was hiding something. Gordon, on the other hand, couldn't help but look at Ilona up and down. Ilona straightened her jacket and turned away.

"Already scanning," Huang said, waving his hand at the tall stacks of machinery and monitors. "We have both infrared and electromagnetic equipment searching the area. No promises as to when we'll find anything. We're learning as we go. But excuse me, I need to grab some hard drives."

With a last harsh look at his son, Huang ducked out of the tent.

As he turned knobs and flipped switches, Gordon said, lightly, "How many of those *dinophants* did you see?"

"Dinophants?" Ilona asked. She moved closer to Gordon. "That's a very smart name for them. I think you just put your name into the history books, even if nothing else happens on this mission. But yes, just the two. Mother and child. I didn't realize the whole team saw what we encountered."

Gordon nodded, keeping his thoughts to himself.

"Gordon," Ilona said sweetly, "you really are the brains of the family, aren't you?"

Gordon chuckled, accepting the compliment. "My father is brilliant. Objectively speaking, though, it is my work that has brought us here more than his."

"So, you're obviously more brilliant."

Gordon laughed but didn't disagree. "And your father," he said, "is Admiral Wells. Maybe we both know something about achieving much at a young age. And about having more potential than our fathers."

"Hmmm." Ilona stood quietly for a moment. Gordon's words made sense. It was something she had thought about from time to time but had never said out loud. There was more to Gordon than met the eye, Ilona realized.

"Tell me about Maya and Joey," Ilona said, giving his arm a small squeeze. "You were on board the *Barracuda* with them, right?"

"I was," Gordon said as he cleared his throat. "Essentially, they were my students. Joey was a nuisance, always asking about my work. And the girl, Maya, well, she had a bit of a crush on me."

Ilona opened her eyes wide in mock surprise. "Oh, really?"

Gordon shrugged confidently. "It happens. Some girls like guys with brains. We can't all be soldiers with perfect physiques," he said.

"Come on. We have brains and beauty . . . both." Ilona playfully let out a laugh.

"Then we're two of a kind," Gordon said.

Ilona picked up a vibe from Gordon, and decided that she liked him as well, but this was an important mission. She couldn't afford any distractions or interference. She broke eye contact and said, "There's no sign of the kids, but it seems they entered a cave. Maybe they've already made contact with the portal here. We might be able to use some of these clues to our advantage."

Gordon grinned. "I like the way you think."

Ilona leaned her hip on his desk. "On a mission like this, we need to use *every* resource we have to ensure our success."

"I agree," Gordon said running his hand through his hair. "But let me ask you something. Have you even thought about what all of our discoveries will be worth?"

"I have," she said, standing a little taller. "Finding the portal will ensure our country has a distinct defensive advantage over every other nation on earth."

"Defensive *and* offensive," Gordon said, peering into her eyes.

Ilona shrugged. "Maybe."

"But what about us?" Gordon asked. "It's my work that will lead us to the portal. And it's you who's risking your life to protect us. Don't *we* deserve something, too?"

Ilona started nodding. "And then there are the dinophants. They'd be worth a fortune. And who knows what else we'll discover here?"

Gordon clasped her hand. "You're exactly right."

Ilona thought for a moment. "I am here because I have a duty to my country. But Gordon, I agree that there's nothing wrong with us profiting from this mission as well. I won't be a soldier forever. Everyone deserves a reward."

Gordon picked up two bottles of sparkling water, handed one to Ilona, and smirked widely.

"And maybe someone compatible to share it with?" he added.

Ilona smiled flirtatiously. It was the first time Gordon had seen Ilona act not like a lethal soldier. She was so alluring. Her smile seemed to push through Gordon's chest and wrap itself around his heart.

"To our partnership then," he said, raising his bottle.

"And to brains and beauty," Ilona added.

Gordon's eyes lit up as they tapped their bottles together in a toast. Ilona leaned forward, bringing her lips to Gordon's ear. She whispered, "And to our future reward."

CHAPTER NINETEEN

MERMAID SECRETS

EVERYTHING IN THE VAST THRONE ROOM had an organic feel. The turquoise walls glistened and sparkled with enchantment. Atop a raised golden platform, Aquamarisha sat silently on her glowing, emerald throne, staring at Maya with an inscrutable look on her face.

The water drained out of the grand throne room until it reached Maya's waist. Maya looked down at the drainage slots. There was a pattern of long slits all along the floor. The walls seemed to swallow most of the water inside the throne room. They reminded her of gills, and they looked like they were breathing.

A few steps below the throne sat a tired-looking Persolia and Crystalline, Aquamarisha's advisors. Lining the wall behind the throne were dozens of elite mermaid guards, balancing perfectly on their tails that partially remained underwater. They wore purple battle armor with gold accents. Each stood completely still and stared stoically ahead. The tips of their golden spears glinted.

"You may remove the breathing shells," Crystalline said.

Maya lowered her shell and took a deep breath of oxygen. She had never tasted such clean air before. It reminded her of fresh fruit and a pristine beach at the same time.

It troubled Maya to notice that Persolia was taking deep, labored breaths, and she sensed that Persolia was not well. It seemed difficult for the older mermaid to breathe air rather than water.

"Thank you for the air," Maya said to the queen, "but if it's causing Persolia pain, we are happy to raise the water back up and use the shells."

Embarrassed, Persolia straightened in her chair and quieted her breathing.

Aquamarisha raised an eyebrow. "We mermaids are strong, young one. It takes more than a little air to pain us."

"Indeed," Persolia added with reassurance.

"We want you to be comfortable in an environment that is suited to you," Crystalline added, "so we may talk freely."

Maya turned, following Aquamarisha's eyes, to see Morgana and Joey behind her, whispering in each other's ear and laughing together.

"Joey," Maya hissed. Joey hadn't even taken the shell from his mouth. All his attention was on the beautiful mermaid princess, and the two of them were ignoring everything else.

"Joey!" Maya said louder.

"Huh? What?" Joey said innocently. Then he noticed that all eyes were on him and Morgana. "Oh, um, yes. Down to business," he said, lowering his shell. "Whoa, this air is incredible."

Morgana laughed like it was the funniest thing she had ever heard, then covered her mouth with her hands.

"Now that we have your attention," Aquamarisha said with a smirk, "you may leave."

"Leave?" Joey sputtered.

"Your highness," Maya interjected, "I'm sorry for Joey's . . . impertinence. But he's family, and I'd very much like him to stay."

Aquamarisha turned to Maya. "I understand he is your brother. That is why I've allowed him to come so far. But our tradition demands that males are not present when we discuss matters of state."

"Really?" Maya said. "Why is that?"

Aquamarisha shook her head and looked from Persolia to Crystalline. Maya saw that both mermaids looked slightly shocked.

Crystalline blinked at Maya and said, as if explaining to a toddler that one plus one equaled two, "Because menfolk are not to be trusted, of course."

Maya and Joey both raised their eyebrows in disbelief.

"Not to be trusted?" Joey blurted. "Now hold on a second—"

"We understand," Maya interrupted, turning to Joey. "We are happy to be your guests here," she said, taking the few steps through the waist-high water to stand face to face with her brother. "And we have no intention of disrespecting your traditions. Do we, Joey?"

Joey looked from one mermaid to the next. Each returned his gaze, sternly. Realizing there was no way to object, he sighed.

"Right," Joey surrendered. "We're not here to challenge your traditions."

"Then you are wise beyond your years." Aquamarisha nodded. "Morgana?"

Morgana stood at attention. "Yes, Mother."

"Escort our guest to the dining hall. See to it that he has everything he needs to replenish his body. Difficult times are approaching for us all."

"Happily, Mother," Morgana said.

Morgana placed the shell back into Joey's mouth with a smile. Two mermaid guards floated apart, revealing a hallway. Then Morgana pulled him down into the shallow water and, with a swift swish of her tail, rocketed him toward the back of the throne room. In a moment, Joey and Morgana were gone.

"Now," Aquamarisha said, "I'm sure you have questions."

Only about a million of them! Maya thought.

"Thank you, your highness," Maya began. "I guess first I'd like to ask why you don't trust men? I saw some mermen living in caves as we swam here.

And at the market. But I didn't see any when we passed the orchards and homes. And there doesn't seem to be any here in the palace."

Maya felt tension infusing the room. The mermaids stiffened.

"Our civilization is thousands of years old," Queen Aquamarisha explained. "Mermen have proven themselves, over the generations, to be lazy and selfish. They believed it was part of the natural order for mermaids to do all the work. They took pleasure in this. They held no interest in raising their own children. They thought that if Awanata remained hidden, no harm would come to us. This was proven false, time after time, as human ships would catch sight of mermaids and desire us for themselves. If mermaids were abducted, the mermen would claim it was fate. If one of their own wives was taken, they would simply choose another.

"One thousand years ago, we rose up and took matters into our own hands. It was one from my own bloodline who led us in revolt. We were the ones who had been training as warriors and, once the decision was made, it was not difficult to become the ones in power. We banished the mermen to the caves and, under strict control, allowed them to trade their goods. As you saw, the mermen enjoy a humble life. They do so because they don't want to work hard to improve themselves."

Maya tried to conceal her shock. "But you have children. Surely you need the mermen for that?"

Aquamarisha smiled. "Of course. But such arrangements are not for young ears."

Maya didn't think it was wise to ask for more clarification.

"I'm sorry that some humans desired mermaids and abducted them," Maya said, honestly. "Is that why there are so many sunken ships outside your palace?"

A hard look crossed Aquamarisha's elegant face. "Yes. We mermaids decided long ago to fight back when the mermen would not. To protect ourselves. We knew the humans' biggest weakness was breathing air. So, we developed strategies. And weapons."

Aquamarisha nodded to an ancient and curious device hanging on a wall. It was long and thin, with a hand crank. To Maya it looked like part spear, part corkscrew.

"In order to survive, we decided to sink every ship we came in contact with."

Maya was astonished. "Every ship? Even innocent ones?"

Aquamarisha rose up, suddenly, and her words vibrated through the chamber. "None are innocent! It is only necessary to lead ships toward the coral reefs. In their zeal to capture us, sailors only find their own destruction." Aquamarisha swam to the weapon on the wall. She ran her fingers along its long handle like it was a holy relic. "And when that fails, we use the sinkscrew."

Maya's head was reeling. Crystalline looked compassionately upon Maya. It was as if she could read her thoughts. However, Crystalline had a talent for understanding what was happening in people's hearts. It was one of the reasons Crystalline sat as a high counselor to Aquamarisha.

"Maya," Crystalline said. She spoke tenderly, knowing the inner conflict Maya was struggling with. "You have been thrust into a deadly journey you never asked for. You have been through much, and you have performed admirably. But I'm afraid the worst is yet to come. If the prophecy is true, if you and Joey are indeed the chosen ones, the chances are high that neither you nor your brother will survive. But I think you already know that."

Maya furrowed her eyebrows. Her own personal safety was not what was tearing her up inside. She swallowed the lump in her throat.

"Your highness," she said slowly. "Our ship. The *Unstoppable Barracuda—*"

Maya paused for a moment. She needed to know the truth, but at the same time she was terrified of hearing it. She closed her eyes and took a deep breath. Maya remembered all the innocent people on the ship: Clayton, Captain Hazelton, Gordon.

"Did your mermaids sink it?"

Aquamarisha traded looks with Persolia and Crystalline.

"Child," Persolia pronounced slowly. "You must understand that we mermaids have only survived by dedicating ourselves to the art of war. And by developing policies that may sound harsh to your young ears. Humans are not our only enemies. There are dark forces in Maradonia we must protect ourselves from, as well."

"How can you say that?" Maya blurted. "Humans aren't your enemies. You almost killed me and my brother! I would never—"

"You," Aquamarisha bellowed, "are not the average human! How else would we have brought you here? You were destined to come. We have aligned with your destiny."

"B-but . . . at what cost?" Maya felt the tears welling in her eyes. "No one aboard the *Barracuda* wanted to harm you."

"Could you see into the hearts of all the men on that ship?" Aquamarisha demanded.

Maya closed her eyes and let tears roll down her cheeks. Something inside her burned with the injustice of it. So many had died—and for what? She raised her head. "Where I come from, people are presumed innocent until proven guilty," she said, not flinching from the queen's hard gaze.

Persolia cleared her throat. "Child, where we come from, we have no such luxury."

Queen Aquamarisha added, "Maya, you must understand. You were prophesied to arrive in Maradonia. We only fulfilled that promise. Sinking the ship through that storm was the only way to bring you here."

Maya could feel anger rushing through her body. Her heart began to beat faster.

"That's not right, so I'm not interested in helping you anymore. You kill innocent people," Maya blurted. This time, it was her words that echoed through the chamber. "Send me back home to my normal world! I don't want to be here."

Silence entered the grand throne room like an unwanted guest. The queen stared straight ahead. Maya looked into the queen's eyes and, for a moment, noticed a hint of regret crossing her face. Her cobalt fin and scales brushed the surface of the water.

Crystalline spoke up, breaking the silence. "Don't judge others when you haven't lived through what they have."

"I am afraid you have no other choice, Maya," Queen Aquamarisha pronounced coldly. "This is the only way you shall return to your normal world."

The other mermaids nodded in agreement. The queen's aura glowed brighter with indignation. "I'm sorry that we are not the happy little mermaids of your imagination."

CHAPTER TWENTY

DINOPHANTS

GORDON MARCHED out of the science tent in frustration. Earlier, his father and Professor Mundi had set up a small table to pass the time, playing chess. Now Gordon kicked the table, sending the chess pieces flying.

He tilted his head to the early morning sky and said, “Stupid interference! Why can’t I beat it?”

All his high-tech equipment had produced exactly zero results since he had begun scanning the day before. He hadn’t slept, having lain awake thinking about all the problems he was facing that were unlike any he had dealt with before. The infrared scanners couldn’t penetrate the mountains of rock that rose beyond the jungle. The electromagnet detectors were useless because the entire island seemed to pulsate with massive waves of energy. All he saw on those screens were clouds of yellow and red, concealing any possible indication of the location of the portal.

Gordon dropped onto the sand and sat brooding. He wasn’t used to feeling so powerless. He had never been faced with a problem he couldn’t solve.

Their supplies were limited, so there would be no regular showers on this mission. The way the sand crunched beneath his fingers as he passed his hand through his hair caused Gordon to grow even more upset. But when he brought his hands up over his nose and inhaled, he could still smell Ilona's hair on his hands from late last night.

Gordon inhaled deeply. Even without much water for showers, Ilona exuded a scent that pleased him. She and her team used some sort of dry powder to clean themselves, and her hair had smelled more like a hospital than flowers, but still—the smell of it brought back the long minutes they had spent the night before, sitting on her bunk, kissing. It was the one good thing he had experienced on this entire mission so far. Gordon sighed, looked down the beach, and felt more peaceful.

Ilona was walking back toward the command tent after inspecting the three Humvees parked and waiting by the tree line. Lieutenant Kreeger was cleaning his rifle and caught Gordon's gaze, sending the young scientist an obvious look of scorn. The musclebound lieutenant had the unique ability to make Gordon feel weak and helpless. Gordon looked away.

The entire camp was in a state of anxious preparedness. Waiting for the next command, everyone was ready. Thanks to Gordon's failure, though, they simply had nowhere to go.

The scouts Kreeger had sent to explore the cave had come back within a few hours. Yes, there was a cave that led to an underground tunnel. Yes, it was wide enough to walk through, maybe even for the Humvees. But then the scouts had reported that the tunnel ended in a cave-in that blocked the way forward before anything of value had been found.

The scouts who had followed the dinophants had not reported back since leaving the afternoon before. Gordon had hypothesized that the electromagnetic energy enveloping the island might be interfering with their radios. His father had said this could be true—but he had added that there could also be a variety of other explanations, given the fact that everything about this island was unusual and scientifically unexplainable. Gordon hadn't liked agreeing with his father, but it was true. Nothing on this island seemed normal.

Gordon stood as Ilona walked past the nearby command tent. He was happy to see her approaching him.

"Hey," he said, "I was just thinking about last night—"

"Shush!" she demanded. Her hard eyes and stern shake of the head told Gordon that Ilona had no desire for anyone on the mission to know that the two of them were now more than colleagues. Gordon sighed and nodded.

"Still nothing?" she asked, as she motioned her head toward his tent.

"Not yet. I'll go check again," he said.

Walking in, Gordon took a deep breath, trying to create an explanation that would not make him sound like a total disappointment. Before he could speak, though, Ilona raised her hand and cocked her head, listening. They looked out of the tent and saw, down the beach, Kreeger had stopped cleaning his rifle.

Gordon felt the disturbance in his knees. The sand beneath his feet was shifting. The chess pieces he had scattered on the beach were vibrating. Then they began bouncing up and down. Fear gripped Gordon's heart.

Ilona's radio squawked to life.

"Incoming! Do you copy? Is anyone there?" The voice sounded scared and out of breath.

"This is Wells," Ilona snapped into her radio. "Who is this? Report!"

"Sergeant! Get ready! They're coming!"

"Who?" Ilona demanded sternly, keeping her cool. "Who is coming?"

"They are!" Gordon shouted, pointing behind her.

Ilona spun around to see the two Navy men they had sent to follow the dinophants sprinting along the beach toward camp.

Behind them was a raging herd of stampeding dinophants. Countless humungous animals were charging right toward the tents, chasing the Navy scouts.

"Alarm!" Ilona yelled. "Battle stations! Protect the tents!"

All around Gordon, the Navy team jumped into action. The men in the makeshift combat bunkers that had been dug into the sand turned from the jungle to face the oncoming threat. Behind him, Gordon saw his father and Professor Mundi poke their heads outside the science tent—then gasp and disappear back inside.

"Gordon," Ilona commanded, pulling her sidearm from its holster. "Get to the rocks by the tree line. Go!"

It sounded to Gordon like her voice was coming from far away. Paralyzed with fear, all he could do was stare at the huge mass of trumpeting dinophants as they lumbered straight at him, raising a cloud of sandy dust behind them that made it look like the entire beach was on fire. They would topple him in seconds.

The dinophant's bellowing roars filled his ears.

As if in a dream, Gordon watched Kreeger jump onto one of the Humvees to man the machine gun on top, just as the first dinophants reached the vehicles. The beasts stampeded straight into the Humvees.

The lead animals tossed their heads, catching the Humvees with their long tusks, sending the three armored vehicles tumbling into the air like kids' toys. The Humvees somersaulted end-over-end across the beach. With a howl, Kreeger got off a burst of machine gun fire, then still on the vehicle, he flew through the air and landed in the waves, dozens of yards away.

Without breaking stride, the enraged dinophants swept around the Humvees in a swarm and kept racing forward. The men in the bunkers opened fire, but the herd quickly overtook their positions. They ducked down into their holes, covering their heads, hoping not to get trampled as the massive legs ran over them. There was nothing else to do.

"Gordon!" Ilona yelled. "Get out of the way!"

Still, Gordon could not move.

Ilona stepped in front of him and raised her handgun just as the leading dinophants were seconds away. She pulled the trigger. The bullet struck the lead dinophant, larger than the rest, dead center in its forehead. The animal screamed in rage, shook its head, and kept coming. Ilona's second shot pierced the animal's knee, and it veered to its left, passing Gordon so closely that he could have reached out and touched it.

Ilona unloaded shot after shot, each striking a new dinophant in the knee and sending it off course.

"The knees!" she shouted into her radio. "Aim for the knees!"

Gordon looked behind him to see soldiers forming a line to protect the science tent. They were all firing their automatic rifles into the knees of swerving dinophants. A young man screamed as he fired shot after shot at a large dinophant charging the tent. The bullets formed a pattern of holes in the animal's belly but did not stop it. Still running full speed, the dinophant shook its head, impaling the unfortunate soldier on its long tusk. The furious animal charged into the side of the science tent, taking down half of it, and ran out of the other side.

Gordon was on the ground, hands over his head. In front of him, Ilona loaded one magazine after another into her pistol, still aiming for the knees. The injured animals swerved all around her and Gordon as if they were an island in a raging river.

This is it! We're done, Gordon thought closing his eyes in surrender.

Then he heard silence.

He opened his eyes.

The sand around him was covered in mixed puddles of blue and red blood. Gordon gasped and started running his hands over his head and chest, checking he was in one piece. When he looked up at Ilona, she was staring down at him.

"It's not your blood," she said before running toward the science tent. Gordon stood up on trembling knees.

The dust clouds were settling. Some Navy personnel began carrying wounded soldiers toward the medical area. Others were kneeling by the bodies of their comrades.

Doctor Huang grabbed his son in a hug. Huang was crying tears of relief.

"It's okay," Huang said, pulling Gordon's head to his chest. "It's okay. We're alive. I was so frightened for us. Thank God for Wells."

Gordon's fear started to ebb, and with the mention of Ilona, he pulled back from his father's embrace. He could not appear weak in front of the team. Or worse, in front of Ilona.

"Our gear!" Gordon blurted. "Our equipment!"

"Most of it is fine. We'll make do."

Gordon turned to the science tent and saw Professor Mundi lying on the ground in front of it.

Gordon, thinking the worst, said, "Is he?"

"Petrified," his father answered. "Exhausted, like all of us. But alive."

Professor Mundi picked his hat up off the sand and started fanning his round, red face. He was hyperventilating. Ilona stepped around the professor, walking toward Gordon and Huang. Gordon stood up taller and wiped the tears from his face.

"The mother and child dinophants led our scouts through the jungle along the coastline," Ilona explained. "Our men didn't find anything—except the herd. The animals must have spooked and chased them here."

Ilona sighed, lowering her head. "Three dead. Two missing and presumed dead. Six critically injured."

Huang brushed more sand off his clothes. "Gordon and I have emergency medical training, so maybe we can help until we get back to San Diego. Should we get them aboard *Explorer 2* and send a team back?"

Kreeger stalked up and grabbed Huang's arm. "No."

Huang's face registered shock. "Why not? Those men need immediate medical attention!"

"Those men knew the risks," he said, with no emotion. "We all did."

Huang's mouth was hanging open. "Do you mean we're going to keep them here, where they could die, and just continue the mission like nothing happened?"

"That's exactly what I mean," Kreeger said.

"This is unacceptable," Huang shouted. "No one's life is worth this mission!"

"Wrong, doctor," Ilona said icily. "We all agreed this mission is worth all our lives. We cannot waste any time by sending an entire team back. We need each and every man and woman here. We need to keep moving."

"I won't stand for it," Huang said, shaking off Kreeger's hold on him. At that moment, Kreeger's palm struck out like lightning, connecting with Huang's chest. The older man dropped backward and landed in the sand on his behind.

"Then sit for it!" Kreeger spat the words, towering over him. Huang coughed, trying to catch his breath. Gordon immediately rushed at Kreeger.

"Don't you dare touch my father like that!" Gordon pushed Kreeger with force, but he didn't budge. Kreeger shook his head in disgust. His disdain for Gordon's weakness was evident on his face. Gordon huffed, inches away from his face. Kreeger smirked, as if he had pleasure in seeing Gordon in pain.

"Stop it. All of you!" Ilona said.

Kreeger turned to Ilona, eyes flashing. His body trembled with anger and rage. For a moment, everyone thought Kreeger was going to punish her for challenging his authority, but he closed his eyes and quieted his breathing.

"All right. You deal with this little *situation*. I'm gonna get me some chow," Kreeger pronounced loudly and strode away.

Ilona exhaled and turned to look out over the beach. The Humvees were twisted and bashed beyond use. Blood of both dinophant and human streaked the sand. Cries of the wounded filled the air.

"We will send the critically injured and the dead back to the ship, but no one will abort this mission," she said. "Tomorrow, we move forward with our mission, and that includes the two of you." She looked down at Huang. "I'm sorry, but we cannot forfeit this mission. There will be no further discussion. Dismissed."

Huang blinked up at her, panting.

Then Ilona spoke into her radio, "This is Sergeant Ilona. Send out the chopper. We need a full arial overview of this island. Copy?" She then turned to Gordon and added, "We continue the mission. At all costs."

He looked at Ilona then to his father and took a deep breath.

"At all costs," he agreed. Ilona turned and walked away.

"Gordie?" Doctor Huang looked up at his son as if he was a stranger. Gordon took hold of his father's arm and pulled him up to his feet.

"Come on, Dad," he said, leading his stumbling father toward the science tent. "She's right. We have work to do."

CHAPTER TWENTY-ONE

CHOICES

Maya sat alone in the dining hall. Joey and Morgana had beckoned her over to their table when Maya entered, but it was obvious they were happy to be by themselves. That was fine with Maya. She wanted to be alone with her thoughts.

The dining hall, like the rest of Awanata, was underwater but half drained so that the tabletops were dry, and food couldn't float away. But she didn't feel like eating at all. Maya stared down at the untouched plate of raw fish, seaweed, and strange sea fruits. She felt overwhelmed with disappointment and entrapment.

How am I supposed to help these people when it was them who sank our ship?

Everyone on their ship was *dead.* Dead because the mermaids had led their ship to the hidden coral reef—and then watched while everyone drowned. Worse, though, was that they were dead because of her and her little brother and their so-called "destiny."

Something Crystalline had said in the throne room kept repeating in her mind. *Don't judge others when you haven't lived through what they have.* It sounded like something Libertine would have said. Maya sighed. She could use the dove's wisdom and support right now.

Maya scanned the area. Although she felt terrible inside, she could still admire her incredible surroundings. An underwater mermaid city! It was like something from a dream. The huge windows made of soft, pressurized bubbles; the globes of phosphorescent algae hanging in overhead pots as lights; the colorful fish that swam around the submerged floor and under the tables.

Everywhere she looked, something fascinating met her eyes. Mermaids of all ages tried to hide their curiosity, but many of them stole secret glances at Maya and Joey. It was clear that none of them had ever seen humans before. She felt like an animal in a zoo. *And they've all been taught that we're monsters,* Maya thought, *that we all deserve to die, no questions asked.*

The sound of giggling drifted to her ears. She looked toward her brother in time to see Morgana feeding him a fork full of fish. *Maybe Morgana and Joey's attraction to each other is a good thing,* Maya realized. *Maybe the two of them will prove that mermaids and humans can be friends—or more than friends.* She nodded at the idea. *Well,* she thought, *I can't change the fact that the mermaids have suffered at the hands of humans. And I can't change the fact that, out of fear, they sank our ship—like so many ships before. Who knows, if I were one of them, maybe I would feel and act the same way. I'll never know because I'm not them.*

Maya sat up straighter as she followed her thoughts through. *All I can do is my best and try to prove to the mermaids that some humans are worth talking to, rather than destroying because of their fear and mistrust.* Not all challenges are physical, Maya concluded. Maybe this was a challenge she had to overcome in her own mind.

All around Maya, the atmosphere in the dining hall suddenly changed. She heard gasps. Mermaids drifted off their chairs and bowed down. Maya looked toward the door and saw Queen Aquamarisha swimming toward her. Judging by the looks on the faces of the mermaids in the dining hall, Maya realized it was highly unusual for her to be there. Aquamarisha glided to a stop at Maya's table and looked down at her. Several of the Queen's Guards took up position behind her.

"Now that you have been brought here," the queen announced, "and knowing the truth about your ship, the time has come to decide. Will you help us?" Aquamarisha's eyes bore into Maya's.

Maya looked around at the faces of the mermaids in the room. Crystalline had been right: Maya didn't know what it was like to be a mermaid, to have endured their centuries of pain and loss. She also didn't know what it was like to be their queen, with the responsibility of an entire civilization on her shoulders.

"Queen Aquamarisha," Maya murmured, lowering her head. "Yes. I will help you however I can."

"Then you have overcome an internal challenge," she said, "a challenge of conscience." The queen looked down at Maya with respect and nodded.

"Come then. We shall leave your brother here. It is time to show you the portal."

CHAPTER TWENTY-TWO

JOURNEY TO THE PORTAL

SWOOSH!

The water rushed from all sides, sending bioluminescent bubbles into the pathway. Even being pulled along by a very playful Koyo didn't raise Maya's spirits, though. Aquamarisha and her royal guards led the way, and Maya was amazed at how fast they were traveling.

Still, there was a long way to go to reach the far side of the lagoon. Maya hadn't realized how vast the lagoon really was.

Crystalline swam up next to Maya.

"Once we reach the ocean side of the lagoon," Crystalline explained, "we will find the ancient river. This river will lead us to the portal. Only the queen, her personal guards, and her top advisors know the way to the mouth of the universe."

"Is the portal on the banks of the river then?" Maya asked.

Crystalline gave Maya the smile of an understanding mother. "You must stop thinking like one who walks on land."

Just as Maya was about to ask her next question, a mermaid scout team arrived. Everyone stopped swimming as the mermaid, whom Maya and Joey had first met on the lagoon beach, delivered a report directly to the queen. Maya couldn't hear, but it was obvious from Aquamarisha's face that the news was not pleasant. The dark-haired mermaid bowed to her queen, shot Maya a suspicious look, and swam off. Aquamarisha flicked her tail and shot over to Maya and Crystalline.

"Emilia's report is troubling," the queen said to Crystalline.

Emilia, Maya thought. *So, that's the name of that mermaid who seems to hate everything about me.*

"Our scout never made it back from the dark territories," the queen continued.

Crystalline scowled. "Three missing scouts during one moon phase."

Maya could see the concern on her face.

Aquamarisha nodded.

"Palazar," she pronounced slowly. Then the queen looked Maya up and down as if reassessing whether a human could actually help them in their time of greatest need. Finally, the queen said, "We must hurry."

After fifteen minutes of faster swimming, Maya saw that they were approaching the far side of the lagoon. She was thankful for it. Her shoulders hurt from clinging onto the racing dolphin as they hurtled underwater at tremendous speed.

Aquamarisha led the group straight toward the shore. Maya noticed that this side of the lagoon looked much more foreboding than the lush side she had discovered with

Joey. There was no sandy beach, just a tangle of razor-sharp rocks. Behind them was a flat, gray land dominated by one huge crater. Smaller craters surrounded the volcanic area. Nothing grew on the barren landscape.

Just as it felt like they were going to collide with the rocky shore, Aquamarisha turned abruptly, and the rest followed.

They had been traveling close to the surface, but now the queen dove deeper, leading the party diagonally downward. The side of the lagoon they were heading for ended in cliffs that towered high overhead. Seaweed and other vegetation grew on the sides of the underwater walls. As they dove deeper, heading for the rock wall, they approached what looked like submerged forest. Tall strands of thick, glowing kelp grew from the bottom of the lagoon. They grew so closely together that Maya was reminded of the sunflower field.

"What is this place?" she asked Crystalline, who was swimming beside her.

"We call this place the Forest of Alguco. Which is part of the sacred energy river. Alguco is an ancient word that means kelp."

Aquamarisha zipped straight into the jungle of kelp, darting and twisting to avoid the tangles of seaweed. Maya hung onto Koyo tightly as he followed gracefully through broader spaces and turning sharply around tighter ones, all the while ascending and descending at a tremendous pace. Quickly, the kelp forest became so dense that Maya couldn't believe how the mermaids found space between the thick stalks and waving leaves.

She must know the path, Maya thought, *because this is an impossible maze.*

Suddenly, they broke through the forest and Maya gasped. They quickly approached a solid rock wall. Underwater plants hung down in long strands, covering much of it, but if Maya and the mermaids hit the stone wall at their great speed, they would surely be dashed to bits.

They were going to hit, Maya realized. There was no way to stop their momentum. The wall was approaching. Was Aquamarisha lost? Couldn't she see the wall?

Incredibly, Aquamarisha increased her speed, and when she and her guards were only about a dozen feet from the wall, their bodies dipped at an awkward angle. They had been caught in some kind of vertical tide. They were going to hit!

Her snail shell secured tightly over her mouth and nose, Maya held her breath, readying for impact. She closed her eyes and hung onto the dolphin with all her might. Koyo zoomed toward a curtain of long vines. Then the strong down-current washed over Maya and Koyo, like passing through a waterfall—but underwater! Although it was only a few seconds of cold, it left her shivering. Dimly aware, she opened her eyes. The group slowed down. Maya caught her breath and Crystalline appeared next to her.

The rock wall wasn't solid at all, Maya thought as they entered a wide tunnel.

"Sorry to startle you, Maya. We have to reach a certain speed to break through the energy field, but now we've reached the sacred river."

Maya looked around her, confused. They were swimming down a huge tunnel. This tunnel glowed even brighter than Awanata. Fluorescent lights burst in many different shades of turquoise and flowed in streams of water all around them.

"A sacred river?" Maya asked gawking at the unexpected scene.

Crystalline's eyes danced. "Yes. This river is unlike any other river. This one is filled with energy. This energy flows into Awanata, channeling us with the power from the crystals."

Maya shook her head. Aquamarisha swam to Maya's side and Crystalline fell back to give them privacy.

"Young one," the queen said, "we will soon see if you are able to help us or not."

"I've been meaning to ask," Maya began hesitantly. "Your city is so beautiful. Your mermaids are so strong. Your community is thriving. How exactly do you need me to help you?"

Aquamarisha stopped swimming. Those around her did the same.

"We are not thriving," the queen said, with a solemn gaze fixed on Maya. "We are dying. All my people know it."

"Dying?" Maya gasped.

Aquamarisha nodded, sadly. "For centuries, we have been growing weaker. You will see when we reach the portal. The Crystal Cathedral used to glow with radiant power. Those were the times when the Seven Kingdoms were united."

"The Seven Kingdoms?" Maya asked.

"Awanata is only one of the kingdoms of Maradonia," Aquamarisha explained, swimming forward. The rest followed.

"Palazar and his principalities also live in Maradonia, unfortunately. However, the other six kingdoms are spread across the earth. All are hidden. Some use illusion to keep their existence a secret from humans, others are in alternate dimensions, which may never be revealed to mortals."

Maya looked up. They had exited the underwater river tunnel. High above them, through the water, Maya saw the clear sky. Aquamarisha angled the group upward.

"There was a time," the queen said, "when the people from the Seven Kingdoms used the portals daily. We traded, we visited. We were at peace. As human civilization grew, however, the kingdoms became more isolated and eventually disappeared for their own protection. Then came Palazar and his dream of total domination. Kingdoms formed small alliances. Some betrayed others. Magical beings fought long wars. The unity of the Seven Kingdoms crumbled. I don't know why, perhaps from lack of use, but our portal became less powerful. Which didn't matter because we barely use it anymore."

"I see why your portal is so important," Maya said. "In the wrong hands, it could be used to divide, attack, and destroy."

Aquamarisha nodded solemnly. "That is true, young one, but there is more to it than that."

The group broke through to the surface of the water. Maya removed her shell and took a deep breath of clean air. They were floating on top of a large lake, inside one of the craters.

Aquamarisha's guards scanned the area as the queen faced Maya and said, "We now know that the health of the mermaids is tied to the health of the portal. Our very future depends on it. Now that the portal has grown weak, the mermaids have also grown weak. This emerald was my grandmother's." She pointed to her necklace. "It used to glow so brightly. The light even hurt my eyes when I looked at it. And now . . ."

Maya looked at the large, green jewel. It pulsed in soft shades of green, but barely.

"The portal, the emerald, and my people," the queen said, "are all linked. I just don't know exactly how. I hope that this is why you are here."

Maya gulped. Her heart dropped down to her stomach, and a hint of nervousness crossed her face. *How in the world am I supposed to solve all of that?* she thought.

"My queen," Emilia interrupted. "Listen."

The queen raised her hand. Everyone went quiet.

Some of the Queen's Guards looked up and raised their spears. Straining her ears, Maya was the last to hear it. It started as a fast ticking. Then it changed pitch, growing deeper.

Just then, the small, black Navy helicopter appeared over the wall of rock behind them.

"What in Poseidon's name is that?" Emilia hissed, squinting. "It looks like a giant insect!"

"Dive!" Emilia yelled.

The queen's party submerged in a flash. They charged straight down for thirty feet, then stopped and looked up. The beating of the helicopter's rotor was amplified by the tall mountains surrounding the crater. Underwater, it grew very loud. Some of the Queen's Guards looked around in shock and confusion.

"We should attack!" Emilia shouted over the helicopter noise. "Aim for the eyes!"

"Wait!" Maya yelled. "It's not an insect."

Aquamarisha nodded, her eyes tracking the chopper. "It's a human machine," she said.

"It's called a helicopter," Maya explained.

"What is it for?" Emilia asked, raising her glowing spear even higher. The energy pulsed through it rapidly, gaining more and more light.

"Transportation," Maya said.

"And war," Aquamarisha said, turning to give Maya a dangerous look.

"Yeah," Maya admitted. "Sometimes for that, too."

Emilia's eyes bulged. "It's a trap! The human child was a spy after all! She has led her war party to us!"

"No!" Maya shouted. "I would never do that."

"It's approaching fast," Crystalline said with unease. Even she, Maya noticed, looked very worried.

"My queen," Emilia insisted, "if we act now, we may be able to hurl enough spears to take it down."

"It looks like a mighty weapon indeed," Crystalline agreed.

Aquamarisha saw the guns and missiles mounted under the chopper and knew exactly what they were for.

"But if we stay still," Maya said, "they'll never see us."

"You did not bring them?" Aquamarisha asked.

"No!" Maya shook her head. "I think they're looking for me and Joey."

The queen studied Maya as though weighing in her mind on how much she believed her.

"I doubt that," Crystalline said, eyeing the helicopter as it approached. "What I know of humans is that they would not make such an effort to find two lost children."

Emilia gave Maya a poisonous look. "A terrible weapon that spits fire and death, and she led it right to us. My queen, allow me to annihilate it before it is too late. They could be tracking her. Or maybe she told them where we are!"

"Don't attack," Maya objected. "Your spears will bounce right off it, then they'll know we're here. You can't let them find your city. And you definitely can't let them find your portal!"

The helicopter moved closer and closer.

I need to convince them, Maya thought. *What would Joey do? Joey would remember to quote his leadership course in school!*

She drew a breath and said, "A leader knows when to attack, and when to hide—in order to fight another day." Her eyes pleaded with the queen's.

Aquamarisha looked at Maya with a new respect. She realized the girl was more concerned for the mermaids than for her own kind. And her words were true. Only a foolish leader attacked an unknown power.

"We will wait," Aquamarisha finally commanded.

Emilia grimaced and ordered the Queen's Guard to surround the royal party. Maya's heart pounded against her chest.

The chopper's engine and rotor screamed over the surface of the lake as it passed low over the tree line. The sound intensified into a deafening roar. Some of the mermaids covered their ears as the helicopter banked slowly and aimed itself directly at the center of the lake.

Emilia inched herself behind Maya, her spear ready. She muttered under her breath, "You may fool them, but you cannot fool me. I know that this mechanical creature is your doing."

Maya held her breath and said nothing. With so much anticipation, the helicopter had finally passed over, and the mermaids remained unnoticed. Aquamarisha followed it with her eyes until it climbed higher into the sky at the far end of the lake and then disappeared behind the hills.

"You have proven yourself once more," the queen said to Maya.

Maya finally exhaled. She didn't know what to say, so she simply bowed her head. Crystalline placed her hand on her shoulder to comfort her. Emilia scowled.

"We must return at once," Aquamarisha commanded.

"But the portal," Maya objected. "Don't we need to figure out how to fix it?"

Koyo raced to her side and slipped his body under Maya's arm, ready to go.

Aquamarisha shook her head. "The portal will have to wait. Humans have found Maradonia and will soon find our city, Awanata. This is the day we have dreaded for thousands of years."

"I wonder how they found us," Emilia mumbled accusingly, just loud enough for Maya to hear.

Maya stood in awkward silence. She had no answer.

CHAPTER TWENTY-THREE

MOVING FORWARD

ILONA DUCKED into the women's latrine. It was nothing more than a tent covering a toilet seat atop a hole in the ground, but as one of the few women on the team, Ilona used it as a place to be alone from time to time. She closed the tent flap and dropped her head.

Everything was going wrong.

Six honorable men were dead under her command. No, eight. The two who had gone missing during the dinophant stampede had been found down the beach, trampled beyond recognition. The injured and the bodies had been evacuated to *Explorer 2*, and there was a good chance the rest of the personnel wouldn't make it either. Kreeger had become a nuisance, seeming to enjoy the power play. But it was more disappointing that this was after their mutual agreement that Kreeger would work closely with her as a favor for Admiral Wells. He said before they embarked on this mission, "We're a team."

Ilona scoffed. *Yeah, right.*

Then there were those two infuriating scientists, always asking questions, and Gordon, following her around like a puppy. Gordon. He was handsome, brilliant, and completely captivated by her. How far did she return his affection? She knew she was attracted to him, but was all the kissing and flirting simply to manipulate him to her own advantage? Even she didn't know. Ilona sighed. It would take all her strength to maintain her command and control her emotions.

She straightened herself up to her full height. *It's up to me, as a leader,* she thought. *My father is counting on me. My country as well. I didn't exactly choose an easy profession. Maybe I should have gone to veterinarian school after all.* Ilona turned to look into a mirror that wasn't there. She rolled her eyes and brushed a few loose strands of long blonde hair under her field cap and exited the latrine. Immediately, Doctor Huang was upon her. He had been waiting outside.

"Sergeant," Huang said, flushed from the sun exposure, "any word from the chopper?"

"Yes, doctor," Ilona said curtly, "and they have found nothing."

"I knew it," Huang said in a tone that irritated Ilona. "And I don't think that's going to change. The peculiar properties of this island are making all our technology rather worthless."

Ilona looked at him squarely in the eye and said, "Then it's time to take the old-fashioned approach. Boots on the ground. We're going in."

"Sergeant," Huang said, his anxiety clouding his mind, "I beg you to reconsider. We don't know what else lies out there for us—"

Ilona cocked her head and stared at Doctor Huang, making him more nervous. In the back of Huang's mind, he knew that if he did anything wrong on this mission, Ilona would report it to her father, and her father would destroy any, if not all, of his future projects.

"What I mean is that if this is what your heart desires, then go for it. However, it's no place for Professor Mundi and me. We'll only slow you down," Huang said.

"No, no, no. This is where your expertise is truly needed. You're both coming," Ilona said, with an effortless smile, "even if I have to drag you with a rope."

Ilona strode away, amused. Huang blinked in dismay, standing still with his mouth hanging open. At this point, Huang was not sure if Ilona was joking or being serious.

CHAPTER TWENTY-FOUR

THE SCOUT'S SURPRISE

THE QUEEN'S ROYAL PARTY passed through the gates to Awanata, and Maya was again shocked to see the beautiful city materialize beneath her as the illusion of open water was broken.

Why was there a military chopper here in Maradonia? she wondered. Her thoughts raced. *Are they after the portal? No, of course not! How would they even know about it? They must be searching for Joey and me.*

Maya had no intention of watching a magical teleportation device fall into the hands of humankind. She knew enough about the history of humanity to agree with Aquamarisha that there was too much bloodshed and greed for that.

Just then, a young mermaid scout burst through the ancient city gate behind them with a terrible cry. She flapped her tail, painfully, groaning loudly with each movement, and looking delirious with fatigue. Maya beheld her with pity. She was no older than Maya, herself.

"M-my queen!" the exhausted mermaid panted, agony consuming her face. "Th-thank Poseidon I found you here!"

Aquamarisha grabbed the ailing mermaid by the shoulder. The scout's body went limp.

"Report," the queen commanded.

Speaking seemed excruciating for the young mermaid. "P-Palazar's f-forces," the scout huffed. "Many ships. So, so many!"

"Where?" Aquamarisha demanded. "Where!"

The scout's glowing green eyes fluttered. Before losing consciousness, she managed to say, "Here. They're here!"

Aquamarisha looked like she had received a physical blow. Her body jerked backward. Then, in an instant, she regained her composure.

"Prepare our warriors!" she cried. "Mermaids! To battle!"

"Your Majesty," Emilia called out. "What about the human war machine?"

"Not now. First, we must face the foe at our door!"

Emilia's face hardened in anticipation of battle. It was as if she couldn't wait to fight.

"Alert our squadrons," the queen ordered. "The ships will be coming through the channel. If we move fast enough, we will be waiting for them. We know how to deal with Palazar's ships. Soon they will be a welcome addition to our graveyard!"

Emilia nodded, and one of the Queen's Guards took off like a bullet toward the military fields. The queen delivered short commands to other guards, and they too zoomed off to prepare for battle.

"Crystalline," Aquamarisha said. "Take her."

Crystalline nodded and started pulling the mermaid scout gently toward the palace for medical attention.

Aquamarisha turned to Maya. Her hair flowed around her face, energy shimmering through each strand. Maya had never seen anyone exude such power, control, and strength. It sent a shiver down her spine.

"You will come with me. You want to learn about mermaids?" The queen's eyes flashed with fury. "Now you will know all about us!"

Aquamarisha grabbed hold of Maya's hand and took off so fast, it felt like Maya's arm would be ripped off her shoulder.

CHAPTER TWENTY-FIVE

ABBADON'S STRATEGY

THE SUN SANK CLOSE TO THE HORIZON, and the sky turned the shade of twilight. The icy winds from the north swirled. Standing on the prow of his battleship at the center of the armada, Abbadon was pleased. A few strands of his long hair brushed his face as he watched the waterways with eyes as sharp as an eagle's.

His ships filled the horizon in all directions. One hundred ships, each manned with one hundred and twenty of the fiercest warriors the dark realms had ever produced. He knew in the depths of his stone-cold heart that never before had Maradonia experienced such a fighting fleet. And with their new weapon, victory was assured. Abbadon clenched his jaw. Finally, he would prove himself. Finally, his father must acknowledge his rightful place as heir to the dark throne.

"Commander," General Targ said, bowing his massive, misshapen head.

Abbadon's nose twitched. Ogres. He had never gotten used to their repulsive smell. Still, Targ was the deadliest warrior Abbadon had ever seen—apart from himself, of course.

"Yes, General?" Abbadon said, turning his face to the northern wind. The ogre advanced another step toward Abbadon, eyeing him coldly. "Your Lordship, our vanguard ships are ready to enter the channel."

"Proceed," Abbadon replied. "And the land troops?"

"Already in position, Commander," General Targ bowed. "We followed you here," he declared, "and we will follow you into any battle."

"Very well," Abbadon bellowed in a gruff voice.

The advanced troops had been Abbadon's idea. The night before, under the cover of darkness, they took position on each side of the channel, stationed at varying heights. It was an unfortunate necessity for the armada to filter through the Channel of Sumah. There was no other way into Mermaid Lagoon. The narrow opening created a natural bottleneck. Ships would have to proceed two-by-two as all the others waited, and they would be vulnerable to attack as they sailed through the short channel. Geography offered Abbadon no other choice. His solution had been the advance team, and the sheer number of ships at his command.

The advance troops were waiting in hidden positions, up and down the channel's rocky sides. Armed with crossbows that were lethal at one hundred yards, the sharpshooting advance troops would kill any mermaid who so much as poked her head above water. Abbadon knew that most of the mermaids' battle prowess was underwater, but those foul creatures still needed to surface to fire at the ships, and that was their weakness.

The advance troops were as much for his warriors' morale as anything. Abbadon's real advantage was in numbers. The channel was deep. Sunken ships would not block the way for the others. With one hundred ships, and warriors that outnumbered the mermaids five to one, Abbadon was willing to sacrifice half of them to the channel if it meant the other half would make it into lagoon.

Abbadon chuckled as he looked over at the ship next to his, the one sailing extra low in the water, thinking, *We shall finally rid Maradonia of these creatures. They are the last miserable force blocking us from ultimate domination. I have a little surprise for Queen Aquamarisha.*

Far out in the distance, the cliffs on the edges of the mountains glowed with streaks of orange lava, while the summit swirled with gray clouds. A sign that the fairies were already in position. Fumes and clouds of ash poured out of the deep crevasses and billowed into the sky.

General Targ pointed, interrupting Abbadon's musings. "Our first ships are entering the channel."

"Good," said Abbadon, his bright eyes glinting.

Targ began signaling the next round of ships.

We will wipe out every single mermaid in Maradonia, Abbadon thought proudly, *and every last life force that stands between us and the mouth of the universe.*

The icy breeze ruffled his cloak. Abbadon revealed his teeth with a triumphant smile as he said, "Put us into position and let us enter with the first wave. My sword is thirsty for blood."

CHAPTER TWENTY-SIX

BATTLE OF MERMAID LAGOON

FROM THE BOTTOM OF THE LAKE, bubbles began rising from the depths, as if the water was heating up.

Crystalline directed her squadron to take positions on either side of the channel. Her expertise was the first line of defense. It brought her great joy to see how prepared and well trained her warriors were. It had taken only a few moments for her squadron to arm themselves with their energy weapons and assemble on the training field. Crystalline had ordered them not to don their full battle armor—there wasn't time, and speed was of the essence. She hoped it was a decision she would not regret. But conveying a sense of urgency had worked. They had swum into position as if being chased by death itself. Now her warriors were awaiting her order to attack. Their spears glowed intensely.

The mermaid warriors heard what sounded like roaring thunder as the first ships of Abbadon's armada entered the channel. War drums were beating in sync, announcing the arrival of the prince.

Crystalline looked behind her, toward Awanata, and was surprised to see Persolia's Fire Maidens already swimming toward her. The elderly mermaid could not be talked out of joining the battle. For decades, she and her elite Fire Maidens had been the pride of Awanata's warriors. Theirs were the most dangerous missions; thus, every mermaid warrior wanted to be a part of that group. To fight beside the legendary Persolia was something every mermaid cadet dreamed of.

Persolia raised her hand, and her Fire Maidens came to a halt. Emilia, Persolia's daughter and successor, was at her mother's side. Each of the elite mermaids carried a backpack full of gear. The scales on their fins glowed with the same fluorescent colors of turquoise and purple. Their eyes glowed with the intense energy that circulated through their bodies. Crystalline's Sinkscrew Squadron would attack first, while Persolia's group awaited their chance to shed the blood of Palazar's soldiers.

Persolia nodded at Crystalline from a distance. Crystalline nodded back, swelling with pride at the incredulous sight of Persolia in her camouflaged battle armor covered in strong seaweed tinted a dark blue so that she could not be seen from above. Looking up, Crystalline impatiently watched two ships pass overhead. Her squadron was stationed in teams of two. *How many mermaids will die today?* Crystalline asked herself. Then she pushed the thought from her mind. There was no choice. Today they would fight against pure evil. A fight that was inevitable.

Crystalline looked around at the faces of her warrior comrades. She saw no fear, only fury. She felt the blood pumping through her veins. Flashing hand signals, Crystalline gave the order to attack. The time had come. The battle had begun!

Meanwhile, above water, Joey had pulled Maya up the last of the rocks. From their position above the channel, they would have a bird's-eye view of the whole battle. Maya looked down to the surface of the water. She saw no sign of the mermaid warriors. The only thing she knew was that they were hidden.

From a distance, they saw strange plumes rising into the sky.

Suddenly, a dark shape leapt from the water, arced through the air, and landed next to Maya on the rock ledge. Aquamarisha was terrible to behold in her battle gear. Mermaids didn't wear metal armor or helmets, both siblings realized. Of course, they would be too heavy. Aquamarisha's armor and helmet were made of thick seaweed and fluorescent shells. They changed color to match their surroundings, camouflaging the mermaids like chameleons. She held a golden spear, balancing a glowing ball of plasma.

Then another figure shot through the surface of the lagoon and flew up toward the ledge.

"Morgana!" Joey called.

The young mermaid's leap was slightly off. She was going to fall short of the ledge. In an instant, Joey was there, catching Morgana by the wrist, hauling her up to the ledge. With a mighty heave, Joey yanked Morgana up onto the shelf of rock.

Morgana smiled, embarrassed. "Thanks, Joey," she said, blushing, "but I'm sure I would have made it without your help."

Joey shook his head and smirked.

Even on the edge of battle, these two are flirting, Maya thought, rolling her eyes.

"Quiet," the queen ordered.

All fell silent. The sound of war drums echoed in the distance.

"It has begun," Aquamarisha murmured, scanning the waters. The siblings followed her gaze. They realized enemy soldiers on one of Palazar's ships were yelling as the ship tilted sharply.

"Crystalline's Sinkscrew Squadron," Morgana explained, pointing out into the distance. "That ship is their first victim."

They watched the ship sink quickly. Then the group heard more yelling and saw that another ship was going down. Then another, and another.

Aquamarisha nodded. "Let us hope they all sink so easily," she said. "The prophecy tells us that soon, the unseen kingdoms will be pulled into the final conflict," Aquamarisha said as she lifted her arms toward the heavens. Maya was astonished when she saw a whiteness growing across the queen's eyes, consuming the turquoise irises. Dark clouds began to form rapidly, lightning flashed, followed quickly by the rumble of thunder.

"Now, Commander?" General Targ asked.

"Not yet," Abbadon said irritably, standing with one armored foot up on his ship's balustrade. Too many ships had been sunk already, more than he had expected. He needed to enter the battle himself before giving Targ the special order.

"I apologize, Commander, but now might be the time—" Targ protested.

"Not yet!" Abbadon bellowed in a thunderous voice. If their secret weapons were employed before Abbadon was in the fray, glory would slip from him to another ship's captain. Abbadon's pride had no intention of allowing any other being to be heralded as the victor of this battle. That honor would be his and his alone.

Finally, his ship inched out of the channel and into the open water of the bubbling lagoon.

"I urge you, Commander!" General Targ growled.

Abbadon grinned. The mermaids had no idea what he had in store for them.

"Now!" Abbadon finally shouted.

Targ turned and bellowed into his battle horn, "All ships release the barrels!"

Dozens of covers were pulled back and large pointed barrels were revealed. Many had been painted with scriptures and incantations. Others featured images of dying mermaids. The creatures of Abbadon's league opened the tops of the barrels and touched their flaming torches to long wicks connected to a mysterious black powder that Andromeda and her fairy sisters had provided. Once the wicks were lit, the warriors swiftly closed the lids and hammered on them. The warriors on each ship worked in pairs to heave the heavy barrels overboard.

The three fairies gazed down upon the battle. From the edge of the cliffs, their piercing eyes watched every movement. Their wings shimmered in the cold wind. Andromeda, Mui, and Lilith felt some of their power evaporate as each barrel was lit. They had enchanted the black powder in each barrel with their own magic spells.

"My spells shall be the most powerful," tiny Mui giggled.

"Mine shall be the deadliest," Lilith added.

Andromeda thought for a moment. "My dear sisters, through the power of the one we serve, we shall rid the lagoon of the mermaids forever."

They chanted together, "So may it be."

Underneath one of the ships, Crystalline was working feverishly with her partner. This would be their third ship. Her Sinkscrew Squadron was split into teams of two, and each duo worked together with four other teams—ten mermaids per ship.

Crystalline held the tip of the sinkscrew in place against the side of the ship while her partner operated the screw by hand-cranking a rotary blade. The screw dug into the side of the ship, sending glowing energy volts through their weapons.

Around Crystalline, the four other duos were fast at work in the same manner. It normally took twenty to thirty cranks before the ship would spring a leak. Palazar must have scoured the land for the hardiest trees because these ships were taking fifty or more turns to break through. Crystalline looked at her team; they were all panting with effort but moving quickly.

Then, behind her teammate, Crystalline saw something curious. It was a pointed barrel, sinking slowly. She cocked her head as she tried to figure out what the barrel was.

Twenty feet away, two of the mermaids had finished drilling. The mermaids looked quizzically at the barrel and inched over to it. They ran their hands across it, examining it. At that moment, a horrible dread filled Crystalline's stomach.

"No!" she screamed. "Get away from it!"

A high-pitched sound pierced the lake. The mermaid team turned just as the barrel exploded. It felt like an underwater earthquake.

Up on the cliffs, Joey strained his eyes. "Do you feel that?" he asked. Maya had felt it herself. They exchanged a nervous look.

Crystalline had been slammed against the side of the ship. Dazed, dizzy, and with her ears filled with an endless ringing, Crystalline saw blood floating up from one of her sister mermaids. As if in a dream, Crystalline reached out to touch her face. There was no response. The eyes were open and lifeless. Another barrel, closer this time, drifted toward Crystalline. Then everything went black.

Thunder rumbled again, and rain started to beat against the surface of the water. Abbadon laughed as he watched the explosions send plumes of water shooting up into the air. There were hundreds of them, all around Mermaid Lagoon. The fairies had not disappointed him.

An oily substance covered the surface of the lagoon. Abbadon scanned the water, seeing the bodies of a hundred mermaids rising quickly to the surface, then sinking slowly, dead.

"Targ!" he bellowed. "Bring the second wave into position. We're losing light."

Targ turned to the nearby ship sailing low in the water and screamed into his horn, "Go!"

A fountain of water erupted just off the bow of Abbadon's command ship. Abbadon felt cold water shower down on him. He looked over the side into the water. A young mermaid with black hair was holding another mermaid who was unconscious. Tears streamed down the mermaid's cheeks as she slapped her friend's face, calling her name. Abbadon grabbed the crossbow from Targ's hands. He took aim at the young mermaid. She looked up. Abbadon cocked his head. He breathed deeply and then stopped.

What a beautiful little thing. His mind overcame his own judgment. *Perhaps I shall keep one for myself.* Abbadon even surprised himself with the idea.

The mermaid held Abbadon's eye, unwilling to leave her comrade, awaiting the arrow with all the pride and bravery her kind was known for. Then suddenly, her comrade awoke, moaning. The attractive mermaid looked wildly down at her friend, then back to Abbadon. Abbadon chuckled, then tilted the crossbow. He pulled the trigger, and the arrow flew, not into the pretty mermaid, but into the heart of her already stricken friend. Abbadon handed the weapon back to Targ in amusement.

"Capture that mermaid for me. Tie her up, but make sure you keep her alive. She may be useful."

The icy wind picked up and rain began to beat harder against the sails of the ship.

"Something's wrong," Morgana whispered, tears welling in her eyes.

"Terribly wrong," Aquamarisha pronounced with dread.

In shock and horror, the small group had been watching the plumes of water erupting in the air. Just then, Maya and Joey were knocked to their knees. If it wasn't for Morgana's strong and quick hands, Joey would have fallen off the ledge.

Underwater, frightened fish darted away, fleeing the deadly vibrations. It was something the lake creatures had never seen before. Immediately after impact, the warriors started clutching at their hearts and writhing in pain. Mermaid bodies floated to the surface of the lagoon, still and lifeless. Elsewhere, dozens of ships were burning and careening out of control, suffering the lethal effects of Persolia's Fire Maidens. But those small victories paled in comparison to the havoc and death the barrels were wreaking. Furthermore, Abbadon's elite troops had taken position on rock ledges high above them, firing their crossbows at every unfortunate mermaid who broke the surface.

The sharpshooters were too far away for the queen to engage, and she could only watch helplessly as their arrows ended the lives of too many of her warriors.

"What evil magic is Palazar unleashing against us?" Aquamarisha asked through her anguish. "What are those cursed barrels?"

"I'm pretty sure those are depth charges," Joey said. All eyes turned to him. "Probably similar to the ones from our world. They must be explosives that are timed to go off underwater."

"Tell the mermaids to stay away from them!" Maya cried out helplessly.

"They know by now," Aquamarisha said ominously, her crystal flashing between bright to dull colors.

Then Maya felt a small tornado of wings flap against the side of her head. "But there's more," the dove said, landing on Maya's shoulder. The other doves fluttered in the sky.

"Libertine!" Maya shouted.

"My queen," Libertine said to Aquamarisha, bowing her feathered head, "see the ship that's running low in the water? There." The bird motioned its head to the ship next to Abbadon's. "It carries barrels fifty times as large."

"That would knock out hundreds of mermaid warriors," Joey gasped.

Aquamarisha's eyes narrowed. "There could only be one target for those."

Maya's hands jumped to her mouth.

A single tear trailed down Aquamarisha's face. Maya and Joey both looked out to see what had to be more than half of the mermaid warriors floating lifelessly on the surface of the lagoon. Then, one by one, sinking.

Startled, surviving mermaids rose to the surface, realizing what was happening. Some shook their motionless friends. Others began to weep. Aquamarisha wailed. It was a long, harsh sound of pure pain and fury. Every surviving mermaid turned to the cliff, then answered the wail with their own. The shrill sound of mourning filled the air, bouncing off the steep sides of the channel. Even Abbadon's evil forces were shocked into silence.

All eyes turned to Aquamarisha on her ledge. The queen raised herself to full height.

"Awanata," she whispered to herself.

"Awanata," Morgana repeated, louder.

"Awanata," Maya and Joey called out, even louder.

Then the queen was screaming it, the battle cry: "Awanata! Awanata!"

Mermaids across the lagoon were inspired and enraged. Against all odds, the mermaids were fighting for their home, for their very survival. Mermaid warriors returned their queen's call with one tremendous voice: "Awanata!"

The surviving mermaids sank into the water, filled with a new courage to defeat their ruthless enemy. Aquamarisha plunged into the water. Morgana turned to Joey and caressed him on the cheek. She said nothing and then went after her mother.

"Wait, Morgana!" Joey shouted.

"Joey, don't!" Maya cried, knowing her brother's intentions. But it was too late. He leapt into the water far below, feet first.

Meanwhile, the mermaid Persolia rose out of the water, kicking her tail with great power, her upper half exposed to the air. She lit her fire grenade with the golden firemaker. She drew her arm back and threw the grenade just as Emilia pulled her mother back underwater. A crossbow arrow followed them under.

Persolia's aim with the fire grenade had been true. The ship above erupted into flames.

Emilia had never seen her mother look more exhausted. But she swallowed her concern and focused on the battle at hand.

"Mother," Emilia panted, "word from the queen."

Eyes blazing with battle, Persolia turned her glare from the burning ship above to her daughter.

"Speak to me!"

Only then did Emilia see the arrow—the one sticking out of her mother's shoulder. *How much more can she withstand?* Emilia had never felt more concern—or respect—for her mother.

Persolia followed her daughter's gaze, reached up, and snapped off the shaft, painfully. The arrowhead was still embedded deep in her flesh.

"Speak!" the old mermaid demanded again.

"That," Emilia said, pointing to a ship in the distance, "is Abbadon's command vessel. And that one next to it is filled with barrels so large they could destroy all of Awanata."

Persolia's mind whirled. The exploding barrels were already turning the tide of battle against the mermaids. A terrible understanding crossed her face. Without a word, Persolia turned and flapped her mighty tail through the icy waters. Emilia followed. As they sped through the channels, Aquamarisha caught up to them. Nodding to each other, the three mermaids made for the ship sailing low in the water. It was already approaching a position directly above the underwater city. Princess Morgana began to follow them, until she heard a splash behind her. Morgana had no choice but to grab Joey and pull him with her.

As they were approaching Abbadon's ship, they saw the full effect of the explosive barrels. Fish scales floated down like tiny crystals glistening in the beams of light. All around them, lifeless bodies sank. Many of them had hideous wounds all over their bodies. Strangely though, some of them looked peaceful as they floated down to the depths, almost like they were sleeping.

Ahead of them, a sinkscrew was falling toward the lagoon floor. Joey grabbed it just as Morgana pulled them under Abbadon's ship.

Joey bit down on his breathing shell, freeing up both of his hands. Nodding to each other, the two of them set to work drilling holes in Abbadon's ship. Morgana positioned them directly underneath it, where they hoped to be shielded from the depth charges. Morgana quickly placed the drill tip to the wooden hull. Joey started working the hand crank furiously.

"Protect that ship!" Abbadon bellowed through the pounding rain. "More barrels!"

Targ's crew of ogres hefted the barrels as far as they could. Successfully, the barrels landed near the side of the bomb ship, sank, and exploded. Every mermaid body that floated to the surface brought a smile to Abbadon's face.

"We are almost there, Commander," Targ said jubilantly, spittle flying from his twisted mouth.

Abbadon peered down into the water. A flash of movement caught his eye as it disappeared under his ship. Abbadon quickly picked up one of his harpoons, rushed across the deck, and took position. He made sure not to step on the connecting harpoon rope.

In his head, he counted the time it would take. Then, with a mighty heave, he launched the huge harpoon into the water.

As Aquamarisha, Persolia, and Emilia cleared the far side of Abbadon's ship, the harpoon rocketed through the water and struck Persolia.

"Mother!" Emilia screamed, coming to a stop.

Aquamarisha stopped, turned to see the lethal injury, and dropped her head.

"Go," Persolia whispered. Her daughter was frozen in place. "Go!" Persolia shouted.

Aquamarisha grabbed Emilia's hand and pulled. Persolia twisted with a scream of pain and pulled off her weapon holster. She took items from it into her hands and let the pack fall into the depths. Emilia gave her mother one last look.

Persolia found her daughter's eyes and said, "Save the city." Then her body was yanked mercilessly upward.

Above, Abbadon chuckled as he pulled on the rope, hand over hand. "Look, Targ," he said, beaming. "I caught a big one!"

General Targ chuckled horribly, his mismatched eyes bulging. Persolia's still body broke the surface, her hands falling lifelessly behind her.

With ease, Abbadon pulled on the harpoon rope, reeling her up the side of his ship slowly.

"You might not know this, Commander," Targ said reaching down to lift Persolia's body onto the deck and dropping her near a few barrels ready to be tossed over the side, "but mermaid is quite delicious when fresh."

Abbadon shook his head in disgust, but advanced to gloat over his prize. This one looked like an officer. He touched the inert body with his boot. Though the mermaid was old, her armor suggested she must have been somewhat important.

Abbadon placed his foot on top of her head.

"Perhaps I'll have her stuffed," Abbadon crowed, "to one day hang on the wall of the throne room when I am king!"

Abbadon suddenly lost his balance and stumbled back. Wide-eyed, he glared back at the mermaid. *The old fish is still alive! Well, not for long.*

Targ raised his sword.

"No! Let me finish this one with my own hands," Abbadon called. He reached out, already relishing the feel of his enemy's throat in his hands.

But the mermaid brought the last of her strength together. She looked, unblinking, into Abbadon's eyes. Abbadon stopped. He had never seen such resolve.

She drew her hands out from behind her back. In one hand she held a metal globe, one of which Abbadon had seen before. It was a mermaid fire grenade. In the other, she clutched a strange, golden shaft that resembled a burning candle. In shock, Abbadon watched the old mermaid touch the flame to the grenade.

"For Awanata!" she screamed and threw the grenade at her own tail. Abbadon grabbed Targ, yanking the ogre in front of him like a shield just before the grenade exploded. The immense spray of sizzling fire ravaged the wood of the nearby barrels, immediately detonating the powder inside. There was an almighty boom.

Persolia's victorious smile was the last thing Targ saw before she and everything around him erupted in a fiery explosion. Targ's body was blasted backward. Abbadon, only partially shielded by the general's bulk, screamed in agony and rage as his burning body flew into the air and out over the water.

Morgana and Joey finished drilling their fifth hole in the bomb ship's hull. The muscles in Joey's arms burned, and his jaw ached from clamping the breathing shell tightly in his mouth. But it was working. The ship was leaning to one side: still on course but sinking. Joey looked down and saw that the ancient gate of Awanata was not far off. If the ship didn't sink or change course quickly, it could still deliver its massive explosives to the city.

Just as Aquamarisha and Emilia reached Joey and Morgana, the sound of an explosion sent a shockwave pulsing through the water around them. The burnt head of an ugly ogre sank past them, its eyes bulging.

"Come on," Joey called. "I have an idea!"

Blown dozens of yards, Abbadon's smoking body slammed into the bomb ship's main sail. Flailing his arms, he caught hold of the canvas. The barbs on his armor pierced the fabric, and he fell, ripping the sail in two as he plummeted to the deck.

Astonished dwarf warriors splashed water at their commander as he patted out the last of the flames on his body. Above them, the sails were on fire. Abbadon stood, gasping. His body was in so much agony, he couldn't believe he wasn't still on fire. He grabbed one of the unfortunate dwarves' shields off the ground and looked at his reflection. His face was charred like a piece of grilled meat. His skin was black and smoking.

"My lord," the dwarf captain said, gawking at his commander, "I—I don't know how to say this but—"

Abbadon turned on him, viciously. "Spit it out, you fool!"

"This ship is sinking," the captain said, wincing. He fully expected Abbadon to throw him overboard, or worse.

Abbadon shuddered with wrath. "How far to the city?" he bellowed, grabbing the captain by his long beard.

"Not far! We are almost there!"

Abbadon felt water slosh across his boots. The deck was nearly submerged. He would have to act fast. "Man the barrels!" he yelled. "We will still be victorious!"

"Yes, Commander!" the captain said. When he spun away, part of his beard remained in Abbadon's hand.

Dwarf warriors pulled the coverings. They fell away, revealing twelve enormous barrels.

"Thirty seconds!" the captain called.

"Get ready!" Abbadon screamed.

Teams of dwarves stood ready with levers, waiting to send the huge barrels over the side of the tilting ship.

Abbadon kept his eyes on the horizon. He spotted a purple-topped mountain in the distance and used it as a landmark. As long as the ship kept heading straight for that mountaintop, he would steal ultimate victory from the hands of defeat.

The ship shuddered under Abbadon's feet.

"What was that?" he demanded.

"I don't know," the captain said, fearfully.

Again, the ship shook. Abbadon peered out. It seemed as if the purple mountaintop was drifting to one side. The ship was no longer sailing straight.

"What's happening?" Abbadon screamed into the cold air.

Meanwhile, under the ship, Joey yelled, "Again!"

Hundreds of warrior mermaids backed away from the submerged bow of the ship and once again took position. Joey raised his hand.

"Now!" he screamed.

As one, the mermaids charged the underside of the largest ship and struck it at full speed with their hands or shoulders. Again, the ship shifted direction slightly.

Screams of pain flooded Joey's ears.

"It's working!" Morgana shouted.

"Again!" Joey called.

The mermaids reformed their line. But it was clear that all were exhausted. Their bodies were battered, their shoulders or hands broken.

"You can do it!" Joey shouted, encouraging them. "Just once more! For Awanata!"

Inspired, the mermaids screamed back, "For Awanata!"

"Now!" Joey yelled again.

They charged the hull again in unison, using their bodies as living battering rams, and collided with the ship, once more knocking it just a little off course.

"I think that will do it!" Morgana said, looking up at the ship. Joey looked around at the bruised and bleeding mermaids who had followed his order—and paid the price.

"It will have to," he whispered sadly.

"Turn!" Abbadon roared. "Turn the ship and release the barrels!"

"We can't," the dwarf captain pleaded. "The mermaids have destroyed the rudder. We have no control."

Abbadon swung his arm and connected with the captain's chest. The dwarf was dead before he hit the water.

The other dwarf warriors traded terrified looks, dropped their axes and shields, and jumped overboard, preferring to take their chances in the lagoon rather than face the insane wrath of Abbadon.

The prince, in all his smoldering glory, looked around. His main ship was mostly underwater, the black powder ruined. He stared out at what was left of his armada. Only a handful of ships remained. The rest had been sunk by the mermaids.

The beautiful faces of dead mermaids floated beside his ship, but even they gave Abbadon no pleasure. He turned to the purple mountaintop, now in a new position. All was lost and Abbadon knew it. *How could this be? We were so close.*

"Son of Palazar!" The voice was both regal and lethal.

Abbadon looked down. There in the water was the mermaid queen herself. An aura of green glowed around her as she somehow balanced in the air with only the tip of her tail underwater.

"You have been defeated," she said. "And I want you to see the face of the one who caused your final downfall."

Abbadon watched as a small head broke the surface of the water. It was Joey. Abbadon squinted. *That's no mermaid,* Abbadon thought. *It's . . . it's a child . . . a human child!* Abbadon reeled. *The prophecy was true?* His mind raced. The mermaid queen then disappeared underwater.

Abbadon looked around in dismay. A moment later, the queen exploded from the water. Her body sped upward and hovered in mid air for a moment. He could see she was more beautiful than he ever imagined. Then the look in her eye made it feel like his heart swallowed itself. The queen spun around gracefully and whipped her powerful tail with unbelievable strength and dexterity. The fluke of her tail struck Abbadon's head with the might of a lightning bolt. Abbadon flew backward. He slammed into the water, two full ship lengths away. His body started to sink.

Aquamarisha returned to the water without a splash.

Emilia immediately surfaced. "The survivors, my queen. What are your orders?"

Aquamarisha heard the screams of dwarves, ogres, trolls, and all the other warriors of darkness swimming around the dead bodies. She saw the advanced troops jumping into the lagoon from their positions on the cliffs. The few remaining enemy vessels were sailing back toward the channel at top speed, hoping to escape. Aquamarisha's eyes narrowed.

"Let there be no survivors."

Alone on her ledge with Libertine, Maya's elation at the mermaid victory quickly turned to horror. Palazar's remaining ships were set ablaze. Even from that distance, she saw the waters of the lagoon stained red with blood. Thousands of screams pierced the air, combined with thunder in the distance. The mermaids were following Aquamarisha's order mercilessly.

"Oh, Libertine. I cannot watch this anymore," Maya wailed, covering her eyes. Darkness fell over the entire land as the day gave itself to the night.

CHAPTER TWENTY-SEVEN

NAVY TEAM APPROACHES

The explosives technician sprinted back around the corner of the tunnel and took cover against the wall.

BOOM!

Even with his hands over his ears and the protective earplugs in, Huang grimaced. This was the third blast they had used in the attempt to clear away the cave-in they had found in the tunnel. Huang could never get used to such a noise. The sound was deafening. Ilona was the first to her feet. She disappeared around the corner into the dust.

Gordon rose from his crouching position and once again beat the dust off his khaki pants and once white shirt. Huang looked over at his son and shook his head. His son had always been vain, but there was no way to clean off the dust and grime.

"Again!" came Ilona's command.

The explosions officer picked up his duffel bag and jogged down the tunnel, out of sight.

"Quick bite?" Professor Mundi was at Huang's side, chewing on some trail mix. Huang chuckled.

Ilona returned and took her position against the wall.

"Wells to base camp. Wells to base camp," she repeated into her radio.

There was no response. Radio communications had gone silent the moment they had turned their first corner in the cave, hours ago. Huang had foretold this. The unique properties of Husario seemed to make the radios useless. Huang shook his head. What use were he and Mundi on this expedition if Ilona never listened to them?

"Sergeant," Mundi said, a mouthful of peanuts, raisins, and granola, "have you given any thought to those sounds we heard earlier?"

Ilona turned to the robust professor. "We've been over this. No one else heard them."

"But I heard them. Don't you believe me?" Mundi said incredulously, his eyes wide. "You're paying big bucks. Don't you want my opinion?"

"Like I said earlier, Professor," Ilona said, checking her watch, "they were probably echoes of our own munitions."

Irritated, Mundi said slowly, "And like *I* said earlier, Sergeant, I heard them before we started blasting."

From around the bend came the cry, "Fire in the hole!"

The technician burst around the corner and took his position.

Ilona grimaced at Mundi. "Get down, Professor."

Mundi crouched against the wall, shoveling a handful of trail mix into his mouth.

BOOM!

Again, dust rose from the floor. Huang looked up. How they were able to be sure the whole tunnel wouldn't come down on their heads, he'd never know. Ilona rose to her feet to check the progress.

"Wait!" Mundi called out, bits of granola spraying down his shirt. He cocked his head, listening, and held up his hand.

Ilona had heard enough. "Professor Mundi," she began, "I strongly advise you—"

"Sergeant, listen." This time it was the explosives expert.

Ilona took a deep breath but stopped. She attuned her ears. Yes. There was a noise coming from farther down the tunnel.

"It sounds like a thousand electric fans," Huang suggested.

"Oh no," Mundi pronounced, his face ashen. "I've heard that sound before, in eastern Africa. It's—"

"Bats!" Kreeger yelled, pointing.

Ilona turned to see what looked like a black tornado appear around the corner of the tunnel. Thousands of bats were swirling in a whirlwind of wings. Their screeching was horribly loud now that they were close—and heading right for them.

"Get down!" Mundi yelled, dropping on his knees. "Cover your faces!"

Lieutenant Kreeger's eyes narrowed. "Rifles!"

"No!" Mundi shouted. "They're harmless! We've spooked them, that's all! They'll pass us by!"

The soldiers stood their ground, raising their weapons.

"Fire!" Kreeger shouted.

"No!" Mundi cried.

Ilona and her men started firing. The automatic rifles made a terrible din. Huang dropped to his knees, covering his ears. The ear-splitting racket intensified as injured bats started screaming. Something wet fell on Mundi's head. Instinctively, he knocked it to the ground. He opened his eyes to see a bloody bat flapping on the ground between his knees. One of its wings had been shot off.

"No, no, no," Mundi was chanting. "They're harmless!"

The maddening sound of seven automatic rifles firing nonstop combined with the shrieking of thousands of terrified bats for several more seconds. To Huang, it felt like a lifetime.

"Hold your fire!" Gordan stepped in and shouted. He grabbed the dirty little creature stuck in his hair by the wings and slammed it to the ground. It twitched by his feet.

Huang looked up as Mundi raced to Ilona.

"Why did you do that?" Mundi demanded. "They're simple creatures!

They meant us no harm! We invaded their home, not the other way around!"

Ilona was breathing heavily. The bullets had done little more than confuse the bats, she admitted to herself. Only a handful were on the ground, dead or dying.

She sighed down at the poor creatures. A voice jumped into her mind, as if a younger version of herself was talking to her through the years. *This is the exact opposite of being a veterinarian,* the voice said. Ilona swallowed. Her saliva tasted bitter. She steadied herself and turned away from the professor.

"The safety of this party is my responsibility," she defended herself quietly.

Mundi stared down at an injured bat limping around in a circle at Gordon's feet.

"You've done a terrible thing," Mundi said softly. "Just terrible."

Gordon brought his boot down on the bat. The squeaking stopped. Mundi gasped.

"What's done is done. Let's move on," Gordon said, scraping his boot along the rock wall to remove bits of bat.

Kreeger chuckled, reloading his weapon. Gordon looked at Ilona, but she didn't meet his eyes. She started walking down the tunnel.

At the corner, she paused. "The way is clear. We will proceed."

Ilona and then Gordon disappeared around the bend. Huang stood next to the professor silently as the Navy soldiers reloaded their weapons, collected their gear, and followed. A dark look crossed Huang's face. Gordon had never been prone to senseless cruelty before. The strains of the mission were obviously getting to his son.

Professor Mundi sighed. "The man who kills the animals today is the man who kills the people who get in his way tomorrow," he said.

Huang placed his hand on his friend's shoulder. Mundi wiped a tear from his eye. His shoulders drooped. "This is not what I signed up for."

CHAPTER TWENTY-EIGHT

MERMAID TEARS

Maya couldn't understand the ancient language, but it was the saddest song she had ever heard. Aquamarisha's throne room was filled with hundreds of grieving sirens singing their song.

Mesmerized, Maya watched thousands of tiny bubbles float up toward the vaulted ceiling, climbing up in strands from different places around the vast room. The bubbles sparkled as they rose, catching the light and reflecting it back in an array of colors.

Maya was in the front row of the crowd, where the queen had commanded her to stand. Next to her was Joey, holding Morgana's hand. Bubbles formed at the edges of Morgana's eyes, and when she blinked, the bubbles detached from her eyes and floated upward. It was then that Maya realized all the bubbles were mermaid tears. She watched one of Morgana's tears twisting and spiraling among the multitudes of others, until she lost sight of it among the many bubbles that inched along the turquoise-stone ceiling and finally disappeared into a gill-like slit.

No one sobbed. The tears were a silent accompaniment to the heart wrenching song they sang. *Such a proud people,* Maya thought. Just by hearing the song, Maya was moved. When she closed her eyes, she felt her own tears trickle out and disappear in the water. She realized that both her and her brother were so close to losing their lives, as well. A soft sniffle escaped her nose. She adjusted her breathing shell and looked up at the queen. Aquamarisha sat on her emerald throne, motionless. No tears were rising from her eyes. Instead, the queen stared at the chair that used to be occupied by Persolia, her top advisor.

Standing behind Persolia's chair, Emilia kept her face still. No tears floated from Persolia's daughter either. Emilia's face looked set in stone.

With her arm wrapped in a seaweed sling, Crystalline stood in front of her own chair on the other side of the queen. A steady stream of bubbles rose from Crystalline's eyes, although her face was otherwise stoic.

The siblings had been uplifted to hear that Crystalline had been found, alive. Her arm would heal. It had been one of the only bits of good news anyone had heard. So many had died.

Maya's heart was so heavy with awful memories of watching the battle that she didn't realize the song had finished. Silence crept through the palace walls as Queen Aquamarisha rose from her throne and floated above it.

"My daughters," she addressed the mermaids. "As is our tradition, we mourn the deaths of our sisters for only one day. Our loss has been great," she said, with a glance at Persolia's chair. "Today we release our emotions. But tomorrow we stop."

The mermaids all stood a little taller.

"No ruler has ever been so proud of her people," Aquamarisha said, her eyes flashing. "We met the foe with very little warning. We were greatly outnumbered. Yet we were fearless."

The queen's eyes turned toward Emilia, acknowledging her mother's courage.

"We were alone," she said forebodingly. Then Aquamarisha raised her eyes triumphantly, looking at her people. "And in the face of all that hardship, all that opposition, we were victorious!"

Hundreds of mermaid tails struck the stone floor as one. Maya felt the shockwave pass over her in the water. It took her a moment to find herself again.

"The battle was barely won, but now the war is upon us," Aquamarisha said solemnly, staring out at her subjects. "The realm of darkness is not completely defeated. We must prepare for an even greater war than this."

Again, the mermaid tails beat the floor, hard. This time the siblings were ready for it. Bioluminescent light pulsed through the throne room.

"Although I was not ready to believe it before," the queen continued, turning to the siblings, "I now know that we have been given an advantage. A gift. A gift we have heard whispered for generations. The prophecy!"

All eyes turned to Joey and Maya. Joey swallowed, uncomfortable with so much attention.

"Two human children have come. And we will be sure to make use of them, just as the prophecy has foretold. Joey, step forward."

Morgana nodded to Joey, and he took a step up onto the first stair in front of him.

"Young one," the queen said to Joey, "it was your plan that pushed Abbadon's barrel ship off course."

Joey bowed his head. "Yes, your highness, but it was your mermaids who executed it. Many of them paying for it dearly."

Aquamarisha nodded appreciatively. Joey stepped back to his spot next to Morgana.

"Maya," Aquamarisha said.

Maya stepped forward.

Aquamarisha caught Emilia's eye and nodded.

"Human child," Emilia said clearly. "I have no skill at reading prophecy. I am a warrior. Born of warriors," she said, placing her hand on her mother's chair. "This seat will remain vacant until our queen chooses her next advisor. But in the memory of my mother, I will say this."

Emilia looked out over the crowd of mermaids.

"Persolia always said that there was only one way to gain trust. It is not something to be given freely." Emilia took a deep breath, quivering with grief over the death of her mother. "My mother gave her life so that we may live. Her sacrifice will live forever in our hearts, and in our legends after we are gone. She told us all, many times, that trust can only be earned. Today, Maya and Joey, you have earned that trust."

"Your mother was a hero," Maya said softly, once the echo of agreement had died. "And both the strongest and fairest woman I have ever met."

Maya and Emilia nodded to each other.

"You know not our ways. And you know not the ways of war," Aquamarisha said to Maya. "But I see now—we all see—that your hearts are pure. Both of you have our eternal gratitude."

Maya thanked her and then stepped back.

A Queen's Guard quickly emerged from the tunnel behind the throne and swam to Aquamarisha to whisper in the queen's ear. Aquamarisha's surprise at being interrupted was quickly replaced by a fire in her eyes.

"Where?" she said sharply to the guard. After hearing the response, Aquamarisha turned back to the crowd.

"We have mourned," she announced. "We will miss our sisters," she said, again glancing at the empty chair. "And we will not stop searching for the twelve unaccounted for. But let not a single tear rise about it again. For thousands of years, it has been our way. Your tears belong only in this room, and only for today, where they have mingled with those of your sisters, and returned to the lagoon. Cry them no more. We have endured hardships for eons. This too we shall overcome. We will endure!"

"We will endure!" hundreds of mermaid voices repeated.

Aquamarisha nodded and the crowd started to disperse.

Maya gazed upon the faces of each of the mermaids as they swam in different directions. Each face was full of unbearable pain, grief, anger, fear, and uncertainty. This mix of emotions began to stir within Maya, as well. Indeed, death is a horrible thing.

She looked at her brother. He was quiet. As the older sister, she could tell he did not comprehend the entirety of what really happened, just hours ago.

Could this battle have been avoided entirely? Maya thought. *The mermaids were only defending their home. War is what they've always known, but maybe I could have suggested a different approach. War is not always the answer to resolving conflict.* Her thoughts and emotions collided with each other.

She may not be a warrior, she decided, but she had other strengths. Perhaps the mermaids needed her more than they knew.

Maya watched Emilia whisper something in the queen's ear. Then Emilia bowed and disappeared into the tunnel behind the throne. When Maya's eyes found the queen's, she could see she was troubled. The queen turned and floated into the tunnel.

"What now?" Joey asked Morgana.

"Now we feast," the young mermaid said, matter-of-factly.

"Feast?" Joey asked. "Isn't that disrespectful?"

Morgana smiled. "On the contrary. It is the most respectful thing we could do. Our sisters died so that we may live. Let us honor them by living."

Maya thought for a moment. She had to admit, it made sense. And she was hungry!

Morgana turned to Maya. "Go. There are many who want to meet you."

"And, what about you two?" Maya asked.

Morgana grinned. "Maybe later. There's something I want to show Joey first."

Morgana grabbed Joey's hand and took off for the main doors. Joey looked behind him to give his sister a shrug and a smile.

CHAPTER TWENTY-NINE

PALAZAR'S RAGE

"THE MERMAIDS KILLED MOST OF OUR WARRIORS," the raven informed Andromeda. He shuffled his black feathers, adding, "A gruesome battle indeed, mistress."

"Where is the prince now?" Andromeda said through clenched teeth.

"The body has not yet been found." The crow let out a rattling caw and continued, "Not all ships have been accounted for."

Andromeda shoved the raven off her shoulder. The bird squawked in surprise, its wings beating furiously to avoid slamming into the wall. It cast a wild eye back at the fairy and left Palazar's throne room at full speed, his brothers hot on his tail.

To Andromeda, none of the terrible news had come as a surprise.

Lilith and Mui traded dark looks. Tensions in Mount Hailstone had never been so high. Andromeda decided that now was not the time to pass this news on to her king.

He would know anyway.

Ever since Palazar began his reign three hundred years earlier, he had never traded hostages. Enemy prisoners were interrogated and then disposed of mercilessly. Andromeda knew her history.

During the mermaids' rebellion one thousand years before, the females of their kind had taken control from the males, and since that time they had never spared a human life. And as far back as Maradonian history went, for thousands of years, merfolk had been merciless in battle with other Maradonian forces, yet always fair with hostages. After Palazar's rise to power though, with his brutal and barbaric practices, all that had changed. Andromeda took a deep breath and looked around the Council Chamber's oval table. The twelve rulers of darkness were seated, all staring down at their hands. In what used to be his brother Remmilos's seat, the Titan Marcarios glanced up while keeping his head down. He quickly looked down again.

Palazar was glaring at the remaining Titan brothers. Andromeda believed that Palazar was hoping for a reaction from Marcarios or Orphilios. It would be a most welcome confrontation, allowing Palazar to unleash some small portion of his rage. However, the titans gave Palazar no excuse to execute them. Andromeda had seen Palazar angry before. She had seen him exact revenge, punish failure, even take out his frustrations on innocents. But Andromeda had never seen Palazar like this. The king had ordered his magnificent black throne moved to the Council Chamber. This was unprecedented.

Wisely, Palazar had always encouraged the idea that the twelve rulers of darkness would be heard. That their opinions and counsel mattered. *Those days are over now,* Andromeda thought bitterly.

Palazar glared down from his throne in an unmistakable display of pure power. Only Palazar's rage would govern the dark realm. Judging by the twelve rulers' faces, Andromeda surmised, no one present was going to challenge that.

Floating before Palazar were twelve balls of fire. Palazar turned his lethal focus to them. He cocked his head and scowled at them, twitching his fingers. Andromeda watched in astonishment as each of the twelve burning globes slightly shifted form. The one aimed at the dwarf ruler grew smaller, to match the size of the dwarf's head. Palazar squinted at his deadly plaything like a deranged sculptor. The circular shape morphed into an exact, fiery bust of the dwarf, complete with long beard and deep-set eyes.

Palazar turned to the fire globe aimed at Marcarios. It grew in size and shaped itself into a burning representation of the Titan's particularly high forehead and broad nose. Andromeda watched as Palazar continued sculpting his fireballs into the likenesses of the other ten rulers. She had never seen him do this before. The intricacy, the detail. His power was greater than she had imagined.

It was one thing to have seen Palazar shout, break things, and burn alive those who drew his wrath. It was quite another to now watch him sitting still, staring madly into his fiery creations.

The deadliest anger is the quietest, Andromeda thought. Palazar's rage seemed so consuming that he felt no desire to vent it. Rather, he appeared to be bottling it. Feeding it. Allowing it to boil inside and grow.

Andromeda shuddered. She shot a look at her sisters, trying to tell them to stay quiet and not draw attention to themselves. There was no need. Lilith and Mui were staring fearfully at their king and apparently thinking the same thoughts.

Unable to sit still any longer, Palazar rose and started pacing around the table, stopping now and then behind one terrified ruler or another. The twelve fireballs orbited his head like flaming little moons.

"In three days," Palazar said quietly, "each of you will produce two thousand more warriors. They will be stationed outside Mount Hailstone on foot and ready to march."

Andromeda knew full well that three days was not enough time for warriors from the further realms to make it to Mount Hailstone unless they sprinted the entire way. The ogres and trolls certainly would never make it in time.

"This campaign will be without mercy, and without chance," Palazar said with what Andromeda considered amazing self-control. As Palazar passed the fairies, the insane thought crossed Andromeda's mind that the burning smell she inhaled was not coming from Palazar's fireballs, but from his boiling blood.

"It seems the mermaids are immune to fairy illusion," Palazar said in his low baritone. "So, they will join us like all others—to fight with their other skills, even if it means with their own hands."

Andromeda stared at the floor, not even wanting to nod.

"No one will watch this battle from afar, this time," Palazar said through clenched teeth. "All will fight. I declare that this war shall never be forgotten, nor those who fought in it."

Palazar was behind his throne now. Andromeda noticed that his body was vibrating and his lips quivering. She took a deep breath and looked around, furtively locating the nearest exit, should he lose it completely and rain mindless destruction down upon all in the room.

Palazar closed his eyes, relishing his own words as if they were a balm to his burning soul. "We will make an example of these children. We will cause them such pain and torment that no living thing will dare to harbor hope in their hearts ever again! They will beg for death, but we will not give it to them. They will plead to be put out of their misery every second of every day. For hundreds of years!"

Andromeda felt hot pinpricks of panic as Palazar seemed to be finally losing the battle with his own fury. Thankfully for everyone in the Council Chamber, he had chosen to focus his wrath on the human children.

Andromeda tensed her legs, ready to flee. Palazar's rage was bursting from his body in hot waves of steam now. The force of his voice was a

physical thing, knocking into the twelve rulers, their heads bobbing back and forth as if being slapped with every syllable.

Spittle sprayed from Palazar's lips as he continued, his voice rising, "Do you hear me?"

The twelve rulers were buffeted with his exclamation like it was a hurricane gale. No one spoke.

King Palazar pushed his hands forward and all twelve fireballs raced over the table, joining into one element. Then he opened his mouth and inhaled the fire element deeply, as if it nourished his body.

"You know," he said, exhaling vapor and smoke, "every once in a while, it'd be nice to get a reply."

Words burst from all twelve rulers:

"Yes, my king!"

"Hail Palazar!"

"Death to the mermaids!"

Andromeda stood still, in shock. She had always known Palazar was unpredictable. At times, she knew him to be erratic. This was the first time she thought he was truly insane. She stole glances at the dark rulers. These were the most dangerous beings in Maradonia. Every one of them had risen to power by their own iron will, unrivaled skill in battle and treachery. Now they were all so petrified by King Palazar's power and unpredictable actions that they looked like school children too scared to raise their hands. Palazar slumped his shoulders and raised his hands in mock frustration.

"Well?" he said. "Don't just sit there! Is three days too long?"

The twelve rulers jumped from their seats, colliding and fighting with each other at the doors as they raced to escape.

Palazar plopped down onto his throne and threw one leg over the other, rakishly. He waved nonchalantly at Andromeda's amazed expression.

"What?" he said innocently. "You didn't like my speech?"

Andromeda held her tongue, unsure.

Palazar leaned forward, conspiratorially, with a broad smile. "Not motivational enough?"

"Of course, my king," Andromeda finally said, staring at the ground.

Palazar sniggered at Andromeda's discomfort. The snigger turned into a chuckle. The chuckle turned into a fit of laughter that lasted a long, long time.

"Relax, witches," he said when the fit had passed, wiping his eyes. "We will throw such a force at the mermaids that they will be like blades of grass in our typhoon. And this time, I will lead the forces, myself."

The three sister fairies caught the look of blood lust in Palazar's eyes. It had been two hundred years since Palazar had led an army himself. He was looking forward to it.

"I was serious about the humans, though," he said, darkly. "Just how long can you extend those children's lives?" Palazar raised his eyebrows. It was a real question.

Andromeda paused. She would have to choose her words carefully. His manner disturbed her greatly. *Is he truly mad? Or is he a greater manipulator? Either way,* she thought, *he is all-powerful.*

A terrible feeling gripped Andromeda's heart. It wasn't fear for the children. It was fear for herself in case she couldn't make the human children endure hundreds of years of Palazar's torture and, thus, bring something worse upon herself and her sisters.

CHAPTER THIRTY

MORGANA'S SURPRISE

JOEY BIT DOWN on his breathing shell as Morgana zipped him through tall masts of sunken ships in the graveyard. The ride was exhilarating. Just for fun, Morgana darted through a gaping hole in the hull of an ancient sailing ship. She obviously knew her way very well as she made sharp turns through the submerged decks. The ship's hallways were narrow, but Morgana navigated them with ease.

They paused for a moment, and Joey laughed when they surprised a little orange octopus that quickly squeezed itself into its hole. Joey's eyes went wide. It had to be the captain's quarters. There were old fashioned navigating instruments, including a compass and telescope.

"These artifacts would be worth lots of money to historians or museums," he said.

Morgana smiled. "Oh, this is nothing. Just wait!"

With a flick of her tail, they shot out the door, up a tight stairway, and emerged back into open water. Morgana turned and they zoomed off.

Quickly, the sunken ships disappeared behind them as they entered an unpopulated part of the mermaid realm.

Joey looked down. There was a huge crack beneath them in the ocean floor. Joey had noticed a few of these during their initial trip to Awanata. The long, winding crevices seemed to naturally separate different parts of the city. Although the water was crystal clear, staring down into the crevice below him, he couldn't see the bottom. Joey was about to ask Morgana about the crevice when she aimed them straight down into it.

They entered the wide crevice and kept descending, plunging down into a bottomless canyon. Eccentric looking fish swam close to the rock walls on both sides. Surprised, the fish darted out of their way or hid themselves in the rocks, obviously not used to visitors. Joey began to worry about the pressure so far down, but he didn't feel any troubling effects. Nothing about this kingdom obeyed the usual laws of nature.

After what felt like hundreds of feet straight down, Morgana angled them toward one of the walls, and Joey saw the mouth of a cave. When they entered it, the opening kept going. Morgana twisted them around a few corners at full speed. Quickly, it became pitch black. Joey tightened his grip on Morgana's hand. He couldn't see a thing; could she? If they became separated, there was no way he would find his way out. He felt Morgana pull him into her, wrapping her arm around his waist as they swam through the blackness. The touch of her made his body tingle.

With relief, Joey finally saw a light. Once they could see where they were going, Morgana would probably go back to holding his hand, he realized with a pang of regret.

Suddenly, they burst through the exit of the tunnel and into an open area. There was some sort of light source high above them. Morgana started swimming upward.

Joey turned to look back at the tunnel and noticed something incredible. Behind them was a long trail of light, perfectly tracing the path they had taken. It was exactly like pictures Joey had seen of comets.

"Whoa!" Joey exclaimed. "Look at that!"

"Aren't they beautiful?" Morgana gushed. "I believe that in your world they call them bioluminescent microorganisms."

"Bio-whats?" Joey said, suddenly wishing he had paid more attention in biology class.

Morgana giggled. "They glow when you touch them. Look."

Morgana stopped swimming and reached her arm out in front of them. It was immediately covered in pinpoints of white light. Joey grabbed her arm and inspected it. Tiny, round beads of light outlined Morgana's arm. His own, too, he realized. Joey did a jumping jack. Hundreds of light points started glowing on his arms and legs. Morgana giggled.

"It's like swimming through the stars," Joey said, amazed.

Morgana beamed. "I knew you'd like it! But that's not what I brought you here to see. Come on!"

The mermaid princess grabbed Joey's hand. A mighty swish of her tail sent them racing farther upward. Joey couldn't stop staring at their comet tail behind as they hurtled the last few hundred feet.

Suddenly, they broke the surface. Joey felt the surprise of air on his face. They were inside a huge cavern. He turned to gawk around them, but as his jaw dropped, his breathing shell fell. Morgana grabbed it before it fell out of reach.

"Welcome to my secret cave," she said, proudly.

Joey whistled. The sound bounced back to him in echoes. The cavern was as wide as several houses put together, and even taller. The rock walls were slick and sparkling. Morgana led them to a small sandy beach that gave way to a rocky shelf attached to one wall. The place was dimly lit by the same globes Joey had seen in the mermaid cafeteria. When they reached the shoreline, Joey pulled himself onto the sand and stood.

"I'm speechless," Joey confessed. "This place is amazing!"

The princess slid onto the beach and propped herself on an elbow, grinning at Joey. "I'm so happy you think so," she replied.

"How can this be?" Joey asked, spinning around. "The air, I mean."

"It's an air pocket," Morgana explained. "You don't usually find them so big. Which is part of why this place is so unique. Nobody knows about it but me. And now you. But there's more," she added, mysteriously.

"Oh yeah?" Joey said, thinking how beautiful she looked, lying there on the beach. "I think the air—and you—are special enough." Joey's cheeks reddened as his mind caught up to his words. "I mean . . ."

"I know what you mean," Morgana said, blushing. "I think you're special, too."

Joey couldn't stop the grin that spread so wide, he felt it in his ears.

"But you haven't seen the best part," Morgana said, slipping back into the water gracefully. Joey didn't understand. If there was something better than being in this incredible place, alone with Morgana, he couldn't imagine what it was.

"Look," the mermaid said, nodding her head. Joey turned. At the edge of the beach that ended in the rock wall, Joey saw a collection of large boxes. He looked at Morgana with a question in his eyes. She tilted her head toward the boxes. Joey walked to the mysterious chests. There were fifteen or so of them, each old and weathered. Joey knelt in the sand. As he opened the box, the hinges creaked. Sparkles of reflected light played across Joey's face. He reached into the chest and lifted out a blue sapphire as big as his fist.

With his other hand, he scooped up gold coins. "Are these . . . ?"

Joey couldn't believe his eyes. As if in slow motion, he let the jewel and coins fall. He opened another chest gently, as if not to break the spell, and saw gold ingots. He needed both hands to lift just one of them. He dropped the bar, looked around at the other dozen or so chests, and sat back on his ankles.

"Treasure chests," he said slowly. "Like, actual treasure?"

Morgana laughed with glee and leapt into the air, turning a somersault before returning to the dark water in a perfect dive.

"I can't believe it," Joey whispered. It was as if his entire life had led him to this moment.

Morgana's smiling face broke the surface. "This is my gift to you, Joey."

"For me? What? Why?"

The shock of so much treasure made his mind whirl. He felt like he just won the lottery! Then he began thinking about the cars he would buy, the clothes, the houses. With this treasure, he could buy anything he ever wanted, for the rest of his life. A mansion? Forget it. He could buy his own island. He sat in amazement, his head turning slightly back and forth in disbelief.

"Most are from pirate ships." Morgana's voice sounded farther away. "Others are from vessels sunk during one human war or another, dating back hundreds of years. I know how much humans like this stuff—gold, you call it, right?"

Joey was nodding, dazed, running his hand through the hundreds of coins in one of the chests. "Gold," he drawled. "Yes. And diamonds, sapphires, emeralds, pearls!"

"We mermaids have no use for it," Morgana said, her voice fading again. "I never understood why humans have such an excitement for these things. I just thought it was pretty and might be useful one day. I've been collecting it since I was a little girl. When we met, I knew right away. I knew why I had done it: it was all for *you*."

Joey chuckled. It wasn't a dream. It was real. He leapt to another chest, pulled it open, and yanked out a jeweled crown. He placed it on his head.

He grabbed heavy necklaces of gold and diamonds and threw them around his neck, laughing.

"Oh, Joey," he heard the princess say faintly. "Everything will be perfect now."

"Perfect!" Joey shouted, letting piles of gold coins spill from his hands. "Yes!"

"So, you're happy?" she asked, her voice a whisper.

"Happy?" Joey yelled. "Oh, Morgana! You have no idea."

The necklaces and crown were too heavy for Joey to jump, he realized with a laugh, so he struggled to his feet and turned to find Morgana. He scanned the surface of the water.

"I've never been . . ." The dark waters of the lagoon were still. The only sound was Joey's own panting. "Happier?" Joey finished saying, confused. An eerie silence surrounded him, with only tiny droplets echoing in the distance. The beautiful Morgana was nowhere to be seen.

CHAPTER THIRTY-ONE

MOONLIGHT ENCOUNTER

I NEED TO FIND OUT ABOUT THE HELICOPTER! Maya thought, clutching Koyo even tighter as he upped his speed. They were zipping through the ocean several feet under the surface.

An hour earlier, Maya had left the mermaid feast by herself. It was funny how alone she felt, despite being surrounded by so many beings who adored her.

After the feast, she decided to take a swim through the curious fruit orchards. To her delight, she saw Koyo frolicking with his dolphin friends, chasing each other through the tall, seaweed plants. Koyo approached her immediately, and when she wrapped her arm around his body, he had taken off at once, as if knowing where to go. The dolphin had whisked them through the lagoon channel and out into the open sea, speeding along the coastline. The trip had taken Maya's breath away. Racing through the water had forced every troubling thought from Maya's mind until there was nothing but speed, sky, and water. It was a glorious release. After a while, Koyo had turned them back toward the lagoon.

Still no sign of the helicopter.

Just as she was thinking her search was unsuccessful, something caught Maya's eye up the river. It was a reflection, like sunlight glinting off metal. Koyo stopped and chattered. Something about the dolphin's tone gave Maya pause. She got the feeling he was trying to tell her something.

"You think you see something?" Maya asked.

The dolphin nodded his head vigorously and then sped them upriver.

In the distance, Gordon held his radio up one last time, as if getting it a foot higher in the air would help. He heard the one and only sound every radio had made since landing on this awful island. Static. Nothing but static. He dropped his arm, feeling foolish. He kicked a rock. He considered yelling out, but that would mean the others would know he had gotten himself lost. He didn't want that. And he didn't want Ilona thinking he couldn't take care of himself.

If he hadn't drunk so much water, he wouldn't have had to wander off by himself in the first place. After finding a secluded spot to relieve himself, Gordon had realized he had gotten turned around. The rest of the Navy team couldn't be far away. It was obvious that the jungle here was different to the ones back home. He had only walked for a minute or two. He listened. Nothing. Ilona made sure the group traveled quietly. He turned around to look into the dense foliage. Visibility was low because of the night, but the bright moonlight was some help.

At that moment, someone shouted his name. Gordon dropped his radio in surprise. It had come from behind him. He whipped his head around and had to blink his eyes. Splashing up out of the river was—he couldn't believe it.

"Maya?"

The girl raced to him and grabbed him in a wet hug. Gordon staggered back. His first reaction was irritation at getting wet.

"I knew it! You're alive!" Maya exclaimed.

Gordon peeled himself from Maya's soggy embrace and held her at arm's length, gawking at her. Rat-a-tat laughter came from the river. Gordon looked behind Maya. “Is that a dolphin?” he asked. This was getting even weirder.

Maya patted down her disheveled, wet hair, hoping it made her look a bit more presentable.

Gordon shook his head, incredulous. “Where have you been? How have you survived?”

“Honestly, I have so much to tell you. I don’t even know where to begin,” Maya said with excitement. “I mean, this world is like no other. We’ve met real, actual mermaids! We just experienced a terrible battle . . . there were so many dead people! I don’t mean people—creatures, beings.”

Gordon’s eyes grew wider.

She continued, “And this all has to do with a magic portal that we’re supposed to heal or something. Somehow these mermaids are connected to it—”

Astounded, Gordon asked, “What’s this about a portal?” Then, shaking his head, added, “Uh, wait. Did you say mermaids?”

“I’m sorry,” she said, blushing. Her crush on Gordon didn’t help with the nervousness in her voice. “I know I must sound crazy. I don’t want you to think I’m nuts.” Maya quickly changed the subject and asked, “Are you here all by yourself?”

“I’m not by myself. Our team just set up camp.” Then he softened his face and added, “Of course, we came here to find you and your brother.”

“Of course! That’s why I saw the helicopter. You were looking for us.” Maya felt hope, security, and peace. She and her brother finally had a way to return home. “Can you take me to the camp?” Maya asked.

Gordon nodded. “But first, tell me about this portal. It sounds important.”

Then she heard a rustling by her ear. Gordon staggered back a few steps as Libertine the dove landed on Maya’s shoulder.

“What is that?” Gordon blurted, stepping back, as if afraid of catching a disease from the bird.

“Oh, it’s just Libertine.”

"You need to go!" the dove whispered so that only Maya could hear.

"What?" Maya said, turning to the bird. "But I need to talk to Gordon. They're going to take us home."

"Now!" the dove commanded, harshly. Libertine started flapping her wings, knocking them into Maya's face. Maya shielded her cheeks with her hands and demanded, "What's gotten into you?"

Gordon, more astonished, said, "You're talking to that bird?"

"Of course, I am!" Maya blinked at Gordon. "You didn't hear her?"

Eyes wide, Gordon shook his head.

Maya looked sheepishly at Gordon. "No, really, she talks. Libertine, speak up so he can hear you!"

Libertine bit into some of Maya's hair and took off, pulling her gently back toward the river.

"Let go!" Maya gasped.

Behind her, the dolphin made a worried chittering sound. She turned to the dolphin. "What? You, too?"

"Maya," Gordon choked out. Maya was aghast to see the look in his eyes that said it all: the girl's lost her mind.

"Wait, you don't understand," she objected, but stepped backward into the river, obeying her new friends' demands. As soon as he could, the dolphin wedged himself under Maya's arm and started swimming down river. Libertine circled above, squawking.

"I will get Joey and then we can leave with you!" Maya shouted to Gordon.

Libertine gave one last loud squawk that sounded like she was chastising Maya. Maya could have sworn she saw Libertine's eyes flash with frustration as the dove took off into the sky.

Koyo pulled Maya under and raced down river. She sputtered out water and quickly jammed the breathing shell into her mouth. The last Maya saw of Gordon was him standing in the moonlight with his mouth open, too stunned to speak.

CHAPTER THIRTY-TWO

JOEY'S TREASURE

JOEY'S HEAD BURST through the surface of the water. He gasped, pulling oxygen deep into his starving lungs. Then he slammed both hands into the water, sending splashes of droplets high into the air.

It was useless. With his deepest breath and hardest swimming, he couldn't even reach the tunnel opening. It was insane to think he could make it down to the opening, through the dark tunnel, and up the crevice on the other side to the lagoon surface with just one breath—but he had felt the need to try. He pulled himself up onto the narrow beach on his hands and knees, then fell onto his back.

"Where is my breathing shell?" he called out to no one. His voice echoed back to him. He sighed. "Where are you, Morgana?" he added, quietly, sitting up.

Joey reached over and ran his fingers through the closest treasure chest. He pulled out a large gold coin. He stared at it, watching it glinting as he turned it over and over in his hand. Joey shook his head. It was old and, more than likely, valuable. He drew his arm back and threw the coin, sidearm, like a skipping stone. He watched it skim across the top of the water until a petite hand reached up and grabbed it. Morgana's pretty face emerged after her hand. She giggled.

"Morgana!" Joey exclaimed, jumping to his feet. "Thank God! I was so worried. I didn't know when you were coming back!"

Morgana grinned. "You never have to worry, Joey. I'll *always* take care of you."

Joey cocked his head, silent for a moment. It wasn't exactly what he had wanted to hear. Morgana approached the shoreline.

"I hope you're hungry. I brought you something delicious," Morgana said, as she placed a large conch shell on the beach. "You will enjoy the taste."

Joey sniffed at the strange root contained in the conch shell. It smelled like seaweed, carrots, and ginger all rolled into one. It wasn't entirely disgusting, and his stomach was grumbling. Joey immediately grabbed it and began to eat.

"You're happy to see me?" she asked, coyly.

"Of course!" he replied, rushing to the edge of the water and kneeling.

"And do you love me?"

Joey's mouth opened and closed. "That's um . . . it's awful soon, I think. I mean, I don't know. I really do *like* you—"

Morgana suddenly rose from the water and kissed him on the mouth. Joey's eyes opened wide, then closed. Her lips tasted salty and fresh. Finally, Morgana pulled back and smiled. Her eyes glistened as they reflected the globes of light.

Joey opened his eyes, slowly. "You're, like, the most beautiful thing I've ever seen," he whispered, honestly.

Her smile widened. "The first moment I saw you on the beach, I fell deeply in love with you."

"You did?" Joey asked, blushing.

"I knew you were the one I was waiting for all of my life," she replied.

Conflicted and confused, Joey blinked at her. "That's um—wow. I, uh, am looking forward to getting to know you better."

"Me, too," Morgana whispered, lowering back into the water, and drifting back. "And we have all the time in the world."

"Wait for me," Joey said. "I can't find my breathing shell. I might have lost it."

Morgana grinned. "No, you didn't," she said, then she revealed the shell in her hand.

Joey's face lit up. "Yes!" He pumped the air with both fists.

"But soon you won't need it at all," Morgana said sweetly. Her lashes fluttered, revealing her deep green eyes.

"What do you mean?"

"You'll see," Morgana said, raising her eyebrows playfully.

"Wait, Morgana," Joey pleaded. "Please give me the shell. Maya must be wondering where I am."

Morgana shook her head and teased. "Don't worry. You just wait here, okay? I'll be back soon."

Joey looked at her incredulously and raised his voice. "Wait here? Come on, enough already. This isn't funny!"

"It's not funny, no," Morgana agreed, shaking her head. "It's perfect! And we will be together," she said.

"What do you mean?"

Morgana blew Joey a kiss and quickly disappeared under the water with his breathing shell. Joey jumped to his feet.

"But wait! Morgana! Morgana?"

Joey sat down on the sand with a sigh, tormented with confusion. He looked over at the chests of coins, gold, and jewels and thought, *I've got more wealth than I could ever want. More than I could even spend. And it can't help me one bit!*

CHAPTER THIRTY-THREE

KAYATONGA ROOT

RETURNING FROM THEIR RIVER JOURNEY, Koyo had taken her through the oldest part of Awanata. Maya left in such a hurry that she didn't have a chance to ask Libertine what the rush was all about. It must have been important. She would find out soon.

Huge stalagmites rose from the floor of the lagoon, leaning at impossible angles, covered in ancient algae and waving water plants. The rising towers of coral were so thick, they were dotted with cave mouths. Homes and stores were built inside them. Squinting through the rushing water, Maya thought she caught a glimpse of Morgana. This was perfect. She needed to tell Joey about Gordon and how he had come to save them.

"Morgana! It's me Maya!"

Maya leaned slightly to her left. Koyo took the cue and turned toward the cave mouth, where Maya thought she had seen the mermaid princess enter.

Morgana acted quickly. She had heard Maya's voice, and the last thing she wanted was to be found inside the apothecary—or seen buying what she was buying. Morgana conducted her business with the ancient apothecarist in a flash and swam out the shop's rear exit just as Maya and her dolphin rushed through the front opening.

Maya slipped her arm from around Koyo and settled to the ground of the wide cave. She turned around, taking it all in. Even through her breathing shell, strange and curious scents greeted her nose from sweet and pleasant, to stinging and bitter. It was a place filled with odd plants and colored glass jars.

"Can I help you with anything?" came the sing-song voice from behind her.

Maya turned to see the oldest mermaid she'd seen yet. Her skin was wrinkled, yet it strangely radiated a youthful glow. Her hair was so long that it was wrapped around and around her head, like a crown. Seaweed and seashells drifted out from the coiled, violet-silver hair. Her face held years of wisdom and grace. From a smile, though, the mermaid's face suddenly grew serious.

"A piece of the Crystal Cathedral," she said, nodding at the shining stone necklace that Maya was admiring. The old mermaid lifted the tiny crystal to the light to appreciate its turquoise color.

"A shame that the cathedral is dying out and no one knows why." She replaced the crystal necklace on the shelf and looked Maya up and down.

"I've heard good things about you, young one," she said.

Maya bowed her head.

"I am Florina," the apothecarist said, "keeper of the ancient ways. I possess the oldest shop in Awanata."

"Pleased to meet you," Maya said. "I'm sure you already know my name is Maya."

Florina nodded.

"My father always told me the old ways are often the best ways," Maya continued. "He would say, 'Old ways last for a reason, because they work!'"

"Your father sounds wise, young Maya," Florina said, impressed. "I wish blessings upon you and your father both." Florina swept open her arms. "What is it that brings you to my shop? Are you in need of healing?"

"Actually," Maya began, "I saw my friend, Morgana, come in and I was hoping to talk with her."

"You are friends with our young princess?" Florina asked.

"I am. And she is especially, um, close, to my brother."

Florina grinned. Then her eyes narrowed. "I see. But I can tell that you are unsure if it is a good match or not."

Maya went quiet for a moment. Florina was certainly perceptive.

"You know," Maya said slowly, "I never put it into words like that, but yes, you're right."

Florina reached out and stroked Koyo's head. The dolphin made a cooing sound and rolled over. Florina chuckled and started stroking his belly. She kept her attention on the dolphin, but her words were for Maya. "This dolphin has come to love you," she said. "I can tell he would do anything for you. And yet, you two are very different, aren't you?"

Maya considered this. "We're about as different as two beings could be," she said.

Florina nodded. "You were born far apart. You live on land; he lives in the water. You cannot even speak a common language."

"Yet we are close friends," Maya said, realizing just how deeply she cared for the dolphin. "We're like family."

"You know," Florina said kindly, "I was just thinking that it's entirely possible that this fellow's sister wouldn't approve of your friendship at all!" Florina let out a laugh.

Maya burst out laughing. "You know, you may be right!"

It took a moment for the laughing to pass. Eventually, Florina lifted the crystal necklace off the shelf and placed it around Maya's neck.

"Wait," Maya protested, "I don't have any of—whatever it is you use for currency."

"No need," Florina whispered. "It is a gift."

Maya gazed at the beautiful crystal on her chest admiringly. "I couldn't accept it. It seems too valuable."

"It's yours already. I insist."

"Well, okay then," Maya said, bowing her head. "Thank you very much."

Florina nodded. Her smile lingered for a moment, and then she grew more serious.

"I'm sorry you missed the princess, but Morgana was here only briefly." Florina turned toward the back of her shop. "Then she darted out the back. Looking behind her as if she was in a bit of a hurry, I might add."

"Did she say where she was going?" Maya asked.

"No," Florina said, pensively. "She was very specific though. She came in for Kayatonga root."

Maya was lost in thought, staring at the back door.

"You say your brother and Morgana have grown close?" Florina asked.

"That's for sure," Maya replied, rolling her eyes.

Florina touched Maya on the arm. Maya turned to see concern in the old mermaid's violet eyes. "And has your brother told you of any plans he has? For his future with Morgana?"

"Future?" Maya snickered. "Joey never thinks past his next meal. I know he likes Morgana, but he's never even had a girlfriend before."

Maya noticed that Florina lowered her eyes in thought and grew quiet.

"What is it?" she asked.

Florina bit her lip briefly. "I didn't think much of it. Kayatonga root, when boiled and rubbed onto our tails, gives mermaids a fresh glow to our scales. It's full of nutrients and natural oils."

"Okay. And?" Maya said, sensing there was more to come.

Florina took a deep breath. Maya had the distinct feeling that the older mermaid was sizing her up and trying to decide what to say—and what not to say.

"When not boiled," Florina said, "when chewed fresh, Kayatonga root has another use entirely."

Maya cocked her head, waiting for an explanation.

Florina sighed. "It is something that has not been attempted for hundreds of years. Something very rare. Only in the most peculiar circumstances has it even ever been attempted."

Maya didn't like the sound of this one bit. It felt like a stone was rolling around in her stomach.

"Please," she said. "What is it?"

She blinked at Maya. "I fear that Morgana is going to feed the root to your brother."

"What will that do?" Maya heard herself saying as if from far away.

"It will cause him three days of excruciating pain. And then, after that, he will no longer be human. He will be one of us. A merman." Florina added, "If, that is, he survives at all."

CHAPTER THIRTY-FOUR

THE EYE

The rocks scattered across the table, skittering to a stop in a random pattern. Andromeda bent down to investigate their exact position. Satisfied, she nodded to her sister. Lilith snapped her fingers and small pillars of flame ignited at different spots atop the table. Next, Mui made a flicking motion. Droplets of water flew from her fingers and sprayed across the table. The heat and moisture collided on the tabletop with a sizzling effect.

Earth, fire, and water all smoldered together on the black, stone table. A thick, gray smoke rose. All three fairies made circles in the air with their hands, chanting in a language that very few still alive in Maradonia even remembered.

A wind funnel appeared over the table, pulling the smoke inside it. The scene looked like a miniature ocean caught in the grip of a raging, gray hurricane. The fairies' chanting grew louder. They were speaking in perfect unison. All three threw their heads back and closed their eyes, losing themselves in deep concentration. As the fairies' wild incantation reached its highest intensity, Andromeda tossed a leaf into the wind over the table. It spun and spun in the funnel of smoke, until, as one, the fairies abruptly stopped chanting.

In the deathly silence, the wind funnel immediately dissipated. The leaf then drifted down to the table. Andromeda and her sisters leaned forward in anticipation.

The leaf drifted to a stop next to two especially tall rocks. Andromeda grinned at her sisters, then nodded. Together, all three exhaled. Long streams of dark purple smoke emerged from their mouths, engulfing the table. When finally, the fairies closed their mouths, the purple smoke began to clear. The tabletop was transformed.

Where there had been pebbles, small drops of water, and tiny pillars of fire, now there was a realistic scene of a particular stretch of ocean. It was like a window had been opened. The three fairies gazed down on the scene like giants looking through the clouds.

Where the two big pebbles had been were now two jagged islands in the middle of the ocean. Where the leaf had been, now was a ship. Standing on the bow of the ship, staring into the sea, was Abbadon.

Andromeda exhaled in relief. “He lives.”

“Yessss,” Lilith hissed.

“But wait,” Mui chirped in her dainty voice. “Where does he embark?”

Andromeda shook her head. “He opposes our direction.”

Mui’s face fell into a pout. “Afraid of facing his father after his failure.”

Lilith snickered. “Can you blame him?”

Mui giggled. “So hopeless. He just needs a little . . . help.”

Andromeda narrowed her eyes and spun to look into the dark corners of the room. Her eyes flashed with urgency.

“The time has come. We shall make concrete our alliances with Prince Abbadon. Then King Palazar will have no other choice but to oblige, and both of you shall rule beside me. Our plan shall unfold sooner than expected.”

The two sisters nodded in silence. They knew that their unspoken conspiracy was slowly becoming a reality. Andromeda extended her fairy wings and called, “My little ones. Come to me!”

Howling winds pummeled against the walls like a giant fist. In V-formation, a murder of crows rushed to Andromeda, flapping and shrieking. Gently, thirty or forty birds each took a piece of Andromeda’s black cloak into their mouths. As one, they rose, carrying her into the air. She smiled in triumph, looking both terrifying and majestic.

Andromeda gestured and the birds flew out of the huge window. Mui and Lilith watched as the ravens carried their sister away from the icy towers of Mount Hailstone and out over the open, frozen sea. Roaring waves crashed over the jagged rocks surrounding the neighboring mountains.

CHAPTER THIRTY-FIVE

THE ROOT OF LOVE

MAYA HELD ONTO KOYO for dear life. The dolphin had never swum so fast with her! The clear crystal necklace glowed on her chest. Before leaving Florina's shop, Maya had watched the ancient apothecarist wave Kayatonga root under Koyo's nose as if the dolphin was a bloodhound. The effect had been immediate. Koyo had gone stiff, spun around, and motioned Maya to grab hold before speeding through the water. It was so fast that she couldn't even say goodbye to Florina.

Now they were rocketing straight down through one of the wide crevices that cut through the lagoon floor. Koyo never hesitated a moment. The dolphin knew exactly where he was going. Still, Maya urged the dolphin on.

"Faster, Koyo!" she called out. Somehow the dolphin kicked into an even higher gear. Maya closed her eyes against the intense rush of water as they raced downward.

Meanwhile, Joey was watching the surface of the water intently for any sign of Morgana. *Why would she bring me here and leave?* It was just strange. Everyone was probably wondering where he was.

He finally noticed bubbles rising from the depths of the water. Out of the darkness emerged a glowing beam. Joey's heart skipped a beat. He immediately ran behind one of the treasure chests for cover and hid himself. For a long moment, he heard water droplets echoing from the cave walls. Then there was silence.

He slowly looked around the chest and saw that Morgana returned. He let out a sigh of relief. She brought more roots for him to eat. The mermaid pulled herself out of the dark water. Her silver-blue tail sparkled with each scale reflecting the dim light in the cave. Morgana smiled at him and then at the roots in a way that made him uncomfortable. He lowered the roots back into the large conch shell that served as his bowl.

Morgana sighed coyly. "You don't like the food I brought you?"

"It's not that, Morgana. It's just that, well, somehow, I feel like a prisoner."

"I thought you liked me," she whispered, lowering her head. Her eyes began to water. Joey felt a pang in his heart as if someone jabbed it with a red-hot needle.

"Of course, I like you!" Joey blurted.

Morgana sniffled, "But you don't *really* like me."

"I do," Joey said, sitting down next to her. "I really, *really* like you."

A small smile pulled at Morgana's lips, but then disappeared. "I've shown you my secret place," she said bitterly. "I've offered you the treasure that I've collected my whole life."

"And I appreciate it!"

"But still," Morgana said, louder, "it's not enough for you! Humans always want more, don't they?" She sat up and turned away from him. Joey was torn. He had true, strong feelings for Morgana. But he couldn't help but feel manipulated. Trapped, against his will.

"Morgana," he said, touching her shoulder, "I've never felt this strongly for anyone before. Ever."

Unseen by Joey, Morgana smiled.

"But still," Joey continued, "I've known you only a few days."

Morgana whipped her hair around and faced him. "You don't believe in love at first sight? We don't need more time, not if we feel this way for each other."

Light danced in Morgana's eyes.

Joey pulled back, starting to feel irritated. "Look, you need to bring me back to Awanata. This is not what love is."

"I guess sometimes things just need a little push," Morgana said and looked down at the Kayatonga root in Joey's hand. Joey shook his head. He felt like he was in a corner and nothing he said made it better.

"You can't push love," he said. "Everyone has their own pace. Their own comfort zone. You might feel right making a commitment already. I might not. It doesn't mean either one of us is wrong."

Morgana still staring down at the root as if mesmerized—contemplating if she were making a terrible decision. Joey noticed.

"Okay," Joey said. "I get it."

"You do?" Morgana asked.

Joey nodded. "I'm being rude by not accepting the gifts you've given me."

Joey lifted the root toward his mouth. Morgana watched Joey intently. Her gaze lowered to the Kayatonga root as it approached his lips. Joey opened his mouth, bit into the bitter root, and chewed.

Then at that moment, the dolphin Koyo appeared through the surface of the water, followed by Maya.

"Don't eat it! Don't eat anything she gives you!" Maya was sputtering.

Joey turned to Morgana with questioning eyes, but he had already swallowed the entire root.

CHAPTER THIRTY-SIX

A VISION

MERMAIDS SLEPT WITH THEIR TAILS wrapped around something to keep them from floating off, like seahorses. Knowing something of human habits, Aquamarisha's palace staff had furnished Maya and Joey with beds inside air bubbles that the siblings could cross through at will—one side water, one side air. Maya inhaled the air inside her bubble, which smelled of spring grass and wildflowers. Even though her eyes were closed, it took her a long while to fall asleep. So much had happened.

There was the horrible gruesome battle, the grieving mermaids, meeting Gordon, and then saving Joey from turning into a merman! Maya sighed, listening to the sound of her brother snoring across the room. At least Joey was safe. For now. The fact that he had eaten part of the Kayatonga root was concerning; however, Florina had advised that it would have to be eaten for three consecutive days in order to be effective.

Maya wanted to head straight to Queen Aquamarisha and let her know what her daughter had done, but Joey had refused. For whatever reason, her brother wanted to protect the princess. To Maya, it was odd. If someone tried to change her into something without her consent, she would be furious! Joey, however, had been quiet since they returned to their quarters from Morgana's secret cave. She did not sense any anger in her brother. Instead, Joey seemed introspective and embarrassed, maybe even a little regretful. The queen would eventually find out about it. Just not tonight.

Maya rubbed the crystal pendant tucked against her chest under the blanket and finally fell into a deep sleep. Instantly, a vision came.

Maya was a spirit with no body. She sensed herself underwater, then saw herself rising from a murky substance; it reminded her of the Pool of Bacchus. She began floating high over Awanata. She could see the mermaid buildings and deep crevices below her. Then with a burst of speed, she took off past the ship graveyard and out over a barren region of the lagoon floor.

The speed was exhilarating, but Maya also felt a sense of foreboding and danger. She was not aiming herself anywhere. It was more like she was a passenger, going where her spirit knew it needed to go.

The route seemed familiar though. Maya saw herself zooming through the lagoon, past hanging plants, through a tunnel, out into a lake. Maya realized where she was traveling. It was the same way she had gone with Aquamarisha when the queen had planned to show her the portal.

She angled down, toward the bottom. Off in the distance, she saw glimmers. Reflections bounced off the walls, like diamonds catching the light. As she approached, she saw a tall structure reaching up from the lagoon floor. This was the source of the sparkles and flickers.

The Crystal Cathedral, Maya realized. *It must be the secret location of the portal.*

As Maya approached, she felt overcome with awe. She stopped traveling and hovered, appreciating the beauty of the Crystal Cathedral. The spectacular building was rectangular, with tall buttresses and towers. The cathedral was breathtaking in its beauty. Rays of sunlight from the surface struck the walls of the cathedral, making a rainbow of colors. It was huge, intricately built, and breathtaking. The cathedral felt both fragile and invincible at the same time. All of it seemed to be made of crystal, and a glow came from deep inside, forming a soft halo around the structure, much like a sun's corona.

But suddenly, something changed.

Maya felt the water around her grow cold. She felt the chill in her bones.

A vibration traveled through the lake. She heard a crackling sound and looked down to see a jagged line of ice speeding across the lake toward the cathedral. The icy lightning struck the cathedral with a crack.

She screamed to herself, fearing the worst.

Icy fingers of energy shot up the walls of the Crystal Cathedral. The entire structure started shaking. Then several of its towers cracked loose and started toppling over. As if in slow motion, the tall towers hit the lake floor hard, sending up plumes of sand and rock. The once sparkling towers broke apart into dull heaps of rubble. What was, only seconds earlier, stunning crystal reflecting angelic light, was now piles of dull rock. Next, whole portions of the walls broke off and fell to the lake floor, leaving gaping holes in the sides of the cathedral. It all happened fast. Maya gawked at the destruction.

Then she felt as if someone was yanking hard on a chain that had been tied around her torso. She seemed to travel many miles in less than a second. She slammed to a stop, looking down on Mermaid Lagoon. It was solid ice. She shivered. There, deep below, she saw hundreds of mermaids stuck in place, some of them at awkward angles, and all of them with looks of terrible surprise and horror on their faces. They had been flash-frozen in the ice.

Before Maya could even process the scene, she felt herself transported high up into the sky. Beyond the lagoon, thick, black smoke rose over the forests of Maradonia. Trees were being burnt by the thousands. The once emerald-green, lush lands of Maradonia were now reduced to gray and brown rubble. In the distance, she heard snarls of vile laughter and inhumane cries. Then something streaked through the sky and caught Maya's gaze. The speeding object came to a stop near where Maya hovered, high over the land.

The small, familiar face struck a chord of longing in Maya's heart. She tried to call out to it, but the sound only echoed inside her own head: *Libertine!*

Still, the dove turned. Maya could swear the dove knew she was there, that Libertine could see her.

Libertine! Maya tried calling again. *What's happening?*

A tear appeared in the dove's eye, then it slowly trailed down her feathered neck.

Suddenly, Maya heard a swooshing sound. There was no time to act or scream. A large fire comet exploded in the sky. The searing flames rained on the land, and a massive piece of burning rock struck Libertine full force. The beautiful dove was gone, like the land, consumed in fire, smoke, and ash.

In that moment, Maya woke up. Shocked, sweat dripped down her face. It was the most vivid dream she ever encountered in her life. She knew this wasn't just a nightmare; it was a warning.

CHAPTER THIRTY-SEVEN

CALL TO ACTION

THE EARLY MORNING SUN gave the lagoon a dim hue. Surprisingly, Joey woke up before Maya. Brooding in thought, he aimlessly watched the fish outside his air bubble. They swam without a care in the world. *They aren't anxious about when they will eat, and yet they are always well. Such a simple creature,* Joey thought. *And me? Always anxious. Always wanting more.* He had dreamed all night long about the treasure in the cave he'd had to leave behind.

When Maya woke, she could see the inner conflict consuming her brother. There was so much to talk about. Today was important, she realized.

"I have good news and bad news!" Maya started.

"Some good news, please," Joey groaned, scratching his back.

"Gordon Huang is alive! He brought an entire rescue team. They're here and want to help us get home safely," Maya exclaimed.

Joey snapped out of his thoughts, sitting up. His eyes brightened and were suddenly filled with hope. "I never thought I'd be excited to see that guy again. When are we leaving? Where are they now?"

"Well, I'm not sure. The last I saw him was on the riverbank. I'm assuming they set up camp close by there. Libertine hurried me away." Maya paused. "Actually, I never had a chance to ask her why. Or maybe, it was about saving you."

Joey scratched his back again, harder. "And what's the bad news?"

"That's the thing. We still have unfinished business here with the mermaids. Gordon can wait. Right now, we need to get to the portal and help the mermaids figure out what's happening. I have a strong feeling they need us. Something bad is going to happen if we don't."

Joey groaned again. He stretched his arms.

"What's up with you?" Maya teased.

"I don't know. Can you check my back? It's been itching all morning. I can't reach it."

Maya got up from her seaweed bed and plopped next to Joey.

She gasped. "What. Is. This?"

"What. What is it?" Joey tensed, straining his neck. "Tell me!"

There was a cluster of five green fish scales growing out of his skin. In disbelief, Maya tugged at a scale. It didn't budge and Joey jolted.

"Ow! Is that a pimple?"

"No, it's . . . a fish scale."

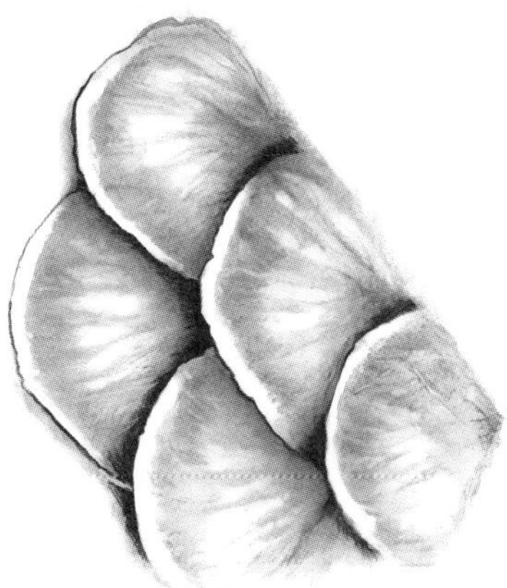

"Don't lie!" Joey said.

"Why would I lie? The root must have begun to take effect," Maya said.

"Ewww! I don't want to be scaly!" Joey said.

Maya stifled a smirk. Served him right for following Morgana like a lovesick puppy. "Look, there's no time for this right now."

After a few moments of argument and discussion over the cluster of fish scales, the siblings hurried along the stone corridor. They needed to see the queen immediately. There was so much to discuss.

Once the guards opened the tall stone doors and ushered the siblings inside, they swam slowly, still trying to figure out how exactly to address the delicate issues. It was as if the mermaids were already waiting for the siblings to arrive. At the end of the lavish throne room, Persolia's seat was still vacant, but her daughter, Emilia, floated behind it. Crystalline sat on the other side of the throne. Both were talking quietly with the queen.

Morgana stared at Joey from behind her mother's throne. He had mixed emotions about what had happened with the princess and her Kayatonga root scheme. *How could I have been tricked like that?* Then he shook his head and chuckled. He said to Maya, "I could've been a merman today."

Maya caught Joey's childish smile and rolled her eyes. As the siblings arrived before the throne, the mermaids stopped talking.

"I sense your hesitancy, young ones," the queen said, seated on her emerald throne. "It has come to my attention that Morgana has acted foolishly toward you. One must never try and make certain decisions for others, especially one as important and permanent as changing from human to merman."

Morgana sobbed, "Please, forgive me."

Her eyes rose from the floor to meet Joey's. Their connection was undeniable.

"Your majesty," Joey said. "I hope Princess Morgana didn't get punished too severely. Nobody is perfect, including me. And I forgive her."

The queen looked at him with the eyes of an understanding mother.

"Love is not only blind, young one. It is also sometimes rather foolish." Aquamarisha nodded to Morgana, and the young mermaid swam immediately to Joey's side. Joey took her hand, blushing. The queen smiled.

"However, it is an exceptional thing for us mermaids to find love. So, if one of us is fortunate enough to find love, it is logical that she may not have the tools and experiences to deal with it intelligently. We have been forgiving and lenient with the young princess. Just as you seem to be."

Joey exhaled through his breathing shell in relief, sending a tumble of bubbles rushing up through the water. The queen couldn't help but laugh. Then she turned her attention to Maya.

"Something else troubles you, young one," the queen surmised.

Maya nodded clutching the crystal pendant around her neck. "Ever since I fell into the Pool of Bacchus, I've had vivid dreams, well, more like visions, really."

"Proceed," the queen commanded.

Maya took a deep breath. She related her dream to the queen. The council grew serious as Maya described her journey through the rivers, to the lake, and then the Crystal Cathedral. Maya spoke of the frozen mermaids and how the land was covered in ice. When she finished, silence filled the hall. For a long moment, no one said a word. The queen was frowning.

"That was no dream," Aquamarisha pronounced. "You have been blessed by higher powers. Given a spiritual gift. What you have received was a prophetic vision."

Maya followed the queen's eyes down to the pendant around her neck. It was glowing brighter. The queen rose from her throne, floating back and forth in the mermaid version of pacing.

Maya swallowed hard. "Please don't tell me I had a premonition."

"You must meditate on your gift. Your destiny is higher than you realize. It is time for you and your brother to help us reactivate the portal."

"Yes, we will try," Joey added. "But what about Gordon and his team?"

Emilia muttered negatively in her native tongue for the council to hear.

Immediately, the room began chattering. Each sibling grew uneasy as the mermaids began looking at them more fearfully.

"The military is here to help us," Joey defended.

"So it seems," Aquamarisha added.

Emilia pounded her spear. It emitted high energy streaks of blue and green. "I shall investigate and report back to you."

The mermaids nodded in unity.

Aquamarisha approved. "We have learned from past mistakes. We trust no one."

The siblings looked at each other but knew that this moment was not the time to speak.

"What you've seen is the most probable future, Maya," the queen said. She sighed and added, "We lost more than half of our mermaids. We are weak. And so is our portal. Without strengthening the portal, we will die."

Silence filled the hall again.

"The principalities of darkness will stop at nothing to eliminate us, and gain control of our portal. As its guardians, we must protect our kingdom, otherwise we shall perish and all the remaining kingdoms of Maradonia shall be enslaved."

Maya shook her head. "We have to do something."

Joey's mind raced, too. "What about the other kingdoms? You need to unite with them."

"There are a total of seven kingdoms." Aquamarisha's eyes bore into Joey's. "But we have closed ourselves off and grown distrustful of each other. With the passing of many moons, times have changed."

Maya's hands were balled into fists. "Well, if they changed once, they can change again."

"You don't understand, child—" the queen began.

"Oh, I understand," Maya interrupted.

Aquamarisha turned to face the girl, surprised by the interruption—and by the fire in her voice.

"I understand that we can't sit here doing nothing," Maya continued.

"We need to try at least," Joey added.

Crystalline nodded to her queen. "They are right. Securing our alliances should be our immediate concern."

The meeting ended and bright sunbeams traveled through the waters of the lagoon in a soft glow. The sparkling, golden rays touched the Palace of Awanata and reflected on the turquoise walls. It was as if hope and reassurance had entered the palace and begun to fill the atmosphere with a sense of peace.

Maya turned to face her brother, remembering the words of Oraculus: "In our time of greatest need, the Encouragers will arrive."

CHAPTER THIRTY-EIGHT

ANDROMEDA'S BARGAIN

The mermaid, Dariya, sighed and drew the moist sponge across her dry tail. She had protested as long as possible, but now it was necessary. Her body needed water. Her tail was already cracked and dull. She had no choice but to accept the gift of water in the bucket.

She heard the tiny clicking noise and shuddered. She turned her body away from the door so all he might see was her back. Abbadon stared through the small hole in the wooden door. He swallowed, hard. *Why am I so consumed with this mermaid?*

After the battle, Abbadon's warship was one of only a few ships to escape. Before the damned mermaids had turned the tide of battle, he had ordered his men to pull the mermaid from the sea—the young one who had stared at him so defiantly when he had killed her friend. He could still hear her screams when his arrow pierced her comrade's heart. He could still see her rebelliousness as another arrow entered her own shoulder—until she had fainted from the pain.

He did not know why he had chosen to wound rather than kill her with that arrow. He also did not know why he had given the order for her unconscious body to be pulled from the sea.

He blinked into the peephole.

She was unlike any creature he had ever seen. He had seen mermaids before, but only from afar. All his life, his father had spoken of how disgusting mermaids were. How they were soft, frail, and unworthy. How they were slimy to the touch and smelled of rotten seaweed. This one was nothing like that. She was strong. Fierce. And mesmerizing.

"Dariya," he whispered to himself. Even her name was sweet, dripping off his lips like honey.

In the nearby cell were a handful of other mermaids. They had been hauled onto his ship in nets as his flagship had fled the battle. Abbadon was a collector of fine things, and these mermaids were fascinating to him. But, somehow, this one mermaid was different. Special.

Abbadon remembered vividly how her skin had shimmered in all the colors of the rainbow when she had first been dropped onto the deck of his ship, unconscious. He had lifted her himself and carried her here, to the brig. The ocean scent of her was nothing like his father had described. Her skin had been soft and smooth, and her luscious black hair had glistened like the rarest treasure. He wanted to save this mermaid but didn't want her to be free. It was a strange conflict.

Abbadon sighed and closed the peephole covering. He felt the need for open space and strode to the bow of the ship. The decisions he now had to face were very difficult. His father must believe him to be dead by now. If he returned, it would not be in glory. But the alternative was what? A life on the run? Where in Maradonia would he be welcomed? Nowhere. A coward, indeed.

He stared out into the sea. He was hated by his enemies. His allies would be happy to turn him over to Palazar in hopes of the dark king's favor. Somehow, none of it mattered to him. He was hopeless. Gazing up at the stars, Abbadon's eye was drawn to a certain area of the night sky. Stars were being blotted out, winking away and then back again, almost as if something was . . . flying toward him.

He heard the cries of ravens. He took a few involuntary steps back, not believing his own ears. Then he heard a voice he knew well calling out.

"Abbadon!"

Astonished, he watched as the host of shrieking crows lowered Andromeda to the deck of the ship in front of him, gracefully. She looked tall and strong. Next to such power, especially after his recent defeat, Abbadon felt small and cowardly. He had to stop himself kneeling before her.

"My prince," Andromeda said, lowering her head. When she looked up, though, there was no reverence in her eyes. There was only a sense of authority.

"How did you find me?" Prince Abbadon asked.

"I am a fairy, after all. I am not without my strengths." She grinned, knowing she was the one in complete control.

"You, however," she said, stepping closer to him, "have not exactly been the triumphant one." Andromeda shook her head as if scolding a toddler. "Your father is not happy with you, Abbadon."

He raised his chin proudly. He was, after all, a prince, and not to be trifled with.

"My father will understand," he said with more conviction than he felt. "The mermaids had help. The human children. They are, indeed, the ones from the prophecy."

Andromeda smirked. "My lord, I delight in your enthusiasm. However, I don't think your father will like hearing that excuse."

"He doesn't understand these creatures," Abbadon blurted. "They fought differently. We were so close. We were nearly victorious! Is it my fault that our soldiers were not able to execute the final explosion?"

"Well, as their leader, yes." Andromeda blinked at him, innocently. "It is absolutely your fault." Sniffing the air, she said, "You have multiple mermaids on your ship. Why?"

Abbadon's mouth opened and closed for a moment as his mind raced. "She's a prisoner," he said, finally. And then he quickly added, "They. They are prisoners."

The slip of the tongue was not lost on Andromeda. She shook her head, grinning. "We both know your father keeps no prisoners."

"Things are different now," Abbadon said, reaching for a line of reasoning to convince Andromeda—and ultimately, his father. "We may need them once we conquer the portal. The mermaid entrance has been dormant for centuries. Opening it will be a challenge." An idea struck Abbadon as he peered deeply at Andromeda. "With all your power, do you know how to do it? How to operate the mermaid portal?"

Andromeda thought seriously about this. "No, I don't."

"Well then, who does?" Abbadon said, triumphantly. His desperate grasping for a reason to keep Dariya alive was actually going somewhere. He stood up a little taller. "Indeed, we need them alive. To assist with the portal."

A smile teased at the corners of Andromeda's lips. "You had my curiosity, but now you have my attention."

Abbadon swallowed and nodded.

"I have an idea, my prince," she said.

"I do not need your ideas," Abbadon scoffed.

"I believe you do, and it would serve you well to listen."

Abbadon scowled as the fairy continued, "Your father is furious about your failure. We both remember what he did to your brother when he lost his battle all those years ago. I'm not sure he'll treat you any differently."

Abbadon looked down to the deck. The fairy spoke the truth.

"But maybe we can help each other with a simple transaction," Andromeda said. "I think your idea about using a mermaid to operate the portal makes sense. And I think I can talk that sense into your father. I am, after all, his most trusted advisor. If we are successful in operating the portal with your captives, he will reward you with his forgiveness."

"And in return for this favor, you would ask what of me?" Abbadon said.

"If I can convince your father not to kill you, one day you will be king. You will need a real queen. Someone on your side. Someone powerful."

"Someone like you," Abbadon said, quietly.

Andromeda could sense his disappointment. She shot a look at the mermaid and winced. The smell of the mermaids reached her nose.

"Don't worry, my prince," Andromeda said. "I won't share your secret. You can keep the mermaids for yourself. Build them a water palace at Mount Hailstone and let them live there for your amusement. What does it matter to me? Just make me your queen."

Inside, Abbadon knew that nothing else mattered—he got to keep Dariya, and with the fairy's help, he would return to the good graces of his father. Would he ever become king? He could not be sure. But if he did, Andromeda would be an excellent queen at his side—although Dariya had his heart. Abbadon stepped forward and extended his hand. The fairy smirked and took it in her own.

CHAPTER THIRTY-NINE

THE CRYSTAL CATHEDRAL

To Maya it all felt too familiar. The tunnels and rivers she and the queen's party were traveling through were exactly what she had seen in her vision. Aquamarisha must have been correct. It hadn't been a dream at all, but a vision of the future. Maya shuddered with the memory. Then she furrowed her eyebrows in concentration and determination.

"Look!" Joey's exclamation broke the spell of Maya's melancholy thoughts. As they swam, she followed his finger. There it was. The Crystal Cathedral. As they approached, the first thing Maya noticed was its sheer size. Maya, Joey, and the seven mermaids escorting them were dwarfed by the huge, open cathedral gates as they swam through them.

It wasn't the shining, beautiful structure that the mermaids painted it out to be. But it wasn't the rocky ruins she had seen in her vision, either, damaged by Palazar's forces. It was somewhere in between.

The next thing that struck them was the depressing state of the walls. Maya knew they must have been crystal clear, magnificent, and glowing, as she saw in her vision. Now, though, they appeared like ancient stone. They were dark, gray, and pitted with age.

The siblings shivered. It was cold inside. She and Joey were near the end of the mermaid procession. Crystalline was first, holding globes of glowing algae. Then came Morgana, two mermaid royal guards, the queen, and the siblings. An eerie feeling floated around as they traveled deeper into its grand hall, as if entering a haunted house. The whole place gave Maya an anxious feeling that death itself was not far away.

Two more guards followed behind Maya and Joey, also carrying glow globes. The light from them, however, was quickly swallowed by the immense size and darkness of the cathedral. The globes were no more than pinpricks of light inside the gaping, icy blackness.

Deep, eerie echoes, similar to the calling of whales, were heard in the depths. Bulging-eyed eels and strange, skeletal fish dashed toward the group, then scurried from the glowing globes once caught in their light. Every few moments Maya would feel something slimy brush against her skin, then slither off. She had the terrible thought that if she were alone here, in the dark, she would be nothing more than a quick dinner for an unknown creature.

Crystalline steered the group toward the very back of the cathedral. Finally, they reached their destination. Maya saw the mermaids in front disappear through a small door. She took a deep breath and followed. The mermaid guards placed their glow globes upon high shelves. They filled the entrance with a soft, green-yellow light.

Scanning the walls, Joey saw frescoes that depicted centuries of mermaid battles against all types of evil creatures. He also saw painted scenes of what looked to be the signing of treaties and alliances, images of mermaids raising fists of victory alongside other fantastic creatures. And then, at the back of the room, they saw it. The portal.

It was a free-standing, tall archway. The archway was half in the water and half sticking out in the open air, hidden inside the crater. On first look, the structure appeared to be made of stone, but Maya now knew better—it was made of crystal that, at the moment, was gray and dull. Behind the crystals were fluted columns intricately carved. At the very top, where the two columns arched and met in the middle, Maya saw seven short vertical lines. She felt a warmth on her chest. Gazing downward, she noticed that the crystal pendant around her neck was glowing softly now that it was near the portal.

The mermaid guards were all silent, staring in reverence at the portal. Queen Aquamarisha's eyes were closed, as if lost in memory. Of course, Joey had a different reaction. He swam right through it.

"Well," Joey said, "I'm still here. Looks like it's not working."

Maya rolled her eyes.

Aquamarisha removed the emerald pendant and chain from around her neck. She swam to one of the portal's columns. There was a notch, perfectly shaped to fit the pendant. Aquamarisha took a deep breath and slipped the jewel into it. Everyone held their breath. But nothing happened.

The queen shook her head. "It's useless," she said. "The portal won't awaken."

"It could only be sleeping," Princess Morgana offered, quietly.

"Or it could be damaged," Crystalline said.

Maya chewed her lip, deep in thought.

Crystalline stared out the door through which they had entered. "My queen, we have tried. I suggest we return home. As you know, there are creatures in this ancient lake that awaken with the moon. We wouldn't want to face them with such a small party."

"It was worth our time," the queen said, discouraged.

"Wait, please," Maya said. "You said this portal flows with energy that connects all seven kingdoms?"

"Yes, child," Aquamarisha said, lowering her defeated eyes to the ground.

"And now, because the kingdoms have become disconnected, that energy has stopped flowing," Joey added with some thought.

He floated close to the portal, gazing up at the seven marks close to the top. Maya followed. They both felt a slight current flowing through the room, pushing a little to the right. The siblings began to study the markings on the columns. There were carvings of seaweed, bent to the right. There were schools of tiny fish, all carved swimming from left to right. The mermaid was swimming left to right. Then they saw a carving of a mermaid circling a crystal.

"Looks like everything is leaning toward the right," Joey said.

"Queen Aquamarisha," Maya said softly, "may I borrow your emerald please?"

Princess Morgana whipped her head around to gawk at Maya. The guards took sharp breaths and even tensed their hands on their spears, as if what Maya had asked was both sacrilegious and dishonorable. The queen frowned, her fingers instinctively closing on the pendant in her hand.

"No hand but mine has touched this pendant since it was put around my neck when I was young."

"You have an idea?" Crystalline questioned, peering at Maya.

"I do," Maya said. Bravely, she faced the queen and stretched out her hand.

Aquamarisha stared at her hand, hesitantly. Then she placed her pendant in it.

Maya nodded. "Thank you for your faith," she said.

The queen bowed her head. Already she had learned to trust these human children.

Maya placed herself in front of the portal. She took a deep breath, then swam around the portal, left to right. When she was facing it again, she slipped the pendant into the notch. All waited expectantly. Still nothing happened.

"My queen," Crystalline urged. "I have as much belief in these humans as any. But night is falling and—"

"Look!" Joey shouted through his breathing shell. All eyes followed his finger to the top of the portal.

The first of the seven carved lines slowly flickered. It pulsed from gray and dark, to a soft blue light.

"Yes!" Maya whispered to herself, gaining more faith. She took off, swimming again around the portal. Left to right. When she pushed the pendant into the notch again, the second carving lit up on top of the portal.

"Ingenious!" Crystalline remarked.

"It's brilliant!" Joey said, grabbing Morgana in a hug.

Maya continued swimming around the portal. As she swam, she said, "There are seven portals for the Seven Kingdoms. There were seven doves, including Libertine. Seven seems to be a magical number in Maradonia. A power number!"

Aquamarisha placed her hands on her hips. "It's clever thinking, young one. Very clever indeed."

Maya circled the seventh time.

Everyone watched in silent anticipation as the last point sputtered to life. The glow from all seven points filled the room with more light than the glow globes. Suddenly, veins of light raced down each of its columns. Trails of blue light reached the emerald in its notch, and all the carvings around the portal exploded in a bloom of light. The crystals shimmered through every shade of green imaginable—from deep, dark emerald to bright green to a pale tone of honeydew melon.

The group shaded their eyes for a moment, until the flash had passed. When they all opened their eyes again, the portal was unrecognizable. It looked more like a giant cluster of crystals than a palace. The light shone through the faceted walls, sending a myriad of rainbows shimmering around them. Light danced and refracted as if the portal had been cut from one gigantic, translucent diamond.

Aquamarisha lifted her arms up in a gesture of delight. "I've never seen anything like it!"

"I think it's filled to the brim with energy now," Maya said. She twirled around, disrupting the patterns of light on her skin and watching them reform.

"Once again, you have done what I would have thought impossible," the queen said with thankfulness.

"I couldn't have done this without Joey's help, though," Maya reminded her. Princess Morgana nodded in agreement. "Now we need to decide where we need to go."

The queen's face clouded over with the new challenge. She turned to trace her fingers across the wall carvings of the other six kingdoms.

"It is difficult to say where we should travel," she said. "None of the other six kingdoms have been friendly to us in so long."

"To be fair, you haven't been so friendly to them either," Maya offered.

Crystalline's eyes widened at Maya's audacity to address the queen this way. But the queen turned to Maya and acknowledged her clever tongue.

"You are right," she said. "We are not enemies, but we have not been friends either. You got us this far. What do you suggest?"

Maya thought for a moment. The answer wasn't coming so quickly.

"A good leader knows that the enemy of his enemy is his friend," Joey said, swimming toward the queen. "Let me ask you this. In the old days, the oldest days, back when all the kingdoms were close and united, which kingdom strongly opposed King Palazar's forces?"

Aquamarisha nodded. "The giants. They were our closest allies. We fought many battles together over the eons."

"Then that's where we should go," Joey said. "To the giants."

"The challenge," Crystalline said, "is that the giants are the deadliest warriors in all of Maradonia. Next to us mermaids, of course. If they do not greet our party with open arms, chances are no one will return alive."

"The bigger challenge, though," the queen added, "is that the giants' kingdom is one of fire."

"Fire?" Joey said, gulping.

"Fire and lava," Morgana confirmed. "It is too dry and too hot. Mermaids cannot survive there, not even for a moment."

Around the room, eyes and heads were lowering toward the ground. The truth of the situation was sinking in.

"But we can," Maya said, giving voice to what all were thinking.

"Yes," Joey echoed. "We can."

Morgana took Joey's hand and closed her eyes in fear of losing him. Joey lifted her hand and kissed it. His eyes said it all. This was too important. It was something the siblings had to do. Without a word, Morgana knew—and agreed.

Aquamarisha floated to the top of the portal and touched her emerald to the first carved line. It glowed turquoise—the color of water. It was the mark that represented the mermaid kingdom. Then she touched her emerald to the third mark. This time, it flashed bright red—this mark surely represented the giants' land of fire.

The portal started humming. The water between its columns began glowing bright red. Quickly, the water between the portal columns was roiling and bubbling, like the top of a volcano.

Standing before it, Maya and Joey could even feel heat emanating from the portal. They looked at each other.

"Be cautious of your surroundings," Crystalline warned.

"Great advice," Joey said. "Thanks for that."

Both him and Maya drifted closer to the portal entrance. They could feel themselves being pulled toward it as if by a magnet. The portal's hum was building in intensity, starting to sound like a jet engine revving up.

"This is it," Joey called out over the noise, giving Morgana one last nod. Maya clenched her teeth. She tried to stay brave, watching the long strands of her hair being pulled past her own face and toward the portal.

"And don't forget about the giants' guardians!" Crystalline called, just remembering.

"Yes!" Aquamarisha shouted. "They are trained to kill first, ask questions second."

"Wait, what?" Joey called out behind him. "What guardians?"

"The guardians are—" Morgana shouted.

The last part was swallowed by the ear-splitting noise of the portal.

"They're what?" Joey shouted.

Morgana cupped her hands and yelled even louder. "They're—"

WHOOOOOSH!

Before they could hear about the guardians, Maya and Joey were yanked violently into the portal. In the blink of an eye, they disappeared from the small room in the Crystal Cathedral and into the unknown.

CHAPTER FORTY

DISMISSED

"I AM NOT CRAZY!" Ilona felt Gordon's hot breath on her cheek as he hissed the whisper into her ear. She brushed him away, like he was a mosquito on her face and leaned over to pick up more dead branches for the fire. In the process, she turned her back on Gordon to conceal her irritation.

"Enough, Gordon," she said sternly yet quietly, so the others wouldn't hear. "The sun plays tricks on us all. We've been through a lot in the past few days. You could, very well be dehydrated."

"Arrrrrgh!" Gordon's head and hands trembled with frustration. "I didn't imagine it!"

Ilona bit her lip and rose back up to face him.

"Maya appeared in the river, riding a dolphin, talking to a bird, and told you she had found a group of mermaids who had fought a terrible battle, and she also just so happens to know where the portal is. That's the gist of it, right?"

"Okay, sure, it sounds a little odd when you put it like that."

"How else would you put it?" Ilona asked. "And why didn't you bring her to the lieutenant?"

"She took off before I could do anything!" Gordon protested. "But I told you we'd find this lagoon, right? We're going in the right direction."

Ilona had to admit that part was true.

She sighed. "Look. I know we're searching for a portal that exists at the point where science meets magic. But now you're talking about mermaids and talking doves."

Gordon gazed past Ilona, his eyes seeming to fall out of focus.

Ilona said, more gently, "You must know how crazy it sounds."

In the distance, Ilona's men were milling around the campsite. However, there was a commotion by the shore where a few of the men were gathered, looking at the water, pointing, and shouting with wild excitement. Ilona watched them, with her hands cupped around her eyes to shield her sight from the sun. Now she could finally see what her team was gawking at. Were they seals? Dolphins?

Ilona walked past the tents toward the edge of the beach. Lieutenant Kreeger and the other Navy personnel took position around Ilona. Gordon was right behind.

Ilona stopped at the water's edge. There were three mermaids. *Mermaids?* Real, live mermaids! They were just like the ones in fairy tale books she read as a child. One was lying on a large, flat volcanic rock at the spot where sand met water. The other two were floating in the water. Those two carried sharp, glowing spears held at the ready, like guardians. The one on the rock held no weapon but carried an air of authority and control. All three mermaids had long hair. The two guards had brown reddish hair. The mermaid on the rock had hair the color of dark lavender. All three wore armor made of shells and fibrous plants.

Glancing around, she was glad neither Professor Mundi nor Doctor Huang were in sight. The scientists would only confound and confuse this first contact. Then the mermaid on the rock announced to Ilona, proudly,

"I am Emilia, Leader of Awanata's Royal Scouts. Identify yourselves and your intentions."

Ilona had no idea what the mermaid's title meant, but she was impressed with her tone. It was commanding but not threatening, strong but not hostile. Just as Ilona opened her mouth to speak, Kreeger stepped forward.

"We've come to find a port—"

"We've come to find our friends," Ilona interrupted him. "Maybe you've met them? Maya and Joey?"

The mermaids exchanged nods and raised eyebrows. The tight knot of tension in Ilona's back loosened a bit. It had worked; she had chosen her words well. The mermaids seemed to know and approve of the missing teenagers.

Ilona continued. "My name is Sergeant Ilona Wells."

"And I'm Gordon." He flashed a toothy smile. "Maya and I are close friends."

The mermaid realized that these were the humans the siblings had mentioned to them.

"We're here to find them," Ilona said. "There are people from our land who miss them very much."

Ilona feared being caught in a lie. If Maya and Joey were brought to the beach now, they would reveal they didn't know Ilona at all. They might even tell the mermaids that the Navy team was out to control the portal—which was true—but Ilona didn't want Emilia and the other mermaids to leave without sharing the portal's location. It was a tough situation. Ilona decided to press forward for the information.

"Emilia," Ilona said holding her hands out peacefully, "where might we find Maya and Joey?"

Emilia regarded her. These were humans. Humans were to be distrusted. Still, their knowledge of their realm must be limited. Against her usual judgment, her eyes softened. "We trust no one. However, any friend of Maya and Joey is a friend of the mermaids." The other two mermaids nodded in agreement, lowering their spears.

"Last I saw them, they were in the Crystal Cathedral."

Ilona wondered if that would be the location of the portal. It sounded like a place of importance. Ilona looked at her Lieutenant and suspected he was thinking the same thing. A broad grin spread across Kreeger's face as he said, "And where is this Crystal Cathedral then, girlie?"

The mermaid looked Kreeger up and down with the hint of a frown. "My proper title is 'Royal Leader.'"

Emilia turned to Ilona. "Do you always allow your males to talk like that?"

"Oi, talk like what now?" Kreeger croaked, offended.

"Please, Lieutenant," Ilona said, keeping her voice light. No sense raising tensions when everything was still under control.

"I said, talk like what, *Leader Girlie*?" Kreeger snickered.

The two mermaid guards raised their spears. Kreeger and the Navy soldiers raised their automatic rifles. Before Ilona could intervene, Lieutenant Kreeger stepped forward.

"We'll keep it nice and simple," Kreeger said. "Just tell us where the portal is, and everything will be just fine."

"The portal?" Emilia asked. "I do not know what you're talking about."

Kreeger brought his rifle up higher so that his eye looked straight down the gun sight at the mermaid. Emilia looked back at her guards, a question in her eyes. One of her guards shook her head.

"He holds it like a weapon. Like a crossbow. But I see no arrow."

"Nor do I," Emilia replied calmly. "You claim that you are friends, yet revealed that your intentions are unclear."

"Where's the portal?" Kreeger demanded, louder.

"You need to teach your male some manners," another of the mermaids said.

Kreeger's eyes grew wider. It was at this moment that Ilona perceived that the mermaids respected feminine authority rather than male.

"I know nothing of what you call a portal," Emilia claimed, growing uneasy.

"Lying fish!" Kreeger shouted.

The mermaids raised their weapons. Electricity pulsed through their spears, ready to engage. "I sense subversiveness within you. Remove yourselves from our territory immediately! You are not welcome here."

Kreeger stepped forward again, now shaking with anger. "Enough of this chit-chat. Now, you tell us where that portal is."

"Lieutenant, please," Ilona hissed.

"Right now!" Kreeger yelled, his eye narrowing down the gunsight. His finger tightened on the trigger.

Emilia's eyes narrowed. Immediately, both mermaid guards launched their spears with lightning speed. Kreeger was far enough away to avoid the spears by diving and rolling. When he came up to his knees, three shots rang out from his rifle. Both mermaids fell back into the water. Emilia looked down at her chest and saw the blossom of red blood. She turned to Ilona with a look of disappointment and regret. Then she closed her eyes, slipped off the flat, black rock elegantly and dropped into the lagoon.

Having finally learned what was happening on the beach, Professor Mundi and Doctor Huang ran onto the shore. Each carried plants and berries from the forest where they had been foraging.

"What happened?" Mundi asked, looking around.

"Were those gunshots?" Huang asked frantically.

Lieutenant Kreeger stood at attention. His face was blank. He looked straight ahead as if nothing out of the ordinary had happened. Ilona stomped over to Kreeger, stopping mere inches from the bulky man. She rose up onto her tiptoes to get right in his face.

"How could you do that?" she shouted. "We're supposed to be a team. We talk to each other."

Lieutenant Kreeger didn't blink.

"How else would you have handled a direct threat? I am protecting my team. I'm the one in charge here," he sneered. "And I ain't takin' orders from a mermaid."

Ilona couldn't believe it. Their first contact with the local power and Kreeger had killed them for the sake of his ego. Any hope of diplomacy and the mermaids' help in finding the portal were shattered.

"Did you say, mermaid?" Huang pronounced slowly. Professor Mundi's mouth was hanging open. "You saw mermaids? And you shot them?"

Ignoring the scientists, Lieutenant Kreeger trained his eyes on Ilona and said with venom in his words, "It doesn't matter what your daddy says anymore. Aye? From this point forward, you follow my orders and do exactly as I command. Otherwise, you will be dishonorably withdrawn. Do you understand?"

Ilona looked down with sadness and defeat. "Yes, sir," she sputtered.

"Dismissed."

CHAPTER FORTY-ONE

SEEDS OF DISCORD

ILONA PUNCHED THE BUTTON on her cell phone hard. She hadn't really expected it to work. But any word from her father, the admiral, would be most welcome right about now. She sighed and looked around the beach. Professor Mundi and Doctor Huang were pretending to work outside of the campsite, but really, they were whispering to each other and stealing hurt looks at Kreeger.

Lieutenant Kreeger's orders were simple. To shoot at anything that threatened the team. He also commanded a few of his men to dig a hole for the mermaid's body. Sipping on a beer, he watched his men dig, as if he didn't have a care in the world. Gordon was in full obsessive mode, headphones on, absorbed in whatever sound his high-tech gear made in his ears. Whenever his father approached, Gordon would lift up a finger to silence him and press the earphones against his ears as if he was listening for the most important sound in the world. Maybe he was, Ilona reasoned.

But mermaids. They were the most incredible creatures she had ever seen. What a discovery in itself! They had found real, live mermaids. Except now they were dead. Kreeger had killed them. The pain of it stung Ilona. Taking live mermaids back home would have been the most amazing discovery in the history of anthropology, or even veterinary medicine for that matter. Who knew what else was waiting to be discovered in this fantastic place besides the portal?

The portal would be enough. It would be plenty, in fact. A portal that instantly teleported you from one place on earth to another would be the most significant discovery in the history of—well, in the history of history. Her father would be so proud. For the first time that day, Ilona was able to smile.

She looked over again at Mundi and Huang. Now they were peeking at Ilona out of the corner of their eyes. They had the look of conspirators planning something secret. Did she have to worry about them too, now? Ilona shook her head. Give her a nice, plain target, a rifle, and two thousand yards. Give her rampaging rhino-elephants and a handgun. These tasks, she could handle. But dealing with the emotions and relationships of a handful of people under Kreeger's command? Not her forte.

What was it her father had said about command? About managing people's hopes and weaknesses? "It is the hardest job you'll never love." Yes. She had to agree.

"Oi! Egghead!" Kreeger shouted, leaning on his spade and wiping his thick forehead with an already filthy handkerchief. "Ain't you found nothing on that billion-dollar iPod of yours yet?"

Gordon blinked but kept his eyes on his gear. Ilona knew he had heard Kreeger. He just didn't know how to respond. Kreeger snickered, shook his head, and went back to digging. Then Ilona saw Gordon sneak a scared, sideways glance at her. *Great,* she thought. *Now I have to deal with Gordon's hurt feelings, too.*

Just then, she heard a beeping. Mundi and Huang scrambled to adjust dials. Gordon whipped off his headphones. Ilona strode quickly to Gordon's side, and he pointed at moving lines on a computer screen that looked to

Ilona like a seismograph showing one huge earthquake on it.

"There!" he said, proudly.

"What?" Ilona said, hopefully. "What am I looking at?"

"You're looking at the biggest surge of electromagnetic energy anyone has ever seen," Gordon said, excitedly.

"What does that mean?" Ilona asked.

Gordon stood up tall. "It means that if there's a portal, someone just used it."

Ilona's eyes went wide, and Gordon turned to look in triumph at Kreeger. Kreeger shrugged and threw down his shovel. "Lay her in there," Kreeger commanded two Navy men.

Slowly, the Navy men lifted Emilia's body and reverently lowered her into the grave as they dug. They had already wrapped her, respectfully, in long strands of seaweed. They had searched the waters for the bodies of the other two mermaid guards but to no avail. Kreeger grinned maliciously and started shoveling sand onto the mermaid's body.

Gordon walked up to Ilona's side.

"Your lieutenant got us in real deep with that one," Gordon said, nodding to Emilia's grave.

Ilona huffed. "Unfortunately, our lieutenant is the reason those mermaids won't be welcoming us with open arms."

"You know that grave isn't deep enough," Gordon said quietly. Ilona didn't respond. A deep grave wasn't the issue.

There was no way she could let Emilia's remains stay here in eternal rest. Her body was too important. A trophy, an experiment to autopsy—it didn't matter. All Ilona knew was that they should be taking the mermaid's body back to civilization to be studied. But no one needed to know about that now. Neither did Gordon. They just needed to be morally and emotionally satisfied so that they would keep working.

Ilona sighed. Indeed, managing the weaknesses of these civilians was not something she enjoyed. But hopefully it would pay off.

"Gordon," Ilona said, turning to the young scientist. She smiled at him, batted her eyelids, and shifted her weight onto one foot to accentuate the curve of her hip. It had the desired effect.

Gordon leaned toward her without even knowing it, as if magnetically attracted.

She bit her lip the way she had seen Hollywood starlets do in movies. "I don't know how the mermaids will respond to all this. But I know one thing."

"Yes? Ilona, what do you know?" he managed to say.

Ilona leaned even closer to him. "I believe you now, and I'm confident that Maya will show you the portal. We have to do absolutely everything we can to get to that portal," she breathed.

"Yes," Gordon croaked. "Yes, we do."

Ilona pulled back, pouting. "Can I trust you?" she asked, blinking innocently.

"Always," Gordon whispered.

"Then lead the way."

CHAPTER FORTY-TWO

PROVE IT

Maya was screaming, but she just couldn't hear it, which made everything even scarier. She knew Joey was next to her. He had to be.

All Maya knew for sure was that she was flying at an impossible speed. She was being pulled from her chest, like her heart was steel and the strongest magnet in all creation was drawing her forward. Her arms and legs trailed behind her. Try as she might, she couldn't move them. She couldn't move anything.

Then, suddenly, it all stopped.

With a whooshing sound that flooded her ears, she came to an abrupt halt. She wobbled on her feet, struggling to maintain her balance. What made her tremble, however, was the dizzying sight before her eyes.

She was standing on the edge of an incredibly high, rocky cliff. The mountainside at her feet disappeared, straight down, into a purple mist. With one step, just six inches forward, she would fall into the yawning chasm and fall for what looked like forever. Turning, she saw her brother staring, dumbfounded, at the spectacle all around them.

The siblings didn't know what time it was in this realm, but the sky was dark, filled with smoke and thick black clouds. Rumbling sounds of distant thunder made the ground roll beneath their feet. Far-off, shards of red lightning broke the sky into a jumble of pieces.

A mountain range of jagged volcanoes stretched out into the horizon. The cliffs were streaked with zigzags of glowing orange as if huge claws had raked them open, exposing the raw flesh underneath. Thick rivers of lava flowed through these wounds like blood. Molten lava slowly and endlessly tumbled down the sides of the volcanoes, and chunks of rock fell into the rivers, boiled, and disappeared. A wind carried the toxic smell of sulfur, assaulting their noses. The summits of the volcanoes were topped by twisters of smoke that spun madly around the volcanoes' craters.

Maya covered her mouth and began to sway with vertigo.

Joey felt Maya's grip on his shoulder loosen. It shocked him back to reality, and he grabbed his sister by the arm and led her away from the cliff edge.

The two of them dropped to the hard ground, panting. Now that they were away from the cliff, Joey saw the portal they had emerged from. Black and steaming, it looked like it had been hewn from a huge chunk of lava rock. It had none of the intricate carvings of the mermaid portal. Instead, it was all sharp angles. However, the same straight vertical lines burned red atop the portal's arch.

Joey calmed Maya and surveyed their surroundings. The mountaintop they were on was another volcano. On their side of the volcano there was no soft, gradual slope downward, just the sharp cliff they had appeared on.

Joey stood and offered Maya his hand. She took it and Joey pulled her to her feet.

"I can see why the mermaids can't survive here," Maya said, covering her mouth again. "The heat, the smell. It's dry and it's—" Maya coughed, struggling for the right word.

"Disgusting?" Joey offered, looking back over his shoulder at her. He was walking slowly to the edge of the cliff.

Maya controlled her cough. "I was thinking more like 'toxic,' but yeah, disgusting works, too." She felt a rush of wind and turned around.

"Who the heck puts their portal on the edge of a cliff?" Joey said, cautiously peering over the edge. Maya didn't answer immediately. She was staring at the huge, burning red eyes that had appeared behind them, floating in the air.

"Um," she said, swallowing hard, "maybe something that can fly?"

Joey turned with a question on his face that quickly fell into a look of astonishment. The red and black beast stopped beating its veiny wings and stretched them out to their full width. There was only one possible word for what this was.

"Dragon," Joey whispered.

The creature's body, thirty or forty feet long, paused in midair, its long neck fully stretched, its head high in the sky. For one perfect moment, it was still and silent, hanging in midair. Looking at this magnificent creature took their breath away.

Then the dragon dropped to the ground and settled forward, falling onto its pointed talons and folding its thin, fleshy wings against its body. On the ground, it looked like an awkward bird. Its body was surely made more for the air than the earth. Now that they were closer to it, the siblings both noticed that the dragon's body shimmered in more than just red and black. From different angles, its scales and sharp bumps reflected the surrounding light and glistened with every color. It was somehow terrifying and beautiful at the same time.

"Good dragon?" Joey said, holding out his hand as if to pet it.

"Joey!" Maya hissed.

Joey shot her a wild look. "What? You have a better idea?"

"Silence!" The dragon's voice flowed hot and menacing, like the lava on the distant volcanoes.

"Guess that answers that," Joey mumbled to himself.

Maya stopped herself from waving her hand in front of her face. The

dragon's breath smelled like rotten eggs. Sulfur. Maya wondered if this amazing creature breathed fire, like in the stories she had read. Never in her life had she thought she'd ever be face to face with a real-life dragon. Then again, after mermaids and everything else she had seen recently, talking dragons weren't too much of a surprise.

Joey took a small step forward. "Sir," he said. Then quickly he added, "Or ma'am . . . I'm sorry, I'm not sure, um, which you are."

Maya knew she had to step in. "Mighty dragon," she said, "my name is Maya. This is my brother, Joey. We come in peace. We mean you no harm."

The dragon's laugh made the ground tremble under their feet. It sounded like deep thunder. The dragon's eyes narrowed. Two pairs of eyelids, one horizontal and one vertical, blinked over its eyes in quick succession. Its face scrunched into what the siblings recognized as a sneer.

"You mean *me* no harm?" it said. The dragon stretched its long neck, and its head snaked forward until it was face to face with Maya and Joey. Its breath was hot and toxic on their cheeks.

Joey's throat immediately ran dry. His eyes started burning and watering.

"What possible harm might you do to me?" the dragon hissed.

It took all of Maya's strength to stand tall and not run away screaming. Her palms began to sweat. She raised her chin.

"We have come from Awanata. Seeking help."

The dragon blinked its eyes in recognition. It drew its head back, away from them.

"The mermaids sent you? Ha."

"They couldn't come themselves because of how hot and dry it is here," Joey offered. "We're their emissaries. The forces of evil are marching through Maradonia and—"

The dragon turned its head to the sky and roared. Joey shut his mouth and covered his head. The sound hit Maya's ears like the blast from an explosion. Then the booming sound turned into a pillar of blazing red fire spouting straight up into the air from the dragon's mouth. Maya and Joey could hardly believe their eyes. The heat from the dragon's fire made sweat break out on their faces. Finally, the dragon stopped spewing flame and turned to face the children again.

"Prove it!" the dragon rumbled, loudly. "Prove you come from the mermaids."

"It was Queen Aquamarisha," Joey gasped, cupping his ears. "She sent us."

Black, angry steam spewed from the dragon's nose. Its body glowed a dark, dangerous red. Maya knew that Joey and she were only moments away from being burnt alive. If they couldn't prove they had been sent by the mermaids, the dragon was about to turn its fiery breath on them. It would be a terrible death.

"Please," Maya said. "If you would just give us a moment." Her mind raced.

The dragon pulled back its neck. Its terrible, black eyes started glistening. The dragon's belly began to glow an even deeper red.

"You are mere spies sent by Palazar," the dragon breathed, pronouncing the name with pure hatred. "You have the audacity to come to us dragons, pretending to be sent from the mermaids? Have you no shame?"

Maya was trembling. *How can I prove it? What do I have on me? If only Aquamarisha were here. Or Crystalline. Or . . . wait!*

Just as the dragon arched its back and opened its mouth to cook the siblings alive, Maya shouted, "Look!"

Maya pulled out the crystal pendant that had been under her shirt. "This was given to me by a mermaid named Florina," she blurted.

The dragon paused, then leaned closer to peer into the pendant. "Florina?" the dragon said delicately, as if pronouncing the name of a long-forgotten friend.

"Yes," Maya gasped. "This pendant was made from pieces of—"

"The Crystal Cathedral." The dragon was nodding. "Yes, I can see that."

"You can?" Joey asked, bewildered.

The dragon sat back on its haunches, immediately more relaxed and pensive. "A dragon never forgets. We dragons live a long time. Longer than mermaids. Florina and I fought side by side one time. Just like our kind did in the days of old. Before Palazar's rise."

"That's incredible," Maya said. "And, frankly, that's very lucky for us."

The dragon tilted its head and looked at the siblings with a newfound respect, but still skeptical.

"The mermaids need help you say?" the dragon said.

"Palazar has gathered the Forces of Darkness. They've already attacked Awanata once," Joey explained. "And the mermaids were able to repel them."

"Actually," Maya added, gesturing to her brother, "Joey here was one of the heroes of the battle."

The dragon cocked its head to peer at Joey quizzically. The dragon's stare made Joey shiver.

"Is that so?" the dragon said doubtfully.

"But now Palazar is coming, himself," Maya said. "With an army larger than anyone has ever seen."

"So," Joey said, "we have been sent by Queen Aquamarisha to come here and ask for help."

"The Seven Kingdoms must unite again," Maya said. "The old alliances must be renewed. The portals must be used once more. For the good of all Maradonia."

"Will you help us?" Joey said.

The dragon did not hesitate. “I would help the mermaids.”

Maya and Joey turned to each other. They breathed a sigh of relief and smiled at each other.

“But it is not up to me,” the dragon said as smoke escaped his nostrils. “It is not up to any dragon.”

“What do you mean?”

The dragon turned its head skyward. A shrill call erupted from its mouth. Maya and Joey looked up to see two other dragons break through the dark clouds like arrows shot from above, heading straight down at them at astonishing speed.

With a sudden, mighty heave of its wings, the dragon took flight in front of the siblings. It hovered and addressed them.

“It is not me you need to convince, young ones. It is the rulers of this land, the giants.”

“Will they listen to us?” Joey called out.

The dragon closed its eyes. “At this time, that is unknown.”

The dragon beat its wings and lifted into the sky. Right behind it, the two diving dragons swooped down. Quick as lightning, the dragons grabbed Maya and Joey, one child each. The dragons were surprising gentle, and the children were not hurt at all by their claws. Suddenly they were flying at great speed over the volcanic landscape, away from the portal.

CHAPTER FORTY-THREE

GORGONIA

Once again, Joey was speeding through the air. At least this time, he could see what was around him. The dragon's claw gripping each sibling was both gentle and firm, and Joey trusted the creature. In fact, both siblings felt no danger of either being ripped apart or falling to their doom. Below them, Gorgonia, the Kingdom of the Giants, unfolded.

Joey's and Maya's dragons flew behind the larger one they had spoken with. They flew over more volcanoes. Far below them, the lava that flowed down the sides of the volcanoes met in large, steaming rivers and lakes of lava. Even hundreds of feet overhead, Joey could feel the extreme heat.

Up ahead he saw a lake, and soon enough they were flying over a narrow beach of black sand and tall, sharp columns of clear crystal. The rivers of lava flowed around the spiky pillars of crystal and met the water in huge plumes of white smoke. Maya's dragon flew straight through one of these plumes, and she was relieved it was not hot. Rather, it was cold, wet, and refreshing, like flying through a cloud. She came out feeling clean.

Then they were approaching solid land again. They arrived at a thin shoreline comprising shelves of cliff that looked like many enormous staircases. This land was less formidable than the range of volcanoes they had just been on. It was rocky and full of lava rivers, but it also had stretches of greenery. The air was not full of toxic fumes, like the air over the volcanoes. The clouds were turning from gray to golden. As they flew over the shore, Maya thought she was looking down on hundreds of orange and red waterfalls. Then she realized they were actually lava flows pouring off cliffs and into the sea. Maya exhaled in astonishment.

The leading dragon noticed and slowed to fly next to Maya's dragon.

"What do you think of Gorgonia?" it said, peering closely at her.

"I can't believe that's lava," Maya said, truthfully. "It's strange to me that something so deadly can also be so beautiful." She turned to look into the dragon's ebony, sparkling eye. "Kind of like you and your friends," Maya added, appreciating the magnificent dragon in flight. The dragon's eye told her that it knew she was telling the truth, not just trying to find favor with a compliment.

Without a word, the three dragons turned as one and flew north, over the shoreline. The light was growing softer and streaks of pink and purple clouds started appearing in the sky. Below, odd vegetation appeared. Trees with long branches of fiery red and purple leaves clung to the cliffs, leaning toward the sea. Rays of sunlight shot through the pillars of golden smoke, lending the land a magical quality. Maya smiled and gasped at the natural beauty around her.

"Maya," the dragon pronounced slowly.

"Yes?" It was the first time the dragon had used her name.

"I owe you an apology," the dragon began. "I did not introduce myself to you because I am the guardian of our portal, and it has been hundreds of years since anyone emerged from it. I was shocked, and I did not know if you were friend or foe. But I can see into your heart, and I know you are not deceptive."

"I'm glad to hear that," Maya replied, bowing her head slightly.

"My name is Oomrath, Captain of the Dragon Legion, sworn to protect the giants' portal and lands."

"Pleased to meet you, Captain Oomrath," Maya said. "Have the dragons always served the giants?"

Oomrath huffed. "My kind were born from the core of the earth. But many thousands of years ago, Palazar's ancestors imprisoned us and made us serve them in the kingdom of snow and ice. We dragons were not suited to that environment. Most died because our element is fire. The rest were enslaved for many generations. We dragons live for hundreds of years. We lived in pain and misery in our prisons under Mount Hailstone. It was the giants who saved us in a great battle hundreds of years ago. Since then, we have served them, here, as their guards and soldiers. We are proud to serve the giants. They are fair and kind to us." Oomrath added mysteriously, "Or, they have been up to now."

"And the mermaids?" Maya asked.

"As I mentioned, over the centuries, we dragons have fought alongside the mermaids against the powers of darkness. The giants and the mermaids enjoyed a very favorable alliance until all the kingdoms grew jealous of each other and stopped using the portals."

"I think that's a shame," Maya said. "How can you ever learn or progress if you're stuck in your own little bubble? No one is alone on this planet. Diversity is key to survival for all beings."

Oomrath again looked appreciatively at Maya. "These are wise words from someone so young," his voice rumbled.

Maya bowed her head.

"A leader sees friends where others see strangers," Joey added with a smile, eavesdropping on them from below his dragon. Oomrath turned to nod at him. "That is, indeed, a deep thought."

"I wish it were mine," Joey called out.

The dragons turned left, heading inland.

"Look!" Joey called from his dragon. He pointed down.

Down below, the land was changing. It was no longer covered in rivers of lava. The tone of the land was changing from red, to purple, to midnight blue.

The sun was still high in the air, but everything below had a tint of nightfall. The siblings looked ahead to see something that took a moment to process.

It was a city, but unlike any city they had ever seen. The first thing Maya thought of was pictures she had seen of cities in ancient Japan. The buildings had a pagoda style to them, with buildings that had many stories, each level smaller than the one under it, like stacked pyramids. They appeared to be made of clay bricks with upturned roof corners. Many were surrounded by bodies of water crisscrossed by many footbridges. The buildings were built amongst many tall trees, joining them with the natural landscape in perfect harmony. As the dragons began to descend, Joey was struck by the strangest feature of this city: its size. Everything was huge!

The footbridges were wide as freeways back home. Each story of every building was many times higher than the buildings he was used to. The towers stretched high into the clouds. It made sense, since this was a city of giants, but to see it for the first time was quite a shock. *These giants,* he thought, *must be truly giant!*

The dragons were heading for the brightest spot in the city. It was also the tallest. The compound at the heart of the city reminded Joey of emperors' palaces in old martial arts movies. Gates and walls as tall as skyscrapers surrounded a huge courtyard. Turrets and towers rose from the massive, long central building. Ponds and streams dotted the enclosure and green ivy grew all around it. How perfectly the structure fit into its natural surroundings. The whole palace seemed to be made of crystal that was both absorbing and reflecting the cobalt blue color of the land.

A long, deep rumbling noise filled the air. In a distant tower, an enormous animal horn was being blown. The doleful sound traveled for many, many miles.

"Is that for us?" Joey called out. "A welcome call?"

Oomrath sighed with a deep sadness. "No, Joey," he pronounced. "That is a call of mourning. Our emperor," Oomrath said solemnly, "is dying."

CHAPTER FORTY-FOUR

FEAST OF THE GIANTS

MAYA AND JOEY had never felt so small. The siblings were like two mice inching down the impossibly long aisle in the incredibly huge hall. Giants were seated at wooden tables as large as buses, eating and drinking loudly and messily. As Maya and Joey passed them, followed by Oomrath, no one noticed. The siblings' heads didn't even reach the top of the tables.

The hall was the giants' meeting place, and they were in the middle of a rowdy feast. Oomrath had told them earlier, as they landed inside the palace compound, that this was the giants' way. Their emperor, Neolith, was close to death. It was their tradition to celebrate his life by eating, drinking, laughing, wrestling, and telling stories of Neolith's exploits.

No one announced their arrival. Oomrath had not alerted the emperor or anyone about the siblings—he had simply flown them straight there, nodded to the dragon guards outside the hall, opened the great doors, and walked them inside. This was also the giants' way: they had no secrets from each other, no strict hierarchy. The emperor ruled, but apart from that, all were considered equal—young or old, male or female, rich or poor.

Maya and Joey could not see over the tables to the far end of the room where the emperor was seated. The architecture in the palace was breathtaking. Each cornerstone was engraved with strange markings and along the walls were dragon images and snake sculptures.

Just as the siblings were rounding a corner and about to approach the head table, a wrestling match between two giants broke out. Joey pushed Maya out of the way at the last moment as enormous wine goblets crashed down around them like boulders. Two giants rolled past, roaring and grappling good-naturedly, big as dinosaurs. A huge chair exploded from one of their kicks. Oomrath quickly sheltered the siblings under his folded wings as splinters of wood, like enormous arrows, flew all around.

Oomrath pushed the siblings forward, still protecting them in his wings, until Maya and Joey felt him stop and say, "Sire. I bring you travelers. Strangers have come through the portal."

Suddenly, the entire hall went dead silent. All the fighting and laughing stopped at once. In the quiet, Maya and Joey heard a thin voice say, "From the portal you say? Well, well. What a treat. Show us them."

Oomrath's wings unfolded, and he lifted them higher. Maya and Joey found themselves looking up at three giants seated behind a massive table laden with food. In the middle was Neolith, the emperor. His tall frame was thin and bony. His face was ashen. Indeed, he looked ill.

To his left was a young, giant woman who, in human years, appeared to be in her teens. In giant years, that put her somewhere around fifty or sixty. She wore a thin, gold crown on top of long, fiery red hair that cascaded down to her waist. Though she was three times as big as him, Joey couldn't help but admire her strong muscles and sharp, chiseled face. She looked down on them with confidence and curiosity.

"They're so puny," said the third figure, distastefully, raising a handkerchief to his nose. He was a middle-aged giant seated on the emperor's other side. His fancy clothes and rigid posture conveyed the fact that he must be important and powerful.

A look of astonishment crossed the young giantess's face. "Of course, they're small, Cephais. They're human."

Whispers encircled the hall: "Human children?" and "The prophecy!"

"Nonsense!" shouted Cephais, turning to the crowd. "Rubbish! Superstitious drivel." His black, beady eyes stared around the room, daring anyone to contradict him. He snorted. "I shall not place my confidence in a myth. Who even believes it to be true?"

Grinning mischievously, the young giantess raised her hand up, straight and proud. Cephais rolled his eyes and sank back into his chair.

"Brunhilda," he breathed. "Of course, you would deem this to be true."

As much as he would have liked to, Cephais seemed unable to fully ridicule or confront her in public.

Emperor Neolith smiled. "Soon to be *Empress* Brunhilda, Cephais," he corrected.

Cephais bowed his head with a sneer. "Yes, of course, sire. Empress Brunhilda."

"Ah, my daughter," Neolith said, fondly taking Brunhilda's hand. "I knew you would not forget the old ways. It gives me great peace to know the kingdom will be in your hands soon enough."

Brunhilda lowered her eyes, already feeling the loss of her loving father.

"Sire," Cephais interrupted. "Send these younglings away. I strongly advise it. Today is about celebrating your greatness and all your achievements! Do not cloud the people's heads with irrational stories of saviors and Encouragers and other nonsense."

Brunhilda raised her eyes. "Tread softly, Cephais," she said, raising her chin at him. Now there was power and strength in her words. "Empresses choose their own High Advisors."

Giants in the hall murmured amongst themselves. Cephais had very few fans in the crowd, Maya and Joey realized, looking around at the aggressive and disapproving looks the giants were aiming at the emperor's advisor.

Neolith chuckled. "Ah, my princess, every day you prove yourself worthy of the throne. And stronger than I have ever been."

A coughing fit struck the emperor. His frail body doubled over in his chair, wracked with spasms. Brunhilda patted him on the back and held out his wine goblet.

"Your highnesses," Maya said, seizing her opportunity and bowing deeply. "My name is Maya, and this is my brother, Joey. It pains us to see the emperor in poor health. And we beg your forgiveness if we seem rash and disrespectful. But time is of the essence.

"We have been sent by Queen Aquamarisha. Only days ago, the mermaids defeated Abbadon in a terrible battle, but now Palazar himself marches on Awanata with the largest fighting force anyone has ever seen.

It is not only the mermaid kingdom that is in danger. Once he destroys Awanata, he will control the portal and then turn his sights on the other six kingdoms, including yours. Surely you know what I say is true.

"My brother and I have come to ask for your help. The time has come to reunite the kingdoms, put away your grudges, and defeat the forces of evil the only way possible—together."

The hall grew quiet as all processed what Maya had said. Oomrath looked down, approvingly, at Maya. It was a stirring speech. Neolith's coughing fit had passed. Now he was leaning back in his chair with his eyes closed and a look of pain frozen on his face.

Brunhilda turned from her father to Maya. "You speak truth, but our traditions demand that no such business shall be addressed tonight. As you see, my father is in his final hours. Tonight, we shall honor the emperor, and you are welcome to join us. Tomorrow, with the rise of the sun, we can discuss the situation about the dark realm."

Maya opened her mouth to object, but Joey grabbed her hand to quiet her.

"A leader," he began, looking from Maya to Brunhilda, saying it for both of them, "knows there is a right time and a right place for everything. We appreciate your hospitality." Joey bowed. Maya followed suit. Brunhilda looked down on them favorably.

CLANK!

Neolith banged his goblet on the arm of his chair. "What's an emperor to do to get a refill around this place?" he said with the last bit of his strength. Slowly and weakly, he raised his goblet with a smile. The giants in the hall roared their approval and appreciation.

"To the emperor," Brunhilda called out, raising her glass.

Hundreds of stone goblets collided in an earsplitting toast: "To Neolith!"

Instruments sprang to life, voices joined in song. Young giants leapt up to dance in the aisles, shaking the walls of the hall. Maya and Joey were served morsels of the giants' delicious food.

For the rest of the night, neither the giants, nor Maya and Joey, would mention the battle between Palazar and the mermaids. However, in the commotion, no one noticed Cephais silently creeping into the shadows and out of the hall.

CHAPTER FORTY-FIVE

CURSE OF CEPHAIS

Cephais didn't bother knocking. Isobel was so shocked by his barging through her front door that she dropped the broom she had been using to clean up.

Cephais sneered. "What kind of a seer doesn't see visitors coming?"

Isobel bowed so deeply that her long, brittle, gray hair brushed the floor as she inched away from the door.

"Forgive me, my lord, I am only a mortal," she said in her ragged, thin voice. "The spirits speak to me, of course they do. But only when I ask them to."

A look of distaste crossed Cephais's face. The old hag's appearance—and the awful smell in her dingy forest cabin—never failed to make him feel sick to his stomach.

"Enough," he said bringing a handkerchief to his mouth. "Conduct a séance immediately."

Isobel blinked. "A séance? Your lordship has never asked this before.

The emperor has outlawed such divinations. And then, the information you learn may not be exactly what you hope—"

"Silence!" Cephais said with haste. "Just do it."

He sat down at her table without being asked—after dusting off the chair with the bottom of his black cloak.

"Yes, yes," Isobel said obediently, bowing. "Of course. I survive only through your lordship's generosity and patronage."

Cephais looked down with scorn at her outstretched, wrinkled hand, but dropped a few coins into it, careful not to touch the moles growing out of her trembling fingers. Isobel, her spine bent with age, pocketed the money and then circled the table three times, chanting.

At one point, she grabbed a plant off a shelf, ripped up its leaves and scattered them across the floor. After lighting a few candles, she poured different powders over the floor. Finally satisfied, she sat opposite Cephais.

"Who is it, my lord, you wish to speak to?" she asked.

Cephais thought for a moment, then sat up taller. Isobel glanced at him from the corner of her eye and realized, with surprise, that the high minister was summoning his courage. She wondered what it was that scared him. He had always seemed confident and assertive before.

"Bring me my father, Keritan," Cephais said, jutting out his chin. "Leader of the Black Tribe. He's the only one I ever trusted."

Now Isobel knew why Cephais was afraid. Keritan had been a ruthless giant leader. He was rumored to have killed off half his own family during his rise to become chief of the Black Tribe. He died in a terrible rebellion, betrayed by his best friend.

Isobel lowered her head and started chanting. Cephais did not recognize the language, but he heard his father's name. He took a deep breath, preparing to speak with him.

A circle of thick, white smoke hovered over the table and suddenly the spirit of Keritan appeared. As in death, his throat was wet with blood. His fine bedclothes were stained crimson. Now Isobel knew the rumors were true—he had been murdered in his sleep.

The spirit of Keritan peered through the smoke. "Who beckons me?" the spirit roared. "Who dares to disturb my peace and bring me to this place against my will?"

Cephais swallowed. "It is I, father."

Keritan blinked his eyes. "Cephais? Bah! Leave me in peace!"

Cephais was sweating and breathing hard. Even in death his father terrified him, but he knew he had to persevere. "Father, please answer my question."

Keritan laughed darkly. "Stop wasting my time. I don't like it here. What is it that you wish to ask me?"

Cephais focused his eyes. "Emperor Neolith will not last the night. He has named his daughter, Brunhilda, his successor. Now two human children have come, as the prophecy forewarned, and urge us to interfere in their fight with King Palazar. I have spoken against them, but the people will not listen. You told me that I should be the rightful ruler of Gorgonia. Answer me this. How may I take my rightful place as emperor? How may I seize control of Gorgonia?"

An awful grin spread slowly across Keritan's face. "I told you many years ago that a man who cannot obey cannot command! You have never learned your lesson: that one who cannot see the ultimate becomes a slave to the immediate. Command is already out of your grasp. The people will not love you. They love Brunhilda. And now they don't fear you either. They fear the news the human children bring. You will never rule Gorgonia, so long as the empress and these children live," Keritan pronounced, rising even taller. "And tomorrow, you shall rule with me."

The vision of his father faded away until nothing appeared over the table but a thin wisp of white smoke. Isobel trembled. Cephais fell to the dirt floor of the cabin, dreadfully frightened by his father's words.

Finally, Cephais stopped panting and opened his eyes. Isobel was looking down at him. The pity in her eyes was enough to shock him from his terror.

"Don't look at me that way!" he yelled.

Isobel jumped back.

"I'm not weak," he whispered to himself. "I will take my rightful place as emperor."

The thought gave him courage. Cephais looked frantically around the dirty cottage. His eyes fell on several bottles, and a malicious grin tugged at the corners of his lips.

"Watch me," Cephais started ranting. "He who lives longest, laughs longest. And laughs last! The old fool doesn't believe in me because of his own pride and the downfall of his own state of weakness. But that is not me." Cephais leapt to his feet. Isobel swallowed and stepped backward, afraid of the look in Cephais's eye.

"Curare," he pronounced slowly, inching toward her, murder in his eyes.

Sweat broke out on Isobel's forehead.

"What are you going to do with curare?" she said, shaking her head innocently.

Cephais reached out and wrapped his fingers around her throat. "It all comes down to this. You know the forest people use curare as an arrow poison. You know it is a deadly toxin that, when administered, looks like a heart attack. You will give it to me. Now."

Isobel cried out for air. The room was swimming, darkening.

Cephais's enraged face was close to hers. He said, "I'll show them all what it means to become a powerful ruler. More powerful than they could ever imagine. My father will roll in his grave with disbelief. Indeed, tomorrow I shall rule, just as he said."

CHAPTER FORTY-SIX

CURARE

A FIRE FUNERAL had taken place at sunrise. During the night, Neolith had passed away, peacefully, in his sleep. The gathering the following morning was somber, in contrast to the feast that had been filled with celebration the night before. Now, the giants were assembled back in the hall, speaking to each other, eating, crying, or sitting in silence, each remembering the emperor in their own way.

At the center sat Maya and Joey. Small compared to the giants, they could barely see over the table. However, it had been the empress's wish for them to be there, beside her. On Brunhilda's head was a heavy crown of gold, diamonds, and rubies, but her face was covered in grief.

The royal advisor, Cephais, rose and walked over to the table filled with meats, food, and fruits. He picked up a plate, forked a few things onto it, turned his back for a moment, and then returned to the head table. In his hand, he was holding a plate with three pieces of juicy yellow fruit.

Cephais stood before Brunhilda and bowed deeply. "You are an empress now, Brunhilda. Our hearts are all heavy with the loss of our emperor. Please, accept this token of my loyalty. These fruits were grown in my own garden. They are ripe and decadent." He held out the plate. "Allow me to nourish your body, as you now nourish the soul of Gorgonia."

Maya didn't think much of it, but Joey eyed him warily. Even though Joey barely knew him, it felt very out of character. Brunhilda reached out mechanically and took a piece of fruit. Cephais stretched the plate over toward the siblings and nodded to them.

"You two are also most welcome in Gorgonia, our honored guests," Cephais bowed to Maya and Joey.

After they took the enormous fruit, Cephais wiped his hand on his robe.

Joey watched carefully. He noticed that the slightest smirk played on the advisor's lips.

Just as Brunhilda was lifting the fruit toward her mouth, Joey yelled, "Stop!" His action seemed to snap her from her stupor. The giants in the hall gasped.

"What is the meaning of this?" Brunhilda demanded.

"Don't eat it," Joey yelled as loud as he could. "It's poisoned!"

"That's absurd!" Cephais exclaimed. His hand flew to his chest in a gesture of disbelief. An exaggerated look of shock washed over his face.

"That is a very serious accusation," the empress said, "especially of our royal advisors." Brunhilda looked back and forth from Cephais to Joey.

"Your highness," Cephais said, shaking his head as if greatly insulted. "I have been a trusted advisor to your family for so many years. With all due respect, those who make false accusations in Gorgonia must be whipped, banished, and—"

Brunhilda raised her hand to silence Cephais. She was staring quizzically at Joey. "I know the law very well, Cephais," she said. "It was my father who decreed it."

"I'm very sorry," Joey apologized. "It was dishonorable to accuse your royal advisor."

Cephais sighed. "I shall accept your apology. It is the only proper thing to do after all."

"Of course, we will accept the fruit and eat." Then Joey added, "But first you must eat one of the fruits yourself."

"Oh, I cannot. These were grown just for the empress. I am not worthy to eat the royal fruits," Cephais sputtered, his face turning red.

Joey held out the piece of fruit.

Brunhilda carefully analyzed Cephais's face. Then her demeanor changed, and she immediately commanded, "You *will* eat it, Cephais."

Some giants found some humor in the situation and started chanting, "Eat, eat, eat!" Their voices echoed in unity throughout the hall. Of course, no one thought their own royal advisor would ever poison the new empress!

Cephais looked like a lonely sea captain standing on the bridge of his sinking ship. There was no way out. He had been trapped by this child! His plans were foiled. Now that he was caught in this murder attempt on the queen, he would be put to death most horribly. There was only one thing to do. And this way, he would die with some thin shred of dignity. Curare was painless. He reached out and picked up Joey's piece of fruit. The giants continued to chant in unison.

Cephais stood up tall. He lifted the fruit into his mouth and chewed. It wasn't bitter. It was soft and delicious. Hope sprang in Cephais. Perhaps the poison Isobel had given him had been faulty. Or too old to work. Or—

Then Cephais's face sagged into a look of sorrowful resignation. The last thought that went through his mind was of his father's prediction had come to pass, that on this day, he would indeed stand by his father, Keritan, and rule with him. The giant's heart stopped beating and he fell to the floor, dead.

All chanting ended immediately. The giants looked at each other in confusion. Immediately, the captain of Brunhilda's guards strode to the body. He felt for a pulse. There was none. He reached inside Cephais's black robe and removed a vial. He uncorked it and sniffed, then staggered back and dropped it on the ground where the vial shattered.

"Curare," the captain said, his face twisted with the noxious fumes of the poison.

Death walked through the hallway and not a single soul said a word. The empress stood up immediately. All eyes looked to her.

"Treason," she said. Her voice boomed throughout the hall.

Then an eerie silence fell across the entire room as two giants pulled the body of Cephais out. With one heave, they threw him off the palace balcony. Not a sound was heard, but it was evident that he was completely consumed by the lava river down below.

Maya gasped in disbelief. She cupped her hand over her mouth.

Brunhilda straightened the crown that lay on her head. In this moment, she understood the responsibility of her power. It was the first attempt on her life, and she had been empress for less than a day. Her brown eyes sparkled with thankfulness as they reflected fire from the table candles.

"We have you to thank for our very lives," Brunhilda said as a new glow of leadership embraced her posture and tone. "In this strange time of need, you have proven yourselves beyond any doubt. We believe you are truly the Encouragers."

"So, you'll come fight?" Maya asked, hopefully.

Brunhilda closed her eyes and shook her head. "Unfortunately, no. We giants must grieve for Neolith for seven days. It is our tradition and honor."

"But—" Joey started.

"But indeed, because you protected me with your great gift of discernment," Brunhilda interrupted, kindly, "we shall grant you the greatest warriors in all of Maradonia to aid you. The dragons shall fight in our place."

In the back of the hall, the dragon Oomrath lifted his head and bellowed a loud, frightful roar of approval.

"You will forever hold my gratitude, and I know we will be lifelong friends. Go now, Encouragers," Brunhilda commanded, "and defend the kingdoms of Maradonia!"

The giants started chanting: "En-cou-ra-gers! En-cou-ra-gers!"

CHAPTER FORTY-SEVEN

FATHER AND SON

FROM ATOP HIS ENORMOUS throne wagon, King Palazar looked down upon his army. Between his own forces and those of his allies, his soldiers numbered almost thirty thousand. They sluggishly swarmed down the mountain pass before and behind him like ants in slow motion. Palazar grinned.

After all the losses the mermaids faced in their previous battle, Palazar's fighting force now outnumbered the mermaid warriors at least four to one.

Within hours he would reach the lagoon, where the final battle would be waged—and won. Soon Aquamarisha would be dead, and her portal would be under his control. Palazar pondered which of the other six kingdoms he should attack next. Gazing out at the two deformed giants pulling his throne vehicle, Palazar thought, *Perhaps the giants next? As punishment for freeing the dragons from our ancestors so many centuries ago.*

"Sire?"

Palazar was annoyed to be roused from his thoughts of conquest. It was his new second in command, the leader of the ogres, the two-headed General Frab. "What is it, Frab?" he demanded.

"Look, sire," his two voices spoke in synchronicity.

Palazar followed Frab's gnarled finger. A swirling cloud of black was approaching. The cloud was more like a whirlwind in the air.

"It . . . it's unnatural," Frab sniveled.

"Of course it is, you brainless ogre," Palazar sneered. "It's my witch."

Palazar raised his hand and the entire procession ground to a halt. As the strange funnel cloud grew closer, Frab realized that it was made of black wings. Hundreds of screeching crows were flying around two blurred shapes in the center of the tornado. The spinning madness of wings hovered in front of Palazar's massive throne carriage for a moment, then settled on the ground. The cawing murder of crows dispersed. Frab blinked in shock. There, kneeling before Palazar, was Abbadon, his son. Palazar raised an eyebrow.

"You live?" he said drily.

Abbadon's courage was shaken. His father did not seem to care in the slightest that he was alive.

"Father," Abbadon began, about to recite the words he had been practicing over and over, "I come to ask—"

Palazar waved his hand as if shooing a pesky fly. "Yes, yes. You come to beg my forgiveness for your abysmal failure at Mermaid Lagoon."

"Well," Abbadon started, "I suppose—"

"Andromeda," Palazar again interrupted, "did any others survive? Tell me what you've seen."

"My lord and king," Andromeda said with a bow, "thanks to Abbadon's leadership and bravery, his ship survived. They are moored nearby and, although their numbers are small, your son was successful in securing several mermaid prisoners. I know your royal highness does not bargain with his enemies but perhaps they could be used as bait somehow, for your entertainment, or as a way to operate the portal for us. One of them is of royal blood, kin to the queen herself."

Abbadon closed his eyes. The one thing he knew about Dariya was that she was the queen's niece. His beautiful mermaid captive had not shared it; one of the other mermaid prisoners had admitted the fact after being tortured by the fairy.

"My sisters have already secured them at Mount Hailstone. Mui and Lilith will join us in battle later," Andromeda concluded.

Palazar considered for a moment. It was true, he never liked trading hostages. But maybe, as Andromeda suggested, there would be some amusement in killing mermaid prisoners in front of their queen. Especially one of her own family. Just to see the look on her face.

"If you lie to me, I shall rip your guts from your indecent throat," Palazar said, eager to continue the march. The king nodded impatiently to the ogre general, signaling his desire to resume the procession.

"My king," Andromeda added, "one more thing, if you please. Your son and I are engaged."

Palazar furrowed his brow. "Engaged?" *What was the fairy playing at now?* he thought.

"Yes, sire," Andromeda continued. "We have recently discovered our feelings for each other. And since Abbadon is your last remaining heir, forgive me for saying so, but perhaps some thought should be given to how your lineage shall be continued deep into the future."

Palazar glared down at the fairy. "You dare speak about my death?" he said darkly.

Andromeda shook her head and bowed even lower. “My lord,” she said. “You are all powerful. You are invincible. I seek only to serve, as does your last surviving son.”

Abbadon would not meet his father’s eye. Palazar looked down on him in scorn. But Andromeda’s words did stir something inside of him.

“You, are my *son*,” Palazar pronounced the word bitterly, “and the witch is correct. Indeed, you are my last remaining offspring. If you die childless, my line ends. I will never allow that to happen. You shall live and marry Andromeda. The one thing you can do for me now, Abbadon, is produce an heir.”

“Yes, Father,” Abbadon whispered.

“Pray you can perform that one, simple task.” With that, Palazar chuckled. Frab joined in, chortling in his ogre’s rat-a-tat laugh. The king picked up the long whip at his feet and used it to strike one of the slave giants across the back. The giant howled in pain, then started lumbering forward.

Frab shouted orders. Soldiers marched.

Once more the procession inched forward toward the fateful battle that would decide the future of all Maradonia.

CHAPTER FOURTY-EIGHT

DRAGON SCALES

HALF IN AND HALF OUT of the water, Queen Aquamarisha waited at the waterside to greet the dragons. She glowed with the pleasure of knowing that the siblings were successful.

When Oomrath emerged from the portal, he was also greeted by the mermaid queen. She bowed her head and raised both hands above her head, pressing her wrists together. Oomrath repeated the gesture, his mighty wings coming together at his head and forming a huge umbrella shape. This seemed to be the dragons' greeting of respect. Oomrath lowered his scaly wings, and, with one motion, the great dragon took off, roaring into the sky. Behind him, thirty dragons poured out of the portal and emerged through the open crater one-by-one. With each flap of their wings, they lifted higher into the sky.

Just before the dragons, Maya and Joey had emerged from the portal. The siblings swam to the beach that made up the lakeshore and walked out of the water. The dragon, Oomrath, was already waiting for them on the sand. Maya and Joey bowed the same way they had seen Aquamarisha bow. The corners of Oomrath's mouth rose in a smile as he returned the gesture.

"Encouragers," he said in his low, gravelly voice, "I have gifts for you from Empress Brunhilda." Oomrath was carrying a burlap sack in his talon. He placed it at the siblings' feet.

Joey opened the sack and pulled out two sets of black clothes. They were made of very hard-yet-flexible overlapping plates. Maya studied the small outfits for a moment.

"Dragon scales," Oomrath explained. He stretched his neck out so the siblings could see the thousands of small scales that made up his own black hide. "The toughest material in Maradonia," Oomrath said proudly. "No mortal weapon can pierce this armor."

The siblings held the armor in their hands. Though black, it shimmered in different reflections of colors as it moved. The armor was stretchy and lightweight, yet somehow harder than stone.

"Whoa. What an amazing gift," Joey said, impressed. "Thank you. And give Brunhilda our thanks, as well."

The dragon nodded solemnly. "When this battle passes, you may thank her, yourself."

Joey thought for a moment, "Wait. I have something for the empress too!"

Joey rummaged through his backpack for a moment before pulling out a banana leaf. It was the bejeweled snakehead.

"C'mon Joey. That's not a gift," Maya scolded and rolled her eyes.

Oomrath intervened. "Somehow Joey understood our customs. The snake appears on Gorgonia's emblem. This gift will be accepted with gratitude. With this, I will leave you; I must gather the rest of the dragons and discuss our strategy."

Joey wrapped the bejeweled gift back into the banana leaf and placed it in the burlap sack. The great dragon curled his talons and secured the sack. With this, he beat his wings and rose into the air. The siblings watched him fly away, toward the group of dragons circling overhead. Once Oomrath reached the others, they followed him to the mountainside at the far end of the lake, close to where the mermaid forces were also gathered, in formation, awaiting war.

Maya and Joey sat on the shore. Lush, tropical plants formed a protective wall of jungle around them. They both were exhausted mentally and physically, and it took a moment for them to speak.

"Only weeks ago," Maya said, "we were fighting over what to stream on TV for movie night."

"And who was going to do the dishes," Joey added.

After a moment, Maya admitted, wearily, "I really miss our old life back home. I miss my friends. I miss Mom and Dad. I hope Gordon and the rescue team find their way and get here soon."

"Me, too," Joey agreed. "We've just got to save, you know, Seven Kingdoms first."

Joey's grin made Maya's heart feel warm. After the events of the past few days, she had never been prouder of her brother.

Joey put on the dragon-scale armor, pronouncing, "I look awesome!" Then he peered over at the dragons and mermaids congregated on the far side of the lake. "Well," he said, "we better get over there soon."

"Missing your girlfriend already?" Maya teased.

Joey blushed. It was true. Even though he wouldn't admit it, Maya could tell he loved Morgana.

"You go ahead," Maya said. "I need a few minutes to gather my thoughts."

Joey nodded, affixed his breathing shell, and walked into the water until he disappeared under its calm surface. A couple of seconds later, with a huge splash, he reappeared.

"Holy smokes!" Joey exclaimed in full excitement. "I can breathe underwater!"

Maya rose to her feet. "What! How?"

"I was adjusting my breathing shell and accidentally swallowed a bunch of water. Except, it didn't bother me. Look, I'll do it again!"

Joey jumped back into the lagoon and after about thirty seconds, he returned to the shore triumphant.

"I don't understand," Maya said, stunned.

"Maybe it's because I got those fish scales now. That root stuff must have had some effect. I'll have to ask Morgana what's up with that." Without another word, Joey tossed her his breathing shell, waved, and leaped back into the water. Maya stood in dismay. Could it be? Could Joey have been changed? Was the change forever?

Taking a few moments to process what Joey told her, she slipped on the dragon-scale armor. Immediately, it gave her a sense of power and strength. In fact, she felt ready for anything. She tucked her dirty clothes into her backpack.

Walking along the border of sand and greenery, Maya came to a path that cut into the jungle. She walked down it and was soon surrounded by tall palm trees and thick tropical plants. Somehow the dragon-scale armor helped her move more quickly and nimbly.

She turned a corner on the jungle path and suddenly came upon a small lake. She stopped for a moment to take in the peaceful scene and calm her breathing. Then, something caught her attention.

Maya heard muffled sounds in the near distance. She walked up to the wall of tropical shrubs in front of her and parted the long, red leaves. Maya's heart fluttered with overwhelming happiness. It was the Navy team. They made it!

They had set up some kind of mobile base. There were a few simple tents, and logs for sitting. A few Navy men were cleaning their guns and chatting. Maya heard the sound of people talking inside one of the tents. And then Gordon appeared, exiting one of the other tents. He leaned back, stretching his back and shading his eyes from the sun with his hand. Maya's heart tightened in her chest. Just the sight of him sent a rush of butterflies coursing through her body. But looking at the rifles and handguns the soldiers were cleaning, Maya felt apprehensive. But she knew she had to talk to Gordon.

Maya waved at him. He stopped stretching and squinted at her, leaning forward, his mouth open, as if couldn't believe his eyes. Maya raised her finger to her lips and beckoned him toward her with her other hand. Gordon looked around at the other team members, shook his head, then walked the short way to the wall of shrubs. The shrubs were dense, and Gordon struggled to break through.

Maya stepped out from behind a tree and said, "Fancy meeting you here."

"M-Maya?" Gordon stammered. His eyes widened. It was obvious he was caught off guard.

"I don't know what you've seen so far but this place is just magical!" Maya gushed.

There was a long pause. Gordon felt his throat tighten. "Yeah," he said, clearing his throat, "you're right. We've, uh, seen mermaids. And other things."

"You came to save us at the right time," Maya said. "When I saw you last, we were so rushed! I realized I didn't even get to tell you about what's about to happen at the lake."

A sharp cry from above pierced the air. Gordon opened his eyes and saw a massive . . . dragon? It was flying off into the distance.

Maya nodded. "Yup, that's a dragon," she said, guessing his confusion.

It took Gordon a moment to process what he saw, but eventually he snapped back to reality and his mind whirled.

"I believed everything you told me," he said, thinking quickly. "And all of this is so dangerous. The best thing you can do right now is tell me where that portal is so that I can document it and then I—*I mean we*—can get out of here in one piece. That's a very important part of this process. That's, you know, just something we need to do."

Maya grinned. "That's the thing. We can't leave yet. There is a real war about to happen. We really need to get through this and then we can talk about the portal. Can your Navy team help in battle?"

"Maybe. That's not my call, but will this battle take place near the portal?" Gordon asked.

At that moment, a loud sound, like a wailing horn, came from the direction of the lagoon and war drums beat in the distance.

Maya started backing away. "It's happening! Look, I have to go. I'll see you soon?"

"Wait," Gordon called, not wanting her to leave without sharing the location of the portal. But Maya was already backing up toward the trail.

"The important thing," she called back, "is that we all fight together. It's the right thing to do. You need to get the Navy team to join us there. It's due east of here, a big lagoon. Where the dragons are headed."

"Due east! Okay. And you're sure this lagoon is near the portal?" Gordon said, stepping toward her as she backed away.

Maya smiled. "Just meet us at the lagoon with your team!"

Maya turned and sprinted away.

From behind him, Gordon heard, "Well, lover boy, that went well." Suddenly, Ilona was at his side.

"Uh, yeah," Gordon said. "You heard her. Due east."

Back at the campsite, the Navy team began to prepare themselves for an all-out offensive. It was obvious that they were all alarmed by the strange sounds in the distance.

Ilona stole glances at Gordon as they walked the short distance back to camp. She casually brushed her fingers against Gordon's as they walked toward the tents. For what lay ahead, she needed his allegiance. The contact didn't have any desired effect though; Gordon ignored it. In fact, the only effect it had, regrettably, was that Kreeger and the boys saw it.

The lieutenant started whistling a romantic tune, which infuriated Ilona. But what could she do? Red faced, she kept walking, acting like she didn't hear it. There was no such thing as privacy on a mission like this, but Ilona prided herself on her professionalism and was annoyed she had been caught out. But the guys didn't understand that her femininity was one more weapon she could use to her advantage. Or did she genuinely like

Gordon? No, no time for such thoughts. Ilona pushed the conversation she was having with herself to a corner of her mind.

Ilona didn't love the idea of fighting a battle she might otherwise avoid. But it seemed inevitable: in order to secure the portal, they would have to be involved in this battle. When it came to engaging with an enemy, she believed in her team and her technology. She didn't know much about this "evil army," but she was sure it was no match for her modern military force.

Her father's words echoed through her mind. Ilona had no choice but to fulfil this mission successfully, which meant finding the exact location of the portal. With all the science at her disposal, the best her scientists could do was tell her the general area. It had to be somewhere near this lagoon! She thought a bit more selfishly about the coming battle. *The quickest way to promotion is through combat—even if it's fighting whatever ridiculous, primitive creatures the mermaids are against.* Ilona rolled her eyes at how bizarre her own thoughts sounded.

Ilona grabbed Gordon by the arm and stopped walking through camp. She brought her fingers up to her lips and blew, creating a shrill whistle. Huang and Mundi emerged from the science tent. Kreeger and the half-dozen remaining Navy soldiers stopped cleaning and preparing their machinery to look up at Ilona.

"Break camp!" Ilona shouted, oozing authority.

Excitedly, Huang whispered to Mundi, "They must know where the portal is!"

Ilona stood up tall. "We travel immediately."

Everyone but Kreeger jumped into action.

"To where?" Huang asked.

"Aye, what did I tell you? I make the orders 'round here." Kreeger said, insolently.

Professor Mundi and Doctor Huang looked at each other, confused with the order of command.

Ilona glared at the beefy lieutenant. "You heard those war drums! And whether you like it or not, we're going to have to defend ourselves. We're all about to go to battle."

A sly grin snuck across Kreeger's face. "Well, I like the sounds of that. It's about time." He shouted to the Navy team, "You heard the lady. Pack it up! Time to fight!"

CHAPTER FORTY-NINE

WAVES OF DESTRUCTION

Oomrath and his dragons had gathered inside the mouth of a huge cave at the edge of the shore. Maya made her way toward the cliff side. When she entered the cave, Oomrath immediately sensed her presence.

"The armor becomes you," he said, sizing her up with his enormous eyes. Maya gestured to the dozens of dragons and asked, "Why are your forces not in the sky?"

The dragon captain replied, "Palazar knows not that we are here. It is best to use the element of surprise where my forces are concerned, and conserve our energy. It is difficult to wait and do nothing, but the queen's thinking is sound. Thus, we are in this cave, unseen." He added, darkly, "For now."

Maya nodded at the cleverness of it. Then the shrill wailing of a horn cut through the air, this time louder and closer than before. It was not a mermaid horn, nor was it a dragon's bugling. It could only mean one thing.

What they saw took their breath away.

"Oh no," Maya whispered to herself. The image that came to her mind was that of an ocean wave. Palazar's forces were so numerous that they seemed to consume the hill they were marching down, like a tidal wave.

"There are thousands of them," Maya said quietly.

Oomrath's sharp eyes scanned the horizon, calculating. "Thirty thousand, I'd say. Maybe more."

Maya's breath caught in her throat. "But we have what? Ten thousand?"

Oomrath shook his head, "No, young one. We have *seven* thousand mermaid warriors."

Legions of mermaids were positioned under the water. The precision of their formations was impressive. They floated at various depths in groups ranging from small platoons of a dozen or so in camouflaged armor to huge arrangements of hundreds of archers. Every mermaid was prepared. Mermaids as young as ten or eleven were positioned alongside elderly mermaids who could be their grandmothers. Maya was impressed with what she saw.

Alongside Maya, Crystalline fixed her gaze sternly on the shore they were approaching. The unspoken answer was clear: many warriors had been lost in the Battle of Mermaid Lagoon. Now every mermaid who could raise a spear was here, ready to lay down her life for the survival of their species. Against Palazar now, it was all or nothing. Extinction hung in the balance.

Crystalline and Maya broke the surface near the shore. They had arrived at the command center. After hearing the news of Emilia and her missing scouts, Queen Aquamarisha spun around in the shallows, barking orders. She was fierce and breathtaking in her shimmering armor. Her aides sped away, carrying her orders to the various fighting forces stationed around the lake.

On the beach, Joey and the princess were sharing their last peaceful moments with each other, both half in and half out of the water.

Crystalline placed a hand on Maya's shoulder. "I admit that I doubted you once. For that, I apologize. You have proven yourself. I only regret that you are here now to share this danger."

Maya took Crystalline's hand. "I never believed in fighting. But now, I see that this is our only option. Your fight is now my fight."

Crystalline smiled, briefly, before hardening her eyes. "Then I shall see you after the battle . . . or in the next life."

With that, the mermaid spun around, and with one flick of her tail, she swam to Aquamarisha's side. The queen's gaze was locked, watching the hilltops cautiously.

"My queen, I ask your permission to invoke the contingency plan we spoke of," said Crystalline.

Aquamarisha turned to her top advisor, incredulous. "Already? But they are untrained and their loyalty untested." The queen lowered her head, obviously not comfortable with what she was about to authorize. "Very well. Let it be done."

Crystalline bowed, caught Maya's eye for a moment, gave a quick smile, then dove underwater and raced away.

Joey whispered to Morgana, "What was that all about?"

Without an answer, Joey turned back to look up at the many thousands of evil warriors marching down the hill and assembling on the field between lake and mountain. He didn't like admitting it to himself, but the sight struck true fear in his heart.

What he saw was an army of the most revolting creatures he could've ever imagined. There were ogres, imps, trolls—and other gruesome creatures he didn't know the names of. At the front of the dark horde, was a humongous vehicle, pulled by two prisoner giants. In the center stood a man in black battle armor. But was he a man? He was too tall to be human. It must be King Palazar.

Joey could see him now, whipping the giants mercilessly.

Green and yellow energy bolts crackled around him. On his face was a look of pure malice—and victory. He roared in laughter. The battle vehicle crested the hill and descended.

Joey's mind raced. He felt Morgana, by his side, take his hand. He turned to look into her eyes and saw the reflection of his own affection—and his own fear.

"We will not only defeat them," Palazar announced, malice punctuating each word, "we will destroy them. Let not one escape. The minstrels will forever sing of the most decisive—and shortest—battle in the history of Maradonia!" Palazar was laughing. The sound of it chilled Andromeda's soul.

"Sire," General Frab said, bowing deeply. "It is my duty to ask if we should deviate from such a plan."

"Coward!" Palazar shouted. "Send them all in!"

Andromeda had to admit—the two-headed ogre general was right. Palazar was being rash, sending in all the foot soldiers at once. It would be more prudent, as they had planned, to reserve some and direct them more specifically into the battle, should they be needed. Palazar's soldiers outnumbered the mermaids so greatly that it made little sense to commit the entire force to the first wave of attack. But Palazar would not be deterred. He insisted on a swift victory.

Andromeda turned to Prince Abbadon. The prince only stared ahead, clearly not ready to oppose his father. Andromeda grimaced at her choice of future husband.

General Frab signaled the horn to be blown. As one, thirty thousand ogre soldiers in black and brown armor marched forward. Behind the ogre soldiers, the trolls pushing the huge, wheeled catapults stopped. Dwarves scurried around the bases of the tall war machines, preparing the depth charges to be hurled into the lake. Palazar had been very clear—the charges must be set to detonate just under the water's surface. He did not want any possibility of harming the Crystal Cathedral and its precious portal. Also, that's where most of the mermaids would be gathered with their longbows and crossbows. The shallow depth charges should perform perfectly.

"Witch!" Palazar shouted. Andromeda obediently stepped forward. "Your time has come."

She nodded. Lilith and Mui stepped forward, by her side.

All three fairies held hands and concentrated. Andromeda felt an unnatural wind tussle her long, black hair. Its cold touch made her shiver. Soon, their incantations raised a waterspout. Its funnel looked like a black tornado hovering over the water. The fairies chanted something in their harsh, ancient tongue, and water started gushing up into the waterspout. Thick jets of lake water began pouring from the top of the spinning funnel with such force that the water shot clear through the sky and landed, in a massive stream, in the jungle past the far beach.

Lilith slithered forward, concentrating on the waterspout. Andromeda and Mui turned to their left and continued chanting. A second waterspout formed. Andromeda stepped to the side, chanting, and now a third waterspout began draining the lake. Just then, the catapults started hurtling depth charge barrels through the sky and into the lake.

BOOM! BOOM-BOOM-BOOM!

The charges exploded almost as soon as they hit the surface of the lake.

By now, the thirty thousand ogre soldiers had reached the shore of the lake. They raised their bows and fired thousands of arrows high into the air. For a moment, all went dark in the sky as the massive black cloud of arrows nearly blocked out the sunlight. Then the arrows plunged straight down, into the water.

"Look out!" Morgana dove onto the shore and tried to knock Joey aside at the last moment but was unsuccessful. An arrow struck Joey's back.

"Oh no! My love!" Morgana shrieked.

But to her surprise, the arrow was on the floor, bent out of shape. They looked at each other, realizing that he had been totally protected by the dragon-scale armor. They smiled briefly before they turned their attention back to the action.

Screams erupted from the lake as mermaid bodies floated to the surface, pierced with massive arrows. Palazar chuckled. Everything was going as he planned.

The ogre soldiers were close to the lakeshore. As soon as the mermaids emerged from underwater, the ogres started rushing forward, screaming their battle cries, their swords and axes held high.

Crystalline looked around at the faces of her warrior comrades. She saw no fear, only fury. She felt the blood pumping through her veins. Flashing hand signals, Crystalline gave the order to attack. The time had come. The battle had begun!

Five hundred mermaid warriors suddenly erupted through the surface of the water, headfirst, in perfect unison. They rose into the air as one, their bodies fully above the lake, tails glistening. Hovering for an instant in midair, they drew back on their bows, and let loose their glowing arrows. Effortlessly, they returned to the water in perfect harmony, in a synchronized dive.

The forward lines of Palazar's army exploded into chaos.

A second wave of mermaid archers flew into the air and released their energy arrows as perfectly as the first. But the water from the lake was being lifted by the fairies' magic rapidly.

More barrels of depth charges plunged into the lake. Palazar roared. With a single movement he leapt from his battle vehicle and drew his radiant sword. Distracted, the fairies turned to their king. The lake was already significantly drained. Only half the water remained in it. The waterspouts sputtered and stopped. Palazar spun on the fairies.

"Don't stop. Finish it!" he screamed, eyes red. "Drain it!"

The fairies immediately focused back on their tasks and the waterspouts grew into the sky again, even bigger than before.

Ilona couldn't believe her eyes. She rubbed them, then she shook her head. But still, the incredible scene remained before her eyes. She and her team had just broken through a thick line of brush to discover themselves standing on a beach and looking out at the craziest vision they had ever seen. Even Kreeger was silent, the cigar dangling from his lower lip.

Huang and Mundi, on the contrary, took it all in their stride.

"No, I think I'd call those ogres," Mundi was saying casually.

"How do you know it's not a troll?" Huang said, nodding.

"The shape of the head, I'd say," Mundi said matter-of-factly, as if they were merely discussing an unusual creature at a zoo. "Note the high, sloped forehead. Turns out many of the fifteenth century Chinese etchings got it quite right, didn't they? More accurate than their European counterparts I'd say."

Huang nodded, snapping pictures with his digital camera.

"Enough," Lieutenant Kreeger barked, yanked back to reality by the scientists' surreal chatter. He stared at the scene, shaking his head in disbelief. "Crikey. There's just so many of them."

"B-but," Gordon stammered, "so many of what?"

Ilona turned to face Kreeger. "Lieutenant? Orders?"

"I'll admit, I didn't know what to expect. But I didn't expect this!" he said.

"Look out!" Gordon shouted, raising his rifle.

A platoon of Palazar's dwarf soldiers broke through the foliage behind them, racing to flank the mermaids on this side of the lake. Ilona didn't have time to think. Bursts of automatic rifle fire sprayed the oncoming dwarves. The bullets pierced their armor and their axes fell to the ground. It was over in seconds.

Kreeger bent over to pick up a battle axe.

"Well now," he chuckled. "Gimme a clip of armor-piercing rounds over one of these little pointy jobbies any day, I'd say."

"Lieutenant! Get down!" Ilona yelled.

Reacting mostly to the look in her eye—and the fact that the sergeant raised her rifle right at him—Kreeger fell to the ground just as Ilona unloaded a dozen bullets into a nine-foot-tall troll soldier.

"Now that's a troll," Mundi said, nudging the open-mouthed Huang from their hiding position.

Forty or fifty more of the huge, foul creatures followed. The trolls were shocked to find a small force of fighters they had never seen before—humans—but lost no time attacking with their spears and clubs.

Kreeger fired off rounds at various trolls as they appeared through the bushes, then dove out of the way of a huge, barbed club. There were too many of these—things. They had to move.

"On me!" Kreeger shouted, leaping to his feet.

With the scientists protected in the middle, the Navy men formed a tight circle, each facing out and firing at the trolls, taking them down, keeping them at bay. As a group, they inched down the beach and toward the water, unloading clip after clip into the huge, marauding creatures.

Through the chaos, Ilona caught sight of something striking in the far-off distance: a massive glowing mountain.

Standing just inside the cave, Maya's heart sank. She was staring at the top half of the Crystal Cathedral. It was no longer covered in water. The fairies' water funnels were doing their job. The lake was draining, and it was almost dry!

Breathing hard from battle, Queen Aquamarisha looked around quickly, taking stock of the situation. Her warrior mermaids were fighting hard. They were exhausted, injured, and now completely out of their element, balancing on their tails in just a few feet of water.

They had started the battle outnumbered roughly four to one. There had been seven thousand mermaid warriors against Palazar's thirty thousand soldiers, and at least half the mermaids had given their lives.

At that moment, Oomrath stepped proudly out of the mouth of his cave. Aquamarisha held his gaze, then nodded. With one flash of his mighty wings, the dragon took flight. Behind him, thirty more dragons emerged and took to the sky in tight formations. The dragon legion rose up then swooped down, and blasted fire down onto Palazar's screaming soldiers.

From their vantage point on the hill, the fairies watched Palazar form a ball of protective magic around himself, then send orb after orb of power up at the dragons as they wheeled in the sky. An orb collided with one large dragon, sending the creature screeching and burning down to the ground, where Palazar's foot soldiers converged on it with sword and club.

"Sisters!" Andromeda screamed.

Lilith and Mui ceased their incantations. Their jobs done; all three water funnels dissipated. Andromeda pointed to the dragons and her sisters nodded.

The fairies concentrated their powers on the dragons. They formed three dark clouds, and soon, raging fingers of red lightning bolted from each of the clouds, striking down three more dragons, quickly followed by the rumble of thunder. The dragons flew across the fields, spewing more fire.

Behind the front ranks were still at least ten thousand fresh soldiers eager to fight. They looked like a sea of black armor. Then, that sea started parting. From the back of the fighting force, something was carving a path through the mass of soldiers. Bodies were flying through the air. It almost looked like a river, or a comet was scattering the great mass of soldiers. As the tip of it grew closer, Maya finally saw him. Palazar. The dark king was swinging his tremendous sword back and forth as he walked. Ten or more of his own soldiers flew high into the air. With every swing of his arm, flames erupted from the sword. Maya gasped at Palazar's sheer physical power—and his complete disregard for the lives of his soldiers. Finally, the king reached the front line. He was magnificent in all his powerful glory.

Maya surveyed the lake. Palazar's army continued to march into the shallow lake. Exploding barrels kept rolling through the battlefield. Because the water had drained, the Crystal Cathedral was fully revealed. Mermaids were no longer able to submerge into the safety of the lake. Only their tails remained in just a few feet of murky water.

The entrances to the tunnels that connected Crystal Lake back to Mermaid Lagoon were no longer underwater. It was now simply a cave opening in the bare rock cliffs. Then the sound of a conch shell, the signature trumpet, blew from behind the queen.

Through that opening, Crystalline appeared, saying, "It is time."

A smile pulled the corner of the queen's mouth.

The conch shell blew again. Immediately, thousands of merpeople arrived . . . not mermaids but mermen! But because of the low water levels, they advanced slowly, holding their electric weapons. Nevertheless, they were full of new energy, and this alone strengthened the mermaids.

Florina's mouth fell open. "The lazy mermen? My queen. It has been eons since they fought by our side."

Queen Aquamarisha looked over to the entrance of the cave. Her eyes found Maya's. They nodded to each other.

"Today, that changes! We should have always been united," said the queen. "All we needed was a little . . . *encouragement.*"

The united merfolk began moving forward with full force, but the armies of darkness continued to bring death to many. Queen Aquamarisha cut down the troll in front of her with an elegant spin and slice of her enchanted sword. She knew there wasn't much time. Even with the mermen reinforcements by their side, her warriors would not hold up to Palazar's superior numbers.

The king raised his hand and pointed into the muddy lakebed. His remaining ten thousand soldiers roared and raced into the muck. The surviving merfolk stood their ground against the new onslaught, drew their energy swords, and met their foes. Everywhere Aquamarisha looked, an untrained merman or exhausted mermaid was fighting for his or her life with a much larger enemy soldier.

Joey picked up one of the energy swords from a fallen mermaid, and with Morgana by his side, they began fighting a huge ogre in flaming armor, together.

Hearing thunder overhead, Aquamarisha looked up to see another bolt of lightning about to strike a young dragon. At the last moment, Oomrath dove between the dragon and the bolt, taking the lightning strike in his own chest. Ablaze, Oomrath spiraled down and crashed into the sand of the opposite beach. Aquamarisha's breath caught in her throat. Miraculously, the dragon captain rolled over and over, quelling the flames, and leapt onto nearby trolls. Without missing a beat, Oomrath continued fighting valiantly.

Though inspired by the bravery of her allies, the queen knew now, more than ever, that they would not last long against their overwhelming foe, Palazar. Yet she was determined. And even if it meant the choice between life or death, the time had come to confront him. Aquamarisha dropped down onto her belly in the remaining few feet of water, swished her tail, and shot off toward the shore, her stomach scraping the lake bottom.

Maya helplessly watched the queen set out toward Palazar and gasped. She didn't know how she could help. Given what she had seen so far, Maya believed that the fatigued Mermaid Queen would be no match for Palazar's evil power.

Maya sprinted away from the secure cave, over the sand, and into the shallow lakebed. She weaved her way through the battle, ducking under the sword swipes of the soldiers, protected and empowered by the dragon-scale suit. Just as a troll was about to bring his axe down on a stunned mermaid, Maya knocked into him at a full run, sending him sprawling into the mud. The mermaid came to her senses, drew her dagger, and leapt onto the troll with a ferocious battle cry.

Sensing an approach, Palazar turned just in time to see Aquamarisha leap out of the shallow water and brandish her golden spear-sword, balancing, what looked like a glowing energy plasma ball. Palazar's protective orb disappeared, as if the mermaid had pierced it. He raised his own sword and blocked her overhead swing at the last moment. Aquamarisha landed on the sand, maintained her balance on her tail, and pressed the attack on the king.

In between thrusts of his blade, Palazar threw swift orbs of energy at the queen, but she either ducked out of the way or shattered them in midair with her enchanted spear-sword. The two leaders seemed evenly matched, and each fought with a ferocity that revealed their mutual hatred of the other.

Suddenly, blue lightning streaked from behind Aquamarisha and struck her in the back. Her body lifted into the air, electricity coursing through her body. She screamed in agony.

When the lightning finally finished, the queen dropped into the mud, quivering. Palazar cast an approving look at the nearby hilltop where Andromeda stood proudly. The king stepped forward in triumph. Then his eyes fell on something curious.

It was a youngling. A human. Maya jumped into the space between the

Queen of the Mermaids and the King of Darkness. Maya grabbed Aquamarisha's heavy sword and lifted it up in her trembling arms, aimed at Palazar. The dark king stopped walking, widened his eyes, then threw back his head in uproarious laughter.

"Ah, the human," he said, wiping the mirth from his eyes. Palazar found humor in the situation and danced lightly, raising his blade. "Shall we fight then?"

Maya awkwardly swung the sword around to face him. Then the weight of it was simply too much and she dropped it to the ground. She had acted without thinking, on instinct. Now she wasn't quite sure what to do.

With one smooth swing, Palazar struck Maya with his backhand. The blow knocked Maya to her knees on the muddy floor. Her lungs ached for oxygen. Her heart raced. She didn't know what to do. From afar, Joey's heart dropped when he saw his sister on the ground. He ran the fastest he had ever run.

Palazar shook his head, sizing up Maya disapprovingly. "And to think that all this bloodshed is your fault. You know that, don't you?" Palazar said. All amusement had left his voice. "You have an eternity of pain ahead of you, my dear. You shall be an example of my power for generations."

Maya still trying to catch her breath, straightened herself up. All the battle cries around them seemed to merge into silence, and all the fighting around them became a blur.

Now it was only Maya and the king, facing each other.

"Didn't you try to *encourage* them?" the king sneered. "You can't even encourage yourself."

Finally, Joey made it over to lift Maya up.

"Don't you dare touch my sister again!" Joey yelled.

With her brother's support and her ears still ringing, Maya slowly brought herself up.

Staring down at them, Palazar chuckled. "Enough chit-chat. Let's come to a conclusion. Command and *encourage* the mermaids to bow down to me, your new king, and instead of death, I shall grant you life."

"We will never bow down to you! You are not our king!" Joey said, growing bolder, surer of himself. "And the people of Maradonia will never stand by you either. It doesn't matter if we survive this battle or not! But you will always remember these words."

Behind Joey, Maya grew stronger with each word she heard. Joey's strength was both medicine and power. She felt the courage returning to her body, but deep in her heart, she knew this was the end. They were no match for the powerful king.

Behind them, Aquamarisha pushed herself up on shaky hands. Palazar eyed the queen, only to find that the queen's eyes were staring straight ahead, as if in a trance. Aquamarisha's hand was clutching the emerald around her neck. It started glowing.

Palazar wiped his hands and felt heat on his face. He noticed curiously that, in the distance, the Crystal Cathedral was revealed, glowing a bright golden color.

"Palazar, do not harm these children. This battle is between us!" the queen said serenely, her eyes now on Palazar. "Step away now, my friends."

Maya and Joey obeyed, backing away.

Palazar gazed down at the mermaid with disdain and arrogance and spit out one venomous word: "Pathetic."

He stood up tall and grinned at this last, feeble effort. He was triumphant. No weak, leftover abilities of the fish queen and her glass cathedral could hurt him. They were his. The portal was his.

"Your kingdom is mine and you will serve me for the rest of my reign," Palazar announced in triumph.

Meanwhile, miles away, streams of bubbles were rising up from the bottom of the water. At the lake bottom, the Crystal Cathedral reflected light like a prism. Rainbow colors glinted off its high towers. The entire edifice was humming, sending out waves of energy that pushed the sea plants back and forth.

Suddenly, the cathedral stopped humming. The water grew colder. For a moment, the sky fell dark as the cathedral seemed to inhale the light. Like a black hole, the cathedral pulled all the light around it into itself.

Just as the area was enshrouded in complete, impenetrable blackness, a high-pitched whine shot out from deep inside the cathedral, piercing the air. The Crystal Cathedral and the rocky floor around it started vibrating in an earthquake, growing stronger and stronger.

Then the queen clutched her emerald pendant and spun around to face the south. The Crystal Cathedral, shaking so strongly that the water around it was shimmering, let out a tremendous explosion of light and sound.

Maya turned to follow Aquamarisha's eyes and saw a brilliant flash of white light explode over the far mountain. The shockwave sped across Maradonia, but the following sound was deafening. Like a chain reaction, everyone on the battlefield stopped fighting. Then an eerie silence filled the entire area. All the surrounding water started to withdraw from the lake, leaving it nearly barren. It was so powerful that it even sucked in the water that was withdrawn by the fairies.

"Run!" Aquamarisha screamed. A single tear trailed down her chiseled face.

Far out in the distance, an abnormal wall of water slowly began to form as high as a mountain. Chaos broke out on the battlefield when the ogres and trolls realized what was about to happen. They immediately dropped their weapons on the ground and began running up the hillside.

The mermaids and mermen were now totally crawling on their hands, bracing themselves for the crash.

"Whose sorcery is this?" Palazar bellowed with rage and disbelief. He was in complete astonishment when he saw his army flee in all directions.

The enormous wave raced over the ground, consuming anything and everything in its path. It bucked and roiled like a wild creature as it shifted across the battlefield, throwing mud high up into the sky.

As the howling tsunami raged with full speed, the siblings braced for impact. They watched in fear as the deadly tsunami sucked in hundreds of beings from both forces into its foamy frigid grasp, just in front of them.

Realizing that a supernatural tsunami was about to take place, Palazar started building a protective orb around himself, feeding it with hateful power into a bigger and bigger bubble.

Aquamarisha turned to look at the siblings, yelling inaudible words full of pain and loss. The tidal wave crashed and consumed the queen in its spiral.

With a second to spare, a massive dragon swooped in and grabbed Maya and Joey with his claws and immediately shot back into the sky.

On the hillside, Abbadon and the fairies were in shock as they witnessed their own king swept away before their eyes. He spun out of control, head over heels, arms flailing. Even though Palazar shielded himself with a protective orb, the massive wave devoured the entire orb into its raging wall of frigid water and crashed down again.

"What happened?" Maya screamed through the tears welling up in her eyes.

"Did they all die?" Joey shouted in confusion.

The dragon gave them no answer, and instead tightened his grip on the siblings as he flew. They watched the wave crash again and again, until all the water in the lake was level. After a few moments, the dragon dropped them on the shoreline and landed nearby. Both siblings stood blinking, in shock from the events of the last few moments.

Maya fell onto her bruised knees and began wailing. Joey sat not too far from her and breathed hard. It was all too much to take in. In denial of what had happened, the siblings now watched in horror as bodies started floating to the surface of the lagoon, still and lifeless. However, the most bodies on the surface belonged to the dark army, rather than the mermaid forces.

Behind them, Oomrath the magnificent dragon stretched his fire-scarred neck and bugled mournfully to the sky. The other dragons spread about the battlefield joined in the desolate sounding cry. It was a long, harsh sound of pure pain and fury.

Palazar's remaining soldiers stood on the banks, silently, jaws open. Then, as if on command, all of them fled to the hillside.

Andromeda and Prince Abbadon watched as the entire lake began to fill up again. All the water that the fairies had drained out was somehow drawn back into the lake by this supernatural phenomenon. Abbadon lost his breath completely. He watched two trolls staggering up the hillside. The next moment, with total rage and fury, he ripped the sword from its holster and stabbed one in his gut and sliced the other through his chest. They fell down trembling in shock.

The fairy Andromeda grabbed Prince Abbadon by his collar and said with a commanding voice, "Look at me! Stop this despicable behavior. You are king now, Abbadon."

Abbadon pulled away, throwing his sword into the grass. Many of the ogres and trolls looked at their new king with nervousness. However, he frowned and remained quiet.

The fairy-witch extended her glistening wings. Her wings reflected the sunlight in all directions. Andromeda realized it was her moment to take the initiative. Abbadon was in no place to command. With enchanting words, she caused a dark cloud to surround her feet. The ravens lifted her high up into the air.

With a powerful voice, she shouted, "Armies of darkness. Well done!"

The survivors grunted and groaned. Mui and Lilith sneered as they watched power and control surge through their sister's veins.

"Return to your tribes with honor. Provisions shall be granted to you in three days. The gods were not on our side during this battle. We shall call upon you when we have regained our strength."

The dark army cheered in relief and, without another command, they began marching home.

"My little ravens," Andromeda commanded, "return Abbadon to Mount Hailstone in one piece. We must protect him and rebuild our kingdom."

Minions of ravens swooped down in a swirling fury of black wings and lifted Abbadon into the sky, followed by the fairies. In the blink of an eye, the black clouds disappeared into the horizon, toward the icy wilds of Mount Hailstone.

CHAPTER FIFTY

REPLENISHING

SOMEHOW, THERE WAS A SENSE OF PEACE over the lake. Now that the lake was leveled, peaceful waves kissed the shoreline in sweet harmony. The sun broke through the clouds, and a rainbow appeared over the forest. It was almost like a little paradise on earth. Yet Maya and Joey were grief stricken.

Libertine landed on Maya's shoulder. "Don't fret, child. It is over," Libertine cooed.

Maya gave her no answer. Her tears were never ending.

"We failed!" was the only thing Maya could say.

Joey nodded in agreement, tears in his eyes. "This can't be happening."

Libertine said in a faint voice, "Life and death are one, like the rivers that flow from the lagoon to the sea are also one." Her golden tail feather sparkled in the sunlight.

"No, no, no, no, no," Maya repeated. Her ears were buzzing, and everything looked too bright. In her grief, she felt a million miles away from everyone else. The two siblings played the scenario in their head over and over again.

"Why did that happen? That tsunami wave came out of nowhere!"

On the surface of the lagoon, one by one, the bodies began to sink. Maya put her head down. She couldn't bear to see any more death. A shadow fell across Maya, and she looked up through her tears to see the mermaid Florina in all her tranquility, greeting her.

"Child," the elderly mermaid cooed, softly. "You are the one who has given us hope. Surely you saved just a little for yourself?" Florina smiled down at Maya and pointed.

Maya followed the direction of Florina's finger down to see that now heads began emerging from the surface of the water. Joey stood up immediately and ran into the water. Morgana calmly swam to meet Joey and they embraced in a wet hug.

"But how?" Maya asked. "How did you survive?"

"Don't you know that water is our element? As warriors, we thrive in water," Florina said. "We live for Awanata."

All the surviving mermaids and mermen rose to the surface, realizing what had happened. Together they fought to keep the portal safe. Although it was a mixture of grief and triumph, the merfolk were inspired and embraced each other in unity. Triumph rose from the survivors and dragons around the lakebed. Mermaid warriors glowed, and with one synchronized voice they screamed: "Awanata!"

"Where is the queen?" Joey questioned. The others scanned the lake, until a few mermaids rose to the surface of the water. They were carrying Queen Aquamarisha in their hands. She was motionless. Her pendant was almost dim, but glowing softly. They brought her to the shoreline and pushed lightly on her chest. But the queen moved no more.

"There isn't much time. Our only chance is that she can get replenished by the portal's enchanting power. Because there is still light in her pendant, there may be hope," Florina said.

"Hurry," Maya said. "Help me bring the queen to the Crystal Cathedral."

The group made their way into the portal's entrance and brought the queen to the stone table built into the center of the Crystal Cathedral room. Gently, Maya, Joey, Morgana, and Crystalline lifted Aquamarisha's prone body onto the table. Maya had stopped crying, but the way the queen's limp body felt in her arms did not give her much hope. Sensing this, Florina laid a hand on Maya's shoulder.

"All is not lost, child," the elderly mermaid said, balancing on her tail. "Not as long as there is breath in those who love her."

With that, Florina turned to the queen. She placed one hand on Aquamarisha's forehead and the other on the queen's emerald pendant, now barely radiating a dull green. Florina took a deep breath, blew into the pendant, then touched the crystal walls. She repeated the process, one wall after the other.

Soon, Joey noticed that the emerald pendant glowed a little brighter with each breath Florina breathed into it. Trembling with concern over her mother, Morgana wiped a tear but kept her silence. Joey took her hand in his. Some of the mermaids who had arrived to help held their faces in their hands, sobbing. Others struggled to stay quiet in honor and respect of the queen.

After a number of breaths, Florina straightened up, her hands still on Aquamarisha's forehead and pendant. She looked up at the portal's arch stone, closed her eyes, and focused.

The portal began to emit a golden color. The queen started glowing in response. It was not only light, Maya noticed, but heat as well. She could feel the warmth coming from the portal and entering the queen. Then, multicolored light exploded from the Crystal Cathedral in an intense, rainbow beam that struck Queen Aquamarisha in the back. The energy focused through her body and joined the golden glow and became a bright ray of pure white light.

Finally, Maya saw the queen's chest rise. Aquamarisha's eyes opened. The color emanating from her pendant had been restored. Maya was clutching her necklace, which was likewise radiating a brilliant hue. Everyone in the room had been holding their breath. Now all of them exhaled loudly.

"Mother!" Morgana gasped, kneeling at Aquamarisha's side.

"You're alive!" Maya breathed, kneeling with Joey.

"I am," the queen said. Her voice was frail and weak. Her eyes still heavy as they slowly opened.

Florina smiled. "The pendant and the portal," she told the siblings, "cannot exist without one another. As it has always been."

At the entrance of the portal, the Navy team appeared.

"Oi, what's all this commotion?" Lieutenant Kreeger sneered, his rifle not exactly pointed at the mermaid group, but not exactly hanging loose either. He sloshed through the water that was up to his waist. Some of the science team started making measurements and began examining the portal.

"Quite a pretty little chapel you she-guppies have here. I don't suppose that this might be where the 'teleportation portal' we've heard so much about would be?"

"Gordon," Maya said, stepping forward. "You made it."

Ilona stepped between Maya and Gordon. "We're here to save you, but before we leave, you must tell us how to work it," the sergeant said matter-of-factly.

Aquamarisha pulled herself off the table, balanced on her tail, and drew herself up to her full height. "Who is asking?" she said.

Doctor Huang stepped forward. "Please excuse us, your royal highness," he began, bowing. "We are scientists. Humans. We have heard of the power of your portal, and we are eager to understand it."

"And we are eager to understand your world," Mundi said, also stepping forward and bowing.

"To be friends," Huang added, smiling.

Crystalline eyed the rifles in the Navy team's hands. "What type of friends bring weapons into a sacred place?"

"It matters not," the queen said. "Humankind is not ready to access the portals. Your history is one of power, greed, and division. In your hands, the portals would become destructive."

Huang blinked. "I admit, your highness, our history is one of war. But so is your own. We come here as scientists. To discover, not to make war."

Florina shook her head, staring from one team member to the next. Finally, her eyes fell on Ilona. "I can sense that your purposes are not only science, as you say. Your armies plan to use the portals for conquest. Don't they?"

"It's . . . complicated," Ilona finally said, searching her heart. Now that she was here, in this incredible place, in the presence of these brave and proud mermaids, she found herself having only respect for them. They were strong. Honest. Not like she had been lately.

"It's not complicated," Kreeger said. "It's just business. Lover boy is behind the whole thing, girlie. He's had you fooled pretty good, I'd say. Right from the get-go," he chuckled.

Maya turned to search Gordon's eyes.

"Gordon?" Maya asked confused. "I thought you were here to save my brother and me."

Gordon stepped forward, boldly. "It's time for you to grow up," he began, sounding like a schoolteacher. "This portal will mean world domination for whoever controls it. That means it's worth a fortune. We're here to bring this technology back to our world—and to finally profit from our brilliance."

"Gordon," Huang whispered. "Son. No."

"Be quiet," Gordon hissed, stepping to the portal. He rubbed his hands on it as if it was a holy relic. "Finally. Finally, we have it!" Gordon turned to Ilona, smiling. The Navy team members smiled as well, each thinking about the fortunes that awaited them.

Maya furrowed her eyebrows. "Why would you do this?"

Gordon's eyes were wet and shining. He looked mad with greed. "Oh, I can give you about a billion reasons why. And don't worry, I'm sure you'll be included in the profit margin." He cackled with glee. "Sorry, Maya," he said, putting on a fake pout. "Turns out you are just a silly little girl after all."

"You don't understand!" Joey interrupted. "This portal is what brings life to all the kingdoms of Maradonia. It is their life. If you remove it from them, everyone is going to die. They are at one with each other."

"Look, we are not your enemies," Ilona said with an understanding voice. "I can see that you've bonded with these mermaids, but you must understand that our country needs us. *Our world needs this.*"

"We understand, but we just can't allow that," Joey said, looking at everyone around him.

"Let's cut the crap. Shall we?" Kreeger said, angered by all the chit-chat. "We don't need you; we are taking over this portal with or without you."

Without a second thought, Kreeger raised his rifle and shot into the air. Every mermaid instinctively moved to attack Kreeger but stopped when the handful of Navy soldiers raised their rifles. He strode up to the weakened Aquamarisha, who stood her ground.

"Now then," Kreeger said, "which of you nice little fishies is going to show us how to work this teleportie thing-a-ma-bob?"

Everyone remained silent. No one moved. No one spoke. Maya looked to Ilona, who lowered her eyes. Kreeger reached up to grab the glowing pendant and was shocked to find it burning hot to the touch. He leapt back with a yelp.

Enraged, Kreeger raised his rifle to Florina's temple. "Fine. We'll do it the fun way. One at a time until someone talks."

Kreeger's finger tightened on the trigger. "Five, four, three, two—"

"Wait!" Maya stepped forward. "The pendant and the portal. They are one." She looked deeply into the queen's eyes, willing her to understand. "One cannot exist without the other."

"Halt—" Aquamarisha began.

Joey instantly caught his sister's idea. He had started to see her as a different kind of leader, one whose instincts and compassion made her decision-making swift and sound. He had much to learn from her. He stepped toward Kreeger and said, "Yeah! She's right. I can show you what to do with the pendant."

Joey turned back to Aquamarisha, secretly glancing down to the stone hilt of his dagger. "Please, my queen. Please let us do this one act. For our people."

Kreeger narrowed his eyes suspiciously. "For humans, you mean?"

"Who else would be our people?" Joey said, smirking.

Princess Morgana watched with a confused look. Her mother took her hand and said quietly, "The portal must never fall into the wrong hands under any circumstances."

Questioning the siblings' plan, the queen stood tall when Maya reached out for her pendant. Then it all clicked. If they destroyed the queen's enchanted necklace, the portal's energy would also explode, evaporate, and become an idle stone.

Gordon was surprised to see Maya lift the necklace from around the queen's neck without getting burned. Maya moved slowly, knowing these might be her last moments. She realized that for her plan to work, she would have to give up her own life to keep the portal from falling into human hands and keep the rest of the mermaids alive. Aquamarisha had been right. Humanity was not ready for that kind of power. Her only regret was that Joey, too, needed to make the sacrifice.

"Now," Maya said, thinking fast, "for the portal to work, I stand right here, with my necklace." She positioned herself just right. "Yes. And Joey stands at the table, with the pendant."

"Don't you know what you are doing?" the princess Morgana whimpered. "Please don't."

"The rest of you need to leave the Crystal Cathedral," Joey added with a stern tone.

"I'll be staying right here, watching, thank you very much," Kreeger bellowed.

"Me too," Gordon hissed, moving over to stand by the table, eager to see every detail of how to operate the portal.

Mundi lowered his head and took Huang by the arm. "Come, old friend, it is best that we leave. We cannot be part of this."

Huang gave one last disappointed look to his lost son and followed Mundi out of the room, silently.

Ilona stared at the ground. Contrary thoughts blazed through her mind. Her allegiance to her country. To her father. These valiant and wise mermaids. The honorable scientists. Gordon. Who was she to believe? Who was she to trust?

"Go," Maya said to everyone in the room. "Go outside the cathedral. That's how this works."

The team members turned to Ilona, questioningly. She nodded. "Kreeger, Gordan, and I will stay. The rest of you, out."

The Navy team members walked through the waterway toward the outside of the crater, while the mermaids swam away. Maya held her gaze with the queen, until she nodded, and turned to go. Now it was only Kreeger, Ilona, Gordon, Maya, and Joey.

Joey took a deep breath and took his position at the table. He placed the queen's pendant on the table and felt the dagger in his hand. He secretly turned it upside down, so he was holding the blade. The sharp edge bit into his palm.

Maya lifted her pendant. Even though doing this was a mere distraction of what Joey was about to do, the pendant started glowing gold. It worked.

Kreeger's eyes shined. "Now that little bauble will look beautiful around the next Mrs. Kreeger's neck I'd say."

Maya turned to her brother, a tear in her eye. They nodded at each other, unable to say what they wanted to say—but each knowing exactly what the other would say. It had been quite an adventure. An emotional roller coaster. And it was all about to end, but end it must. Maya closed her eyes, lifting her own pendant as a distraction.

Joey looked down at the queen's pendant. Then he quickly raised the dagger overhead, poised to slam it down onto the pendant. When the queen's pendant was destroyed, so would the entrance to the portal. And probably everyone in the room. Maya only hoped the mermaids were far enough away not to be killed in the blast, as she and Joey would. Joey raised his arm high above him, the dagger hilt glinted in the air. Maya mouthed *I love you* to her brother, and he nodded back.

Just as Joey moved to slam the stone hilt of his dagger down onto the pendant, to crush it, a brilliant white light blazed from the portal. Instinctively, Joey turned his dagger hand to shield his eyes from the blinding light. Kreeger caught the light full in the face; he dropped to his knees, clutching his eyes, screaming.

Maya felt a rush of air and the beating of wings all around her. She opened her eyes to see not only Libertine but her six dove sisters circling overhead. She had never been so happy to see anything in her life.

Ilona's sight was returning just as she saw a tall, olive-skinned man with dreadlocks step through the portal followed by a chattering monkey. It was a testament to how incredible the past few days had been that she didn't lose her mind completely right there. It was the man from the beginning of Maya and Joey's journey! Oraculus.

This time, Oraculus was dressed in a shining gold robe. His staff glowed with a shining crystal.

"What's going on now?" Kreeger exclaimed, his eye streaming and face sweating.

Bubah leapt on the lieutenant and grabbed his rifle away.

"What the—?" Kreeger yelled, failing around for the thief, half blind.

Oraculus smiled down at Ilona, who lowered her own gun. Then the tall man turned to Maya and Joey who were just overcoming the bright light and shock.

"Well," he said. "Will you look at that? Bubah, I believe we're in the presence of two true leaders. Yes. Two inspirations. Two . . . Encouragers."

"Wait," Joey said, "was all this a test?"

"No," Oraculus said. "I would never put you through all this for a test. No, it has been all too real. And if Bubah and I could have come to help earlier, we would have. But those aren't the rules," he smiled gently. "Let's just say I was sent by a higher power." Oraculus's eyes twinkled.

Maya opened her mouth to ask about this mysterious higher power, but Oraculus raised his finger and spoke. "By being willing to sacrificing yourselves, you two have unlocked the true meaning of leadership."

Bubah jumped up and down and chirped in agreement.

"I think there are others here," Oraculus said, looking at Maya, "who have learned a thing or two about leadership as well."

Ilona lowered her head, ashamed. Bubah leapt onto her leg, climbed up to her shoulder, and nipped her on the ear.

"Ow!" Ilona yelped. She tried to unseat the monkey, but it remained on her shoulder.

"It's never too late for a change of heart, my dear," Oraculus said. "There is always room for improvement. And forgiveness." Ilona met Oraculus's eyes and nodded, gratefully.

Oraculus looked down on Kreeger in pity and then at Gordon with scorn. "But some of us cannot bear the bright light of truth. Some of us don't have the strength of mind for anything but hate and vanity."

Overwhelmed with anger and defeat, Gordon reached into his back pocket, grabbed the handgun given to him by his father and squeezed the trigger.

BLAM!

The noise was deafening in the stone and crystal chamber. Maya closed her eyes. When she opened them, she saw the bullet hanging in midair, inches in front of Oraculus's face. The wise man stared at it, curiously, for a moment. Then he cocked his head and the bullet dropped to the ground.

"Primitive," he sighed. "And then there are those of us who just never learn."

Oraculus flipped his hand, and Gordon was swept off the floor as if by a giant invisible broom. His body flew straight through the far wall of the portal chamber—without breaking it—and simply disappeared. Maya saw the look of surprise and fury on his face as he vanished.

Just outside the Crystal Cathedral, the mermaids and dragons were shocked to see a small, screaming human figure materialize out of the wall and zoom high into the air, its arms and legs flailing. The scream diminished as the wriggling body arced through the sky, descended, and disappeared into the far-off jungle.

CHAPTER FIFTY-ONE

NEW BEGINNINGS

THE NEXT MOMENTS in the Crystal Cathedral were a mixture of many emotions. The mermaids swam back with happiness when they realized that the portal would be safe. Without a second thought, Joey embraced Morgana, and they kissed for a long moment.

When the queen arrived, she saw Oraculus standing near the portal. The two old friends smiled, then bowed their heads to each other. Bubah leapt onto his friend's robe and climbed up to Oraculus's shoulder. Without another word, they stepped through the portal and disappeared.

After much debate, Sergeant Ilona persuaded Lieutenant Kreeger to leave the portal alone and leave Maradonia for the greater good. Kreeger had been visibly humbled by the experience of being powerless against a stronger force, although Maya suspected he would assert more of his own power when he returned to more familiar territory.

With that, the Navy team began their journey back to the beach shore and began to pack away their equipment. A search party would be sent out to look for Gordon, but everyone feared he would be nowhere to be found.

Out in the water, dozens of glittering mermaids and mermen, together, broke through the surface of the lagoon in unison. They sailed into the air and executed perfectly timed somersaults, then dove back down into the water as one magnificent water show.

Just then, the mighty dragon Oomrath emerged from underwater, floating on his back. He spewed a great spout of water high into the air. It shot out of his mouth as if from a fire hose. The line of water arched through the air, heading straight for the royal table.

Maya held her breath, wondering why Oomrath would soak them all, then watched a handful of younger dragons swoop in at the last moment and exhale short bursts of fire. Overhead, the water sizzled out of existence and was replaced by fluffy, white clouds of steam and mist.

Applause rose from the delighted mermaids seated at various tables around the shoreline. Out of deference for the humans, the mermaids were holding this celebration on the beach of Mermaid Lagoon rather than in its depths. Their tables were half in and half out of the water.

After the battles and terrible losses of the recent past, the sound of laughter sounded foreign and unnatural. Maya realized, it wasn't just laughter, it was giggling, gleeful whispering, and kissing—all coming from Joey. Maya smiled to herself when she noticed her brother holding Morgana in his arms. He kissed Morgana's cheek, and the mermaid princess blushed. Maya no longer resented it. *Let them have their joy*, she thought. Her brother, in love. Who would have imagined? Just a few weeks ago, Maya would have bet that all her brother cared about was finding a way to convince their parents to buy him the newest Xbox. *Things certainly have changed.*

Floating in the lagoon, Oomrath turned to Maya, amusement in his great, rainbow eyes. Maya smiled back. She watched him lumber out of the water and lie down, laboriously, on the beach near a table of mer-children, who were delighted to talk to the dragon captain, already one of the famous heroes of the Battle of Crystal Lake. Maya felt a pang of regret, though.

The wounds Oomrath had suffered during battle had injured his wings. No one knew if he would ever fly again. The captain had taken the news with great strength, boasting that there was plenty of work to do on the ground as well as in the air.

Queen Aquamarisha turned to Maya. Her eyes glinted in a vibrant blue-green color, the same as the jewels on her shell crown. "On behalf of the mermaids, I just wanted to say thank you. You knew in the depths of your heart that as guardians of the portal, we would rather destroy the portal completely before the control would go into the wrong hands. You are one of us."

Maya nodded in return. "I am happy things played out the way they did, but I still don't understand what happened with that tsunami wave. What was that? How did that happen?"

"Maybe our good friend can answer that," Aquamarisha said, gesturing to the side. Maya followed her gaze and was shocked to see Empress Brunhilda approaching with giants beside her and, of course, a new royal advisor. She looked fierce in her long black-and-red armored dress. It matched her fiery hair. She first greeted her dragons then greeted the mermaid queen before sitting down next to her at the royal table. Everyone looked at the giants with awe.

"I have come here not just to celebrate your victory, but to join you in alliance," said Empress Brunhilda. "We believe that the reason for the wave may have been due to interference with the portal's sacred energy. Perhaps, this is all because the Seven Kingdoms are meant to be united," Brunhilda said with her heavy Gorgonian accent.

Aquamarisha added, "For centuries, our portal has been tuned into our energy and frequency levels, almost as if with a mind of its own. Since we are the guardians of this portal, it is connected to the pendants we wear, to our very thoughts and feelings. In our time of need, the portal engages. And reaches out to the other kingdoms."

"Unfortunately, their portals must be awakened to receive this call," Brunhilda said. "The power had nowhere to go. The energy must have had no choice but to explode outward. And with this, I want to tell you that our advisors have granted the full awakening of our portal in hopes that the other kingdoms will join us."

Brunhilda beckoned her aide, and the young giant brought over a small, wrapped package.

"Joey, we accept your last gift with gratitude. The snake's head is a symbol in our country used as the Gorgonian emblem," Brunhilda said. Joey gave Maya a self-satisfied look. Maya pursed her lips but was proud of him.

The empress continued, "However, I would like to present one last gift to you both. It's an artifact from before time has been counted. It is one of the oldest known talismans in Maradonian history. We giants have kept it safe for eons but now, I realize, it does not belong hidden away in a vault."

She unwrapped the package, and her servants held up the two gifts. All went quiet. They were gold armbands that fit around human-sized forearms. Many sitting at the table gasped in recognition.

Joey gazed at the two shiny armbands. Each had a seven-pointed star engraved on it. Each of the seven points had a small, circular indentation.

"The Armlets of Maradon," Florina whispered reverently. "I thought they had been lost."

Brunhilda then took two jewels from her aide. They were shiny and black, resembling polished onyx. She placed a black jewel into one of the star points on each of the armbands. Aquamarisha rose from her seat, balanced on her tail next to her fellow queen. She too held small jewels in her hand. They were deep green, shining emeralds.

"The Armlets were forged in the fires of Mount Hailstone many moons ago," Aquamarisha said, "as a gift for the first empress who united all the lands, Empress Maradon. They represent a time when all kingdoms were united. Equal and free, but stronger together than they ever could be apart." Aquamarisha took the talismans from Brunhilda and fitted an emerald into a star point on each of the armbands.

"There is one stone for each of the kingdoms," she said.

"We beings of Maradonia," Brunhilda said, her voice rising, "have been isolated in separate kingdoms for too long. And we might still be there, alone and stagnant, if it were not for our two guests of honor, Maya and Joey. Rise, my new friends."

The siblings both stood up. Both queens beckoned the children to approach. Brunhilda clasped one of the armbands around Maya's forearm as Aquamarisha placed the other around Joey's. In both cases, the Armbands locked in with a metallic "clank."

Maya felt the armband tighten just a bit around her forearm. It was comforting, as if the talisman's mere presence on her arm caused her to feel safer and stronger.

Aquamarisha turned back to address the crowd. "We two kingdoms are now as one," she said, loudly. The dragons and mermaids in the crowd erupted in agreement. "But we are only two of seven. Palazar has been defeated, but it won't be long before the dark armies return."

"Now the real battle begins," Brunhilda concluded fiercely, the streams of overhead dragon fire burning in her eyes. The two queens turned to each other and spoke in unison: "This day, our two great kingdoms celebrate our friendship and our unity."

"Friendship and unity," the crowd repeated in agreement.

Aquamarisha raised her hand. The crowd quieted.

"Still," Aquamarisha continued, more somberly, "five more kingdoms remain to be included in the renewal of our ancient pact."

Brunhilda turned to Maya and Joey. "Queen Aquamarisha and I pledge to use every resource we have to convince the five remaining kingdoms to unite with us once again, as in the days of old. But we are not sure if we can do it alone. After all, we would not be here, together, today without your help."

Aquamarisha raised her glass. "To the Encouragers!" she proclaimed.

"Encouragers! Encouragers! Encouragers!" the crowd started chanting.

Mermaids and mermen leapt from the water. Dragons took to the air in a great flurry of powerful wings. Some bugled and roared their approval. Others spat great, blazing rivers of fire high into the darkening sky.

"We want to ask you," Queen Aquamarisha began, and Empress Brunhilda finished her sentence, "will you stay and help us? Will you work with us to encourage the other five kingdoms to join our union?"

EPILOGUE

HOVERING ABOVE, a Maradonian hummingbird blinked in surprise. Just below, was a strange creature lying silently in the meadow. The hummingbird continued to analyze the creature when a bitter wind suddenly chilled the air. She ruffled her neon feathers. Tiny sparkles trickled off her green crest all the way down to her long violet and yellow tail. When the creature began to move, she became startled and instinctively darted away.

Pulling himself up from the grass, Gordon slowly sat up. His whole body ached in tremendous pain. But somehow, he was alive. How he had survived his flight and fall, he would never know. He rose to his feet on wobbly legs. Now he, too, felt the unusual chill in the air. Scanning the area, Gordon recognized where he was. He had traveled this way before, when the Navy team had marched from Mermaid Lagoon to lake of the Crystal Cathedral. He was standing on the side of the well-worn forest path that connected the two bodies of water.

Gordon took a deep breath and winced. He felt a sharp pain in his face. He raised his hand to his cheek, drew it back, and saw blood. His eyes widened. Nervously, he scanned the ground and found a puddle. Gazing into it, he was greatly dismayed to see the long, thick wound running across his face, connecting lip to ear. A wound that deep would scar him forever, he realized in shock.

Gordon's jaw set. *Those little kids,* he thought, darkly. *They are responsible.*

Hatred filled his heart as he marched down the path, aimlessly, continuing in his mind to list those who had betrayed him until it became a hateful chant. *I can't trust anybody,* he thought. *Not even my own family.*

"Nobody!" he screamed at the top of his lungs.

Gordon's mind raced. It had been a mistake to trust anybody, especially Ilona. In the end, she had proven her weakness. He had been a fool to care about any of them. None of them had his vision. His strength. Of course, he didn't need any of them. A soft crunching sound rose from his footsteps. *Is that—frost?* he wondered. Curiously, he watched his cold breath puff from his mouth. He stopped walking as the path opened onto a view of Mermaid Lagoon.

The edges of Mermaid Lagoon were covered in a blue-white mist. Tentacles of icy fog rose from the areas where water met sand. Then he noticed that the very edges of the shore were starting to freeze over. The water was still and silent. Crystals of ice were forming. His smirk widened.

Palazar, he thought. There was no other explanation. Palazar was alive.

Gordon started breathing faster. He looked north, behind him. Unnaturally, it seemed like the skies were darkening. Gray clouds lit up with lightning. There was no doubt that a storm was brewing.

He turned back to the lagoon, hoping to see it already frozen solid. If only he could see the bodies of the mermaids and two particular human teenagers flash-frozen in its icy depths. It was nothing more than a fantasy, Gordon realized, gloomily. He felt betrayed, lost, and disoriented.

What was his purpose? He could rush back to the Navy ship, but what would that do? It seemed that his future was unknown at this point. He felt like a failure.

What am I supposed to do now? he screamed inside.

Then his face brightened as he thought, *I'm close to the portal. Perhaps, there is still hope. I would be the one who discovered the portal.* They would have no other option but to present a solid contract to him and him alone for *his* discovery. Gordon's thought process was suddenly disrupted when he was knocked to the ground, as if by an invisible fist.

Fear grasped his heart when he heard a deep voice hiss behind him, "You're neither troll nor ogre."

Gordon's body was flipped over violently by this invisible force. He found himself staring up at the most powerful individual he had ever seen. His flowing cloak was made of bumpy, black leathery skin. King Palazar's bulky frame stood a full ten feet tall. Up close, the raw energy seemed to crackle off his skin.

Gordon knew whose company he was now in.

Palazar squinted, then a look of bitter distaste crossed his face. "I see now. You're a human. You must have come with those damned children. A mortal of your kind is destined to be wiped from this world." Palazar chuckled and added, "The only good human is a dead human."

Gordon was horrified to see orbs of red energy forming in Palazar's hands. He realized that he only had moments before the king would destroy him as easily as swatting a fly.

"Wait!" Gordon pleaded. "You need me! I can help you."

Palazar's eyebrows arched in arrogant disbelief. The orbs in his hands grew larger. "You think I need help from you?"

"No! Not at all!" Gordon gulped, thinking fast. "But I know that you're after Maya and Joey. They're the ones you want. And I know them, personally. I will deliver them to you on a silver platter. I hate them just as much as you do. Believe me! I hate her, her stinking brother, that traitor Ilona, my father—I hate them all!"

Palazar cocked his head. "Ahh, it is true. The most underestimated human emotion is hatred." When he spoke, his dark, icy voice boomed in echoes.

"I'm a scientist, too, you know," Gordon continued. "My father was the top scientist in the Navy team. I have everything we need to fulfil your wishes. I'm telling you. Just, please spare my life."

Palazar's eyes narrowed in satisfaction, "You seek revenge."

"Yes!" Gordon shouted. He spread both of his arms out wide in a humble bow.

"A mortal human. Ha. How interesting it is to see something in you that I've never seen in my own sons."

Palazar's cloak shifted in the wind as a light snow began to fall. "And what is it you want in return? If you bring me these children, I will give you anything you wish."

"I want my life spared," Gordon pronounced, slowly. "And access to the portal." Gordon looked to the ground in anticipation of violence.

"Vengeance," Palazar said, releasing his remote control over Gordon's body. His laugh echoed through the trees.

"Yes," Gordon said as he scrambled to his feet before the dark king.

It was at that moment that Palazar began to speak strange chants into the air. His booming voice spun through the wind and the echoes of his words carried through the ice-cold air.

Gordon saw two horses materialize in the sky. The two horses landed and stomped their massive hooves on the ground. Their toned muscles bulged and rippled across their whole body. The horses grunted, letting out large clouds of mist in the declining temperature.

"I will teach you," Palazar said, his mind scheming. His smirk grew wider across his dark face. "You will be respected," Palazar continued, as he grabbed the reins of the black horse and pulled himself upon its back. "You shall be honored. Worshipped."

Gordon stood up taller, his eyes wild with this new idea.

"You shall have everything you've ever wanted," Palazar continued. "Power. Riches. Females. Lands. Influence."

"Yes," Gordon whispered. "This is even better than I expected. Yes! I want *all* of it."

"And in return I ask for only one thing."

Gordon bowed his head. "And what is that?"

"You shall give me this in return. You shall have the whole world within your grasp," Palazar said, the corner of his lip rising. King Palazar let down his hand, "Just give me your *soul*."

Gordon was trembling with his desire and lust for power. For importance. For riches. For revenge. But to give up his soul? What did that mean? Still, at this point, Gordon could see no alternative. He kneeled before Palazar. "It is yours."

The king stared down at his new disciple.

Gordon grabbed the king's hand, which pulled him up with one mighty heave. "You shall be my new son," King Palazar proclaimed, "and you shall be called Apophis, for you will bring great chaos and darkness to all the worlds in this universe."

Gordon sat upon the other fiery horse. When he held onto the reins of the mighty beast, he immediately felt power flow through his arms, like electricity, transforming his entire body. He followed Palazar on his steed and did not look back.

ABOUT THE AUTHOR

SOFIA NOVA was born in San Diego, California. Her love for writing began at a young age, fueled by a deep fascination with the power of words and their ability to shape narratives that captivate and inspire. Driven by her passion for creating stories, Sofia pursued a degree in communications at St. Petersburg College. When she isn't working, Sofia enjoys traveling, swimming in the ocean, creating art, music, and acts of philanthropy. Rooted in spirituality, Sofia radiates positivity and believes in finding the silver lining in all circumstances. She enjoys sharing her knowledge, positive nature, and motivation to others, and hopes this book inspires readers to follow their dreams too.